SHARON
SALA

Out of the
Dark

MIRA

ISBN 0-7783-2402-8

OUT OF THE DARK

Copyright © 2003 by Sharon Sala.

All rights reserved. Except for use in any review, the reproduction or utilization of this work in whole or in part in any form by any electronic, mechanical or other means, now known or hereafter invented, including xerography, photocopying and recording, or in any information storage or retrieval system, is forbidden without the written permission of the publisher, MIRA Books, 225 Duncan Mill Road, Don Mills, Ontario, Canada M3B 3K9.

All characters in this book have no existence outside the imagination of the author and have no relation whatsoever to anyone bearing the same name or names. They are not even distantly inspired by any individual known or unknown to the author, and all incidents are pure invention.

MIRA and the Star Colophon are trademarks used under license and registered in Australia, New Zealand, Philippines, United States Patent and Trademark Office and in other countries.

www.MIRABooks.com

Printed in U.S.A.

I struggled through the writing of this book in a way that I've never done before. The tragedies of incurable illnesses and child abuse seem impossible to comprehend, let alone to find a way to acknowledge. But acknowledge them we must, because they come to us despite every good intention we have.

Once having acknowledged them, we must then strive to find answers, and after answers, solutions. All the money, all the research and all the commitments in the world will not solve a thing until we first search within ourselves to see what it is that makes us look away instead of reach out.

Know that anyone can become a victim of illness or crime; for shame to those who blame and denounce a disease as just punishment for a certain lifestyle, when in truth, disease has no boundaries. And for shame to all who blame crime on poverty and lack of education, when we know it comes from every walk of life.

And so I dedicate this book to those who have been stricken with diseases that have no cures, and to the children who have suffered hell on earth from abuse at others' hands. Fate was often not kind to you, but know that we have cried for you when you could not cry for yourself.

One

It was just after midnight when Margaret Cochrane opened her eyes to look at the face of her sleeping husband. She'd been Sam Cochrane's wife for seven years and Jade's mother for four, and once she'd loved Sam Cochrane more than life. But during the past year, she'd struggled unsuccessfully to hide her unhappiness with herself and with life. Times were changing. The country had been at war for years in a land she could barely pronounce. Young men had abdicated their military duty by escaping to countries outside of the U.S. to keep from being drafted. People Margaret's age had staged sit-ins in protest, burned flags and marched on Washington, D.C. She felt as if life had passed her by. She had so wanted to be a part of it—to make a change in the world. But her responsibilities as a wife and mother had precluded those options. To satisfy her emotional drought, she had decided to enroll in a self-realization course at a local community college.

Then one day, less than two weeks into the course, she had taken a shortcut across the campus greens to the bus stop and found the path blocked by a large gathering of people. She'd seen their kind before, but never up close. Both men and women wore their hair long and hanging loose about their faces. Some had flowers woven into their hair; others carried bouquets and handed out a flower to anyone who

wandered by. They dressed like gypsies from some Hollywood movie, in bright, colorful fabrics—the women in dresses that brushed against their ankles, the men in tight pants and long psychedelic print shirts that hung halfway to their knees. They referred to themselves as the People of Joy and were led by a man who called himself Solomon.

Margaret stopped out of curiosity, listening halfheartedly to their talk of free love and making peace, not war, until the man who called himself Solomon stepped off the low wall on which he'd been standing and started toward her.

One look from the dark-eyed, charismatic leader and she'd been hooked. He'd smiled at her, touched her face, then her hair, with the back of his hand. She felt the warmth of his breath as he bent down and placed a flower in her hair above her ear. As he did, the crowd around them had laughed then applauded, and something within Margaret had soared. One day ran into the next, and then the next, until she was at the campus almost daily. Seven days after her first encounter with Solomon, she'd gone again, only this time with Jade.

The People treated her child as if she was a princess, exclaiming over Jade's stunning beauty, even weaving flowers into her curly black hair and painting a tiny butterfly on the baby doll curve of her cheek. They praised Margaret until she felt as if she'd given birth to a holy child. Within the short space of that week, the emptiness in her heart had been replaced with a false sense of family. And so the brainwashing of Margaret Cochrane had begun.

Six months later, she was about to break her marriage vows to the man she'd sworn to love, honor and cherish. If that wasn't daunting enough, she was also about to steal away his only child. More than once she'd thought about telling him, but she knew he would never understand.

She slipped out of bed, careful not to wake Sam, then stood within the darkness of the room, looking down at his face. He was so good-looking, and he did love her. But he was always busy, and he didn't understand her. It seemed to

Margaret as if everything mattered more to him than she did. There was a brief moment of hesitation before her eyes narrowed purposefully. Quickly she slipped off her nightgown and dressed, choosing a long, ankle-length dress made of a blue, flowered fabric that she'd purchased yesterday. She picked up her shoes, waiting to put them on until she had stepped into the hall. With a quick backward glance over her shoulder, she hurried next door to Jade's room and slipped inside.

The baby was sleeping like the angel she was. Margaret thought of what she was about to do and hesitated again. Sam was going to be devastated. He doted on Jade, and it would be easier if she left Jade behind. Margaret knew it wouldn't be difficult for him to find a nanny. But then she thought of how the People had praised her for giving birth to such a perfect child and was afraid to leave her behind. Jade had become part of her identity with the People.

Having settled that in her mind, she bent down, and as she did, her long blond hair fell forward, hiding her face like a veil. She brushed the dark tangles from her baby's cheek then whispered softly in her ear.

"Jade...wake up, honey. We're going for a ride."

Four-year-old Jade Cochrane rolled over onto her side, subconsciously pulling away from her mother's grasp.

"No, Mommy," she muttered, her voice thick with sleep. "Don't wanna go."

Margaret glanced nervously over her shoulder, then grabbed the pink blanket that was Jade's sleeping companion and wrapped her up in a larger blanket before lifting her out of the bed.

"Sure you do," Margaret whispered. "You're Mommy's girl, and Mommy can't go without you."

Unaware that the pink blanket had fallen onto the floor, Margaret carried Jade out of the room, then hurried down the stairs of the old family mansion. Within seconds, she was out the door and running down the long drive toward an old

blue Volkswagen van parked at the curb. As she approached, the side door slid open. Two bearded men wearing soft flowing robes and ponytails met her with open arms, took Jade out of her arms, then followed her into the van. Within seconds, the door slid shut. There was a moment when Margaret looked up at the two men in the darkness and started to panic. Then one of the men took a hand-rolled joint out of his mouth and offered it to her.

"Here, pretty lady...have a toke."

Margaret shivered as she put the marijuana cigarette into her mouth. She inhaled sharply, held her breath for a moment to let the drug cycle through her brain, then exhaled through her nose. The kick of the drug silenced her conscience as competently as if she'd put a gun to her head and pulled the trigger. Two more pulls from the joint and she knew that she was right where she wanted to be.

Jade whimpered. One of the men pulled the covers up over her shoulder, then shifted her to the back of the van as the other man reached for the joint dangling between Margaret's fingers. He took a long drag, then put the vehicle in gear and sped away.

Inside the house, Sam Cochrane rolled over in bed, felt the empty pillow beside his head and sat upright with a jerk. His wife's absence wasn't unusual. She often got up in the night to check on Jade. But there was something about the silence of the house that felt different. There was a vacuum in the space where love was supposed to be.

"Maggie?"

No one answered.

He got up out of bed and hurried next door to their daughter's room. The room was dark, the door ajar. He shoved it aside and walked in, only to find the bed empty and his daughter gone. When he saw the pink blanket lying on the floor next to the bed and Jade nowhere in sight, his heart skipped a beat. Jade never slept without it. This time, when he called his wife's name, he was yelling.

"Maggie!"

Still no answer.

He turned on lights as he ran through the house, running up to the third floor, then back through the second, before going down the stairs to the main floor. It wasn't until he got to the foyer and found the door standing open that reality hit.

They were gone, and while the possibility of foul play couldn't be ruled out, in his heart, he knew what she'd done. The signs had been right in front of him for weeks, but he'd ignored them, refusing to believe Maggie was that unhappy, unwilling to admit that any part of it was his fault. He'd seen the love beads lying on her dresser, noticed the changes she'd made in her hairstyle and clothes. Last week he'd come home early and seen what society called a "hippie" van pulling out of the driveway. When he'd questioned Maggie about it, she'd shrugged it off by saying it was only people asking for directions. He hadn't believed her, but he'd been unwilling to broach the subject. And now it was too late.

He ran out onto the lawn and then down the driveway just in time to see a pair of taillights disappearing down the street.

"Maggie! Come back! Come back! For God's sake… come back!"

His screams shattered the silence of the night as he raced down the street chasing the taillights, but it was no use. The vehicle disappeared. She was gone, and she'd taken their baby with her.

1997

Pink and green reflections from the flashing neon sign outside the bedroom window painted the couple sleeping on the bed in eerie, garish flashes of color, giving their faces a harlequined appearance.

Outside the hotel, a police car sped past with sirens

screaming. At the sound, the woman flinched and then started to moan, which quickly roused the man sleeping beside her.

His name was Raphael, and for as long as he could remember, Jade had been the only person he had ever loved. He rose up on one elbow to look at her, wincing as movement caused the room to tilt. Ignoring a slight wave of nausea, he swiped a shaky hand across his face, then looked down at Jade.

She was dreaming again. He could see it on her face. The hell of their childhood had scarred them both in ways no one could know. If he had believed in God, he would have prayed for peace in their hearts, but the way he figured it, God was just a myth. If He had existed, He would never have let happen what had happened to them. So it was up to him to ease Jade's nightmares.

He bent down until his mouth was only inches away from her ear, then whispered softly, "Jade... Jade...it's all right, baby...it's all right. No one's going to hurt you...not anymore."

Then he slipped his arm beneath the curve of her neck and pulled her close against his chest.

Somewhere within the depths of Jade's mind, the familiarity of Raphael's voice registered. When it did, her panic subsided. She shuddered, then sighed.

"Yes, that's it," Raphael whispered, stroking her hair until he felt her body relax. "You're safe. You're safe. You're always safe with me."

Jade slept again, but Raphael did not. Sleep had become his nemesis, stealing time he was reluctant to waste. There was a knot in his stomach that had nothing to do with the nausea he'd suffered only moments ago. It was fear, pure and simple. Jade was his life—his world—but in his need to protect her from the hell of their past, he'd done something wrong, something that he had to put right. She'd come to depend upon him so much that he wasn't sure if she would

ever be able to function on her own. He hadn't meant to do it, but it had happened just the same.

Still asleep, she turned in his arms and then laid her cheek against his chest. The warmth of her sigh was a caress upon his skin. He swallowed past the knot in his throat, then threaded his fingers through her hair, unconsciously fisting the length of it in his palm.

"Love you, pretty girl," he said softly, then turned his head toward the window, waiting for dawn.

"Are you sure you want to take this?" Raphael asked, as he steadied the oversized painting Jade had just handed him against his leg.

Jade glanced up from the stack of paintings she was packing, eyed the one Raphael was holding, then shrugged.

"It's just a painting. We need the money."

Raphael frowned. "We always need the money, but this is a painting of your mother."

Jade straightened, then turned, fixing him with a cool, pointed look.

"That's not my mother. That's Ivy."

Raphael's frown deepened. "They are one and the same, and you know it."

"No, they aren't. My mother was a…she…damn it, Rafie, I can barely remember her *or* Ivy. My mother turned into some mushroom smoking hippie named Ivy. When she died, she left me in hell. Why should I care about some stupid picture of her? I don't even know why I painted it to begin with, so pack it."

"Yes, ma'am."

Jade glared at the smirk on Raphael's face, trying to maintain her anger, but she couldn't. Instead they packed up their stuff and headed out the door. A neighbor was giving them a ride in his truck to the street fair. The sun was shining; the sky was clear. It was promising to be a good day.

Jade smiled at Raphael as they rode in the back of the

truck, holding on to the paintings she was hoping to sell. He glanced at her and winked, then focused on the stack of canvases he was holding.

Jade sighed. She could never be mad at the man who'd saved her life. He wasn't just her best friend, he was the other half of her heart. And the fact that she'd taken the last of their savings to pay booth rent at a street fair in downtown San Francisco had been risky. They'd been hungry too often and homeless far more than she cared to count, so saving back any of her paintings, even the one of Ivy, was not only foolish, it was wasteful. Yet as they rode through the busy San Francisco streets, Jade couldn't help staring at the faces of the people they passed—convinced that one day their past would catch up with them and terrified of what would happen when it did.

She had little to no memory of anything before Ivy. Only now and then did she dream about a tall, dark-haired man who had played with her in a wading pool and rocked her to sleep. But the facial features were always vague, and when she woke, the image was always gone.

Most of the time, the face in her nightmares belonged to Solomon. Solomon of the smiling face—who smelled of incense and smoke—who brushed her hair and stroked her face and, the day after Ivy had died, had sold her tiny, six-year-old prepubescent body to a pedophile who preyed on little girls. He had been the first, but certainly not the last, man who'd paid money to ravage her body. And for the ensuing six years, she, like Raphael, became a marketable product for the People of Joy.

She couldn't remember a time when Raphael had not been part of her life—the young, beautiful boy/child three years her senior who had never known a mother or a father and, to the best of his knowledge, didn't have a last name. He was a product of the same commune in which Ivy had died and had no existence outside of Solomon's control. Solomon

had been his father figure. He had known nothing beyond obeying the wishes of the charismatic leader—doing anything to garner the rare moments of affection Solomon had bestowed upon him. He'd suffered the "uncles" who Solomon had brought for him to play with, not knowing that there was any other kind of life.

Then one day something happened that shattered his perception. It was a small crack—hardly more than a weakness in the ties that bound him to the world into which he'd been born. But to a child who'd never had a say in one waking moment of his life, it was huge. Raphael hadn't known it was possible to say no until he'd witnessed Jade throw a screaming fit and refuse to obey Solomon's demand.

She'd been screaming for her mother, and Solomon had laughed and told her that her mother was gone and was never coming back. Raphael wanted to tell her that it would be okay, that the uncles wouldn't keep her, that they always left after they were through playing, but he didn't get the chance.

And even though her tiny rebellion had been futile, it had planted a seed in his head that had slowly taken root. He hadn't known, until he'd witnessed Jade's rebellion, that it was okay to have an opinion of his own.

The bond that was forged between the two children grew stronger with each passing year, so that by the time Jade was twelve and Raphael fifteen, they had become inseparable.

Then the unthinkable happened. Jade began to mature. Her body was no longer that of a thin, hairless doll. She was becoming a woman, which made one "uncle" very unhappy.

Frank Lawson had paid Solomon five hundred dollars for an entire night with Jade. He'd been with her numerous times before, but never for the whole night, and not in the past six months. When she'd arrived in his room and he had seen what nature had done to her body, it infuriated him. The sight of her budding breasts and shapely hips had ended his erection in a way that nothing else could have done. Angry and embarrassed that he couldn't "get it up," he tried a little

acid. Within minutes, her tiny breasts seemed to grow before him, turning colors, then changing shapes, while the terror on her face turned her into a laughing, shrieking bitch.

Horrified by what he was seeing, he lashed out, hitting her over and over with his fists. By now, her body seemed a voluptuous symbol of what he should want but did not. He staggered, and as he did, reached out to steady himself. When his hand closed over a bottle of wine, he grabbed it by the neck and swung. It missed the girl by inches, instead shattering on the bedpost. Wine and glass went everywhere, turning colors and then exploding in Frank's mind like fireworks on the Fourth of July.

Suddenly the jagged neck of the bottle morphed into a sword. He spun abruptly, swinging it toward the shrieking, screaming bitch, wanting to silence her forever.

The slash of glass against skin was sudden—the skin parting like a hot knife through soft butter. Through a drug-induced fog, he saw the woman reaching for her body, then trying to hold it together with both hands.

When the child sank to the floor in a puddle of her own blood, what Frank saw was the body of a headless serpent.

''Yes!'' he shouted, and thrust his arm upward in a gesture of victory, still clutching the sword.

Raphael had been awakened by the sound of Jade's screams. At fifteen, he was already six feet tall and strong beyond his years. With heart racing, he dashed out of his room and then down the hall. He kicked in the door with one blow, saw Jade lying in a pool of her own blood, picked up an overturned chair and swung it across the back of the man's head. There was a loud pop, then the man went limp, dropping to the floor like a felled ox. Raphael shouted for help. Soon, footsteps could be heard running toward them. Expecting that the help that was coming would be for them, Raphael picked Jade up off the floor.

Solomon was the first in the room, followed closely by

two of his trusted assistants. They took one look at all the blood and then at Frank's limp body.

"You've killed him!" Solomon shouted.

"But look what he did to her," Raphael moaned.

"You stupid bastard!" Solomon said, then kicked a pair of pillows aside. "Fuck this mess." He grabbed a sheet off the bed, tossed it over Jade's body, and waved a hand in Raphael's direction. "Get her out of here."

Raphael bolted for the door. But this time, something inside him snapped. If she wasn't already dead, he had only this one chance to save her. So once again, Jade Cochrane was kidnapped—carried out into the night without her knowledge. Only this time, it was to escape the hell into which she'd been thrust.

Raphael laid Jade in the passenger side of Solomon's van, then ran back into the house, into Solomon's private room, and stole every penny of the money the man kept in his desk. His legs were shaking as he bolted out of the room and back outside to Jade. She hadn't moved, but he could hear her groaning. He jumped in the van. With a prayer on his lips, he turned the key. The engine turned raggedly for several tries and then suddenly started.

Solomon came running out of the house, screaming Jade's name, as Raphael gunned the engine and took off down the driveway. He didn't know where he was going or how badly Jade had been injured, but he did know that their survival hinged upon escaping the old farmhouse and the People of Joy.

Twelve years later, they were still running, living by their wits and the occasional turn of good luck, but certain that if they were found, they would go to prison for murder.

Jade was riding a rare high as she handed over the caricature she'd just drawn of her latest customer and pocketed another ten dollar bill. She'd lost count after her fiftieth customer had come and gone, which meant she'd made over five

hundred dollars alone on the simple ten-minute line drawings that had become her stock in trade. Added to that, Raphael had sold nine of her oil paintings, ranging in price from fifty to one hundred dollars. The money they were making today would make the next two or three months a whole lot easier than they'd expected them to be.

"You want something cold to drink?" Raphael asked, as he stepped out from behind her easel.

Jade touched the side of Raphael's face. He was shivering, although the day was nice and warm, and he looked awfully pale.

"You all right?"

"Sure, baby...lemonade okay?"

She nodded, then frowned as she watched Raphael cross the walkway between the booths to the refreshment stand only a few yards away. It was the first time she'd looked at him—really looked—in ages, and he seemed thinner. She sighed and swiped a weary hand across her forehead, absently swiping a lock of dark hair from her face as she turned around. She was thinner, too. It was what happened when you didn't have enough to eat. Then she smiled, thinking of the money they were making today. At least they would eat well tonight. Maybe she could talk Raphael into steak. He needed to get some meat back on his bones.

Lost in thought, she was startled when she felt a hand on her knee. She flinched, then saw it was a child, and relaxed.

"Well, hello there," she said. "What's your name?"

"Kenny."

She knelt down. "So, Kenny, would you like me to draw your picture?"

"Yes, please," a woman said.

Jade looked up. A young woman, obviously Kenny's mother, was smiling at Jade and handing her a ten-dollar bill. As Jade pocketed the money and set Kenny down on a stool, she saw a man approaching.

"Look, honey," the woman said. "She's going to draw Kenny's picture."

"That's great," the man said. "Sit real still for the pretty lady," he said, and then gave Jade a friendly wink.

She nodded, then turned to her task, but her thoughts quickly wavered. The man and woman appeared to be so happy. They kept touching each other in brief but tender ways, and the smiles on their faces as they looked at their son were nothing short of stunned, as if they could hardly believe that their love had produced something as wonderful as this child.

Soon she was finished. She rolled the drawing into a tube, fastened it with a rubber band and handed it to the woman.

"Great kid," she said.

The woman beamed. "Thank you." And then they were gone.

Jade stood for a moment, unaware of the wistful expression on her face. And while she didn't assume for a minute that she would ever meet a man who could love her in spite of what she'd been, it didn't stop her from thinking, *What if?*

But Jade had long since given up on living a normal life. For now, she was just satisfied that their money troubles were momentarily solved. So she turned back to her easel and began trimming her charcoal pencils for the next customer.

A few minutes later, Raphael set a cup of cold lemonade on the tray beside her, gently stroked his hand down the back of her head as she thanked him with a smile, then walked back to the front of the booth.

There was an empty space on the wall from the last painting he'd sold. He looked around at the assortment of canvases leaning against the table leg for something to replace it. Almost immediately his gaze fell on the painting of Ivy. He hesitated, then turned to ask Jade if she was still sure she wanted to sell it, only to see that she was seating a new

customer. Shrugging off the thought, he picked up the painting and hung it on the empty hook.

It was tradition for Paul and Shelly Hudson to visit San Francisco during the month of May. Not only was it the city where they had met over twenty-seven years earlier, but it was the place where they'd gotten married. Renewing their emotional ties here every year was part of what had kept their marriage so strong. It had also kept the ties of old friendship alive. Tomorrow they would return to their home in St. Louis, but today had been dedicated to visiting old haunts and old friends, which was why Shelly and her friend, Deb Carson, found themselves in the midst of a street fair, while Paul and Deb's husband, Frank, were doing a little deep-sea fishing. Only weeks earlier, Deb had taken up photography as a hobby, and today she was snapping pictures left and right. They'd been at the fair for at least a couple of hours when suddenly she paused, letting her camera dangle from the cord around her neck as she pointed toward a nearby table.

"Oh, look at that darling little lighthouse!" Deb said, pointing to a booth with an array of hand-carved objects. She picked it up, eyeing the price and grimacing as she quickly replaced it on the table. "Good grief! One hundred and twenty dollars! It's not *that* darling."

Shelly laughed and nodded in agreement. As she turned away from the table, she looked up. Seconds later, the smile died on her lips.

"Sweet mother of God."

Deb stared at her friend. Shelly was pale and shaking. She slipped her arm around Shelly's waist and pulled her close.

"Dear…what's wrong? Are you ill?"

Shelly shook her head, then pointed to a nearby artist's booth.

"The woman in that painting! I know her…. At least, I did…once."

"Really? How exciting! How did you know her?"

"She was married to Paul's best friend, Sam."

Deb frowned. "Was? What happened to her?"

"She disappeared one night twenty years ago, taking their four-year-old daughter with her."

Deb's frown deepened. "How sad."

Sad wasn't the word for what had happened to Sam Cochrane's life. The loss of his wife and daughter had almost destroyed him. As far as Shelly knew, this was the first clue as to where Margaret had gone. She twisted out of Deb's grasp.

"I've got to talk to the artist," she said, and hurried toward the tall, dark-haired man manning the booth. "Sir. Sir! Excuse me. How much is this painting?"

Raphael turned around. When he saw which canvas the woman was pointing at, his heart dropped. It was the painting of Ivy.

"I'm not sure," he said.

"The woman in the painting…I know her. At least, I used to. Do you know where she is?"

Raphael stifled a sense of panic. In all their years on the run, they'd never seen even one of the People of Joy. He didn't remember this woman, but twelve years was a long time. People changed. She could have been with the People. She was definitely the right age. Before he could speak, he sensed Jade's presence, then felt her hand on his back before she stepped out from behind him.

"You're interested in buying it?" Jade asked.

It hadn't occurred to Shelly before, but now it seemed vital that she take back proof of what she'd seen. She didn't know what Sam would do with it, but she knew he would want it.

"Yes…yes, I am," Shelly said, then saw the man frown before he slid his arm around the woman's shoulder. "Did you paint it?" Shelly asked.

Jade nodded.

"The woman in the painting—"

"You mean Ivy? She's dead. Been dead for years."

Shelly's eyes filled with tears. "Oh. Oh, no." Then she reached toward the painting, gently touching the smooth, unlined face of the pretty blonde leaning against a trellis of ivy. "I knew her by another name."

Now it was Jade who stiffened. "What do you mean?"

"I met her years ago, when she lived in St. Louis. Her name…was…Margaret Cochrane. She—"

Jade turned abruptly, suddenly terrified of hearing more.

"If she wants the painting, sell it," she told Raphael, and started to walk away.

"How much?" Shelly called.

"Five hundred dollars," Jade yelled, and then disappeared behind the booth, certain that the woman would be unwilling to pay such an exorbitant price.

But she'd underestimated Shelly's determination to bring back some sort of closure for Sam.

Shelly started digging through her purse. "Will you take a check?"

Raphael shook his head. "No. Cash only," he said, and then frowned when he realized the other woman had been taking pictures of them. "No more," he said, holding up his hand.

"Sorry," Deb said, and grinned. "Has anyone told you that you're very photogenic?"

Raphael stifled a curse. His looks were what had gotten him into Solomon's hell.

"Five hundred dollars, take it or leave it," he said, wishing they would leave so he could check on Jade.

"I've only got three hundred and forty-two dollars cash," Shelly muttered, as she spread the bills out onto the table.

"Here," Deb said. "I think I've got enough to make up the difference. You can pay me back later."

To Raphael's dismay, the women came up with the money. He had no choice but to hand over the canvas.

"The woman in the painting…did you know her?" Shelly asked.

"Why would I know her?" Raphael asked. "You heard what she told you. The woman has been dead for years."

"Yes, right," Shelly said. "I was just hoping. She ran away from her family and—"

"Raphael!"

He turned abruptly. The panic in Jade's voice was obvious.

"Got to go," he said shortly, leaving Shelly with more questions than answers.

"Come on, Deb," Shelly said. "Let's get this to the car, then call the guys. Paul is going to be stunned by what I found."

They walked away with their find as Raphael discovered Jade packing up her things.

"Call a cab," she said. "We've got to get out of here."

"But, honey, those people might know if you have any other family."

Jade couldn't focus on anything but running. "We don't know anything of the sort," she muttered. "What if she ran into Ivy again while she was with the People? She would think Solomon was my family." Then she shuddered and clutched Raphael by the arms. "We can't let him find us. We just can't."

"Don't panic, baby...don't panic. It's okay." Then he took her in his arms, holding her tight as a wave of trembling shook her body. "Hell, for all we know, Solomon is dead and gone."

Two

The sun was setting by the time Jade and Raphael got back to their apartment, but her panic had not subsided. The woman who'd purchased the painting of Ivy had started a chain reaction of fear. All Jade could think about was getting away—running, as they had so often in the past. Because of the life they'd lived with Solomon, neither Jade nor Raphael had ever gone a day to a regular school. Thanks to an ex-teacher who'd abdicated responsibility for the People of Joy and taken it upon himself to teach the children who'd gotten caught up in Solomon's web, they were remarkably well read and competent in basic mathematics, but their real skills lay in keeping themselves alive and fed. There was nothing they could put on a job application that would get them hired, and not a high school diploma between them. With no responsibility to anything or anyone but each other, they moved often on little more than a whim.

But tonight it was more than a whim that had Jade stuffing her meager assortment of clothes into her bag. Raphael knew Jade had been rattled by the woman's appearance, and, like Jade, didn't know what to make of it, or of her. If the woman had only known Jade's mother after she called herself Ivy, then she would have had no way of knowing her real name, yet she'd claimed the painting was of a woman named Margaret Cochrane who had lived in St. Louis, Missouri.

Raphael's first urge had been to check out the claim. What if the possibility existed that Jade's father was still alive?

What if he'd spent all these years searching for his daughter? Reuniting Jade with her family would be the answer to Raphael's dilemma, but he knew Jade, and she wasn't in the mood to be reasoned with. Not now. Not yet. He would let her get the panic out of her system, then talk to her about it later, so now he sat on the side of the bed, watching Jade run from the dresser to the closet and back again, packing to leave.

"Don't you think we should at least wait until daylight to run?"

The sarcasm in his voice angered Jade. She turned on him, her dark eyebrows knitting across her forehead.

"Did I say I was leaving right now? No! I don't think so. But I'm by God going to be ready when daylight comes tomorrow."

Raphael held out his hand, then threaded his fingers through hers, gentling her with a touch.

"Honey...I don't think that woman poses any danger."

Jade slumped onto his lap and then curled her arms around Raphael's neck, resting her face against the curve of his neck.

"I'm sorry. I didn't mean to snap at you. Don't be mad at me, Rafie.... I can't bear it when you're mad."

He rubbed his hand up and down the middle of her back as he rocked her where they sat.

"I'm not mad, baby...just worried. We can't run forever."

Jade lifted her head, her eyes wide with fear.

"Yes, we can, Rafie. We have to. I can't go back to that life. I'd rather die."

Raphael's eyes filled with tears. His little Jade had grown up to be a magnificent woman, but inside she was still that frightened and tortured little girl.

"That's not going to happen, honey. And you know why?"

Her voice was shaky as she leaned back to meet his gaze. "Why?"

"Because you're not that same helpless little girl. You're

not only a full-grown woman, you're a survivor. If you have to, you could do anything…even take care of yourself."

She shuddered, then hugged him again. "But I don't have to, do I, Rafie? Not as long as I have you."

Raphael sighed, then hugged her close. "Yes, you're right, honey. Not as long as you have me. So where do you want to go?"

"We've never been to New Orleans. I've always wanted to see the French Quarter…maybe eat some crawfish and dance to some Cajun music. And it would be a perfect place to paint. What do you think?"

He tilted her chin up until they were looking eye to eye. "Wherever you go, I will follow."

Jade stared back, seeing her own reflection in his pupils.

"Rafie?"

"What?"

"Do you ever feel like I'm in your way?"

He frowned. "What makes you say such a crazy thing?"

She shrugged. "You know…you're so beautiful, and I see the way women stare at you. That woman today who was taking our pictures, even she mentioned your looks. Do you ever feel like pursuing a relationship with any of them?"

His face stilled; then she watched his eyes fill with what appeared to be great sadness and regret.

"No. Maybe it has something to do with what I went through as a kid. How about you? Do you ever feel anything when you see a good-looking man?"

She shivered. "Sometimes I wonder, but then I remember, and I put it out of my mind."

"They aren't all like that, you know. They don't all want to hurt you."

Jade's lower lip trembled. "But how do you tell them apart? How would I separate a good man from the others?"

"I don't know honey…but I think that you'd know it in here." He put his hand over her heart. "It's something called trust."

"I trust you," she said.

"And I trust you, but you're like my sister. I could never think of you that way."

Jade grimaced. "Me, either. I didn't mean it that way. I only—"

He pinched her nose in a teasing fashion. "I know. I know. I was just teasing you." Then he gave her a big hug. "Go take a shower and get ready for bed while I pack my stuff. That way we can get an early start tomorrow."

"Okay," she said, and jumped up from the bed. She opened the closet, got down on her knees, then pulled a small box from the depths.

"What's that?" Raphael asked.

Once again she got that look on her face that reminded him of a helpless child. She clutched the box close to her chest, her voice trembling as she suddenly looked away.

"It's the faces. I can't forget them."

He sighed. "Maybe you should."

All the helplessness vanished from her persona as she angrily turned on him.

"Can you?" she asked.

He shrugged. "God knows I try."

She lifted her chin, her eyes flashing with hate.

"I don't! I won't!" Then she took a deep breath and shoved the box in the bottom of her bag, her anger vanishing as swiftly as it had come. "I can't," she added, and walked into the bathroom.

As soon as she closed the door, he dropped his head in his hands, stifling the urge to scream.

God in heaven, help me get through this without coming undone.

When he heard the shower beginning to run, he stifled a sigh and pulled his suitcase from beneath the bed, took out the last of his pills and tossed them down his throat. Tomorrow they would be on the run. Again. Would this ever end?

* * *

At sixty, Sam Cochrane was still a striking man. He had a full head of steel-gray hair and a commanding presence that went well with the man he'd become. During the past twenty years, he'd become one of St. Louis's leading citizens, amassing his wealth through wise investments and a successful law practice, although he'd retired from the court just last year. While he took pride in his accomplishments, he would have traded it all to have a second chance with the wife and daughter he'd lost. For ten years after they had disappeared, he'd spent every spare dime he could muster, hiring one private investigator after another to search for them, but with no success. Finally he'd given up the quest in hopes that one day Jade would come looking for him, which explained why, despite his wealth and status, he was still living in the same location. Not a day went by that he didn't think of them, refusing to accept the notion that they could be dead. Then Paul and Shelly Hudson came back from California.

It was three o'clock on a Sunday afternoon when Sam Cochrane's doorbell began to chime. Normally Velma Shaffer, the housekeeper who'd been with him for the past ten years, would have been on the job to answer the door, but her daughter had gone into labor on Friday, presenting Velma with her first grandchild, and Sam had given her the week off.

He hadn't been expecting company and frowned at the interruption as he put down the book he'd been reading, marking his place with a piece of junk mail he had yet to discard, and started toward the front door. The library was some distance from the entryway, and by the time he got there, the chimes had rung another two times.

His frown deepened, but his disapproval quickly turned to delight when he saw Paul and Shelly on the doorstep.

"Hey, you two! Come in! Come in! I thought you were still in California."

They hurried inside, carrying what appeared to be a large framed painting between them.

"What do you have there?" Sam asked.

Shelly bit her lower lip, searching for a way to explain.

"Just show him," Paul said.

Shelly took a deep breath, slowly turning the painting around until it was facing Sam.

The smile on Sam's face stilled as the breath caught in the back of his throat. His vision blurred. His hands started to shake.

"Oh God...oh God...where did you get it?"

"A street fair in San Francisco."

"Was she there? Did you see her?"

"No, Sam, she wasn't there."

The brief moment of hope that he'd felt faded. But to see her face, after all these years, was staggering. He moved toward the painting, putting the palm of his hand against the face on the canvas, then tracing the shape of her eyebrows and the curve of her cheek.

"Maggie...my Maggie."

Then he looked up. Shelly's eyes were filled with tears. His stomach dropped.

"What aren't you telling me?"

Paul reached for his friend, clasping a hand on Sam's shoulder.

"Shelly was stunned when she saw it. She told the artist that she had known the subject years ago and told her that her name was Margaret Cochrane. The artist said it was a woman who called herself Ivy."

Sam frowned. "Are you saying that this isn't Margaret?"

"No, what I'm saying is exactly what Shelly was told."

Sam looked at Shelly. "What else were you told?"

Shelly hesitated.

"Talk to me," Sam said. "You can't bring this to me now,

not after all this time, and then not tell me everything you know.''

Shelly braced herself, hating to be the one to say the words that were going to hurt their friend.

"Sam, I'm sorry, but she also told us that the woman in the painting was dead.''

It wasn't as if the thought had never gone through his mind, but hearing the words said aloud was like a knife through Sam's heart.

"No,'' he said, then looked back down at the painting and at the pensive smile on his young wife's face. "Not dead. Please, God, not dead.''

"It's what the artist told us.''

But Sam needed a lifeline. "What if he was lying? What if he just told you that to hide Margaret's real location?'' He looked at the painting, searching for a signature, but there was nothing but an odd colored smudge in the bottom right hand corner that looked like a fingerprint.

"The artist was a woman. She didn't seem as if she was trying to hide anything. In fact, she seemed rather matter-of-fact about the subject.''

"I need to talk to her,'' Sam said. "Did you get her name?''

Shelly's shoulders slumped. "No. I'm sorry. I was so excited to see the painting…then they would only take cash, and my girlfriend and I were busy counting out the money we had between us. The artist walked away, leaving the man who was with her to collect our money.''

"Damn it,'' Sam muttered. "I can't leave it like this…not after all this time.''

Shelly looked at Sam, then started to cry.

"I don't know why I thought this would be a good thing. All I've done is make you miserable. Can you ever forgive me?''

Suddenly Sam realized what he'd done. Shelly and Paul had brought him a gift beyond words, and instead of being

grateful for the only clue he'd had to his wife's disappearance in the past twenty years, he'd been thoughtless—even cruel. He swiped his palm across his face and then held out his hands.

"No. No, it's I who should be asking your forgiveness. I'm sorry for reacting so badly, but this caught me by surprise."

"It's okay," Shelly said. "We should have warned you instead of just showing up like this, but I was so excited and then—"

"And so am I," Sam said, interrupting her before she could finish. "I'm also ashamed of my behavior." He held out his arms. Shelly walked into his embrace as he gave her a hug. "Forgive me?"

"Of course," she said. "And the painting is yours to do with as you choose."

"Thank you," Sam said.

He took the painting and set it down, hesitating briefly before turning its face to the wall. "Now come inside and tell me about your trip."

The couple led the way into the living room, with Sam following behind. They didn't see him stop and glance back into the hallway or see the wave of despair cross his face. It wasn't until later, when they finally took their leave, that Sam was able to let go of the emotions he'd been trying to suppress. He took the painting into the library where he'd been reading, took down an original Wyeth that had been hanging over the sideboard and hung the painting of the woman named Ivy in its place.

His hands were shaking as he walked back across the room and sat down in the chair where he'd been reading earlier— before his carefully manufactured world had fallen apart. He picked up the book, removed the piece of junk mail that he'd used as a bookmark and then looked down at the page. The words were little more than a blur.

He inhaled slowly and then wiped his eyes, once again

trying to resume reading where he'd left off. But the words on the page still all ran together, fading in a watery blur. He dropped the book onto the floor between his feet, then leaned back in the chair and stared across the room.

She smiled at him from beneath the arbor of ivy, her long blond hair falling over her shoulders and down across her breasts. Her feet were bare; their painted pink toenails a bright contrast to the yellow fabric of her long gypsy dress. There was a chain of daisies woven through her hair and another dangling from one hand. She looked young and happy and seemingly oblivious to the fact that she'd destroyed his world and stolen his child. Facing her this way— now, after all this time—made him so very, very sad and so very, very angry.

"So they tell me you're dead. Are you, Margaret...or Ivy...or whatever the hell you called yourself? Are you dead?" He shuddered, as if the words were bitter on his tongue. "So be it, my love. One day I will join you. Then maybe you can explain what the hell you were thinking when you did what you did."

Margaret's expression didn't change. Her smile didn't waver. Her eyes didn't blink. The complacency of the woman in the painting began to get under Sam's skin. How could she smile like that when she'd destroyed him? And there was Jade. His sweet little baby girl. If she was still alive, she was no longer a child.

He got up from where he was sitting and walked toward the painting with purpose in his step, stopping only a few feet from where he'd hung the picture to gaze into her face.

"Where is she?" he muttered. "What did you do with Jade?"

But there had never been answers in Margaret Cochrane, only questions, and asking them now was redundant.

He leaned closer, staring at the right-hand corner near the frame. That smudge he'd noticed earlier was still there, and the longer he looked, the more convinced he became that it

was a fingerprint. If so, maybe it would lead to the artist and to the answers he so desperately needed. It was then that he thought of Lucas Kelly. If anyone could make sense of this, it would be Luke. He reached for the phone, then remembered Luke was out of town until tomorrow. Still, he could leave a message. He made the call, unaware that his voice was shaking. Once he was through, he looked up at the painting one last time, then headed for the hall. As he reached the doorway, he flipped off the lights, leaving the picture of his wife just as she'd left him all those years ago—in the dark and without a backward glance.

Luke Kelly walked into his apartment after five days on the road, set down his suitcase and then punched the play button on his answering machine as he sorted through his mail. The last call was from Sam Cochrane.

He smiled when he heard Sam's voice. He had known him for more than ten years and considered Sam one of his best friends. But the more he heard, the more he realized that he had never heard Sam this shaken.

Without hesitation, he dialed Sam's number. Sam answered on the first ring.

"I'm home. What's wrong?"

Sam exhaled slowly. Just hearing Luke's voice was settling.

"How soon can you come over? I need to talk to you."

"I'm on my way," Luke said, and hung up in Sam's ear.

He didn't bother to change or unpack, and ignored the fact that he needed a shave. Not once in the eleven years he'd known Sam had he ever asked for a favor. That he was doing it now was indicative of how important this must be. He reached for his car keys, shoved a hand through his hair in lieu of a comb and headed back out the door.

Twenty minutes later he was pulling into Sam's driveway. Sam met him at the door.

"Where's Velma?" he asked, as Sam let him in.

"Her daughter had a baby. I gave her the week off."

Luke tried a smile. "I'm assuming that's not why you called."

Sam shook his head. "No, it's not." Then he eyed Luke's appearance. "You look like hell."

Luke grinned. "Why, thank you, Sam."

Finally Sam managed a chuckle. "Okay, okay. I'm sorry. It's just that I've never seen St. Louis's most eligible bachelor looking so…casual."

"Five days on the road chasing bad guys."

"Did you find them?" Sam asked.

Luke nodded.

"Good, then you're hired."

Luke's eyes widened. "You're serious, aren't you?"

"More than you can know. Come with me," Sam said, and led the way to the library. Once inside, he turned and pointed to the picture he'd hung last night.

"Hey, what happened to the Wyeth?" Luke asked. "Did someone steal it?"

"No. For the time being, it's in storage."

"Then what's with this? It's good. In fact, it's really good. Who's the artist?"

"I don't know, but I need you to find her for me."

"Why?"

Sam took a deep breath and then turned to face the painting. "Because that's a painting of my wife, Margaret. She's been missing for more than twenty years, and it's the first sign of her I've had since it happened."

Luke was stunned. He'd known of the incident and how deeply Sam had been affected. More than once he'd heard Sam speak of the little girl, Jade, who'd been so dear to his heart, but he'd rarely heard Sam speak of his wife. Now, from the expression on Sam's face, he could only assume that one reason Sam had been quiet about Margaret was that the incident was too painful.

"Where did you get this?" he asked.

"Paul and Shelly found it at a street fair in San Francisco last week."

"My God...what are the odds?" Luke muttered; then he leaned forward, looking for a name on the painting, and saw nothing but a faint image of a fingerprint stamped in red on the grass beneath the woman's bare feet.

"There's no name on the painting," he said.

"Yes, I know, and unfortunately, Shelly didn't get the artist's name when she was buying this. That's where you come in. Will you help?"

"Of course," Luke said. "I'll need to talk to Paul and Shelly before I go any further. They might remember something on questioning."

Sam hesitated, then shoved his hands into his pockets and strode to the window on the other side of the room.

Luke frowned, then followed his friend.

"Is there something else you're not telling me?"

Sam's shoulders slumped. "Shelly said that the artist knew Margaret as Ivy. She also said that Margaret was dead."

Luke flinched. He could only imagine what the news had done to Sam.

"Do you believe her?" he asked.

Sam shrugged. "Hell, Luke, I don't know what to believe. But I need to know the truth, or as much of it as you can determine. Even if it's true...even if Margaret is dead... something might lead me to Jade." Then his voice softened, and it was almost as if he was talking to himself rather than Luke. "All these years, I've managed to exist by telling myself that, while they were no longer with me, they were still somewhere on this earth, breathing the same air that I breathe, rising to the same sun and sleeping beneath the same moon as I do. They can't both be dead. They just can't."

Luke clasped his friend's shoulder and gave it a squeeze.

"I'll do my best," he promised. "If there's an answer to be had, I'll get it."

Sam turned. A muscle was jerking in his jaw as he reached for Luke's hand.

"Thank you, my friend. Find my family and you can name your price."

"There is no price on friendship," Luke countered. "I'll settle for a few prayers."

Sam nodded, choking back tears as he shook Luke's hand.

"Time enough for all this in the upcoming days. For now, you need to go home and get some rest."

"I'll be in touch," Luke said, and started to leave, then hesitated and turned back around. He pointed to the painting.

"Will you let me have this for a bit?"

"Certainly," Sam said. "But why?"

"That fingerprint. Thought I'd run it through channels and see what we come up with."

Sam's eyes widened, and then he started to smile.

"Good thinking," he said.

Luke grinned. "It's what I do."

Three

Shelly Hudson's phone was ringing when she came in from the garage. She ran to answer with a breathless hello.

"Shelly, it's Luke Kelly."

"Luke! How nice to hear from you. I understood you were out of town."

"Yes, I was. Got back yesterday."

"We barely beat you home. Paul and I returned only a couple of days ago ourselves."

"Yes, I know. It's part of why I'm calling. Sam showed me the painting."

"Oh." There was a moment of hesitation then Shelly added. "Is Sam okay? Paul and I have been torn about what we did. I don't know whether bringing that painting home did him a favor or not."

"He's fine. In fact, I'm going to do a little investigating for him, and I would like to talk to you and Paul about the artist. Since there was no signature on the painting, it's possible you heard a name and have just forgotten. Sometimes talking about an incident brings back memories."

"Paul won't be of any help. He wasn't even there. My girlfriend and I were the ones at the street fair. Unfortunately she's in San Francisco. I'd be happy to talk to you, although I'm sure I remembered all there was to tell."

"When can I come over?"

Shelly glanced at the clock. It was almost noon.

"If you're up for some chicken Caesar salad, come now and I'll fix us both some lunch."

"Sounds like a plan," Luke said. "Is thirty minutes okay?"

"Perfect," Shelly said. "I hope I can help. I feel so responsible for opening this Pandora's box."

"Don't worry about it," Luke said. "I'll be there soon."

Less than thirty minutes later, Shelly heard a car pulling up their driveway and looked out. It was Luke. She stood for a moment, admiring the pure physical attraction of the man. Over and above his intelligence and successful career, he was more than a sight to behold. He stood well over six feet tall, with chocolate-brown hair and sharp green eyes. His chin was square, his lips full and often smiling. His eyebrows were almost as expressive as his mouth, often arching with surprise or tilting in a quirky manner that mirrored anything from disdain to surprise. He wore his clothes with a casual indifference, conscious only of their fit. But women saw more than a tall, good-looking man. To them, he was a talking, walking, hunk of alpha male.

Even Shelly, who was almost twenty years his senior and a happily married woman, could appreciate the beauty of a perfect male. She wiped her hands on a towel and hurried to the door and let him in.

"You're just in time," she said, offering her cheek for the kiss she knew would be coming.

"You smell good," Luke said, as he followed Shelly Hudson into the kitchen.

She turned and grinned. "Since I'm not wearing any perfume, it's got to be the chicken."

"Like I said, you smell good."

She laughed aloud and waved him toward a chair in the breakfast nook.

"Hope you don't mind, but I thought we'd eat in here."

"This is perfect," Luke said. "Anything I can do to help?"

"I have iced tea in the fridge. You can get it and the glasses I have chilling in the freezer and put them on the table."

"Will do," Luke said.

Soon they were sitting down to eat, and for a short time, they stuck to safe topics of conversation. It wasn't until Shelly was taking their plates to the dishwasher and pouring them some coffee that Luke shifted the mood.

"Tell me about the street fair," Luke said.

Shelly set a plate of cookies on the table between them, pushed the cream and sugar toward Luke and leaned back in her chair.

Luke sugared and creamed his coffee, then picked up a cookie as Shelly began to talk.

"It was such a perfect day. The last day of our trip. My friend, Deb, took me to this street fair. We'd been there at least a couple of hours when I saw the booth." Then she grinned. "Truthfully, I probably saw the man who was working there first."

"I thought the artist was a woman," Luke said.

"Oh, she was, but there was this man with her." Shelly sighed. "He was absolutely beautiful." She giggled, a little embarrassed at herself. "You know…long black hair, striking blue eyes, and the most stunning face…like some Michelangelo statue come to life."

"Did you get a name?"

Shelly frowned. "I don't think so. I saw the painting almost immediately, and after that forgot everything except—"

"Yeah, I can understand. Sam said something about the artist calling the subject by a different name?"

Shelly nodded. "Oh, yes! That surprised me. I suppose it stood to reason, though. If I ran away from my family, I wouldn't be calling myself Shelly Hudson. I'd use another name, which is what I suppose Margaret did." Then she

leaned forward, resting her elbows on the table. "After all, that was a different time, remember? It was the mid-seventies when Margaret disappeared. She got caught up in some cult, obviously changed her name and got lost in that underground society."

"Yeah, I gathered that much from Sam."

"He was devastated. Looked for them for years, but there wasn't a clue. Then this…" Shelly shrugged, then wiped her hands across her face, as if to clear her thoughts. "I had to bring it to him, didn't I, Luke? Please tell me I did the right thing?"

"Absolutely," Luke said, and covered her hand with his. "The worst thing in life is not knowing what's happened to a missing loved one. Trust me, I've been through this countless times with other people. Which brings me to the next question. They told you that the woman in the painting was dead, right?"

Shelly nodded. "Said she'd been dead for years."

Luke frowned. "Did you ask about her daughter?"

Shelly sighed. "No, and I could kick myself, but I was so stunned, it didn't occur to me to follow up like that."

"And that's where I come in," Luke said. "What I need is the address where the fair was held. People usually have to rent booth space, so they should have a record somewhere of the renters' names."

"Oh, Luke! I never thought of that!"

Luke grinned. "Yeah, well, that's why I get the big bucks and you smell so good."

Shelly threw back her head and laughed, her short blond curls bouncing with mirth.

"You make me feel so much better about all this," she said.

"After that wonderful meal, it's the least I can do."

"You'll have to come back for dinner sometime soon. Paul was saying the other day that it's been ages since we've all been together for a meal."

"Name the day and I'm here," Luke said, then stood. "If you remember anything else—anything at all—call me immediately. In fact, why don't you call your friend, Deb, and see if she remembers something."

"Good idea," Shelly said. "I'll be in touch."

Within minutes Luke was gone, leaving Shelly with a lighter heart and a kitchen full of dirty dishes.

But Luke wasn't through for the day. He had the painting in the back seat of his car and was now on his way to the St. Louis Police Department. There was a detective there who owed him a favor, and he wanted the use of their crime lab. If they were lucky, the fingerprint left in paint on the picture might give him a name. It was a long shot, but nothing he could afford to ignore.

Raphael had the aisle seat on the bus bound for New Orleans, putting himself, as always between Jade and the rest of the world. Jade was asleep, curled up in the window seat with her head against the window. The air conditioner vent was blowing directly on her shoulders. He could tell by the way she was sitting that she was cold, so he reached up over her head to adjust the flow.

Even in her sleep, Jade felt the cessation of air on her face. Almost immediately her sleep went from dreamless to a flashback of a hellish incident from her childhood.

It was almost midnight in the San Fernando Valley, where the People of Joy were now living. The old ranch house belonged to a distant relative of one of the People, but he would never know. The stroke that had robbed him of his senses would keep him hospitalized in the sanatorium where he now resided until death took him to a better place.

The rooms where the children slept were at the far end of the sprawling building, supposedly for their well-being. But some of the children would have argued the excuse. Isolated from the other rooms, it was simple for Solomon to pick and

choose the child of the moment for the "customers" who, from time to time, came calling.

Tonight, Jade slept curled up against a little girl they called Sunshine. Sunshine was blond and chubby and on occasion still wet the bed. Jade liked her well enough but always slept on the edge of the bed for fear she would wake up in Sunshine's pee, and tonight was no exception.

The ceiling fan squeaked with every rotation, but the repetitive sound and the flow of air on seven-year-old Jade's face was oddly soothing. They were familiar things that proved no threat.

She was dreaming about the sweetness of the blackberries that they'd picked earlier in the day when something about the dream began to change. The breeze she'd been feeling on her face was no longer blowing. It had happened before and meant bad things would happen. She started to squirm. There was something that she needed to remember—what happened when the wind stopped blowing. But she was so deep into sleep she couldn't make herself wake up.

Then the mattress beneath her started to shift. Mental warning bells went off so loudly that she sat straight up in bed with a gasp.

"Shh," a voice whispered. "It's okay, my beautiful darling, it's okay. Sunshine wet this bed, so you're going to a clean one."

Jade knew the voice—Solomon's voice. She also knew he didn't care if she slept in Sunshine's pee. He was why the wind quit blowing. Every time he leaned over to pick her up out of bed, he blocked the air from the fan. He was going to take her to the purple room again, and she didn't want to go to the purple room. That was where the uncles were.

"No!" she cried, and started pushing him away. "Don't take me to the purple room. Please, Solomon, please. I don't want to go there."

"Easy, Jade darling. You know it's going to be all right. Solomon always takes care of his baby girl."

"No!" Jade begged, now struggling to get out of Solomon's arms, but he was unwilling to give back the hundred dollars in his pocket.

"Be quiet," he said sharply. *"You'll wake up the other children."*

"I don't care!" Jade screamed, and started to sob. *"Take one of them and not me."*

Within seconds, one of the doors up ahead opened. A young boy walked out into the hallway. He was tall for a ten-year-old and wise beyond his years. Solomon saw him and frowned.

"Raphael! Go back to bed."

But the boy stood his ground.

"Please, Solomon, she doesn't want to go."

"It doesn't matter what she wants," Solomon said.

Raphael grabbed Solomon's sleeve as he passed by.

"Take me. I'll go in her place. Take me. I don't care."

"They don't want you, boy. Not tonight. Now get back inside and close the door before I make you sorry."

By now, Jade was sobbing uncontrollably. Raphael reached for her, but Solomon slapped him away, then shoved him inside the room and slammed the door.

"Stay in there or you'll be sorry!" he yelled.

There was a shuffling sound on the other side of the door and then silence. In that moment, Jade stilled. She knew that if she made any more fuss, Rafie would come after her. If he did, Solomon would get mad—real mad. And when that happened, people got hurt. She didn't want Rafie hurt.

"That's my good girl," Solomon said, and gave her a quick hug.

She turned her face against the sleeve of his shirt and closed her eyes, unable to understand why this was happening to her. In her eyes, her mother had just gone off and left her here. She didn't know that Margaret was dead, and even if she had, in her child's mind, she would never have understood the ramifications of what that meant. All she knew was

that she was alone with people who hurt her. She also knew that if she raised a big fuss, Raphael would get in trouble, and she loved Raphael. He was her best friend. So she stifled her sobs and closed her eyes, already letting her mind go to another place where nothing was bad and Solomon didn't exist.

Solomon had no idea what was going through the little girl's mind, and if he had, wouldn't have cared. He was focused on the business at hand. A couple of seconds later, he turned the corner in the hallway and headed for the room at the far end of the hall. Just before they went inside, he heard Jade whisper.

"Take somebody else," she begged.

"I can't," he said softly, and kissed the tousle of curls on the top of her head. "He wants you, baby girl. They all want you. You know you're special, don't you, baby Jade?"

"I don't want to be special," she whispered.

"But you are," Solomon said, and then opened the door.

Immediately, Jade closed her eyes as Solomon carried her across the room. She felt the silken fabric of the sheets as he laid her on the bed. She heard the murmur of men's voices, then the sound of a lock turning in the door.

She held her breath as footsteps crossed the room, then stopped near where she was lying.

He touched her face, then her arms, then her legs, then tugged her nightgown over her head and put his hand between her legs.

"Open your eyes, honey. Look what I have for you to play with."

Jade woke up with a gasp; her body was shaking, her face covered in sweat. Raphael was not in his seat. She stood up with a jerk and stumbled into the aisle. The woman in the seat behind her looked up, frowning slightly as Jade pointed to Raphael's empty seat.

"Where did he go?"

"If you mean your boyfriend, he's in the john."

Jade looked toward the back of the bus and the closed bathroom door and then started to relax.

"Okay…yes, sure…the bathroom. Uh…thank you," she added, and sat back down in her seat.

A few minutes later Raphael came out of the bathroom with a wet paper towel in his hands. He staggered to his seat and then sat down with a thump.

Jade's relief at seeing him turned to concern when she realized he was pale and shaking.

"Rafie…are you all right? What's wrong?"

He reached over and patted her hand, then leaned back in the seat and closed his eyes.

"Nothing, honey, just a little case of motion sickness."

"Oh, I'm so sorry," she said. "I didn't think to pack anything for that."

"It's all right," he mumbled. "I took something while I was in the bathroom. Maybe it will help."

Jade frowned. She wasn't aware of them having anything resembling medicine.

"What did you take?"

"I had some stuff in my shaving kit. I'll be okay in a bit. I just need to rest."

Jade frowned, but acknowledged his need for quiet by stifling her other questions. She took the handful of wet paper towels from him, folded them into a compress and then laid them across Raphael's eyes.

Raphael's lips curved upward into a gentle smile. He patted Jade's hands, then reclined his seat and pretended to sleep. But his thoughts were troubled. It wasn't motion sickness, and he knew it. He didn't know how much longer he was going to be able to hide his illness from Jade. He kept thinking of that woman in San Francisco who'd purchased the painting of Ivy and the fact that she'd known Margaret Cochrane was from St. Louis. As soon as they got settled in New Orleans, he was going to do a little investigating of his

own. Jade always said she couldn't remember anything of her life before, but maybe if he asked her just right, something would click. Especially since they had the name Margaret Cochrane for reference. Maybe he could get online at one of those Internet coffee shops and check out the phone listings for St. Louis, Missouri. If Jade really had been from St. Louis and her last name was Cochrane, then there was the possibility that she might still have family living in the area.

He took a deep breath, willing the nausea in his belly to settle. He needed a miracle, and he needed it fast.

Two days had passed since Luke had taken the painting to the crime lab, and he was just about to give them a call to see if they'd gotten a hit when he got a phone call from his friend, the detective.

Almost at the same time, Shelly Hudson was seated in her living room, going through a packet of photos that her friend, Deb, had just sent her from their day at the street fair. Shelly had called Deb the same day she and Luke had lunch together, but Deb had been as lost as Shelly when it came to remembering any names. However, she'd mentioned the photos and promised to send copies. Shelly hadn't mentioned them to Luke, since there was no guarantee that they would be any use to him, but these were wonderful. There was even a close-up of the artist herself, talking one-on-one to Shelly.

Shelly stared intently at the photo, once again struck by the woman's beauty. Then a tiny bell rang in the back of the house, and she realized the timer on her stove had gone off. She laid down the photos and went to get her muffins out of the oven.

As Shelly was tending to kitchen duties, Luke was hurrying to answer his phone.

"Hello."

"Kelly, this is Marsh. We got a hit on your fingerprint."

"I had a feeling the artist might be a fly-by-night kind of painter. What kind of rap sheet does she have?"

There was a moment of silence; then Luke heard papers shuffling.

"Marsh?"

"Where did you say you got this painting?" the detective asked.

"San Francisco. Why?"

"Can you meet me at Sam Cochrane's home in about thirty minutes?" he asked.

"Yes, but why? Sam hired me to find the artist. Whatever you need to tell Sam, you can tell me first. I'll pass on the information."

"Look, Kelly, in good conscience, I can't really do that, because in effect, we were looking for her first."

Luke frowned. "I don't get it. What do you mean?"

"This fingerprint belongs to his daughter, Jade."

Luke stifled a gasp. "Holy... Are you sure?"

"You know the drill. Fingerprints don't lie."

"Oh man, this is going to knock Sam off his feet."

"Yeah, that's what I figured, which is why I was wondering if you'd mind being there when we tell him. I know you two are pretty good friends."

"I'm on my way," Luke said. "Don't announce yourself until I get there."

Luke's hands were shaking when he hung up the phone; then he turned and stared at the painting he had leaned against the wall. He picked it up, grabbing his car keys on the way out the door. His heart was pounding, his thoughts in a whirl. All this time without a word of his family and now this. It was almost too good to be true.

He was stopped at a light when his cell phone rang. He answered quickly, thinking it might be Marsh.

"Kelly," he said shortly, then realized it was Shelly.

"Luke, I have something you need to see," she said.

"Like what?"

"Photos. My friend Deb got some great photos of both the man and the woman from the street fair."

Luke's heart skipped a beat. "Where are you?" he asked.

"I'm home."

"Can you meet me at Sam's?"

"Well, sure, but—"

"Just do it, Shelly, and hurry, okay?"

"Luke, you're scaring me. Is anything wrong?"

Luke started to grin. "On the contrary, Shelly. Everything is right…very, very, right."

He disconnected just as the light turned green and shot through the intersection. A few minutes later he was at Sam's. Detective Marsh pulled up the driveway, parking directly behind Luke's car.

Luke got out, then reached back into the car to retrieve Sam's painting.

"Hell of a deal, isn't it?" Marsh said.

"I can hardly belicve it," Luke said, then glanced toward the house. "Maybe we should have called. Sam might not be home."

"He's home and expecting us," Marsh said.

"You didn't tell him anything, did you?"

"No, but he's plenty curious."

"I can only imagine," Luke muttered, and then rang the bell.

As he did, another car pulled up in front of the house. It was Shelly.

She got out on the run, carrying a manila envelope clutched close to her chest. Sam opened the door as she reached the front step. He'd been expecting the detective, but not Luke and Shelly.

"What's going on?" he asked.

"I don't know," Shelly said. "I was asked to meet Luke here."

Luke glanced at Marsh, then handed Sam the painting that he'd borrowed.

"Just let us in and we'll tell you what we know."

Sam took the painting, then stepped aside to let them enter.

"When is Velma coming back to work?" Shelly asked, as they followed Sam back to the library.

"Tomorrow," Sam said, as he hung the painting of Margaret back on the wall. Then he turned around. His expression was grim as he faced the trio. "Somebody start talking."

"We got a hit on the fingerprint," Marsh said.

Sam's expression didn't change. "That's great, but Luke could have told me that. Didn't he tell you that I hired him to find the artist?"

"Yes, sir," Marsh said, "but you don't understand. The identification of the artist turned out to be a clue in one of our cold case files."

Sam grimaced. "Are you telling me that the artist is a criminal?"

"No, sir," Marsh said. "A missing person."

Sam shrugged, then sighed. "Oh, well, I certainly don't begrudge that. Some family's life will take a change for the better." Then he looked at Luke. "So who are we looking for?"

"Your daughter."

Sam's expression froze. He staggered slightly, then steadied himself on the sideboard behind him. Luke took him by the arm.

"Come on, my friend. Let's sit down, okay?"

Sam let himself be led to a nearby chair. Shelly followed and sat down, too. She stared at the men, then laid the envelope in her lap and started to cry.

"Are you telling me that the woman I talked to was Jade?"

"If she is the one who put the thumbprint on the painting, then, yes," Marsh said.

"I was such a fool. If only I'd asked about Margaret's daughter." She dabbed her eyes with a tissue, then leaned back in the chair, unable to grasp all she'd been told. "What

I don't understand is why she didn't say that the painting was of her mother? She just called the woman Ivy."

Luke knew there were several reasons why someone who'd been missing didn't volunteer information, but none of them were encouraging. He chose his words carefully so as not to upset Sam.

"There are all kinds of reasons," he said. "And you shouldn't blame yourself. Jade was so young when Margaret left that what you said may have meant nothing to her. Also, we have no way of knowing what she was told. For all we know, she may not remember enough of her childhood to make any connections to what you said. Lots of times children who are stolen from one parent are told by the other one that the parent is dead…or, in some cases, that the parent doesn't love them anymore."

"Dear God," Sam said. "What are we going to do? This is Margaret all over again. She didn't want to be found and stayed lost for all these years. If Jade doesn't want to be found, what's to stop this from happening all over again?"

"Me," Luke said, and then pointed to the envelope in Shelly's lap. "Are those the pictures?"

She nodded, then handed them to him.

Luke opened the envelope and dumped them out onto the coffee table between them. Almost immediately, his gaze fell on a close-up of the woman in the booth. He knew he should say something, but there were no words for what was going through his mind.

At thirty-seven years old, he'd seen his share of attractive women, but the face in the photo was beyond attractive. She was, without doubt, one of the most beautiful women he'd ever seen in his life. He picked up another, then another and another, staring in disbelief at the delicate curve of her cheek and the thick, black hair falling in waves over her shoulder and down her back. When he finally let himself look at the man with her, his stomach knotted. The man was, in his way, as physically beautiful as a man could be.

"Let me see," Sam said.

"Keep in mind, it still has to be determined if this woman is truly the artist. We only have her word that she put the fingerprint on the canvas."

"I saw her doing caricatures," Shelly said. "And the shirt she was wearing had some tiny paint stains. I remember seeing them and thinking how perfectly bohemian."

Luke handed him the photos, watching his friend's expression for signs of distress. But he need not have worried. The moment Sam's gaze fell on the woman in the photo, he exhaled a deep sigh.

"Oh God…dear God…she looks like my mother."

"Are you sure?" Marsh asked. "You're not just seeing something in her that you want to see?"

Sam looked up, his eyes lit with joy, tears rolling down his face.

"Wait here," he said, and hurried out of the room. A couple of minutes later he was back with a small framed photo. "This is a picture of my mother and father on their wedding day. You judge for yourself."

They crowded around the photo. Marsh and Shelly murmured to each other about the similarity in likenesses, but Luke remained silent. Finally Sam noticed.

"Luke, what do you think?"

"That you have a beautiful daughter," he said, and then picked up the photo with the best view of the couple's faces. "And I need to make plane reservations for San Francisco."

Sam clutched Luke's arm. "Find her, my friend. I need this in my life before I die."

"I'll find her," Luke said, but he didn't voice the other part of what he was thinking. He had to find her or live the rest of his life haunted by her face.

A short while later they were all gone, leaving Sam with more hope for the future of his family than he'd had in years,

Four

Rain peppered the windows of the bus near Jade's face, blurring her view of the passing countryside. She was tired of the travel, but afraid to go back to sleep for fear she would have another nightmare. Besides that, Raphael didn't look well. He'd suffered from motion sickness nearly the entire trip, and she was getting worried. His skin was pale and clammy, and she'd begun to notice for the first time that his face looked drawn—even thin. She always expected him to look after her, while she rarely considered that he might need care. He was her rock—the strong one who never complained. Guilt shafted through her as she leaned over and laid the back of her hand against his forehead. He didn't have a fever, but his eyelids had a bluish, almost translucent appearance. As soon as they reached New Orleans and got settled, she would find the health department and make him get a checkup.

Satisfied with her decision, she looked back out the window, only to realize they were coming into the outskirts of another city. Then she saw the city limits sign and started to smile.

New Orleans.

They were almost there. She grabbed Raphael's arm and shook him awake.

"Rafie...wake up. We're here."

Raphael stifled a groan as he sat up. He combed his fingers

through his hair and rolled his head on his neck, trying to stretch out the kinks.

"I'd give a lot for a shower and a bed," he said. "How about you?"

Happy that he seemed more like his old self, Jade forgot about health departments and doctors and threw her arms around his neck.

"It's raining, Rafie."

He threaded his hands through her hair and then curled them into fists, as if trying to draw energy from her vivacity. Then he grinned, knowing she was waiting for him to finish what she'd started.

"And rain washes our troubles down the drain."

"Yes, yes, yes. All our troubles. Down the drain."

A short while later they were at the bus station retrieving their bags, along with one long cardboard box containing a few small paintings and what was left of Jade's art supplies. But walking to search for lodgings in this weather with all their belongings would have been difficult if not impossible. Either they stayed in the bus station until the rain let up, or splurged and took a cab.

Jade took one look at the weariness on Raphael's face and suggested getting a cab. To her surprise, he didn't argue.

A short while later they were loaded up and on their way to a hotel suggested by the janitor at the bus station. Raphael was only vaguely aware of the water running wildly through the streets and the sodden streamers of Spanish moss hanging far too low to the ground. Instead his gaze was centered on Jade, who was staring out the window. Her nervous, almost fearful, expression was focused on the faces of the people huddled in doorways and standing beneath porches.

But Raphael knew it wasn't curiosity that made her look.

No matter where they went or how far they'd come, she was convinced that one day she would come face to face with one of the abusers from her childhood. He knew the odds of that happening were small, yet he had long ago ac-

cepted that if it did, he would have to kill the man. She would expect it of him as he expected it of himself.

A few moments later, the cab driver stopped at a red light, then looked up into the rearview mirror and caught Raphael's gaze.

"You people just visitin' or you plannin' to stay?"

"If everything works out, we'll probably stay," Raphael said.

The old man nodded, then scratched his head before glancing back toward the light. It was still on red. He looked up again.

"Son…you and your lady look like real nice people, and if you don't mind my suggestion, you might want to try a different hotel."

Suddenly Jade was in on the conversation. She grabbed hold of the back seat and leaned forward.

"Why? What's wrong with it?"

The old man glanced over his shoulder, his dark eyes reading something on Jade's face that he seemed to recognize.

"Ain't none of my business," he said, in a slow, southern-sweet voice, "but the place we headed to does business at night that you might not want to be 'round, if you know what I mean."

Raphael put a hand in the middle of Jade's back. It was just a touch, but enough to settle her anxiety. Although their life had been anything but sheltered, they'd never sought out the lifestyle of the people who lived on the streets—just tried to survive it.

"We appreciate your opinion," Raphael said. "If you have a better suggestion, we're listening."

For the first time, the driver smiled, wreathing his cafe au lait face with time-weathered wrinkles.

"My sista Clarice has a real nice place down in the Quarter. It ain't nothin' fancy, but it's clean, and it's safer than where you was plannin' to go."

"We'd be obliged," Raphael said. "By the way, what's your name?"

"Clarence Deauxville. Clarice is my twin sista."

Raphael nodded. "I'm called Rafe," he said. "This is Jade."

Clarence tilted his head. "You up to tryin' out my suggestion?"

Raphael glanced at Jade, who nodded nervously. "Yes," he said.

Clarence's smile widened. The light turned green, and he accelerated through the intersection, taking a right at the next street as he spoke over his shoulder.

"Only take a few more minutes and we'll have you outa' dis here rain."

Jade frowned at the cabdriver, then leaned against Raphael. There was nothing in her background that told her it was safe to trust the kindness of strangers. But Raphael was holding her close and she was sorely sick of travel. The thought of a bed—any bed—was too enticing to ignore.

"It will be all right," Raphael said softly. "Besides, if it's not, we can always go somewhere else."

She relaxed, but only slightly. It wasn't until they arrived at their new destination that her nervousness began to subside.

The old two-story house was long and narrow, running north to south on the matching lot and bounded on three sides with a tall iron fence. Only the front of the house was open to the street, and the tiny patch of green grass that led to the front porch was standing in water.

"Real sorry about the weather," Clarence said, as Raphael counted out the money owed. "You two hurry on up to the porch. I'll get your bags."

Still, Jade hesitated, suspicious that the man was planning to abandon them there and drive off with their things.

Again Clarence seemed to understand what she was unable to say.

"It's all right, missy," he said softly. "Ain't everybody tryin' to hurt you. I'll bring your things right up. You can count on that."

Jade hesitated, then sighed. "Yes, well, all right and...thank you."

He nodded solemnly. "You welcome, missy."

There was a Welcome sign hanging on the front door. Raphael grabbed the doorknob and turned it, pushing Jade in front of him as they walked inside. What had once been a formal sitting room had been turned into a lobby/reception area. The furnishings were dark and ancient, but there was a clean citrus scent in the air that Jade recognized as orange oil. From the shine on the woodwork, she could tell that someone was religious about its care.

Within seconds, a small, skinny black woman appeared from the hallway. It was evident that Clarence the cabdriver had been truthful about one thing: Clarice was definitely his twin. She smiled cordially until she realized Clarence was with them. At that point, her expression lightened even further as she gave him a hug. The familial welcome relaxed Jade even more.

After a quick word with her brother, the elderly woman turned to her guests.

"Welcome to the Forsythia Inn," she said, eyeing the bedraggled pair with an appraising look. "We need to get you settled in, then you come down to the dining room. Clarice has some hot gumbo that will fix you up just right."

"Sounds good, but we need to settle a little business first," Raphael said, then patted his pocket to make sure their money was safe. "How much per week?"

"You plannin' to stay more than just a visit?" Clarice asked.

Jade nodded.

"Then how about two hundred dollars a week? That includes café au lait and beignets every morning, and my good cookin' at night."

It was a lot of money for people with no jobs, but it was a bargain and they knew it.

"We'll take it," Jade said.

Clarice handed them a key. "I've got rooms on the ground floor, but if this rain don't let up, I'd hate to have you wake up in water. So...up the stairs, third door on your left."

"Flood? The hotel might flood?" Jade asked.

Clarice shrugged. "Honey, the city is in flood warning already. This old hotel won't be exempt. However, don't you worry none. It's lasted through a civil war, more floods than you can count, and a fair amount of hurricanes. This little thunderstorm will pass, just like they all do, and we'll all go on livin' our lives just like always. In the meantime, you hurry back down and I'll have that gumbo ready and waiting."

Raphael grabbed the bags, while Clarence dug an old luggage dolly out of a closet behind the front desk, loaded Jade's box of artwork onto it, and followed them up the stairs.

The room was just like the lower level that they'd seen— furnished with out-of-date furniture, but clean as the proverbial whistle. The bed—an old four-poster with mosquito netting and a care-worn mauve duvet—took centerstage in the room.

"I see Clarice likes you," Clarence said, as he unloaded the box.

Raphael turned around, uncertain what he getting at. "What do you mean?"

Clarence pointed at the bed. "She put you two in the honeymoon suite."

"Why is it the honeymoon suite?" Jade asked.

"Got its own bath," Clarence said, pointing toward a door on their right, then winked at her. "You'll be just fine here."

Jade ignored the man's assumption that she and Raphael had a sexual relationship. It was something people always assumed about them, although it was the farthest thing from

the truth. In fact, the truth of their bond was nothing anyone else could ever have understood.

Jade thrust her hand in her pocket and impulsively pulled out some money to pay him for hauling their box up the stairs.

"Thank you," she said, as she handed him some bills.

Clarence held up his hand in gentle refusal. "Your man done paid me for the ride, missy. No need for more."

Jade put the money back in her pocket and then nodded without knowing what else to say.

The old man was on his way out of the room when he stopped and turned around. An odd expression crossed his face, and it was as if his eyes suddenly lost their focus.

"You be goin' home soon now," he said. "Trust the big man. It will be okay."

A shaft of panic sliced through Jade's belly. She didn't trust any men except Raphael.

"I'm already home," she said, and stepped beneath the shelter of Raphael's arms. "He is my home."

Clarence shuddered just as Clarice entered with an armful of clean towels. She saw the look on her brother's face and frowned.

"Stop that, you old fool! You gonna go and scare off my guests. Get on with you. Go find someone to drive around and don't get yourself drowned now...you hear?"

Clarence blinked, then looked around in confusions.

"What you sayin' to me, sista?"

"Go on now. It's okay. You just slipped outa' you-self...but you back now. I told you not to drown."

He acknowledged her words with a smile, then glanced toward Jade before he left.

"Don't be afraid," he said softly, then left.

Jade shivered, then followed Clarice into the bathroom, where she was putting out the clean linens.

"Ma'am?"

"Honey, you just call me Clarice."

"Yes, all right," Jade said. "Uh…about your brother. What did you mean when you said he slipped out of himself?"

Afraid she was about to lose the only customers she'd had in weeks, Clarice tried to laugh off what had happened.

"Oh, that brother of mine fancies himself a seer."

"A what?"

"He says he has visions, but don't you worry yourself none. We don't pay him no mind in our family. We all think Momma dropped him on his head when he was a baby." Then she laughed, tickled at her own wit. "Hurry on down now. My gumbo is just what you need to set yourself right."

She left quickly, leaving Jade and Raphael alone.

"Rafie?"

"What?"

"What do you think that man meant?"

"I don't know, honey. But that gumbo sure sounds good. Let's unpack later, okay?"

Jade let herself be sidetracked, but she couldn't forget the look on that old man's face. Why would he tell her she was going to go home? In her world, there was no such thing.

It was Luke's second day in San Francisco. He'd located the organizer of the street fair, only to find out that the booth where Shelly Hudson had purchased Margaret's picture had been reserved under the name Laurel Ann Hardy and paid for in cash. He'd laughed when the woman had read off the name. So Sam's daughter had a sense of humor. The name she'd given the organizer was nothing more than a play on the name of the comedy team Laurel and Hardy. To make matters worse, the address that she'd given as her residence didn't exist. He'd questioned the people who'd shared booths on either side of her but learned nothing that would help him in his search.

With only an hour or so until sundown, he was no closer

to finding Jade Cochrane than he'd been when he'd stepped off the plane.

He made a call to Sam but got his answering machine instead. He left him a brief message, with the promise to call again in the morning, then hailed a cab and headed back to his hotel.

Once in his room, he turned on the television, then kicked off his shoes and began stripping off his clothes as he headed for the shower. He had a dinner date with an old college buddy and didn't want to be late.

A short while later he emerged; refreshed and clean-shaven; he was looking forward to seeing his friend. From time to time he would glance at the television, keeping an absent eye on the evening news. It wasn't until he sat down on the foot of the bed to put on his shoes that he really focused on the story being aired.

A storm had moved in off the southern coast of Louisiana and was deluging the state with thunderstorms. New Orleans was in a severe state of flooding, and people in different parts of the old city were being evacuated.

"Hell of a deal," he muttered to himself, then reached for a shoe as the on-air journalist began a voice-over for a piece of film that had been shot earlier in the day.

But it wasn't what the journalist was saying that caught his attention. It was the woman being carried out of a building toward a waiting motorboat. Her hair and clothing were soaked and plastered to her body. Her face was expression-less, her arms wrapped tightly around the neck of the man in whose arms she was held. But he'd seen that face—in Shelly's photos. It was her! Sam's daughter! But what the hell was she doing in New Orleans?

Luke dropped the shoe as he jumped to his feet and began searching for the remote to turn up the volume. All he got before the coverage was over was that the film had been shot earlier in the day, and that the Mississippi River, which was causing all the trouble, had yet to crest.

"Oh man, oh man," he muttered, and tossed down the remote as he reached for the phone. He dialed quickly, without taking his gaze from the television screen. And then his call was answered. "Hey, Carson, it's me, Luke. Listen, I'm going to have to bail on you. My case has taken a weird turn, and I've got to catch the late flight to Louisiana.... Yeah, I'm sorry, too, but this is really important. I'll catch up with you another time, okay?"

Moments later, he disconnected, then dialed the front desk.

"This is Luke Kelly, in 1202. My plans have changed, and I'm checking out tonight. I'll need a cab within the next fifteen minutes."

After that, he made one more call, to LAX, and then began throwing his clothes into his suitcase. He had less than two hours to get to the airport, pass through security and board his flight to New Orleans. He kept thinking of the flooding and wondered if they would be able to land. However, he would worry about that later. He didn't know how or why Jade Cochrane had gotten from California to Louisiana in such a short space of time, but he couldn't afford any more delays.

Five

After a hair-raising landing and the discovery that his baggage was somewhere he was not, Luke Kelly had arrived in New Orleans. After filing a report with the airline about his lost suitcase, he hailed a cab.

"Where to, suh?" the driver asked.

Luke hesitated. He didn't know whether to waste time registering at a hotel or implement his search. The tenuousness of locating people who had already been displaced by the flood made him nervous, but it was almost midnight. It was doubtful that anyone, even transients, would be on the move at this time of night, so, given the circumstances, he opted for getting a room.

"Is it possible to get to the Marriott?" he asked.

"Yes, suh, I believe so, but unless you have a reservation, your chances of staying there aren't good. Heard on the radio some time ago that hotels are fillin' up fast."

"Got any suggestions?" Luke asked.

"Let me make a couple of calls and we'll go from there," the driver said. A minute or so later, he turned around. "We're in luck, suh. There's a fine bed-and-breakfast on the dry side of town that has a couple of spare rooms. They're holdin' one for you."

"I really appreciate this," Luke said.

"It's my pleasure," the cabdriver said. "Just sit back and relax. I'll have you there in no time."

In less than thirty minutes, they had arrived. Luke glanced

at his watch as he got out of the cab. It was fifteen minutes after one in the morning.

"You'll be comfortable here," the cabdriver said. "The owner is a retired detective from the Naw'leans Police Department."

Luke nodded thoughtfully. This was good news. His host might be able to help in more ways than just furnishing a bed. After paying off the driver, he turned around, getting his first good look at the Sleepy Hollow Bed and Breakfast. The house was single-story and surrounded by large weeping willows with limbs that hung low to the ground. Something that might have been wisteria grew up the side of the house and onto the roof. Dodging the puddles and wet shrubbery, he headed toward the well-lit veranda, only to be met by the owner, who was in his pajamas and robe.

Armand Louiston was a tall, spare man with thinning hair and a gimpy leg. He opened the door wide, smiling at Luke as he came up the front steps.

"Welcome to Sleepy Hollow Bed and Breakfast," he said. "My name is Armand Louiston." Then he frowned. "Don't you have any luggage?"

"Last I heard, it's probably somewhere over Iowa," Luke said, as he entered the lobby behind his host. "Now that I have an address, I'll need to call the airline to tell them where to deliver it."

"Did they give you a number to call?" Armand asked, as he scurried behind the desk.

Luke nodded.

"Give it to me. I'll be happy to call them for you. At any rate, they'll need special directions on how to get here. Most of the usual routes are under water."

"Thanks," Luke said, and handed him the card the airline had given him.

"It is my pleasure," Armand said, and picked a room key from the rack behind the desk. "I'm giving you the Blue Room. I trust you will rest well tonight. If you have need of

anything, there is an intercom in your room. Press zero and it will ring in my room."

"I'll be fine," Luke said.

"Follow me, then, and I'll show you to your room."

Luke followed Louiston down the hall, taking absent note of the way his bathrobe flapped about his ankles and the uneven rhythm of his stride.

"Here we are," Armand said, stopped at a room on their right, unlocked a door and then handed Luke the key. "I'm going to call the airline. Sleep well."

Luke stifled a yawn as he entered the room. His first impression was that he'd just entered an Egyptian tomb. Pale blue walls, with a blue and gold geometric border that encircled the walls about a foot below the ceiling. A bronze bust of a Pharaoh set on a faux marble stand opposite a large mirror. A navy-blue futon had been angled into the corner of the room opposite a large wooden bed. The artwork on the walls was an eclectic mix of unknown originals and familiar fakes, but all with a Middle Eastern flair. At that point, he was too tired to wonder if sleeping in a pseudo-tomb would leave any lasting problems.

He tossed his raincoat on the back of a chair, then slumped onto the side of the bed. His head ached, and a scar on his shoulder from an old gunshot wound was throbbing unmercifully. He thought of his shaving kit inside the lost luggage and cursed beneath his breath. Considering the fact that he might have to spend tomorrow in these same clothes, he made himself undress, then crawled between the sheets.

The pillow smelled vaguely of lavender. He thought he remembered reading somewhere that the scent of lavender was supposed to promote sleep, but he didn't need any help in going to sleep tonight. He closed his eyes on a sigh, rolled over on his side and pulled the covers up over his shoulders. The last thing he remembered hearing was a floorboard creak and some tree limbs rubbing against the outside of the house.

* * *

At the same time, in another part of the city, the temporary shelter in the old YMCA was wall-to-wall with flood victims. Dozens upon dozens of cots had been set up in rows running the length of the old building. It was long after midnight and should have been quiet, but the cacophony of sounds in the dormitory-like room ranged from crying babies to loud, intermittent snores. Parents too upset to sleep held their children in their laps while trying not to dwell on the fact that what was left of their worldly possessions was heading toward the Gulf via the Mississippi.

Clarence had dropped Jade and Raphael off at this building, then taken his sister, Clarice, home with him, leaving the cot she might have used for someone with nowhere else to go. Now Jade slept on a cot in the corner of the room with her back to the wall, while Raphael slept on another cot next to her, putting himself between her and the rest of the world as he always did.

Somewhere in the back of Jade's mind, the sounds in the large room were getting mixed up with a long-buried memory and turning it into a full-blown nightmare.

The uncle had fallen asleep. Jade knew because she could hear him snore. She wanted up, but the weight of his arm kept her pinned to the bed. Tears welled, then rolled down her face, but she knew better than to make noise. It would only wake the man up. If he woke up, he would want to play the game all over again, and she didn't want to play.

She closed her eyes and thought of Raphael. Sometimes, if she thought of him hard enough, he would come and find her. She wanted him to find her now and take her away. The uncle's arm was heavy, and his breath smelled bad—real bad.

Raphael. Raphael. Raphael.

She thought of his name, picturing his face, imagining him coming into the room.

Suddenly the uncle's snore turned into a snort, then a deep choking cough.

Jade flinched and then closed her eyes even tighter, wanting him to think she had fallen asleep.

Raphael. Raphael. Raphael.

Suddenly there was a hand on her chest; then it slid between her legs.

"Hey there, my pretty baby…wake up for Uncle Sugar. Wake up. Wake up and we'll play our little game."

Jade stiffened.

Raphael. Raphael.

"Come on, baby girl… Uncle Sugar can't wait all night. I got to get out of this shit hole before daylight."

Raphael. Raphael.

"Open your eyes now. Uncle Sugar likes for you to watch him play the game."

The fingers were probing now. Deeper. Harder.

Raphael. Raphael.

"Open your eyes, damn it! Uncle Sugar wants to play!"

Suddenly the flat of his hand connected with the side of her jaw. Instinctively she opened her eyes with the intent of dodging the next blow.

"There are those pretty eyes. That's what I want to see," he said, and then took her hand and pulled it toward his lap.

Jade felt the force of her scream coming up her throat before it became sound. She was no longer thinking Rafie's name, she was screaming it aloud.

"Raphael! Raphael!"

Jade was crying in her sleep. Raphael woke with a start and was reaching for her before his eyes were completely open. She had crawled to the edge of the cot and plastered herself against the wall; her eyes were open, but he could tell she didn't see where she was—only where she'd been.

He grabbed her arm, shaking her awake.

"Jade. Jade! Honey, wake up. You're having a bad dream."

Jade choked on a sob and then crawled off the cot and into his lap.

"Oh God, oh God," she whispered, then buried her face against his neck.

Suddenly there was a hand on Raphael's shoulder. He looked up. It was a Red Cross volunteer by the name of Charlie.

"Is she ill?" Charlie asked.

Raphael shook his head and pulled her closer. "No, she just had a bad dream," he said softly. "I'm sorry. We didn't mean to disturb anyone."

"Maybe she has a fever," Charlie said, and started to extend a hand. Jade ducked, then rolled back onto her cot out of his reach.

"Sorry. She doesn't like to be touched," Raphael said.

Charlie sighed. "I understand," he said softly. "However, if either of you need any medication, just let me know. There's a doctor up at the office who'll be here at least until morning."

"She's fine," Raphael said. "We'll try not to cause any more disturbance."

Charlie grinned as he looked around. "Are you kidding? It sounds like a buzz-saw convention in here already. Try to get some rest, okay?"

"Yeah, thanks," Raphael said.

Jade looked at Raphael and then shrugged. "I'm sorry. I didn't mean to make a scene. I was—"

"*Shh,*" Raphael said, and then brushed a tangled lock of her hair away from her face. "It doesn't matter. Nothing matters except that we're no longer in danger of winding up at the bottom of the Mississippi."

"I'm sorry we came here," Jade said. "This is all my fault."

"No. It's no one's fault. I wanted to come here, too, remember?"

Jade frowned. "No you didn't. You just let me have my way." Then she shoved her hands through her hair and scooted closer so that their conversation wouldn't disturb their nearby neighbors. "I'm sorry, Rafie. I'm sorry about everything. All I do is cause you trouble." Her voice started to shatter, but she made herself focus. What she had to say should have been said years ago. "I am a grown woman. I will get past this...this...crap, so help me God."

Raphael leaned forward until their foreheads were touching.

"It wasn't crap, baby, it was criminal. Don't ever belittle yourself. I damn sure don't, okay?"

She sighed. "Okay."

He smiled. "Good girl. Think you can go back to sleep?"

"I don't want to sleep," she said.

Raphael frowned. "You were dreaming about one of them, weren't you?"

She hesitated, then nodded.

"Who?"

"The one who called himself Uncle Sugar."

"Is his face in the box?"

"No," Jade said.

"Then in the morning, you draw it and put it with the others. Remember, if you put it on paper, then you don't have to remember what he looks like anymore."

"Yes. Tomorrow. I'll draw his face tomorrow," Jade said, then lay back down on the cot and tried to relax.

Drawing the faces was a mental exercise in exorcising the ghosts. Sometimes it worked. Sometimes it didn't.

She watched as Raphael lay back down on his cot and then scooted as far back toward her as he could. She slid her arm across his waist and then spooned herself against his backside. Despite her fears that the nightmare would return, she slept dreamlessly through the rest of the night.

* * *

It was five minutes after nine o'clock when Luke turned his rental car toward the building at the end of the block. He'd been told it was the old YMCA, which was another temporary shelter for flood victims. The only thing good about the day so far was that his suitcase had arrived sometime during the night, so he had been able to shave and put on clean clothes.

But now this was the third shelter he'd been to since daybreak, and he was beginning to panic. According to the man he'd spoken to at the civil defense office, the city had set up only this one other shelter besides the ones that he'd already visited, and the people there were already being released to go back to their homes. He could only imagine what disasters they would go home to, and he empathized with them. However, there was an old injustice that he needed to solve, and the faster things changed, the more difficult his job became.

He parked as close as he could get, then got out. His stride was long, his steps hurried, as he crossed the street and entered the front door. Immediately he was struck by the sea of moving bodies spread out before him. Some were still reclining on cots, while others were up eating the breakfast the Red Cross was providing. Some children were crying, while others were quietly devouring sweet rolls and oranges.

"Sir, can I help you?"

Luke turned around to find himself face-to-face with a weary, middle-aged woman.

"I'm looking for someone," he said. "Do you have a list of names?"

"Somewhere," she said, and then sidestepped a toddler with a dripping, half-peeled orange as she moved into a small office to their right.

Luke glanced toward the sleeping area, then followed her into the office. The woman shuffled through the same stack of papers three times before she found it.

"Ah, here it is," she said. "What's the name of the person you're looking for?"

"Jade Cochrane. She's in her twenties. Very beautiful woman with long black hair. She might be with a—"

The woman suddenly looked up. "A tall, dark-haired man who looks as if he could have posed for Michelangelo?"

Luke's pulse kicked. The man who'd been photographed with Jade could easily have been described in such a manner. "Is she here?"

"She was, or at least she should be," the woman said. "We haven't checked anyone out, although the place is such a madhouse, I can't swear to anything."

"It's imperative that I find her."

The woman hesitated, then looked him square in the eye.

"I need to see some identification."

Luke pulled out his wallet. "Yeah, sure. Name's Luke Kelly, and among other things, I'm a private investigator. I was hired by a man named Sam Cochrane to find his daughter."

"Is she a runaway? Because if the woman I'm thinking of is the one you're looking for, she's already of age, which means she can't be forced to go anywhere she doesn't want to go."

"She's not a runaway," Luke said. "She was kidnapped by her mother when she was four. He hasn't seen her since."

"Oh dear Lord!" the woman said. "Poor man, but how did you come to think she would be here?"

"I'd already been hired to find her when I saw her...or at least I thought it was her...on the national news during some of the taped flood coverage."

"Oh, yes, that," the woman said. "The media has been all over the place, taking up a whole lot of rooms that we could use for the flood victims, instead. However, that's another story altogether. As for your search, feel free to go look. She's not a child, and she's not alone."

"I still don't want to cause her concern. The less fuss, the

better off we'll be. If Jade Cochrane is here, then it's doubtful she remembers much of anything about the first four years of her life.''

''Of course,'' she said, and then clasped her hands to her breast and tried not to cry. ''This is just so...so moving.''

''Yes, ma'am,'' Luke said, as he left her at the desk.

His heart was pounding as he started down the aisles, focusing on young women with pretty faces and long, dark hair. Twice he thought he'd found her, only to realize at the last moment that he was mistaken. The number of people he had left to see was growing smaller by the minute, and then he stopped to pick up a ball of yarn that an old woman had dropped. When he handed it to her, she started to cry.

''It's all I have left,'' she said softly, then clutched it close to her chest as she stared off into space. ''I can't finish the sweater now, you know. I don't know what to do. I always finish what I start.''

Luke's heart went out to her, but he needed to find Jade. Going back to St. Louis and facing Sam empty-handed wasn't something he wanted to do. He took a couple of twenty-dollar bills out of his wallet, then put them in the old woman's hand.

''Here,'' he said gently, making her look at what he was giving her. ''It's forty dollars. Now you can buy some more pink yarn to finish your sweater.''

For a few seconds she stared at the money, then looked up at Luke.

''More yarn?'' she said, as if the thought had not occurred to her.

He nodded, then closed her fingers over the money.

''Yes, more pink yarn,'' he said.

''To finish the sweater.''

Luke touched the back of her head, a little startled that he could feel the rapid and irregular beat of her pulse against his palm.

''Yes, darlin' to finish your sweater.''

She shuddered, then curled her fingers tightly around the money.

"Why, yes, I can do that," she said, and then looked up at him and smiled. "Thank you, young man. Your mother must be proud of you."

Luke didn't bother to tell her that his mother was dead. It was immaterial to the fact that the old woman's confusion was beginning to subside.

"Yes, ma'am," he said, and then looked up.

It was then he realized there was a group of children gathering at the far end of the room. He moved closer, then closer still, until he saw that they were gathering around a young, dark-haired woman.

She was sitting cross-legged on the floor with a handful of colored markers near her knee. There was a small girl sitting motionless beside her, seemingly enthralled by the fact that a butterfly was being painted on her cheek. Another child with a tiny green turtle on his forehead was running away from the crowd to show his parents, while yet another sat looking in a mirror, mesmerized by the black nose and cat whiskers she'd painted on his face.

At that moment, someone said something that made her look up. When she laughed, the breath caught in the back of Luke's throat. It was the woman from the photograph. There was no mistake about it.

He took a step forward and then caution made him stop. Barging in without explanation could be a big mistake. He needed her cooperation to make Sam's dreams come true, and he had no way of knowing how she would react. So he stayed where he was, watching her work her magic to calm the frantic children and, in turn, give weary parents a moment's rest.

Raphael came out of the bathroom, as always looking for Jade to make sure she was all right, then tossed a handful of wet paper towels into the trash. He patted his pocket, check-

ing to see if the paper with Clarence's phone number was still there, then headed for the makeshift kitchen to see if there was any more coffee. He'd heard on the radio a few minutes ago that the flood waters had crested during the night and were now starting to subside. As far as he was concerned, it would be none too soon. Considering the damage the flood had done and the amount of rebuilding that would have to take place, their best bet would be to move on. Their livelihood depended largely upon the tourist trade and carnival-style gatherings, and the disaster of this flood couldn't help but impact that in a negative way.

He called out to Jade in passing, asking her if she wanted some coffee. Too intent on the little mermaid she was painting on a small child's hand to look up, she just shook her head.

The moment Luke had seen the man coming out of the bathroom, his last doubts as to whether he'd found Jade Cochrane disappeared. It was the same man from the photographs, right down to his Hollywood good-looks and shoulder-length black hair. But there was something in the way his gaze swept the room and the set of his shoulders that told Luke they might be on the run from more than a flood. When he walked away, Luke moved closer to Jade.

The first thing Raphael noticed when he came back with his coffee was the man watching Jade, and not with the abstract attention one might expect from a stranger. He was staring at Jade as if he'd just seen a ghost, and it made Raphael nervous. He discarded his coffee and started across the room, unaware that his fingers had curled into fists. When he was close enough to see a mole on the back of the man's neck, he spoke softly.

"She's none of your business."

Luke jumped, then turned around, surprised that he'd been caught so unaware and by one of the people he'd been look-

ing for. It wasn't the introduction he'd envisioned, but it was too late to change it now.

"I'm Luke Kelly."

The man didn't budge, nor did he return the gesture of introduction, but it didn't dissuade Luke from what he'd come to do. He took out his wallet and flashed his ID.

"Look, I mean her no harm. I'm a private investigator from St. Louis, Missouri."

Raphael's heart skipped a beat. The woman who'd bought the painting of Ivy had claimed to be from St. Louis, too. This couldn't be a coincidence, but he needed to know for sure.

"What are you doing here?" Raphael asked.

"Sam Cochrane hired me to find his daughter."

Raphael tensed. *Oh my God…can this be true?* "Who's Sam Cochrane?"

Luke turned and pointed toward Jade. "Is her name Jade?"

Raphael hesitated, then nodded.

"Was the woman in the painting her mother?"

Raphael's eyes filled with tears, but he blinked them away. "Yes."

"What happened to her?" Luke asked.

"She died when we were kids."

"What are you to her?" Luke asked, pointing at Jade.

Raphael looked at Jade, unaware that every fiber of the love he felt for her was mirrored in his eyes.

"We're family," he finally said.

It wasn't the exact answer Luke wanted, but he figured it was all he would get.

"What's your name?" he asked.

Raphael's chin jutted as he met Luke's gaze. "Raphael."

"So, Raphael, do you have a last name?"

"No."

"Look, I'm not out to cause either of you any trouble. If

you're running from something, it's none of my concern. I'm just trying to find a lost daughter for a friend of mine.''

Raphael thought of the years separating them from Solomon and his people and wondered if it would ever be enough. But that wasn't what this Luke Kelly meant.

''We're not 'on the run' from the law, if that's what you're implying,'' Raphael said. ''And I'm not hiding my identity. I never knew my mother or my father. My earliest memories are of the People of Joy. They called me Raphael.''

''People of Joy? Are you still, uh, involved with them?'' Luke asked.

''No,'' Raphael said shortly. ''If the world is lucky, they no longer exist.'' He felt out of control—afraid of what was coming, but aware that if this panned out, it could be the answer to his prayers. ''Is this Sam Cochrane a good man?''

Luke smiled. ''Oh, yeah. The best.''

Raphael sighed. ''So's she,'' he said softly.

Suddenly sensing that she was being watched, Jade looked up, then saw Raphael talking to a stranger and frowned. They weren't in the habit of chitchatting with people, especially ones they didn't know. She arched an eyebrow at Raphael in a questioning manner.

He shrugged and smiled, then waved her over. ''Got a minute?''

Jade nodded and stood. As she did, the children around her began to scatter.

Raphael held out his hand. ''Then come with me, baby. There's someone I think you should meet.''

Jade's eyes widened as her gaze suddenly moved from Raphael to the man beside him. His expression was fixed, his chin jutting slightly, as if bracing himself for unseen blows. All of a sudden she could hear the old cabdriver's voice telling her not to be afraid and to trust the big man. But she didn't trust anyone except—

''Raphael?''

''It's going to be okay.''

Jade's expression darkened.

Luke felt her distrust as vividly as if it was physical, but he said what had to be said.

"Jade Cochrane, my name is Luke Kelly. I was hired by your father, Sam Cochrane, to find you and bring you home."

Six

"I don't believe you," Jade said, then gave Raphael a panicked look. "How can you? We don't know anything about him. What if Solomon sent him?"

Again Luke removed his wallet and held it toward her.

"I don't know anyone named Solomon. These are my credentials. I'm an ex-cop. I have a private investigation company in St. Louis, Missouri. Twenty-some years ago, a woman named Margaret Cochrane took her four-year-old daughter, Jade, and disappeared. Her husband, Sam, spent every spare penny he had for more than ten years hiring people to try to find them, but with no luck. Years later, Sam Cochrane is still alone and growing old. Then the wife of one of his good friends brings home a painting that she purchased at a San Francisco street fair."

Jade paled.

"The painting was of his wife, Margaret, only the artist called her Ivy. Can you imagine what this did to Sam?"

Jade felt rooted to the spot as she listened with growing disbelief.

"His hopes went from high to low within seconds. Whatever dreams he might have entertained ended the moment he learned she was dead. It was like losing her all over again."

"Oh," Jade whispered, and exhaled a sigh.

The room was starting to spin, and she was beginning to shake. She wanted this to stop and the man to go away, but

it was like witnessing an accident and not being able to look away. As frightening as this was, she had to know the rest.

Luke could tell this was tough on her, but not as tough as it had been on Sam, and it had to be said.

"Initially, Sam just wanted me to find the artist. He figured that since the artist had known Margaret well enough to paint her, she might have known her daughter, too. Never in a million years did he imagine that they were one and the same."

"How did you know?" Raphael asked.

"We ran a fingerprint on the painting through the national registry. No one was more surprised than we were when we learned it belonged to Sam's little girl."

Jade's heart skipped a beat. What made this even more frightening than Solomon was that she was beginning to believe him. But what did this mean to her world? Could she go back and live with a stranger? Even if he was her father, he was still a man—a man she didn't know.

"Oh dear Lord," Jade muttered, then grabbed Raphael's hand. "Raphael?"

"What, baby?"

"What do we do?"

"This isn't about me," he said gently.

Jade froze, looking wildly from Luke to Raphael and back again; then suddenly she grabbed Raphael's shirtsleeves, clinging tightly as she cried out, "This *is* about you, too. We're family! You and me! Me and you. That's the way it's always been, and it's never going to change! I don't care if there are a dozen people trying to claim me, I go nowhere without you, is that understood?"

There was an underlying hysteria to what Jade was saying that told Luke her transition back into Sam Cochrane's household would be impossible without Raphael. He spoke quickly, anxious to reassure her before her panic became full-blown.

"Please, Miss Cochrane…it won't be a problem with Sam, I can promise you that."

But Jade didn't believe him. It wasn't in her to trust. When Luke moved forward, she immediately moved backward until she felt the edge of her cot behind her knees. She sat down with a thump, then shoved her hands forward, as if warding him off.

Unaware of the panic that fed her fears, Luke followed her, then squatted down until they were staring eye to eye.

"Miss Cochrane…Jade?"

"What?"

"You've been without a mother for years. It had to be difficult. But you have another parent who is yearning to reconnect with you. Don't you want to see your father again? I can't believe that your life has been easy…that you don't want to give it up. Help me understand."

"I don't remember having a father," Jade said, and then stared off into space. "I don't remember anything before Solomon."

Luke frowned. "Is he the man your mother ran away with?"

"I don't know about that, but he was the man who—"

Then she stopped. Luke watched Raphael grip her shoulder, then give it a squeeze. When Jade looked up, her face was expressionless.

Without thinking, Luke slid his hand up the length of her arm. It was meant to be a friendly, calming gesture, but it backfired. Jade flinched and then paled. The look on her face so startled him that he stood up and yanked his hand back before she could speak.

"I'm sorry, I'm sorry," he said quickly. "I didn't mean anything by that."

Jade grabbed at the place on her arm where Luke's hand had been and then scooted back on the cot until her back was to the wall. She knew she was acting crazy, but she

didn't have the wherewithal to explain. She was too busy trying not to scream to make herself talk.

Raphael panicked. He needed this to work more than either of these people could ever know. Making peace between them without giving away any of Jade's secrets was imperative. He put his hand on Luke's shoulder.

"It's okay, she just doesn't like to be touched," Raphael said.

Luke exhaled slowly, watching the fading terror on her face. He wouldn't ask why. Not now. Maybe never.

Jade shuddered lightly, then tried to smile. In her heart, she knew he'd meant nothing by it. It had only been a simple gesture that ordinary people pass off as part of the conversation. But Jade wasn't ordinary, and neither was her life. She was flawed—so horribly flawed. If they knew... If this Sam Cochrane knew, he wouldn't want her back. No one but Raphael could love her, because only he could understand.

Luke didn't know what was going through her head. Her reticence was obvious, but he owed it to Sam to push the issue.

"Sam Cochrane is a good man. He's also a very gentle man," Luke said. "Please give yourself, and him, a chance." He shoved a hand through his hair in frustration, afraid that he was going to lose her before Sam had a chance to make amends. "God...lady...I don't know what else to say other than you owe this reunion to yourself...and to him."

Raphael knew Jade. She was incapable of making a decision like this. Her gut reaction to everything was to run, and this was something she should run toward, not away from.

"She'll go," Raphael said, and when he felt her shoulders tense, he added, "we'll both go with you."

Luke breathed a quiet sigh of relief.

Jade's chin jutted. "I can't go without my things."

"We'll get them," Raphael promised.

"What if they got wet?"

"If it's clothes you're concerned about, we can easily replace those for you," Luke said.

Jade shook her head. "It's not the clothes. It's the faces. I can't lose the faces."

Luke started to ask what she meant but caught the look Raphael gave him and shifted mental gears.

"Whatever it is you need, I will get," Luke said gently. "And that's a promise…from me to you."

Jade was staring at him now. He had no way of knowing how many times men had promised great things to the child that she'd been, or how many times she'd been disappointed and hurt. All he knew was that if it took the rest of his life, he was going to gain her trust and see her smile.

"So who do I need to see to get your things?" Luke asked.

Raphael dug the piece of paper from his pocket with Clarence's phone number on it.

"We were staying at a place called The Forsythia Inn. The owner's name is Clarice. She's staying with her brother, Clarence. He took us out of the flood in a motorboat, so if the water hasn't gone down there yet, the only way to get back there is still by boat."

"Give me the number. I'll contact him and see that your things are retrieved. What room were you in?"

"No," Jade said. "We'll do it."

"Why?" Luke asked.

Jade looked taken aback. "What do you mean, why? Because it's our stuff, that's why."

Luke threw up his hands in frustration, then stifled a glare.

"That's all well and good, but if you will pardon me for saying this, you both look like hell, so I suggest you take the help that's offered."

Jade's lips parted in shock. Raphael stifled a grin.

"You might not get it all," Jade muttered. "It might not all fit in Clarence's little boat."

Luke sighed, then softened the tone of his voice.

"Lady, if it will make you happy, I'll commandeer the damned Coast Guard. Just let me do what I was hired to do."

"Fine," Jade said.

"Hallelujah," Luke muttered.

"Now, may I have the phone number?"

Raphael handed it to him. Luke punched in the numbers on his cell phone, then walked a short distance away to make the call.

The moment he was out of hearing distance, Jade grabbed Raphael's arm.

"I'm scared," she muttered. "I don't want to do this."

Raphael put his arms around her and pulled her close. "I know you don't," he said gently. "But you have to. Think about it, honey. You have a father, and a home, and obviously people who cared about you greatly. If the situation was reversed, trust me, I wouldn't hesitate."

Jade looked at him, feeling oddly betrayed by what he'd said.

"Why? Aren't I enough?"

Raphael's stomach knotted. "Oh, honey, you're everything to me, but family is something different. They're people with whom you share the same blood, even the same genetic history, for God's sake. Someday, when I'm gone, no one will even remember that I lived. My picture will not be in someone's old photo album. There will be no one to say, 'I think Raphael looks like his grandfather,' or 'he has his mother's eyes,' because I don't know who the hell they are. No one does. When I die, it will be as if I never existed."

Jade cried out, unable to bear his pain. Tears welled in her eyes, then started to spill down her face. "Don't talk about dying. Ever! I love you. You're my brother and my friend and the only person I could ever trust. *I* will remember you. I will. I *will!*"

Raphael wouldn't let himself dwell on the ugly truth of what he'd admitted. Right now, convincing Jade to reunite with her father was the most important thing he could do.

"I know. I didn't mean to sound all sorry for myself," he said, and made himself smile when he wanted to cry, too. He wiped away her tears with the palms of his hands and then teasingly pinched the end of her nose. "Your nose is all red."

"That's your fault," she muttered. "You made me cry."

"Then I'm sorry," Raphael said. "But you have to go back to your father, and if you don't want to do it for yourself, do it for me."

Said like that, Jade felt ashamed. In her heart, she knew it was the right thing to do, but she wasn't certain that her father would want her back once he knew the truth about her.

"Yes, I'll go," she said. "We'll both go, but if this Sam Cochrane doesn't like us, you have to promise me that we'll leave."

"Honey, there's no way he won't like you."

Jade's eyes glittered angrily. "You're not listening to me. I said *us*. If he doesn't like *us*."

Raphael's heartbeat stuttered. Us. The luxury of that word no longer applied within his world, and he didn't know how he was going to bear it.

"It's going to be okay," Raphael said, and then noticed that Luke Kelly was coming back their way. "Here comes Luke."

Jade wouldn't look.

Raphael tipped her chin, forcing her to meet his gaze.

"I want you to give him a chance. He seems like a man we can trust."

"You trust him for me," she said.

Raphael's voice suddenly deepened, and for one of the few times in their lives, he spoke harshly, almost angrily.

"Damn it, Jade! Try not to be so unforgiving, okay? Every man walking this planet is not out to hurt you, and you cannot live your life in denial of that fact."

Jade was stunned by his anger. It was so unlike Raphael that she was momentarily speechless. When Raphael shoved

his hands through his hair and started to walk away, she grabbed him by the arm.

"Raphael."

He stopped; then his head dropped forward and his shoulders slumped. Immediately he turned, his expression filled with regret.

"I'm sorry, I shouldn't have—"

"I'll do what you say," Jade said, talking quickly before he could say anything more. "Just don't be mad at me, Rafie. I can't bear it when you're mad."

He wanted to crawl in a bed, pull the covers up over his head and wait for it all to be over, but he couldn't. There were things that had yet to be done before he could focus on himself.

"I'm not mad at you, baby. I'm never mad at you. Only at the situation. I understand why you feel like you do, but you've got to get past it." When she started to speak, he held up his hand. "Wait. Let me get this said. I'm not asking you to forget what happened to you…what happened to us…but I'm telling you that we've got to get past it. If we don't, the bastards that fucked with our lives will have won. Do you understand that? Just because we left Solomon all those years ago, doesn't mean we've escaped. As long as you keep that hell alive in your mind, then we're still there."

"Oh, Rafie…why haven't we talked like this before?"

"I don't know. Maybe because before, we didn't have any other options."

"Okay. Okay. I promise we'll go back to St. Louis. If Sam Cochrane is a good man, then we'll stay. We'll have a new life…a good life. I'm sure you're right."

Raphael sighed. He wasn't sure if she was doing it just to make him happy or if she really got what he'd been trying to say, but either way, she was going, and that was all that could matter. Time would take care of the rest.

"That's good, honey. You won't be sorry." Then he turned around to await Luke's arrival.

"I got through," Luke said, as he dropped his cell phone in his pocket. "Strange thing was, his sister said he was already on his way over here with your things. That's pretty lucky, huh?"

"Knowing Clarence, I doubt if it was luck," Raphael mumbled.

"I'm sorry, what did you say?" Luke asked.

Jade tried to laugh it off. "Raphael thinks the old man is psychic or something. I think he's just crazy…nice, but crazy."

Raphael smiled and poked Jade in the arm in a gentle, teasing fashion. She responded by giving his long, black hair a quick tug, then ducked before he could grab her again.

Their laughter and their joy in each other reminded Luke that he was the odd man out. Yet he couldn't take his eyes from Jade's face. Rarely did she leave her expression unguarded as she was doing now. When she smiled, there was an indentation at the right-hand corner of her lips that just missed being a dimple. Remembering her reaction to his touch earlier, he took a deep breath, then turned around, not wanting her to know that he was attracted to her in any way.

"Hey, here comes Clarence," Raphael said.

Luke turned around just as an old, dark-skinned man entered the sleeping area and began weaving his way through the aisles of cots, carrying two large duffel bags in his hands.

"It's Clarence with our things," Jade said, and bolted toward him.

Luke started to follow, when Raphael stopped him with a touch.

"Let her go," he said. "I need to talk to you a minute."

Luke shrugged. "Yeah, sure," he said, and then took a seat on an empty cot next to Raphael.

"I'm sick," Raphael said.

Luke frowned. "Hey, man, why didn't you say something sooner? I think I saw a doctor on duty when I came in the door."

"Not like that," Raphael said. "I've been sick for a long time."

Luke's frown deepened as he took another, longer look at the man's face. It occurred to him then that from the way Raphael was behaving, there was the possibility that Jade didn't know.

"Are you seeing a doctor?"

Raphael grinned wryly. "I've been to local health departments from time to time, but the way we live...the lack of money...no."

Luke put a hand on Raphael's knee. It was a brief, friendly gesture meant to reassure, yet the sudden tension in the muscles beneath his hand told him that Raphael didn't like to be touched any more than Jade did. He moved his hand without comment, making a mental note to tell Sam to keep a hands-off attitude until they made the first moves.

"Don't worry about doctor bills," Luke said. "Jade's father is a very wealthy man. He'll see that you have the best doctors available."

Raphael inhaled slowly, judging the man against what he was about to say. Luke Kelly had an open, honest face. He seemed very much his own man without being easy to sway, hence his gentleness with Jade without being a pushover. Then he exhaled on a short, angry grunt.

"Doctors can't fix what's wrong with me," he said. "I have full-blown AIDS and a cancer that's eating me alive from the inside out."

"Oh Jesus," Luke said softly, then suddenly he got the message. He looked up, watching Jade as she ran to meet Clarence. "And she doesn't know, does she?"

Raphael swallowed past a knot in his throat. "No, she doesn't, and I would appreciate it if you wouldn't—"

"It's okay, man," Luke said. "I understand." Then another thought occurred. One even more frightening than what he'd already been told. "Have you been practicing safe

sex? I mean, if she's been exposed without her knowledge, you—''

Raphael blanched. "We don't have sex. Our relationship isn't like that. She's like my sister...my best friend. Besides, even if I wanted it different, I would never..." He stopped suddenly, then just shook his head, as if the very thought of doing anything to harm Jade was beyond his comprehension.

Luke was surprised. Their relationship with each other was so close, so tender, he would have bet his life that they were in love.

"Okay, it's just that I had to ask, you understand? I didn't mean that there was anything wrong with you two being in love. You just seem so, I don't know...so together."

A muscle jumped in Raphael's jaw. "Yeah, we're together. We've always been together, but not like that. You coming into our lives like this is an answer to a prayer. I've been scared out of my mind, wondering what was going to happen to her when I died. You see how she is. She can't function in the normal world...at least not yet. She needs help...so much help. I've tried for years to get her past what happened in our childhood, but I don't know how. I need to know that she'll be okay. I need to know if I can trust the man who claims to be her father, and I need to know if I can trust you."

Luke didn't quite know what to say. How did you reassure a dying man that strangers would take care of his family?

"Sam is a good man and has accepted the fact that his daughter's life might not have been perfect. As long as he gets her back in his life, I can guarantee he won't give a damn about her past. As for trusting me, I give you my word that I will always make sure Jade is happy and safe."

Raphael sighed. He could tell that Luke Kelly was taken with Jade. Most men were. But he had to know to be careful. He also needed to know that his feelings might never be returned. But there was a limit to what Raphael could say

without betraying Jade, which was something he could never do.

"Yeah, okay," he said. "But I'll judge that for myself. I think I have that much time."

Meanwhile, Jade had come face-to-face with Clarence. He nodded at her and then smiled.

"Hello there, Missy," he said, and handed Jade her bag.

She eyed him suspiciously and then knelt on the floor and unzipped the carryall.

"It's all there," Clarence said. "Your box of pictures and paints is up by the office."

It wasn't the paintings that Jade was concerned with. She thrust her hand into the bag, digging past the jumble of clothes and her other pair of shoes. She was just starting to panic when her fingers brushed across the cool, smooth surface of the old shirt box at the bottom of her bag. After that, she relaxed and stood up. She eyed him curiously, considering the coincidence of Clarence's arrival just when she had committed herself to leaving.

"I'm sort of surprised to see you," she said.

Clarence looked at her, then past her. "You goin' on a trip. You'll be needin' your things."

"How do you know about that?" Jade asked.

"Trust the big man," he said; then a child running past them suddenly tripped and fell. Her wail brought her mother running, but it also brought Clarence out of his fugue.

"Clarice is right sorry about having to put you out, but the hotel is gonna take a lot of fixin' to get it ready for business again."

Jade could tell she wasn't going to get an answer to her earlier question and decided that, while Clarence was strange, he'd been nothing but kind, and so had his sister.

"I'm really sorry for what's happened to Clarice," she said. "The hotel was so beautiful."

"It can be fixed," he said softly; then his focus shifted slightly again. "And so can you."

She flinched. "What are you talking about?"

"Bad things happened and will again. Trust the big man to see you through."

An uneasy feeling swept over her. Impulsively Jade glanced around her, eyeing the roomful of strangers. She didn't see anyone or anything that seemed like a threat—except for the possibility of Luke Kelly. She leaned forward, lowering her voice as she asked, "See me through what?"

"What was...and what is to be."

Jade wanted to scoff, but then he looked at her, and it was as if he'd just walked through her mind without judging the life that she'd lived. Angry with the fear that his presence brought, she spoke out in anger.

"You're crazy, old man, and besides that, do you always talk in riddles?"

His gaze shifted again, and he seemed puzzled by what she'd just said.

"Riddles? Nope. Can't say as I know any," he said.

Jade frowned, telling herself that she would be as crazy as he was if she actually believed any of this "Twilight Zone" stuff. Besides that, she'd been rude when he'd been nothing but kind. It shamed her.

"At any rate, thank you for bringing our things," she said.

"God is with you," he said softly, then turned and walked away.

"There is no God," she retorted, then started to pick up the bags when Luke suddenly appeared.

"I'll get those," he said.

Jade took a single step back, needing the space between them to feel easy, then noticed he was alone.

"Where's Raphael?"

Luke sensed her discomfort and pointedly averted his gaze as he picked up the bags.

"Over there where you slept, making sure that you're leaving nothing behind."

Jade saw him, then relaxed.

"I'll be right back," he said.

Jade realized he was walking away with their things. She was torn between the need to keep him and their belongings in sight, and the fear of leaving the room without Raphael. Then Raphael looked up at her and waved. She waved back, then bolted after Luke.

Luke heard her coming and stifled a smile. He had to admire her. She was uncomfortable around him but still had the guts to stay with him to keep an eye on their worldly goods. Then he realized that he was carrying everything they owned, and the humor of the situation died. It wasn't funny. It was tragic. Thank God he'd found her. Reuniting with her father was going to change her world.

Then she caught up with him. He glanced over at her, smiling as they walked. She looked a bit startled by his friendliness, then a little embarrassed. From that, her expression slowly changed to one of reluctant acceptance. It was then that Luke knew Jade's world wasn't the only one that was going to change. If she ever smiled at him the way she smiled at Raphael, he would be toast.

They reached his rental car and loaded the bags inside.

"I have a box of paintings and art supplies, too," Jade said. "Clarence left it up by the office."

Luke eyed the trunk of the car, then looked up.

"Will it fit in here?" he asked.

Her expression fell. "I don't think so."

"Don't worry," he said. "We'll make things fit. Now, show me where it is, and we'll go from there." Then he grinned. "If we have to, Raphael can ride on the hood and be the new hood ornament."

The image of Raphael clinging to the hood made her giggle, and her giggle shot straight to his heart.

Luke's gaze went straight to her mouth. He quickly looked away, but it was too late. He'd known from the moment he'd seen her picture that she was beautiful, but it was nothing to seeing the real thing. And knowing how rarely joy entered

her life made the interchange of humor special. Even though she was unaware of his feelings, the fact that she'd shared the laughter with him had changed the dynamics between them forever.

And yet he couldn't forget what Raphael had just told him and feared the day when Jade learned the truth. Would she ever laugh again?

"So let's go get that box," Luke said, and led the way back indoors.

Seven

Everything fit perfectly, the car had been loaded, and their thanks had been said to the people who'd given them shelter from the flood, but when it came time to leave, Raphael opted for the back seat, claiming a headache and the need to sleep. That left Jade and Luke to share the front. Jade wanted to argue, to beg Raphael to trade places with her, but she could tell by the strained expression on his face that his headache was real.

"Rafie, did you take something for the pain?"

"No," he said, and then rolled into a ball in the back seat and closed his eyes.

Jade turned to Luke. "I think I have something in my bag. Would it be too much trouble to—"

"Of course not," Luke said, and quickly popped the lid to the trunk.

Jade smiled a quick thanks, unzipped her bag and dug through the contents until she felt the small plastic bottle with the painkillers inside. She shook out a couple and then tossed the bottle back in the bag before hurrying to the back seat. Luke handed her a partially opened bottle of water that he'd had in the car.

"If Raphael doesn't mind drinking after me…"

"We've had worse," Jade said, dropped the pills in Raphael's hand, then handed him the water.

He swallowed the pills, then lay back down with a groan.

Seeing him like this was frightening. This was the second time in less than four days that he'd succumbed to illness.

"I think maybe he's getting sick from something in the flood water," she said, then looked up at Luke, wanting reassurance.

Luke stifled a curse. He almost wished Raphael hadn't told him that he was sick. Now everything he said to Jade was going to be a lie, and the last thing he wanted was lie to her. So he skirted the issue by promising Sam's attention.

"Your father has a really good doctor. He'll be more than happy to give Raphael the once-over as soon as we get to St. Louis."

Jade considered the answer, then nodded. It was a better plan than anything she could have come up with. She started to close the door, then noticed that her jacket was lying on the back floorboard. She picked it up and folded into a makeshift pillow, then tucked it beneath Raphael's head.

"Get some rest," she said, and gently kissed his forehead.

After that, there was nothing left to do but to get in the front seat and pretend that Luke Kelly was not a dominating presence.

Luke watched her tending to Raphael and then looked away, afraid she would see too much in his expression. The more they were together, the more intrigued he became. By the time she was settled, he'd thought of one more thing they needed to do. When she reached for her seat buckle, he picked up his cell phone.

"Since we're already loaded, what do you two say to driving to Missouri, rather than flying? It's not that far, and I'm not sure what would happen to your paintings on a flight without some proper packing."

"Sounds like a good idea to me," Raphael said from the back seat.

"I've never been in an airplane," Jade said. "I'd much rather ride in the car."

"Good," Luke said. "Then it's settled." Yet still he sat

without starting the car, juggling what he wanted to do against the possibility of making Jade upset.

When Luke sat without making a move to leave, Jade began to get nervous. She glanced in the back seat. Raphael looked as if he'd already fallen asleep. If the man meant them harm, he would be of no help. Without thinking, she put her hand on the door handle.

"What's wrong?" Jade asked.

"There's someone I need to call."

She frowned. "Who?"

"Your father. I need to let him know I've found you and that we're on the way home."

Her heartbeat skipped and then picked up again as she let go of the door. So he wasn't intent on harming her after all.

"Oh."

Luke had seen her go pale and her fingers curl into fists. He didn't want to spook her, but he had what he thought was a good plan.

"I was thinking that when I call him, you might like to say hello. You know…sort of an ice-breaker? It wouldn't be anything more than hearing each other's voices, but it might make him more real to you. What do you think?"

Once again, Raphael spoke up from the back seat. "I think it's a good idea."

Jade turned to him and glared. "I thought you were supposed to be asleep," she said. "Besides, I can make my own decisions on this, thank you."

"Then do it," he said, and closed his eyes, thankful that someone else was in charge of Jade's future, because the way he was feeling, his was fading fast.

With the sunlight on his face, Jade saw shadows beneath his eyes that she'd never seen before. His cheeks seemed hollow, and his skin was missing that pink, healthy glow. Suddenly, getting somewhere safe so that he could see a doctor seemed imperative.

She looked at Luke and nodded.

"Yes. I'll talk to him."

Luke exhaled slowly, unwilling to let her know he'd been holding his breath. He started to pat her hand, then remembered what had happened the last time he'd gotten too friendly and settled for a quick wink instead.

"Good for you," he said, and punched in a series of numbers.

Sam Cochrane had been in the board meeting for almost two hours, and his patience was nearly gone. He never used to mind the time it took to run the businesses he owned, but over the past few years, he'd begun to begrudge it, although it wasn't as if he had other things to do. He didn't travel much, and he didn't have a lot of hobbies, other than to play a little golf from time to time. But when he looked back over his life, it seemed that most of it had been spent in courtrooms or rooms like this, with people like the ones encircling the long, oblong table, arguing about things that, in the long run, didn't really matter.

"Mr. Cochrane...what do you think?"

Sam had been gazing out the window, lost in thought. Hearing his name called reminded him that he was not attending to business.

"I'm sorry, what did you say?" Sam asked.

"We were discussing the wisdom of selling the Loflin properties before the end of the year. It would generate a lot of income that we might not be able to offset. What do you think?"

Before Sam could answer, his cell phone rang. He glanced at the caller ID and then stood abruptly.

"Excuse me," he said. "I need to take this call."

He walked toward the windows overlooking downtown St. Louis to give himself a bit of privacy.

"Hello."

"Sam, it's me, Luke."

Sam's pulse accelerated. He hadn't heard from him since right before he caught a plane to New Orleans.

"Do you have news?" Sam asked.

"I have more than that," Luke said. "I found her."

The words rippled through Sam's body like hot water over ice, shifting an unstable foundation toward a complete meltdown.

He reached for the windowsill to steady himself and then leaned against the wall.

"Tell me," he said softly. "Is she all right? Does she remember me?"

"Yes, she's fine, and no, not really, but she would like to say hello."

"Oh, dear God, so would I," Sam said, and then held his breath.

There was a moment of silence at the other end of the line as he supposed Luke was handing over his phone. All Sam remembered was the little girl that she'd been. He'd seen the photos from San Francisco, but that woman was a stranger. It was going to take some time for him to realize that the child had become that woman. And then he heard a nervous cough and a quick intake of breath on the other end of the line and knew that she was there. For the first time in twenty years, he was going to hear his daughter's voice. Tears thickened his own voice as he turned his back to the room and spoke into the phone.

"Jade? Is it you?"

The deep resonance of Sam's voice rolled across Jade's eardrums in a slow, gentle rumble. In that moment, she sensed that everything was going to be all right. She nodded slowly, then realized he couldn't see her and answered.

"Yes, this is Jade. Are you Sam?"

Sam forgot where he was and turned around, unintentionally startling the men sitting at the board table when they saw that he was crying. They began to mutter among themselves

as to what they should do. But Sam was oblivious. All he could hear was the voice on the other end of the phone.

"Yes, this is Sam. Do you remember me, honey?"

There was a slight hesitation, then a sigh. "I don't think so," she whispered. "I'm sorry."

"It doesn't matter," Sam said. "You have all the time in the world to get to know me again." Then he choked on a sob. "I'm sorry. I'm sorry. It's just that I'm so happy. I had just about given up hope of ever seeing you again."

"I didn't know."

It was those few words that put everything into focus for him.

"I understand, and it's all right. All that matters is that you do now. I can't wait to see you. We have so much to catch up on."

Jade's heart skipped a beat. How could she tell anyone what her life had been like and expect to be accepted? Anxious to change the subject, she blurted out the first thing that came to mind.

"I have a friend. His name is Raphael. He and I are together."

"I welcome him as I will welcome you," Sam said. "Just promise me one thing."

Jade shivered, afraid of what he might ask.

"If I can."

Sam heard the fear, and it made him sick at heart.

"Don't be afraid...not of me, honey...never of me. No matter what is in your past, all you have to do is think of the future. Where there's love, anything is possible."

"Yes, okay," Jade said, and handed Luke the phone.

Luke put the phone to his ear. "Sam?"

"Oh God, Luke! You did it, boy! You did it. I can never repay you enough for what you've just done."

Luke could tell Sam was crying. He swallowed around a lump in his own throat.

"You don't owe me anything." Then he looked at Jade,

seeing beyond the worn-out clothes and the long, unruly hair to the beauty of the woman beneath. "Bringing you two back together again was payment enough, understand?"

"Yes, I understand. When will you arrive?"

"I rented a car and we're driving through," Luke said. "As late as it is today, we'll have to stop somewhere along the road and get some rooms, but we should be there late tomorrow. If we're delayed in any way, I'll let you know."

Sam could hardly contain his joy. "Have a safe trip and hurry home."

"You know it," Luke said, and disconnected the call.

"You okay?" he asked Jade.

She nodded.

"Then we're on our way," he said. "Buckle up."

Sam also hung up, then dropped his cell phone back in his pocket. Tears were running down his face, and his hands were shaking.

His secretary, Doris Smith, immediately moved toward him, fearing he was ill.

"Mr. Cochrane, is anything wrong?"

He stared at her for a moment, remembering all the years of faithful service she'd given him, then suddenly picked her up and swung her off her feet as he gave a wild whoop.

"Mr. Cochrane! Mr. Cochrane! Please put me down!"

Sam laughed, but did as she asked.

Shocked at his behavior, Doris fussed with her suit, pulling at the jacket and smoothing down her hair as Sam started to laugh.

"Are you ill?" she asked.

"No. No. Nothing is wrong. In fact, for the first time in years, everything is right. Luke Kelly just found my daughter, and she's on her way home!"

Doris had been with Sam for almost twenty years. She'd known of all the private investigators and the dead ends that had been so disappointing for her boss. But this was some-

thing she'd never believed she would hear. She put her hand on his arm and gave it a squeeze.

"Oh, Mr. Cochrane, what wonderful news!"

The others at the table began talking at once. Some knew what he was talking about, some didn't. But by the time the meeting was adjourned, nine people, including Sam's secretary, were aware of the impending reunion. By morning, it was the headline in all the local papers. After that, it was only a matter of time before the AP wire services picked up the story and released it nationwide.

They'd been on the road for almost three hours. Raphael was snoring lightly in the back seat as Luke topped a hill on the two-lane road that was serving as a detour for another road that had been closed due to the flooding. Suddenly he hit the brakes and slammed the car into park. Water covered the highway below, and without being familiar with the area, he had no way of knowing how deep it might be.

"It's over the road here, too," Jade said.

"Yeah."

Raphael sat up in the back seat. Luke glanced in the rearview mirror, thinking to himself that the man looked like hell, and considering the reasons, he probably felt worse than he looked.

"What's wrong?" Raphael asked.

Jade pointed. "There's water over the highway," she said.

Raphael frowned as he leaned forward. "I could get a long stick, use it as a measure and check it out," he offered.

"I don't think so," Luke said. "You don't want to go wading with snakes."

Raphael grunted, then shuddered. "Ugh. Snakes. I hate snakes."

"Don't we all?" Luke said.

"Then what should we do?" Jade asked.

Before Luke could answer, a pickup truck topped the hill

from the other direction and then continued down the highway.

"There's our answer," Luke said. "We'll be able to tell how deep it is from how high the water goes up on his wheels."

To their relief, it was less than a foot, which meant they could cross easily. When the driver drew even with them, he stopped and rolled down his window.

"You can make it through easy enough," he said. "But if you're going farther than Little Bayou, I'd suggest you get a room at the motel and wait until the flood crests."

"How far is Little Bayou?" Luke asked.

The man pointed behind him. "About four miles. There's a decent enough motel and a couple of places to eat. Weatherman said the waters were due to crest here around midnight. Most of the roads are usually passable within six or eight hours after that."

"Thanks a lot," Luke said.

The driver smiled and nodded, then drove away.

"You guys okay with that?" Luke asked.

Jade glanced at Raphael and then nodded. "Yes."

"Ever been to Little Bayou?" he asked.

"No," Jade said.

"Ever heard of Little Bayou?" he added.

"No."

He grinned. "Me either, so we're all about to break new ground together, so to speak."

After that, he put the car in gear and started down the hill.

Little Bayou Motel and Eats was exactly what one would have expected it to be. The rooms were small and plain, and the Eats portion of the establishment was simple, with a limited amount of choices on the menu. But due to the flooding, a few of the locals had taken rooms in the tiny motel, which left only one vacant room with two double beds. If they

wanted a bed tonight, they were going to have to share the room.

Luke was apologetic about the situation as he paid for the room, but Raphael just shrugged it off with a grin.

"We've slept in lots of places that were worse, haven't we, Jade? Besides, you can't possibly snore any louder than Jade does."

She punched Raphael on the arm, just as he expected her to do, and it eased the tension enough that they shared an easy chuckle.

Jade watched Luke when he wasn't looking, trying to figure out what it was about him that made him different from other men. And he *was* different. That much she'd figured out. He seemed determined to get her back to this man who claimed to be her father, and at whatever cost. Except for Raphael, the men in her past had been sadly lacking in honor. She didn't know what she thought about Luke Kelly, but she was no longer afraid of him.

"We're in number ten," Luke said. "You guys go unlock the door. I'll get the bags."

"I'll help," Raphael said.

Luke stopped him with a hand on his shoulder. "It's okay. I've got them," he said, and gave him the room key. "Stay with Jade."

Raphael hesitated, then nodded. Obviously Luke was trying to help him without giving away his illness to Jade.

"Yeah, right," he said, and headed for the room, with Jade beside him.

The decor of the room was less than inspiring, but it was clean, and for Jade, that was a plus. Luke walked in behind them and set the bags on the floor.

"Take your pick of beds," he said.

"The one next to the bathroom," Jade said.

Raphael touched her face with the back of his hand and then looked at Luke and shrugged.

"She doesn't like the dark. We usually sleep with a small light."

"That's fine," Luke said, and sat down on the other bed. "Anyone hungry besides me?"

Food used to be Raphael's favorite topic, but the past few weeks, it had become the last thing on his mind. However, admitting that would alert Jade that something was wrong with him, so he was the first to speak up.

"I could eat," he said.

Jade grinned. "You can always eat."

"Good," Luke said. "Want to try out the Eats half of this fine establishment, or should we cruise the big town of Little Bayou to see what else is available?"

"I vote for eating here," Raphael said. The closer they were to a bed, the better off he would be.

"Then here it is," Luke said.

It was almost midnight. Luke had tried to sleep, but to no avail, although it wasn't Raphael's soft, uneven snore that was keeping him awake. It was the woman lying in Raphael's arms.

He couldn't see her face for the tangle of black hair spilling over Raphael's forearm. She slept with her back to Raphael's chest and his arms pulled over her like a child would clutch a blanket. Light from the parking lot outside illuminated enough of her body that Luke could tell she was dreaming. Her fingers kept opening and closing, as if she were making fists. Every now and then her leg would jerk and her feet would flatten out, like a person poised to run.

He could only imagine the hell they'd been through, living on the streets for so long. Part of him wanted to know the truth—to find a way to make it better. But another part of him feared it, knowing that the possibility existed that nothing could make it better—ever.

Suddenly there was a loud thump against their door and then the sound of a woman's giggle and a man's muffled

curse. At the moment of impact, Jade started to scream. Before Luke could react, her hands were in the air, fighting off some unseen enemy as her body bucked on the bed.

"The light! The light!" Raphael shouted. "Turn on the light!"

Luke's heart was pounding as he flipped the switch, instantly flooding the room with a soft yellow glow.

"Jade...honey...wake up! It's a dream. It's a dream. It's only a dream."

Her eyelids fluttered; then she went limp in his arms.

There were tears on Raphael's cheeks as he pulled her closer to his chest.

"Oh, Rafie...the dreams...why won't they stop?"

"Maybe because you haven't drawn all the faces," he said softly. "Do you want to draw his face?"

She was still for a moment, then nodded and rolled out of bed. Without looking at Luke, she dug through her bag and pulled out a large drawing pad and a stub of charcoal pencil.

"Do you want me to sit up with you?" Raphael asked.

She looked at him then, as if seeing him for the first time. He was pale and drawn and thinner than he should have been. Clutching the pad against her breast, she took a step forward.

"Rafie?"

"What, baby?"

Her heart was thumping against her rib cage like a trapped bird. She was afraid of the answer, but she had to ask.

"What's wrong with you?"

Stunned by the tableau unfolding before him, Luke could do nothing but hold his breath, like Jade, waiting to hear what Raphael would say.

But Raphael only shook his head and pointed to the pad of paper.

"Draw the face, baby. Draw the face, and then he'll be gone."

She started to argue, then feared to press him for more. It occurred to her that she might not want to hear the truth. Her

focus shifted, her mind sliding back to the face that had haunted her dream. Stumbling toward a chair, she sat down, then crossed her legs beneath her. Using her lap for a table, she opened the pad. Her fingers trembled as the first stroke of charcoal marked the page. After that, everything faded from her mind but recreating the image of the man who had caused her such pain.

Luke sat on the side of the bed, watching the intensity of her face, judging the anger in her by the hard, angry strokes of the pen.

An hour passed, and then another. Just when Luke thought she would pass out from exhaustion, her hand suddenly stopped. She lifted it from the page as if something ugly lay beneath and then laid down the pad.

"Raphael?"

He rose up from the pillow, almost as if he'd been waiting for the call. Without speaking, he lifted up the cover.

Jade stumbled past Luke, then fell into Raphael's arms. He rolled her up within his embrace, resting his chin on the crown of her head as she sighed and closed her eyes.

Luke was shaking as he finally lay back. The window unit of the old air conditioner was blowing across his feet as he pulled the covers up to his waist and closed his eyes. As he lay waiting for sleep, he remembered the drawing pad and quickly sat up. He wanted to look at what she'd drawn but was afraid that if they caught him, they would think he was snooping.

Still, the need to see the face that had caused her such pain was uppermost in his mind. He slid his legs to the side of the bed and then stood. He wouldn't look at them—couldn't look at them without feeling like the outsider that he was. The bond between them was like nothing he'd ever seen. To be that close and share nothing but platonic love seemed impossible, but then, he had not lived in their shoes.

Quietly he moved toward the chair where Jade had been sitting and picked up the drawing pad, then carried it to the

bathroom. But the tiny night-light wasn't enough for him to see what she'd drawn, so he eased the door shut and then turned on the light.

It was then that he realized what a skilled artist Jade Cochrane was. The face on the paper did everything but breathe. The hair on the man's head was drawn so skillfully against the shape of his face that it appeared mobile. The eyes were so lifelike that Luke had to look twice to convince himself that they had not blinked. It was the face of an ordinary man, without artifice or guile, and yet Luke knew that behind that bland smile was a man with an evil soul.

"What did you do to her to make her cry? What hole in hell did you crawl out of to make her come apart like that?"

But there were no answers this night for Luke, only more questions to add to the ones he already had that had gone unanswered.

Reluctantly he turned out the overhead light, laid the pad back in the chair and returned to his bed. Certain that he would never be able to sleep, he closed his eyes. When he opened them, it was morning.

"No, no, baby…not like that. Move a little closer. Right. Now lean forward…okay, perfect! Now, Mario, take her breast in your mouth and cup her hips with your hands." Otis Jacks turned around and pointed to the makeup man. "Ving! Spray them down. I want their skin to have a dewy glow, like they've been fucking for hours."

A small oriental man hurried forward with a spray bottle of oil and water and began misting the actors' nude bodies.

Otis narrowed his eyes, then stepped back for a better view before looking through the camera lens. Obviously he liked what he saw, because when he looked up, he was smiling.

"Yeah, like that. Now get it on, people! We got a film to finish."

The nude couple began writhing and humping in fake ec-

stasy, taking turns with the moans and groans while the cameras rolled.

Otis poured himself a fresh drink, added some ice, then sat back in his director's chair and sipped at the liquor until the scene was finished. Just then the woman arched her back to simulate an orgasm. He took a stiff drink and then pointed toward at the man.

"Okay, stud boy, she's hot. She's wet. She's all over you. Drive it home. I don't have all day."

The stallion-hung male lifted the woman off the bed and slammed her against the wall, where he proceeded to finish the act.

"Cut! Print!" Otis yelled, then downed the rest of his drink and stood. "That's a wrap! I've got an appointment in thirty minutes."

The actor set the woman down on her feet and then slapped her bare rear with the flat of his hand before strutting naked toward his dressing room. The actress picked up a robe and put it on, then took a cell phone out of her pocket. Like Otis Jacks, she was through for the day and planning her night.

Otis paused at the door and yelled at his stage manager. "Hey, Tiny, make sure everything is locked up." Then he strode out the door.

At sixty-three, Otis was on what he called his third life. He'd been born Nigel Bates, in Concord, New Hampshire, and lived with that name until he was thirty. It was during a sermon on Easter Sunday that it occurred to him that there was more to life than selling radios and televisions in Detroit. The following morning he kissed his wife and two children goodbye and left for work as always. Only one thing was different about that Monday from all of the other Mondays in Nigel Bates's life. He didn't bother to come home.

He emptied his bank account with no thought for what would happen to his family, gassed up his Volkswagen van and headed west to San Francisco. Six months later his hair

was hanging past his shoulders and he was wearing Nehru jackets and love beads and calling himself Solomon. That gig lasted long enough to destroy countless lives and families before he began to get nervous. Someone spilled the beans to the Iowa welfare department that there were children living with the People of Joy who'd never seen the inside of a school. Around ten o'clock on a rainy Monday night, he'd packed his bags and left without telling his dwindling followers goodbye. Friends were not something he collected, and it meant nothing to him that he was abandoning them to face the devastation that he'd wrought.

Once again, he found himself heading west. He drove into Hollywood with a new plan on the horizon and the money to make it happen. He cut his hair, bought a half-dozen good suits, traded the van for a black Corvette convertible and rented a house in the hills above L.A. under the name of Otis Jacks.

Within three months, he'd put his first porno film in the can and was in the act of casting the second. Seven years later, he was the accepted kingpin of x-rated films.

So when he strode out of the sound stage and got in his car, he had nothing on his mind but a meeting with his distributor and then dinner. He was contemplating lobster and a good bottle of Cabernet when he unlocked the car door and slid behind the wheel.

"Fuck," he muttered as the hot leather seat burned the backs of his legs.

He started the engine and immediately jacked the air conditioner up on high, then turned on the radio. His favorite radio show was on the air. The DJ was a Howard Stern wannabe with a mouth as filthy as the censors would allow, which was right down Otis Jacks' alley. Otis tuned in just as the DJ was commenting on a news bite; making jokes about a man finding a daughter who'd been missing for more than twenty years. The jokes ranged from back allowances owed to the inevitable clothes and car he was going to have to buy.

Everyone in the station seemed to think it was hilarious and was laughing along with the DJ, tossing in their own comments as to what the poor father had ahead of him.

Otis snorted beneath his breath as he put his car in gear and drove away without one thought as to what his own children might be doing today. Just as he was about to pull out of the security gates, the DJ mentioned the man's name.

Sam Cochrane, from St. Louis, Missouri.

The name seemed familiar, but he shrugged it off. In his lifetime, he'd met thousands of people and been in almost every state in the union. But then the DJ said something about the daughter's name being Jade and speculated that, with that name, she could have been a stripper.

It was at that moment that it all fell in place. Otis broke out in a cold sweat and then slammed on the brakes, skidding and stopping just shy of going over the edge of the canyon road that led back to L.A. His hands were shaking as he put the car in park. In his mind, he saw the beautiful, dark-haired child begging him to take her back to her bed. He put his hands over his ears, but he could still hear her screams as he shut the door behind him on his way out. And there was that last night, when he'd been certain she was dead. He'd had no way of knowing that Frank Lawson was going to flip out and beat the kid within an inch of her life, much less cut her. He closed his eyes, remembering that night. In his mind, it had been the beginning of the end for the People of Joy.

It had been late when Frank Lawson arrived, and Solomon had thought about turning him away. But Lawson had been there several times before, and he was always good for big bucks.

"Come on, Solomon, it's been six months since I've been here. Give me a break."

"Damn it, Lawson, it's almost two in the morning."

Lawson smiled, then started peeling off one-hundred-dollar

bills from a roll in his pocket. At that point, Solomon's greed had overcome his good sense.

"I want the little one with the pretty face and black hair," he said.

Solomon frowned. The last six months had brought about a lot of changes in Jade that he didn't think Lawson would like, but with all that money in his pocket, Solomon willingly agreed. He put Lawson in the purple room to get ready, then dragged Jade out of bed.

She tried to beg off, claiming that she didn't feel well, but Solomon had heard it all before. He walked her down the hall with a vicious warning to do her business or he would make her sorry. After that she clammed up.

Lawson was already high when Solomon arrived, and he frowned when he saw her.

"What the hell are you trying to pull?" he asked.

Solomon frowned back. "What are you talking about? You asked for Jade, didn't you?"

Lawson stared. This wasn't the delicate, flat-chested little girl that he remembered. She had grown in height, and if he wasn't mistaken, she was growing breasts. He didn't like breasts. They represented women, and women made him feel worthless.

"Come on, Lawson, you know Jade. She's your hot little honey, remember?"

Then, before Lawson could answer, Solomon shut them in together and left, telling himself everything was going to be all right. Five, then ten minutes passed before he heard the first scream. It was a mixture of pain and terror like Solomon had never heard. By the time he got out of his room, the others still living under his roof were also responding to the sounds. They came running from every room, flying down the hallway to Jade's defense, but it was Raphael who had been the first on the scene.

"He's dead!" someone cried. "Raphael killed him."

Solomon threw a sheet at Raphael, tossing it over Jade's lifeless body.

"Get her out of here," he said, and then ignored him as he left the room.

Solomon dropped to his knees and felt for Lawson's pulse. Lawson wasn't someone who could go missing without fallout. He couldn't be dead. Then he felt a faint pulse, and he shouted, "No, he's not dead! He's not dead! Someone get me some water."

In all the mess, he'd lost two of his best kids and a van, but by the next morning, he could not have cared less. If she lived, Jade was well past her prime, and Raphael was becoming a danger. He was glad to be rid of them, but just in case, it might be time to find a new home.

Otis felt sick. He hadn't thought of that pair in years. It could have been a coincidence, the lost child named Jade and the man she belonged to being named Sam Cochrane, but he knew it was not. And he knew, as surely as his name was not Otis Jacks, that he might be in trouble. Of all the children he'd pimped, she and that bastard boy who'd dogged her every footstep were the only ones who'd gotten away.

He took out a handkerchief and wiped the sudden sweat from his face. All these years and he'd assumed they were dead. They should have been dead. Most runaways that age wound up dead from one thing or another. Why the hell hadn't they?

His mind was racing as he took his foot off the brake and eased the car onto the canyon road. This time, changing his name might not be enough. He couldn't dye hair that was no longer on his head, and he'd never been able to put on any weight. The way he looked at it, there was only one thing left to do.

Eight

Frank Lawson stood at the window overlooking downtown Nashville, staring at a poster of himself on the giant billboard across the street.

A Vote For Lawson Is A Vote For Law.

He thought the slogan was a bit lame, but he liked his picture. Subconsciously he smoothed his hand over his thinning hair, then knuckled the weight below his jaws and shrugged. A little airbrushing here, a little shadowing there and one could almost believe he still had a full head of hair and no double chins.

Then Frank smiled. Pictures aside, he was on a roll. The polls were predicting him as a shoo-in as Tennessee's new governor, but he didn't need the polls to tell him what he already felt in his bones. It had been a long time coming, but his dreams were about to come true. He was going to win. He just knew it.

There was a brief knock at the door of his office; then his secretary walked in with the morning mail.

"Good morning, Mr. Lawson."

He smiled. "Good morning, Lydia." Then he lifted his coffee cup in a salute. "Great cup of coffee this morning," he said.

She nodded primly. Of course it was great. She prided herself on doing everything correctly, including making a perfect pot of coffee.

"Thank you, Mr. Lawson. You have a meeting in twenty

minutes with your campaign manager and lunch with the mayor at one o'clock.''

"Thank you, Lydia. I don't know what I'd do without you."

Lydia was just as certain that he wouldn't know what to do without her, either, which was why she made herself indispensable to her employers.

"Is there anything else you need?" she asked.

"No, thanks," Frank said.

Lydia left, quietly closing the door behind her, and leaving Frank with his coffee and the morning mail.

He took a quick sip from his cup, then sat down in his chair and picked up the paper. The headlines were nothing special.

And then he turned the page.

It was little more than a human interest story in the bottom right-hand corner, and he wouldn't even have bothered to read it, but the headline, above the story caught his eye.

Man finds missing daughter after twenty years.

He paused, then closed his eyes, thinking about where he'd been that long ago. Haight-Ashbury. Love-ins. And the drugs—lord, the drugs. Unlike what some of the country's leading politicians had claimed, Big Frank Lawson had sinned and inhaled—repeatedly—and admitted to it.

But that had all changed ten years ago due to an act of random violence. In the process, Frank Lawson had become a national hero.

He'd been in California for less than two days, trying to put together a group of financial backers for a shopping mall he wanted to build, but with little success. On his second night in L.A., he'd been asleep in his hotel, only to be awakened by a series of gunshots. At first he'd thought they were the result of a drive-by shooting, then he'd realized they were coming from the room next door. Without thinking, he jumped out of bed and ran into the hall, more to get away

from the bullets flying through the walls of his room than to try to be a hero.

But fate had intervened. He reached the hall just as the shooter came running out. It was a case of fight or die, and Big Frank had never been a quitter. He tackled the surprised gunman before he could take aim at Frank and took him to the floor. Despite the fact that the shooter had the weapon, Big Frank had four inches and seventy-five pounds more of height and weight to his advantage. With his elbow in the man's throat, he wrestled the gun from his hands, then knocked him out cold.

As he staggered to his feet, he heard moans from the room the gunman had exited, and entered to find a woman and three children, lying in their own blood on the floor. He grabbed the phone and called 911, then sat out in the hall with the gun trained on the shooter. Within minutes the police arrived, followed closely by emergency services and then the media. By morning, Frank Lawson had become a star in a city where stars were a dime a dozen. The woman, who'd been on the run from her abusive husband, survived, as did her children. The husband, furious that his wife had left him, had hired a man to kill her and the kids. By the time the truth came out and the trial was over, Big Frank Lawson's name was on everyone's lips. He was a guest on all the big talk shows, appeared at news stations across the country and in every facet of the media that wanted a draw for their weekly shows. After that, investors were a dime a dozen and Frank Lawson was not only famous, but rich, as well.

And now he found himself standing on the precipice of another new venture—one that he wanted more than he'd wanted anything in his entire life.

To be the governor of his home state of Tennessee.

Beyond the windows of his office, a jet plane flew across his line of vision, breaking his thoughts and reminding him that, within minutes, he would be leaving for a meeting. He

glanced back at the story, and as he did, a name caught his eye.

Jade Cochrane.

He frowned. The name seemed familiar, but he couldn't place where he'd heard it before.

Jade? Jade?

He skimmed through the rest of the article, catching only the highlights. Parental kidnapping. Missing since the age of four. Thought to have been living with a cult called the People of Joy.

That was when it hit him.

A delicate, seven-year old girl with long, black wavy hair. Eyes the color of coal and a mouth like a rosebud. Skin so white it looked pearlescent on her fragile, prepubescent body. He choked on a breath and then stood abruptly. The paper slid out of his hands onto the floor as memory surfaced and his knees went weak.

"Oh shit. Oh shit."

That was why the name Jade was familiar. Sweet baby Jade…his Saturday night toy.

Big Frank spun toward the window and then stared across the street toward the billboard.

A Vote For Lawson Is A Vote For Law.

And therein lay his problem. In his lifetime, he'd broken quite a few laws, but after his life-changing role as a hero, most of that had become infinitely forgivable—except for that one.

It was the single weakness he had that the world would not forgive. Even now, thinking about the small bones and satin-smooth skin on a little girl's body made him hard. He closed his eyes, remembering what he'd taught her to do—remembering the feel of her tiny hands and soft mouth, picturing her bloody and lifeless on the floor at his feet.

"Mr. Lawson, you're late for your meeting."

Frank pivoted sharply. Lydia was standing in the doorway and he was on the brink of an orgasm. He was afraid to move

for fear he would come where he stood. He inhaled sharply, then made himself focus. *Don't think of it. Don't think of it. You have too much at stake.*

"Tell them I'll be there as soon as I make a phone call."

She nodded, then left.

The moment the door was closed, Frank reached for the phone. The way he looked at it, this wasn't his mess. He'd paid a lot of money to that son-of-a-bitch Solomon to make sure that his sexual preferences were protected. Granted, when this began, back in the seventies he'd been a nobody on the road to nowhere. How could he have known that he would become a fucking hero? But he was honest enough with himself to admit that, even if he'd known, he doubted he would have lived his life any other way.

What he did know was that the man who called himself Solomon had quit the "cult" business and gone semi-legit, if one could call porno a legitimate occupation. Now all he had to do was find him. He thought he remembered the name of the film company he'd founded. It was a place to start.

He picked up the phone and dialed information. As soon as the operator answered, Frank spoke.

"Los Angeles, California, please."

"Yes, go ahead," the operator said.

"Do you have a listing for Shooting Star Productions?"

"One moment please."

A few seconds later, a recorded message came on, listing the number. Frank wrote quickly, tore the paper from the pad on which he'd written it and stuffed it in his pocket. Then he smoothed down his hair with the palms of both hands, lifted his chin and headed for the door.

Normally the library in Sam's house was a place of comfort to him, but not today. He'd been unable to concentrate on anything and had done little else but pace through the rooms of the house, trying to look at them with a fresh view—wondering if there was anything within the walls of

the old, three-story home that would ring a bell in Jade's memory. Luke had cautioned him carefully about not expecting too much from her, especially at first. He understood. She'd been so young when Margaret had taken her away that it would be a miracle if she remembered anything, especially him.

And ever since Luke's phone call, he'd been inundated with calls from the local media with requests for interviews, as well as one man's request for permission to film their first meeting as part of a documentary.

Sam had refused them all, but it hadn't stopped the stories from appearing in the papers or the reporters from calling.

He'd tried to ignore everything and focus all his energy on getting the house ready for his daughter's homecoming. All he could think was, thank God for Velma. She'd positioned herself between the world and Sam, giving him time to come to terms with everything that was happening.

"Mr. Cochrane, I've cleaned the guest rooms as you requested. The florist delivered the flowers a few minutes ago, so the fresh arrangements you wanted are also in place. Is there anything else you want me to do before they arrive?"

"No, Velma...not that I can think of," Sam said.

She frowned. He'd been distracted ever since he'd gotten up this morning. At first she'd attributed it to anxiety over his long-lost daughter's arrival, but the more time passed, the more convinced she became that something else was bothering him.

She started to leave and then made herself stop and turn around.

"Mr. Cochrane, are you feeling all right?"

Sam sighed. Velma was like a bulldog when it came to pursuing a truth, so he shouldn't be surprised by her astuteness.

"My health is fine. It's everything else. Christ almighty, woman, look out the windows! The papers are full of this

story. There are news crews camped out as close to my doorstep as they can get without getting themselves arrested. I'm scared to death that all this crap will frighten Jade off before she gets a chance to know me again."

Velma sighed. She should have known. This block had become a madhouse.

"It will pass," she said. "Besides, if your daughter has survived the past years on her own, don't you think she's strong enough to survive this, as well?"

Sam sighed. He hadn't thought of it in those terms. He was so used to being the one in charge, but in this case, everything was out of his control.

"You're right," he said, and then gave the little woman a quick hug. "And thank you for caring," he said.

"Of course I'm right," she said, and then fussed with her apron to cover her embarrassment. "I'll be in the kitchen if you need me."

Sam grinned as she left the room. Just like a woman to get the last word and claim righteousness in the process. Then the phone rang, and his smile faded. He thought about letting it ring, but there was always the chance it might be Luke. He circled his desk and picked up the receiver.

"Cochrane residence."

"Sam? What the hell is going on at your house?"

"Luke? Where are you?"

"About two blocks away. News crews are everywhere. What's happening?"

Sam sighed. "You're what's happening," he said. "I'm assuming you haven't been reading the papers or watching the news."

Luke glanced at the woman sitting beside him on the seat and gave her what he hoped was a comforting smile. After what he'd witnessed last night in the motel, the last thing he wanted to do was spook her. She didn't smile back, but at least she no longer looked at him with fear. It was a start. Now if he could find a way not to ruin their tenuous rela-

tionship, he would be happy. He returned his attention to the street and to the man on the other end of the line.

"No, we haven't done much reading the past two days."

"Good," Sam muttered. "But you've got to find a way to get her inside this house without scaring the hell out of her."

Luke stifled a curse. "Yeah. Sure. No problem." A moment of frustration came and went, and then a thought occurred. "Hey, Sam, are they still laying cable in the alley behind your house?"

"No, they finished that job almost a week ago. Why?"

"Good, because we're coming in the back door."

Suddenly Sam understood. "I'll open the gates," he said quickly, then added, "But what if your car won't fit through the opening?"

A muscle jumped in Luke's jaw as he made a sudden turn to the right.

"We'll make it fit," he muttered, then touched Jade's hand.

"Hang on, honey. We're almost there."

Sam heard the tires skidding on pavement before he dropped the phone and started to run.

Jade didn't know what was happening, but it was too late to ask for an explanation.

Raphael roused himself from the back seat as the car began to skid. Thinking they were about to be in an accident, he reached over the seat toward Jade.

"I'm fine," she said. "Buckle up."

Raphael fumbled for his seat belt.

The rental car bounced into and then out of a set of ruts as Luke drove into the unpaved alley.

"Sorry," he muttered, then glanced into the rearview mirror and frowned. A white van was less than a half block behind him and closing fast. "Damn it, they've spotted us."

"Who spotted us?" Raphael asked.

Jade's heart was in her throat. She didn't know what was going on or why these elaborate maneuvers were necessary,

but she suddenly realized that she was trusting Luke Kelly to see them through.

Luke had never done sixty miles an hour down a narrow, one-way alley before and was too busy driving to answer Raphael's question. Added to that was the unexpected confusion of not being able to tell one piece of property from another due to the high brick walls of the estates.

"Look for a big blue gate!" he yelled. "It should be on the right!"

Jade leaned forward, her gaze fixed on the blur of shrub and structures by which they were speeding. Suddenly, she saw a flash of blue up ahead. Before she could focus, the color began to disappear. It took her a moment to realize that it was the double doors to a big gate and they were swinging inward.

"There!" she cried, pointing up ahead. "Someone is opening the gates."

Luke grinned. "Good job. Now let's see if this baby will fit."

He tapped on the brakes just enough to take the turn inside without slamming against the walls, then whipped the steering wheel sharply to the right, correcting the turn. The car fishtailed slightly, then shot through the gap with mere inches to spare. Once inside, he slammed on the brakes and put the car in park, then jumped out on the run.

Despite the excitement, Jade found herself unable to move; instead staring in disbelief at the elegant grounds on which they had stopped, grounds that led up to a three-story edifice of native stone and brick. Suddenly she came to her senses and pivoted in the seat just in time to see Luke and a tall older man pushing the gates shut. When they dropped a long, wooden bar across a pair of large, metal brackets, she had the sensation of having been locked inside the castle walls.

"What in hell was that all about?" Raphael asked.

"I don't know, but I think we've arrived," she said softly, then unbuckled her seat belt and got out of the car.

The sunshine was warm on her face, and there was a slight breeze rustling the leaves in the tops of the trees towering over the brick walls encircling the property. Somewhere overhead a bird chirped. Off to her right, another answered. She looked at Luke and then the man standing beside him and shivered. He was tall, with a full head of silver-gray hair and a look on his face that was just short of pain.

Instinctively Jade took a step backward, then felt Raphael's hand on her shoulder.

"It's all right, honey," he said softly. "Just say hello."

"I can't, Rafie…I'm scared."

"He doesn't want to hurt you, baby."

Jade's stomach was in knots. "How do you know?"

"Just look at his face. There's nothing there but love."

Jade took a deep breath and then made herself look.

Sam held his breath, afraid she would bolt, but whatever she saw convinced her to take that first step forward, and then another and another, until she was so near he could hear the short, rapid sounds of her breathing. She was scared, and he knew just how she felt. He was shaking so hard he could barely stand, but she was beautiful—so beautiful. After all these years, it was nothing less than a miracle that they were standing face-to-face.

Sam started to speak and then had to clear his throat to get past the tears. He reached for her, wanting to hold his daughter in his arms.

"Oh Jade…honey…"

She took a nervous step backward.

"Easy, Sam," Luke said softly. "Let her take the lead."

Sam nodded, then took a deep breath and started over, making sure that he kept his emotions at bay.

"I guess the proper greeting would be 'welcome home.'"

"Thank you," Jade said, and then reached behind her, caught Raphael's hand and pulled him forward. "This is Raphael."

Sam's smile was genuine as he offered his hand.

"Raphael, it's a pleasure to meet you."

Raphael was taken aback by the man's genuineness. It wasn't something he was accustomed to from a person of this man's standing.

"No, sir," Raphael said. "The pleasure is all mine." Then he put his arm around Jade, gently urging her toward the man who'd given her life. He spoke softly, so that only she could hear. "Look in his eyes, honey girl. Trust what you see."

The emotion of this moment was so strong that Luke felt like an intruder, and yet common sense told him that until they were safely inside the house, they weren't really safe from the eyes and ears of the media.

"I think we need to take this inside," he said.

Sam swung toward the gate, as if expecting intruders to come barging through. His first instinct was to protect Jade from all that he'd wrought.

"He's right," Sam said. "Shall we go before they start crawling over the walls?"

Jade's eyes widened. "Who's out there? Why were we trying so hard to get away?"

Sam sighed. "I'm afraid it's partly my fault. I was in a board meeting when Luke called to tell me that he'd found you. Without thinking, I blurted it out to the people there. I have no idea who told the press, but like it or not, your return is news. It's not every day that a parent finds a lost child after twenty years."

Jade eyed the gate again. "You mean all those people were there because of me?"

Sam nodded. "But it will be okay, I swear. We'll make it okay. You don't have to say or do anything that you don't want to. I'll protect you, I promise."

Jade looked in Sam's eyes and saw truth, but there was still a part of her that wished she'd never taken that painting of Ivy to the street fair. If she hadn't, they wouldn't be in

this mess. Then she felt a muscle jump in Raphael's arm and remembered her fears about health.

"Don't worry about us," she said, and then turned her back to the gates in a gesture of dismissal. "A few people with microphones and cameras aren't what's scary in this world...are they, Raphael?"

"No, honey, they're not, and just look where you are. You won't ever have to be afraid again."

"Follow me," Sam said, and hurried toward the house.

Jade and Raphael did as he asked, leaving Luke to bring up the rear.

Nine

Sam led the way into the house through the library, hustling everyone inside. The phone on his desk was ringing as he shut and locked the doors.

"Let it ring," he told Luke.

Luke smiled. "Been rough?"

"You have no idea," Sam muttered, but his concern was for Jade, not himself. "I suppose I was naive about the impact finding Jade would have. I was so concerned with renewing our relationship that it never occurred to me that the rest of the world would find our story remarkable."

Then Sam noticed Jade staring at the room in disbelief. His father had built the house during the 1920s. He'd lived in it all his life, had brought Margaret here from their honeymoon, and then, a few years later, they'd brought their baby daughter home from the hospital to live here. It was so comfortable—so familiar—that he'd taken the elegance for granted, but seeing the shock on his daughter's face reminded him that he lived a privileged lifestyle. Sam stifled a surge of anger. If it hadn't been for Margaret, Jade would not be a stranger in her own home.

Luke could tell Sam was troubled, but he didn't know how to fix it. He'd found Sam's daughter. The rest had to be up to them.

"Some of Jade's paintings and art supplies are still in the car. I'm going to get them, along with the bags, then get out of your hair. You guys have a lot of catching up to do."

Jade heard what Luke said and turned abruptly. It occurred to her as she watched him walking away that she wasn't sure she wanted him to go. She told herself that it was certainly not because she was beginning to think of him as someone she could count on. It was simply a case of the devil you know being better than the one you did not—and she did not know Sam Cochrane.

She gave Sam a nervous look, then glanced at Raphael, who'd seated himself in a large overstuffed chair beneath the painting that had caused their world to unravel.

Sam watched her face, searching her expression for clues as to what she was thinking. When she looked up at the painting of Ivy, she frowned. He decided it was time to make the first move.

He walked up beside her, then pointed to the painting.

"Thank you for that."

Jade looked up at him, uncertain as to what he meant.

"Thank you for what?"

"For giving a little bit of her back to me."

Jade sighed. So Sam had really loved her. She began to understand what losing her must have meant.

"You really loved her?"

Sam sighed. "More than life."

"Then why did she leave you?"

His smile was sad as he met her gaze. "I was hoping that was something you could tell me."

Jade frowned. "I barely remember her. All I know is she died and left me in hell."

Sam hid his surprise as anger exuded from every fiber of his daughter's being.

"I'm sorry I couldn't find you," he said softly. "God knows I looked. I looked so hard and for so long, but there was no sign of you or your mother anywhere."

Jade shrugged and then turned, facing the man who wanted to call himself her father. But to do that, he had to accept her for what she'd become, not who she'd been.

"You couldn't find your little girl because she died, too."

Sam felt the floor shift beneath his feet. "What are you saying? Are you telling me that you're not Jade?"

"Oh, no, I'm Ivy's child. That much I remember. But the little girl I was no longer exists. You may not want what's left of me now."

Sam flinched; then his shoulders straightened as he stared into Jade's face.

"There's something we need to get straight right here and right now. I don't give a damn about your past. Whatever you did, you did to survive, and for that I will be forever grateful. Whether you like it or not…whether you want to admit it or not…you're as much a part of me as you were of Margaret, and I want every goddamned bit of what's left of you. Do you hear me, girl?"

Jade shivered. "I hear you."

"Good," Sam muttered. "Now that we've settled that bit of history, is it too much to ask that I might hold you? Just for a moment, you understand. Just so I can assure myself that I'm not dreaming?"

Luke reentered the library just as Sam delivered his request. He stopped, all but holding his breath as he waited to see what Jade would do. He saw her glance at Raphael, then look back at Sam without speaking a word. Slowly, her shoulders straightened, not unlike Sam's had only moments earlier.

"I don't think it's too much to ask," she said; then, just before Sam's arms began to enfold her, Luke heard her add in a calm, quiet voice, "Don't hold me too tight. I don't like to be touched."

Sam didn't want to consider the reasons why that might be so. For now, it was enough that she'd allowed him the familiarity.

"Certainly," he said, struggling with the urge not to cry; then, banking his fervor, he wrapped his arms around his only child. Like the miracle that it was, he felt the beat of her

heart against his chest and remembered there was a God after all.

Luke exhaled slowly. It wasn't going to be easy, but if he read this right, they just might make it work. Then he looked at Raphael, caught a wry smile on his face and thought he understood the reason why. Everything was starting to work out for Jade, but Raphael's situation was different. On one hand, Luke guessed that he was relieved. At least now he wouldn't have to worry about her welfare and safety. But it had to be the biggest irony of all that he would never live to see it happen.

It was Luke's opinion that the whole situation was one big tragic merry-go-round. Sam had his daughter, but her only memories of the past left her screaming in the night. Jade had Raphael, but not for long. In a way, Raphael was the only one who was close to realizing a goal. He'd been searching for a way out of their lifestyle and a safer place for Jade. Now he had both, but at what cost? Suddenly Luke realized that Jade had been staring at him over Sam's shoulder.

When their gazes met, Jade immediately pushed herself out of Sam's embrace and looked away, but it was too late. She'd been caught. What bothered her most was not that he'd caught her in the act but that she'd been doing it at all. He didn't belong in her world, and she wasn't so sure that she would ever find a way to belong in this one. Then she looked at Raphael and knew that what she thought or wanted didn't matter. Something was wrong with him. She could feel it in her bones.

She looked back at Sam.

"Uh… Sir…uh—"

Sam smiled. "For now, why don't you call me, Sam?"

Jade nodded. "Okay. Sam, it is. Now I have a favor to ask of you."

Sam's smile widened. "Anything!"

"Raphael hasn't been feeling well. I think he needs to see a doctor."

Raphael was unprepared for the abruptness of Jade's request.

He stood quickly, afraid that confronting her father with an ailing houseguest would sour his opinion of her, as well as of him, and he couldn't afford for that to happen.

"There's no need," he said quickly. "I'm just—"

"I think it's a good idea," Luke said quietly.

Jade turned, her eyes narrowing angrily as she looked from Luke to Raphael and then back again. Suddenly she saw something on Raphael's face that she'd never seen before. He was keeping something from her, and whatever the secret, Luke knew it, too.

She pivoted sharply.

"Raphael?"

He took her in his arms. "It's okay, honey. It's okay."

Sam could tell something was amiss but was less concerned with what he didn't know than with granting Jade's wish.

"Of course we'll get you medical care. I'm so sorry I didn't notice you weren't well," Sam said. "I'll show you to your rooms, then call my personal doctor myself. Under the circumstances, I'm sure he'll be more than happy to stop by."

Raphael sighed. There was no way to get around it, and, truth be told, he knew it was time. The pain in his belly was getting worse, as was the nausea. During the past two months, all he had wanted to do was sleep. Now that Jade was safe, it was as if his spirit had started to fade. He didn't have to keep it together for her anymore. It wasn't going to be easy, but the last thing he could do for his sweet baby Jade was teach her how to let him go.

"Thank you, Mr. Cochrane. I would appreciate it."

"Please, call me Sam. Now follow me. I'll show you to your rooms."

"I've got the bags," Luke said.

Jade wouldn't look at him. She didn't want to see anything resembling pity on his face and not know the reason why.

Luke followed them up the staircase, aware that Jade was trying not to stare at the elegance of the old Cochrane mansion. It probably hadn't occurred to her yet that she was heir to all she saw and several million dollars to boot. If only money were all it would take to give her peace, she would be set.

Then, halfway down the hallway, Sam stopped.

"Here we are," he said, then opened the door and stepped inside. "It's quite roomy, with its own bath. I think you'll find everything you need, but just in case, the white phone on the table is a sort of intercom between you and Velma. Just pick it up and dial O. She'll have the answer to any questions you might have."

"Who's Velma?" Jade asked.

Sam smiled. "She calls herself my housekeeper, but she's more like the captain of the ship. If it wasn't for her, I would have sunk years ago." Then he opened another door and pointed inside. "These bedrooms are adjoining. I wasn't sure about your sleeping arrangements, but I wanted to give you both a little space if you felt the need."

Jade's eyes widened perceptibly as she glanced into the second room and saw the large, empty bed.

"We'll be in here," she said quickly.

"That's fine," Sam said, then turned to Luke. "Just set both bags in here, then, will you?"

"Done," Luke said. "And now, why don't I go call Michael Tessler while you finish getting them settled."

"Who's he?" Jade asked.

"Your father's doctor," Luke said, and walked out of the room.

To his surprise, Jade followed him into the hall.

"Hey!"

Luke wanted to keep walking but knew there was no way to ignore her. He pasted a smile on his face and then turned.

"Yes?"

"What's going on?"

"I'm sorry. I don't know what you mean."

Jade moved closer then, her fists doubled, her expression guarded but angry.

"You lie." Then she took a deep breath. "You're no different from the others."

"What others?" Luke asked.

"Men," she said, spitting out the word as if it were a curse. "They all lie. You're no different."

He felt sick to his stomach for reasons he didn't want to examine, but he wouldn't let her have the last word. Not about this.

"I will never hurt you," he said quietly. "And that is no lie."

Then he turned and walked away, leaving her alone in the hall.

Confused by what she was feeling, Jade strode back into the bedroom. If she couldn't get the answers she wanted out of Luke Kelly, she knew who to ask. Except Raphael was already stretched out on the bed with his eyes closed. She knew he wasn't asleep, but she couldn't bring himself to confront him—not like this.

"Are you hungry, my dear?" Sam asked.

She looked at Raphael and then sighed. "A little. Rafie…do you feel like having something to eat?"

"No, but you go ahead," he said. "I think I'll just take a little nap until the doctor gets here."

Sam touched Jade on the shoulder, then quickly removed his hand when he felt her flinch.

"I'll leave you to freshen up. When you're ready, come back downstairs and turn left. At the end of the hallway, turn right. You'll see the dining room from there."

"Yes, all right," Jade said, wanting him to leave so she could talk to Raphael.

Sam made it as far as the doorway before he stopped.

"Jade?"

"Yes?"

"I am so very glad you're home."

She sighed, and for the first time since she'd walked into the house, had to admit her own truth.

"Yes, Sam…so am I."

Sam waved as he closed the door. The moment he was gone, Jade sat down on the bed beside Raphael, then laid a hand on his forehead. His skin felt cold —almost clammy— and there was a muscle jumping at his temple, as if he was battling pain.

"Rafie?"

He stifled a sigh. "Yeah?"

"You're sick, aren't you?"

The fear in her voice made her sound like a child, and he needed her to be strong.

"Yes, baby, I am."

She lay down behind him, spooning herself against his back, and then laid her arm across his waist.

"Why didn't you tell me?"

He grabbed her hand and pulled it against his heart, wishing she could feel the love he had for her through osmosis, because he would never be able to show her the truth of what he felt.

"There was no need," he said.

She was silent for a moment, then took a slow, shuddering breath. She didn't want to think of what it might be. Neither she nor Raphael had ever done drugs, but it was impossible to forget what Solomon had done to them—or ignore the fact that some sexually transmitted diseases were not only incurable but fatal.

She slid her hand beneath his shirt, felt the curvature of his rib cage and the shocking lack of flesh that normally covered it, and stifled an urge to scream.

Not Raphael! Please, not my Raphael.

Then she made herself calm. After all the years that he'd

taken care of her, returning the favor was the least she could do. She rubbed her hand up and down the middle of his back in a gentle, caressing motion.

"It's all right, Rafie. The doctor will come, and he'll make you okay."

She waited for Raphael to agree. She waited, and she waited, and then she started to cry.

Raphael felt her body shaking and struggled with tears of his own. In that moment, if he'd had the energy, he would have cursed God for giving him this fate. But he didn't, and it wouldn't have mattered, anyway. His fate had been sealed from the day he was born.

"You are going to be all right," he said softly.

"I'm not worried about myself. I'm worried about you."

Raphael closed his eyes, willing away a feeling of nausea.

"Go meet Velma...have something to eat. When you come back, maybe you could bring me something cold to drink."

The thought of being able to do anything for him brought Jade to her feet.

"I won't be long," she said. "Maybe they'll have some soup. Rafie...would you like some soup?"

"Yeah, sure," he said. "That would be nice."

He felt her hand on his shoulder, then felt the mattress give as she got up. He held his breath until she was gone, then rolled out of bed and staggered into the bathroom.

The phone number was burning a hole in Big Frank's pocket as he pulled into the underground parking garage beneath his apartment complex. He rolled his considerable girth out from behind the steering wheel and then ambled toward the elevator, nodding and waving to an attendant as he passed. It never hurt to be friendly to a potential voter.

He got on the elevator with a couple who lived on the floor above him and found himself forced into an amiable conversation when all he wanted to do was punch someone's

face. When he reached his floor, he strode off with a casual
"Have a nice evening" and all but bolted into his apartment
before closing and locking the door. Tossing his briefcase
aside, he reached for the phone number, then headed for his
bedroom. Although there were phones in other parts of his
home, somehow the privacy that a bedroom represented
seemed appropriate.

He took off his suit coat and loosened his tie, then dropped
to the side of the bed and picked up the phone. As he did,
he glanced at his watch. It was six o'clock in the evening
here in Tennessee, which meant it would only be four o'clock
in California. He took a deep breath and then made the call.
It rang only twice before a woman's voice chirped in Frank's
ear.

"Shooting Star Productions. How may I help you?"

"I'm trying to locate a man named Otis Jacks. Is he
there?"

"No, I'm sorry, but Mr. Jacks has gone home for the day.
Would you like to leave a message?"

Frank's body went limp. At least the son-of-a-bitch was
still in L.A. That was a positive.

"It's imperative that I reach him as soon as possible. How
about a cell phone number?"

The receptionist hesitated. She'd only been on the job a
few weeks and wasn't certain about the protocol of giving
out the boss's cell number. Then she shrugged. It wasn't as
if she was giving out a home phone number or address. She
rattled off the number to Frank.

"Thank you," he said, and hung up, then quickly called
the new number.

It rang five times, and Frank was bracing himself for a
voice mail when the call was suddenly answered.

"Hello...this is Jacks."

"You used to call yourself Solomon. What was it before
that, huh, Otis?"

Otis froze. To his knowledge, no one from his past had

ever found out about this phase of his life. Obviously he'd been wrong.

"Who is this?" he asked.

"Let's just say I was one of your clients and leave it at that."

"Listen, you son-of-a-bitch. I don't have time to fuck with you. State your business."

"Have you been reading the papers? Do you know about the girl…the one you called Jade?"

Otis grunted. So he wasn't the only one nervous about that little bit of news.

"Yeah, I heard."

"So what are you going to do about it?" Frank asked.

"Nothing," Otis said. "I'm going to do nothing, which is exactly what I suggest that you do, whoever the hell you are."

Big Frank's nostrils flared. No one talked to him like that and got away with it.

"Yeah, well, maybe you don't have as much to lose."

"That's your problem, not mine," Otis said. "So put your dick back in your pants where it belongs and lay low. It'll all blow over. Or you could get a nose job or something and retire to the Bahamas. Hell, don't blame me because you're a sick fuck."

Frank was livid, but there wasn't much pressure he could put on Otis without putting his own dirty secrets in jeopardy of being revealed. Still, he couldn't resist getting in a good dig.

"I know more about you than you think," Frank whispered. "You stole babies… You pimped kids to sick fucks like me.… So what does that make you?"

He hung up in Otis Jacks' ear. He should have known the sorry bastard would be of no use, but he'd had to try. And since Otis hadn't recognized Frank's voice, Frank considered himself still in the clear. Now he had to find out if the man

who was with Jade when she was found was Raphael. If he was, then Frank would make sure he couldn't give him away.

He looked around the room, eyeing the painting on the wall. It was just a print of an original Van Gogh, but he liked the fuzzy confusion of the colors and the paranoia he saw in the brush strokes. Then he lay back on the bed and closed his eyes, cursing the fact that a voluptuous woman turned him off while the flat chest and thin body of a little girl turned him on.

He lay there in the quiet, his mind turning over all the possibilities and weighing the ramifications of ignoring what he'd learned. Finally he sat up with a sigh. The truth was, there was too much at stake for him to ignore.

This time, when he picked up the phone, he had a plan.

It was eight o'clock in the morning when Otis Jacks arrived at the doctor's office. The man was one of the most skilled plastic surgeons in Los Angeles, but more than that, for the right amount of money, he could develop a perfect case of amnesia regarding the names of certain patients. In fact, it was rumored that he had worked on people without ever putting a name on paper. It was just what Otis intended.

Today he was going to start the ball rolling on getting a new look, including a nose job, cheek implants and maybe a few nips and tucks around his eyes and beneath his jaws to remove the excesses of his lifestyle. He knew someone who would buy his film company, although he could walk away from it without a backward glance and still be a very wealthy man. To hell with kids who wouldn't forgive and forget, and to hell with the nervous bastard who'd called him. As soon as the doctor would let him travel, he was going to be going, going, gone.

Michael Tessler had been Sam Cochrane's personal doctor for years, but he'd never been asked to make a house call. To say he was curious would have been putting it mildly,

although when Luke Kelly had called, he had readily agreed. Like everyone else in St. Louis, he knew about Sam's daughter being found and rejoiced for Sam's good fortune. But now, as he drove through the melee of media parked along the street, he began to see the need for the house call. There would have been no way for anyone to leave the house without starting a riot. When the news crews saw him turn up the Cochrane driveway, the cameras began to roll. He averted his face as he hurried up the walk to the house. Velma opened the door to him before he had time to knock.

"Come in, Dr. Tessler. I'll show you to the room upstairs."

Tessler had started up the staircase when Sam suddenly appeared at the head of the stairs.

"Michael… I really appreciate you taking the time to do this for me."

"It's my pleasure," Tessler said. "And congratulations on finding your daughter. Is she my patient?"

"Yes, it's a miracle she was found," Sam said. "But she's not the one who's ill. Follow me."

Sam opened the door. Jade was sitting in a chair near Raphael's bed. The stricken look on her face hurt his heart, but he didn't know how to comfort a stranger who wouldn't let him near.

"Jade, this is Dr. Tessler. He's a marvelous doctor as well as an old friend. He'll take good care of Raphael."

Jade stood, her hands clutched against her belly in a defensive gesture.

"He's asleep," she said.

"Not anymore," Raphael said, and rolled over to the side of the bed and sat up. "Dr. Tessler, my name is Raphael. Thank you for coming."

Michael Tessler had seen lots of patients during his career, and at first glance, this one didn't look so good.

"I'm happy to help," he said, then set down his bag and took off his sports coat. Then he smiled at Sam and Jade.

"If you two will excuse us now, I'd like to examine the patient."

Jade frowned. "Oh, no, I think I should—"

"No, Jade. Go with Sam. We'll talk later, okay?"

"I don't want to," she said.

"I know, but I'm asking just the same."

Blinking away tears, Jade ducked her head and left the room, ignoring Sam's outstretched hand.

As soon as the door was closed, Michael Tessler turned to Raphael.

"So, young man, do you want to tell me what's wrong?"

"I have full-blown AIDS. I also have cancer of the liver, and I'm dying."

Ten

The doctor was gone, but Jade had yet to go back upstairs. She'd seen him speaking to Sam, overheard him suggesting hospitalization, then shaking Sam's hand before leaving. She'd watched the housekeeper come out of the kitchen carrying a tray and take the back stairs to the second floor. It was the soup and cold drink that she'd asked for earlier. She knew she should go up and see if Raphael needed any help, but her legs were too weak to move. So she sat on a chair in the foyer with her hands folded in her lap and waited for the strength of mind to get up.

Suddenly a shadow crossed her line of vision. She turned around and then frowned. It was Luke.

"I thought you were gone."

"I thought I'd wait around a bit…see what the doctor told Raphael."

"You know what's wrong with him, don't you?" she said.

"Don't ask me that, Jade. Don't ask me things I can't answer."

Anger brought her to her feet, but her voice was as shaky as her legs.

"I hate you for this. I hate you for coming between Raphael and me."

She could have cut him with a knife and it wouldn't hurt any worse than what she'd just said.

"Nobody could ever come between you and Raphael. You, above all, should know that."

Her defiance wilted almost instantly. "Then why?" she whispered. "Why would he tell you something so personal and keep it from me?"

"Maybe because he has nothing invested in me. Sometimes it's easier to face a stranger with bad news than someone you love."

Bad news? Jade's vision blurred as she looked down at the floor, then back up at Luke.

"He's not going to get better, is he?"

Luke wanted to hold her, to smooth that ink-black hair away from her perfect face and tell her it was going to be all right. But he couldn't lie, and the truth wasn't his to tell.

"You're talking to the wrong man."

Jade swallowed a sob, then staggered backward, her eyes filled with unshed tears.

"Damn you, Luke Kelly. Damn you straight to hell. We were fine until you came and messed everything up."

Luke flinched, then fired back.

"Fine? *Fine?* What the hell was so fine that I messed up? You tell me! Was it the fact that you were stranded by a flood and sleeping in an abandoned YMCA? Yeah, that must have been a blast. Sorry I screwed up that party. Oh! I know…maybe it was the living from hand to mouth and so goddamned poor that your boyfriend didn't want to tell you what was wrong with him because neither of you could afford the care he needed. Uh-huh…it really sucks that your father can put an end to that."

Then he stopped. The stricken look on Jade's face made him regret losing his temper, but at the same time, she had to face the reality of the situation.

"Damn it, Jade, I'm sorry I lost my temper, I'm sorry as hell that Raphael is not well, and I'm even sorrier that you distrust men so much that you're blaming me for something that is obviously not my fault."

Jade was stunned. She hadn't expected his anger, and at the same time, she was ashamed. He was right, but she didn't

have the guts to admit it. A long moment of uncomfortable silence followed Luke's outburst; then Raphael's voice drifted down from upstairs.

"Jade, tell the man you're sorry and then come up here. I want to talk to you."

Both Luke and Jade jerked at the sound of the voice, then looked upward. Raphael was standing at the top of the staircase.

"I don't need an apology," Luke said shortly, nodding at Raphael. "Call me if you need me," he said, and then walked away without looking back.

Jade was torn between the need to talk to Raphael and the knowledge that she should make it right with Luke, but he'd taken away her decision by leaving. And with Raphael waiting for her, she could not prolong their confrontation. She couldn't remember ever saying a prayer and believing it would be answered, so she didn't bother this time, either. Instead she looked up, focusing on the familiarity of Raphael's face, and started up the stairs.

Down the hall, Luke stepped out of the library where he'd taken shelter and listened to Jade's hesitant footsteps as she moved to join Raphael. His heart hurt for her in a way she would never believe. Even he was hard-pressed to understand how the woman had gotten under his skin so easily. He'd witnessed how fragile she was. It should have turned him off. Instead he'd wanted to take her in his arms and shelter her from everything ugly that was left in the world.

Luke was anything but a green, untried male, yet when he stood in her presence, he felt like a fourteen-year-old teenager without a brain. What he knew about her made him afraid he would offend her even more than he already had, but he couldn't seem to stay away. So he walked to the foot of the stairs and waited, listening for what he knew would be the death knell of her small, fragile world. The silence lengthened, and the only thing Luke heard was the solid, steady beat of his heart.

And then a sound sliced through the silence—a high-pitched, keening wail that made the hair stand up on the back of Luke's neck. He closed his eyes, letting the pain in the sound filter through him until he thought he was the one who might die.

She knew. God in heaven, now she knew.

He turned away from the staircase and stumbled toward the library, swallowing past a knot in the back of his throat. The way he felt right now, he was in no shape to drive.

"Luke?"

Sam was standing in the hall.

"I need to use your phone to call a cab," Luke said.

"I'll drive you," Sam said.

Luke shook his head. "No. You heard her, what the news did to her. You need to stay here."

Sam sighed. "She doesn't want me. You know that."

"She doesn't know what she wants," Luke said. "So go show her what she's been missing all these years."

Sam's voice cracked, and for the first time, he looked all of his sixty years.

"Dear God, Luke... I want to, but I don't know how. Damn it... I don't even know what's going on."

"I'll tell you what's happening. Your daughter is going to lose her best and only friend. Raphael is dying. Now go up those stairs, walk into that room, and help both of them grieve for what they're about to lose. From what they've told me, neither one of them remembers having a father. Go show them what it means before it's too late."

"Lord help me," Sam whispered.

"He will," Luke said. "Now go."

Sam straightened his shoulders and headed for the stairs, leaving Luke to call the cab and make his own way home.

Late that same night, Jade lay curled up beside Raphael, holding him close as he usually held her. His sleep was restless. She now knew it was from pain. The cancer was eating

him alive from the inside out, and according to the doctor, was directly related to the fact that he had full-blown AIDS. Jade didn't know exactly what that meant, other than that he was dying, and didn't care. What mattered to her was that Raphael had known of his condition for more than a year without telling her. And, up until they'd left San Francisco, he had been getting pain medication from a free health clinic. She kept thinking about what he must have felt when she'd announced they needed to move. Had he been afraid? Had he known that it was already the beginning of the end? If only he'd told her then. She swallowed past the lump in her throat. The hard thing to accept was that it wouldn't have mattered.

Jade shifted a little closer, needing to hear the inhale and exhale of his breath to assure herself that he was still here. They were admitting him to the hospital tomorrow, to a ward for HIV patients only. The injustice of that alone was enough to make her furious. Even in death, he was being separated from society, just as he had been in life.

Raphael moaned. Jade rose up on one elbow, checking to see if he was awake and needing medicine. He was still asleep, though, and she wasn't going to wake him up just to give him something to help him sleep. She pulled the covers up around their shoulders, then inhaled softly, savoring the clean, fresh scent of the soft cotton sheets.

It was there, in the quiet of the darkened room, that she finally admitted what a blessing Luke Kelly had been. Were it not for his persistence on behalf of Sam Cochrane, she and Raphael would probably still be at the mercy of the Louisiana flood waters and depending upon the help of the Red Cross. He would be sick and suffering. She stifled a sob. She didn't want him to hurt. She didn't want him to die. But she wasn't going to get what she wanted.

The strange thing was, Raphael seemed at peace. Once he'd told her the truth, it was as if a huge weight had lifted from his shoulders. He kept telling her how lucky they were

that her father had found them, and that he could tell Sam Cochrane was a good man. He had scolded her for fighting with Luke Kelly, warning her not to make an enemy of a man who wanted to be her friend.

Jade hadn't argued with him, but she wasn't going to agree until the men had proved themselves worthy of her trust. She closed her eyes just to give them a rest and, despite her best efforts to the contrary, finally fell asleep.

Luke lay on his back with his hands pillowed under his head, replaying the events of the past few days in his head. The earth had shifted beneath his feet the day he'd seen Jade Cochrane face to face, and he hadn't been the same since. He was angry with himself for dwelling on a woman who so obviously hated his guts and wished that he could turn off the growing feelings in his heart. But he knew himself well enough to know that what was happening to him was out of his control. Despite the fact that he'd been warned, he was falling in love with a woman who was deathly afraid of men. The irony of the situation was not lost on him. With a groan, he rolled over on his belly, punched his pillow a couple of times to rearrange the feathers, then resettled into a different spot on the bed. He needed to sleep and to forget, but he didn't think he was going to get what he needed—at least not tonight.

Frank Lawson had spent all night mapping out a plan. By daylight the next morning, he'd set it in motion. There was a man he knew from the old days—a three-time loser who would kill his own mother just for the chance to watch her bleed. He was a crazy bastard, with a hard-on for violence. Add a bundle of money to the pot and he was relentless. His name was Johnny Newton, and he was already on his way to St. Louis to find out if Raphael was the man with Jade Cochrane. If he was, his orders were to kill them both.

The plan was a good one. The way Frank figured it, it

couldn't fail. No one would ever suspect that their lives would be in danger, so no one would be watching their tails. And Johnny Newton had a phobia when it came to being jailed again, so even if he was caught in the act, he would choose death before he would let himself be incarcerated again. Now all Frank had to do was wait for the next news flash announcing the tragedy to the world.

He smiled at himself in the mirror as he finished his shave. Damned if he wasn't about the smartest son-of-a-bitch walking. He almost wished he could tell the world just so it would be known how really smart he was. Once all of the clutter of his past was swept away, he could concentrate on the governor's race.

He leaned over the sink, peering closely at his image in the steam-shrouded mirror, then thumbed away a tiny droplet of blood just below his chin.

"Drew a little blood myself," he said, and then chuckled at his own wit, slapped aftershave lotion on his face and cursed the burn.

Johnny Newton's daddy always told him that he wouldn't amount to a damn thing. Johnny had reminded him of that right before he'd slipped the rope around the old man's neck and hanged him. Of course, everyone in town had assumed that Arnold Newton had committed suicide after having filed bankruptcy. Johnny had stayed long enough to play the grieving son, then lit out for Washington, D.C. It had taken him exactly six months to establish himself as a man who would do anything for money.

Fifteen years later, his fee had gone up, but it was getting harder and harder to get any kind of joy out of the work. Every new job was just an echo of the last. He wanted some diversion in his work and was determined to make this job a landmark.

He'd been in Denver when he'd gotten the call. Once the priorities had been dealt with, which included wiring a fee

of one hundred thousand dollars into one of Johnny's special accounts, he'd begun to pack. Later, he'd replayed what he knew as he boarded the plane. He knew the target's name and basic location. The target, a man named Raphael, was associated with some prodigal daughter thing that the news had picked up on, which meant that when he snuffed this guy and then the woman, it was going to be news again, which meant he needed to have a solid way in and a solid way out. He was going to take a couple of days to scope out the location, figure out the best way to do the job, and, as always, make sure he had a Plan B that was as workable as Plan A.

Within a half hour, his flight would be landing in St. Louis. All he had to do was catch a cab and get a room at some out of the way motel, pay cash and disappear into the proverbial woodwork.

"Ladies and gentlemen, we are beginning our descent into the St. Louis airport. Please turn off all electronic equipment, return your trays and seats to their upright positions, and buckle your seat belts."

Johnny glanced out the window. *Look out St. Louis.... Johnny Newton is coming to town.*

Raphael had been hospitalized for two days now, and Jade had yet to leave the building except when Sam took her home to shower and change clothes. Shelly Hudson had appeared one morning at Sam's house with an overnight bag for Jade filled with all the necessities, as well as several tubes of creams and lotions for her to rub on Raphael's hands and feet.

Jade had recognized her immediately as the woman who'd purchased the painting. There had been a brief moment of awkwardness; then Shelly had opened her arms and pulled Jade into a gentle embrace.

"I hope you don't hate me," Shelly said. "I want so much for you to consider me a friend."

Jade had seen the sincerity in Shelly's eyes and been too frightened and weary to resist.

"Thank you," Jade said. "I think I'm going to need all the friends I can get."

"Then count Paul and me as two of them," Shelly said, then kissed Jade one more time and left.

Back at the hospital, gloved and gowned, she fed Raphael his meals, rubbed the fragrant unguents of Shelly's gifts into his dry, hot skin, and slept in a chair by his bed each night. Oddly enough, the nightmares that she normally suffered were absent. It was as if her mind had shut down to everything except Raphael's well-being. If it hadn't been for Sam's constant vigilance, she would have passed out from sheer exhaustion. Even now, she stood watch at Raphael's bedside, unwilling to acknowledge his rapid deterioration. His once handsome face was sallow and gaunt, and his skin looked too loose on his frame. Once he'd known that Jade was safe, he'd quit denying his pain. Now he lay in a near comatose state, blanketed with drugs that kept the knives in his belly at bay.

He moaned and then coughed. Jade jumped up from her chair, readjusted the surgical gloves they made her wear and grabbed a wet cloth from the table. She wiped spittle from his lip, then laid the back of her hand against his brow. He was hot. It meant his fever was back.

Sam had provided a private nurse, along with the private room they were in. The nurse had stepped out to get a new bag for his IV. The moment she returned, Jade told her.

"He's hot again," she said softly.

The nurse pulled up her mask and moved toward the bed.

"I need to check him again," the nurse said. "Why don't you step out into the hall for a few minutes? Maybe get yourself something to eat, dear. Have you eaten today?"

Jade shrugged. "I don't remember."

The nurse patted her gently on the shoulder as she pushed her toward the door.

"The cafeteria food isn't nearly as bad as it's made out to be. Try the chicken noodle soup. It's pretty good."

Jade wanted to argue but knew it was futile. She'd already tried and failed at that miserably the first day they'd admitted Raphael. Now she and the nurses had come to a clear understanding of what their roles in Raphael's care would be. And right now, he didn't need Jade. He needed the medicine that the nurse could administer.

"Yes, maybe I will," she said, then stopped at the door and turned around. "You'll call me if there's any change?"

"Yes."

"I'll be in the cafeteria. You can page me if—"

"Go," the nurse urged. "He's stable."

Jade heard what the nurse said, but it was what she didn't say that frightened her most. *For now.* She didn't say "stable for now," but they both knew that was what she meant.

Jade took off the disposable gown, mask and gloves, dumped them into a biohazard container in the hall outside, then walked down the hall. She was startled by the sunlight pouring in from a window on her left and the cool rush of air-conditioning against her face. Nurses busied themselves in and out of different rooms, and there was an underlying murmur of voices coming from a waiting room down the hall. A sudden burst of indignation sent her stomping down the hall toward the elevator.

How dare those people go on as if nothing was wrong? Didn't they know…? Didn't they care? Raphael was dying. Her world was coming apart at the seams while someone was talking about macaroni and cheese.

She strode past the elevator and headed for the Exit sign above the doorway opposite. She didn't want to be in an elevator with people who talked about macaroni and cheese and the state of the nation.

The stairwell was empty and quiet. The moment her footsteps touched the smooth, tiled surface, the echo sounded up and down. She grabbed the railing and started down the steps

with anger in every step, but halfway down toward the first landing, she started to cry. She stumbled as her vision blurred but caught herself before she could fall. Still clutching the handrail, she sank to her knees on the steps and turned her face to the wall.

Sobs tore up her throat, coming out in loud, choking gasps. She couldn't catch her breath, yet she couldn't seem to stop.

Suddenly there were arms around her shoulders and someone was pulling her to her feet. She sensed the masculinity and tried to pull back, but his hand was firm against the back of her head as he pressed her face against his chest. Before she had time to panic, she recognized Luke's voice.

"Ah, Jade, Jade, I am so sorry."

She shook her head, as if shaking off a bad dream, and looked up. The disbelief in her expression broke his heart.

"You seem to have all the answers, so tell me something, Luke Kelly. Raphael has never done a mean thing to anyone in his entire life, so why is this happening?"

"I don't claim to have answers to anything," he said, then handed her his handkerchief as she pulled away from him. "I've been told all my life that God never gives us more than we can handle, so He must believe that you're very strong."

Jade swiped the handkerchief across her face, then slapped it back in Luke's hand.

"There is no God."

Luke flinched. "Yes, there is."

She laughed, and the sound came out like a hard, angry bark.

"Then He must hate my guts, because my life has been hell."

"Did you ever stop to think that the hell was of someone else's making and that God is the reason you're still alive?"

For a moment Jade's face lost all expression. Her eyes widened. Her lips went slack as she absorbed what he'd just said. Then his hand cupped the side of her face.

"Jade."

She shuddered, then blinked.

"What?"

Sam had told Luke that she wasn't eating or sleeping worth a darn. It was one of the reasons he'd come. He wouldn't let himself dwell on the others.

"Would you like to go get something to eat?"

She swiped at the tears on her face. "I was going to get some soup."

He held out his hand. "So, may I go with you?"

She didn't answer.

"I'll buy," he added.

She blinked again, then almost smiled.

"I guess," she said, and then ran her fingers through her hair and took off down the stairs, leaving Luke to follow.

Eleven

A few days later, Raphael woke up just as his nurse was about to inject a syringe full of medicine into the shunt on his IV bag. He blinked, trying to clear his sight, then reached clumsily toward her arm, staying her intent.

"What...what...doing?" he mumbled.

"Just helping make you comfortable."

"No," he said. "No more."

She frowned, not certain that she understood what he meant.

"Sir, I don't think you understand. Without this, the level of your pain will change considerably."

"No. Makes me sleep. Can't think," he said.

She touched his arm gently, then capped the syringe and put it back in her pocket. She'd been ordered to administer the painkiller, but a patient's wishes couldn't be ignored, either. She needed to consult with his doctor.

"Relax, sir. I'll be back in a few minutes."

"No more painkillers for a while," Raphael repeated, then exhaled slowly, as if the mere effort of speaking exhausted him.

Once the woman was gone, he closed his eyes and let his mind go free. He kept trying to focus on Jade, but his body wouldn't cooperate. It was that damned medicine. He needed his head clear. There were things that had to be said, both to Jade and to her father—and to Luke Kelly. Unless they really understood her, they would never be able to help, and she

needed help, but more than that, she needed to feel safe and to be loved.

Pain began to coil in the middle of his belly. He flattened his hands across his stomach, as if to hold back the devil within. He needed time for what had yet to be done, but time was at a minimum.

The door opened. He opened his eyes. It was the nurse. He grimaced. Obviously she'd gone for backup. Not only was Dr. Tessler with her, but so was Jade.

"I understand you want to call some of the shots," the doctor said, then smiled and patted Raphael's leg beneath the sheets.

Raphael blinked slowly, then nodded. "I've been in charge of my own life for years, and I like it. I see no reason to stop."

Jade slid between the doctor and Raphael and then put her hand in his. Raphael gave it a squeeze as he threaded her fingers between his. She felt so warm—so vital. If only he could draw on some of her strength.

"How you doin', baby?"

Jade fought back tears. "I'm doing fine."

He winked. "That's my girl. You're tougher than you realize. You know that, don't you?"

"So you tell me," she said.

Michael Tessler leafed through the chart the nurse handed him.

"I don't advise coming off the painkillers."

"I didn't ask your advice," Raphael said. "I'm just telling you—no more. I don't want to waste what time I have left asleep."

Jade choked on a sob. Hearing Raphael talk so calmly about dying was more than she could bear.

"Please, Rafie..."

He frowned. "No, Jade. This is my call."

She bowed her head, then turned away and walked to the window. Behind her, the doctor and Raphael continued to

discuss his care, but she didn't want to hear it. It was like watching someone building his own coffin. She didn't understand Raphael's ability to distance himself from his illness. It was consuming her.

"Jade."

She turned to find that the doctor and Raphael's private nurse were gone. For the moment, she and Raphael were alone. She hurried to his side.

"What do you need?" she asked, then snatched up his drinking cup. "Are you thirsty? Do you want some fresh water?"

Raphael sighed. "Put the cup down, honey, and sit down beside me."

She did as he asked, then scooted onto the side of his hospital bed.

"I didn't mean for this to happen as quickly as it has," he began.

"Please, don't talk about this, Rafie. I don't want to—"

His voice lowered, the tone of it tougher, even censuring.

"It's not about what you want anymore. This is about me. If you want to make me happy, then you have to listen."

"Okay."

He wouldn't let himself be swayed by the tremor in her voice or the tears in her eyes. There were things that had to be said. Just then the door to his room opened and Luke Kelly walked in.

Luke quickly realized he'd interrupted something.

"Uh, listen, I just stopped by to say hello...see if you needed anything, but I can come back another time."

"No," Raphael said. "You need to hear what I'm about to say, too."

Jade's eyes widened. "No," she whispered. "He doesn't belong."

Raphael's frown deepened. "Damn it, Jade...you're not listening to me. He does belong...even more than I do now, because he's part of your future. I'm part of the past."

Jade doubled up her fists and pounded the mattress beside Raphael's legs.

"Stop saying that," she said. "I don't want to hear you say anything like this again."

"You already promised me you would listen."

Jade shut her mouth, but Raphael could tell by the set of her chin that she was mentally rebelling.

"Okay," he said, and then motioned Luke closer. "I've got things that need to be said."

"I'm listening," Luke said.

Jade sat without answering, but Raphael knew she was listening, too.

"I want you both to know that no amount of money or doctors could change what's happening to me. Don't blame them. If you want to blame someone, blame Solomon."

"What are you saying?" Luke asked.

Jade stiffened. "Raphael...please."

He frowned at Jade. "This is what I'm talking about. How are you ever going to get well if you continue to wallow in the shit that is our past?"

"Okay, okay," she muttered.

Luke wished to hell that he'd gone to the office instead of stopping here first. If he had, he wouldn't be a part of what was happening, and yet every time he looked at Jade, he knew that he would do anything it took for just one chance at a life with her.

"Now, where was I?" Raphael asked.

"Blaming Solomon," Jade muttered.

He smiled softly. "That's my girl. Like I've always said, it's healthier to get pissed at the right person." Then he looked up at Luke. "I need to know that Jade is going to be okay. I guess I'm wanting your reassurance that you'll be her friend."

Luke shoved his hands in his pockets.

"I'll be anything she needs me to be."

Jade hid her shock. She wouldn't look at Luke—couldn't

look at him. She felt like a charity case that had just been put up on the auction block.

"My God, Rafie...do you hear what you're saying?"

Then, despite knowing how she hated to be touched, Luke put his hand on her shoulder.

"Did you hear what *I* said?"

Shocked, she looked up, staring into a face that was becoming more and more familiar.

"I know I make you uncomfortable. I'm sorry. I wish whatever happened to you in your past hadn't happened. I wish to God that your mother hadn't taken you with her when she left. I wish a whole lot of things. But know this. I like you, Jade Cochrane. I think you're beautiful, and strong, and I'm sorry as I can be that this is happening."

Raphael clenched his jaw. It was just as he'd hoped. Luke Kelly was smitten by Jade, and while it was in Jade's best interests, he was surprised by the jealousy he felt. From the first, Jade had been his friend, then his only love. The fact that she looked upon him as something between a brother and a best friend was beside the point. Even after they'd gotten away from Solomon and Jade's battered body had healed—even when he'd watched her mature into the stunning woman she was today—he'd known that she would never be his.

"Okay, honey, Luke told me what I wanted to know. Now it's your turn."

"Anything...I'll do anything," she said.

"Talk to a shrink?"

If he'd slapped her, she wouldn't have been any more surprised. She glanced at Luke, wishing he would disappear. Damn Raphael for starting all this in front of someone else.

"Why? They can't change what happened to me," she said.

"No, but they can help you learn how to deal with it."

"I already deal with it."

Raphael's fingers curled into fists. "How? By cringing

from the touch of every man still walking the face of the earth? By running away to a different city every time you feel threatened? When are you going to stop? Tell me that, baby. When?''

Jade's vision blurred. She took a slow, shuddering breath and then covered her face with her hands.

"Stop, Rafie...don't be mad at me anymore."

Raphael groaned. "I'm not mad at you, baby. I'm worried. You won't let anyone near you but me. You won't let anyone help you but me. You refuse to admit there's anything wrong, and yet we've been on the run for so damned long I've lost count. But we both know there's a horrible flaw in that scenario, don't we?''

She choked on a sob.

"Stop crying and answer me," Raphael said.

"I'll talk to the shrink," she said.

Raphael turned to Luke. "You heard her say it. As her friend, it's going to be up to you to make sure she keeps her promise.''

"If I have to drag her kicking and screaming," Luke said.

Suddenly exhausted, Raphael sighed and then closed his eyes.

"Good. Now will you both go somewhere and make peace? I'm tired. I need to sleep.''

"What you need is a shave and a haircut," Jade mumbled, and then pulled a handful of tissues from a box on the table and blew her nose soundly.

Raphael smiled gently. "What? Are you telling me that I'm starting to look like Jesus again?''

She blew again, then leaned back and let her gaze rest on his face. A few years back, when they'd been down on their luck more than usual, Raphael had let both his hair and beard grow rather than spend money on a package of disposable razors. An old man who'd been begging on a street corner in Oklahoma City had taken one look at him, thought it was the second coming of Christ and dropped to his knees.

They'd been startled by his behavior until the old man had reached up and touched the hem of Raphael's shirt and asked to be healed from the wages of sin and drink. It had taken them a couple of minutes to decipher the man's rambling words, but they'd finally figured out that he believed he was looking into the face of Jesus.

"Don't flatter yourself," she said, and then tossed the tissues into the wastebasket and gave Raphael a quick kiss. "See you later."

He grabbed her hand. "Where are you going?"

"Out, so you can rest."

"That's not the right answer," Raphael said.

She wanted to be angry with him but couldn't bring herself to argue anymore.

"I am going to play with my new friend?"

He grinned. "That's what I thought you said."

"So are you, Jade? Are you my new friend?" Luke asked.

Raphael held his breath as Jade turned around.

"I don't know. Maybe."

He held out his hand. "I'll take that as a yes. Want to go see if we have anything else in common beside wishing for a miracle for Raphael?"

"Yes," she said, and then realized that she meant it. She patted Raphael's leg. "I'll be back in a few minutes. Don't start the party without me."

Raphael smiled and waved them away. But the moment the door closed behind them, he stifled a groan. God, but he hurt. Before, he'd been afraid to die. Now he was starting to think of it as an upcoming blessing. As he was struggling with the decision of whether to breathe or scream, the door opened again. Thinking it was Jade, he was ready to give her grief for coming back so soon; then he realized it was the nurse.

She smiled and held up the syringe of painkiller.

"Still holding out?"

The pain in his belly was ballooning. "I think maybe I

could handle just a little. But don't give me so much that it knocks me out."

"Dr. Tessler changed the medication orders. He said to tell you that this one isn't quite so strong."

"Tell him I said thank you," Raphael said.

He closed his eyes as the nurse began to put the medicine into his IV, anticipating the moment when it would begin to work its magic.

But there was another kind of magic working as Luke and Jade walked toward the elevator.

"How about some lunch?" he asked. "We survived the noodle soup the other day. I'm game for more."

She shrugged and then nodded. "I don't mind as long as it's here in the cafeteria. I don't want to get too far from Raphael."

"Sure, no problem," Luke said.

Once they reached the elevator, the silence between them lengthened again. Finally Luke realized that if anything was going to change between them for the better, it was going to be up to him.

"Jade, I'm not going to pretend this is easy for you, but you've got to understand that in the short time I've known you, I have come to feel great admiration for you."

Jade didn't bother to hide her shock. "Admiration? There is nothing in my life worth admiring."

"I beg to differ with you," he said. "Without having been told any details, I gather your childhood was terrible, and yet you not only survived it, you managed to escape."

"Because of Raphael," she said.

Luke wanted to brush a stray strand of hair from near her eye but restrained himself.

"Yes, honey," he said gently. "Because of Raphael. But somehow you managed to stay away from what happens on the streets."

Then the elevator car arrived. Everyone inside got out, leaving them alone as they started down. Luke Kelly didn't

know what the hell he was talking about, and Jade wasn't sure she had the guts to tell him different. But if this new phase of her life was ever going to work, it would be because of the truth, not the secrets. She glanced up at Luke and caught him watching her.

"Back there...you told Raphael that you would be anything I needed you to be."

Luke's heart skipped a beat. "Yes, and I meant it."

"Maybe," she said. "But you don't know everything about us...about what we did...what Solomon made us do."

Suddenly Luke knew he was about to learn why she screamed in her sleep. The knot in his stomach grew harder.

The elevator stopped on the first floor. Two people got on and rode the rest of the way down with them, forcing Jade to delay what she viewed as a confession of sins. The longer she had to wait, the more difficult it became to regain her courage.

In the cafeteria, she went through the food line, picking and choosing without appetite, knowing that the food was simply a means to survival. Then she chose a table in the back of the room in the hopes that she could finish what needed to be said without interruption.

As they sat, Luke's phone began to ring. He glanced at the caller ID, then turned it off.

"I'll call them back later," he said.

Jade felt guilty. The man had a business to run, and here she was, taking up his time.

"It's okay," she said. "If you need to leave, please don't let me stop you."

"I don't need to leave. If I did, I would tell you. Besides, doing what I want, when I want, is one of the perks of being the boss."

"Oh." She picked up her fork and shoved a green bean around on the plate, then remembered her napkin, laid down her fork and spread her napkin in her lap. "Sorry. I haven't had all that many opportunities to practice my manners."

Luke grinned wryly. "Jade...honey...in the grand scheme of things, how much do you think napkin etiquette matters?"

She paused, sighed. "I'm being defensive again, aren't I?"

She stared down at her plate, absently watching the green bean juice spilling off the edge. Then she looked up. "Damn it, Luke, don't you see?"

He frowned. "See what?"

"How flawed I am."

"Didn't anyone ever tell you that no one's perfect?"

"Don't be flip. I'm serious."

"Then explain it to me," Luke said.

Her voice shook. "It's ugly. Sam will be ashamed of me. You will no longer want to be my friend."

"No, Jade. That will never happen."

"You don't know."

"Then tell me," he said softly.

He laid his hand over hers, expecting resistance. To his surprise, there was none.

She glanced over her shoulder, making sure they were still alone. Then she took a deep breath.

"My mother died when I was six. I can barely remember her."

"That's tough. I can't even imagine what that must be like."

She looked down. Her fingers were trembling. She curled them into fists so that he might not see.

"You slept in the same room with Raphael and me."

"Yes?"

"You heard me...you never talked about it...but you heard just the same, didn't you?"

He didn't know how to answer.

She shrugged. "It doesn't matter. But it's part of what I'm trying to say. I don't remember my mother or my father, but it's what I do remember that has made me the way I am."

"Look, if this is making you that uncomfortable, you don't have to tell me," Luke said.

She sighed, then looked at him, studying the solidity of his jaw and the steady gaze in his eyes.

"Unfortunately, I do."

"Then I'm listening."

"Right after my mother died, Solomon...the man who was the leader of the People of Joy...sold me to a man."

Luke flinched. "Sold you how?"

"For the night."

Shock hit Luke like a fist to the gut.

"Sold you. For the night."

She nodded.

"For sex?"

She laughed, but it sounded more like a sob.

"Yes."

Now it was Luke who looked away. The colors of a painting on the wall behind Jade ran together in a kaleidoscope of hues, but it wasn't until he felt the moisture on his cheeks that he knew he was crying.

The emotion startled, then frightened, Jade. "I'm sorry," she said quickly.

He looked up, his voice deep and angry.

"Don't!"

"Don't what?"

"Don't *ever* apologize again. Not for that. Never for that. God in heaven, Jade, you were a child. Someone was supposed to be taking care of you, not selling you to perverts."

"Someone tried," she said.

Luke knew instantly who she meant. "Raphael."

"Yes, Raphael, but he was only three years older than me, so there wasn't a lot he could do. Solomon did it to all the kids. It has to be how Raphael got sick.... We never did drugs. And once we'd gotten away from Solomon, we never...we couldn't..." She shuddered. "It was easier to be hungry than to take money for sex."

Luke was trying to focus, to ask the right questions so that she would feel safe enough to confide in him, but all he

wanted to do was break something—preferably the sorry son-of-a-bitch's neck who'd done this to them.

"How did you get away?" he asked.

"I'm not real sure. Raphael only talked about it once. After that, we never spoke of it again."

"Again, if you'd rather not, it's okay," Luke said.

"No, you may as well hear it all. It was late in July, I think. At least, I remember how hot it was. The kids slept in rooms sort of like dormitories. I had a couple of bed partners...girls who were about my age or younger. The boys had a larger room down the hall. When Solomon woke me up and started dragging me down the hall to the purple room, I knew one of the uncles had come."

"Uncles?"

"It's what he called the men who paid him money to have sex with the kids."

Luke watched the expression on her face disappear. There was an absence of emotion in her voice as she laid her hands in her lap and leaned back against the chair. He had a moment's impression of someone taking a stance in front of a firing squad, and then she began to talk.

"I knew the man. He'd been there before. He always called me his pretty baby and made me call him Uncle Frank. But it had been a long time since I'd seen him...maybe six months. Solomon always marked the passing years with a group celebration, so I remember someone telling me it was my eighth year with the People, which meant I was probably around twelve. Anyway, my body was changing. I didn't look like a little girl anymore, and when the uncle took off my clothes, he got angry. When I told him it wasn't my fault, he slapped me and told me to shut up. So I did."

Jade didn't realize it, but she had started to rock back and forth, weaving the upper half of her body between the back of the chair and the front of the table. Luke had seen similar trancelike behavior in people who'd suffered emotional traumas.

Then she looked at Luke again, trying to see if she could

tell what he was thinking by the look on his face. It didn't work. Except for the tears on his cheeks, he was motionless.

"As I said, I shut up. But he couldn't...uh, I no longer turned him on. He took his humiliation and anger out on me. I remember the pain from being cut, then I don't remember anything much after that. Raphael said they heard me screaming all over the house. And at fifteen, Raphael was big for his age. He got to me first and nearly killed the man with his fists. Solomon came next. Told Raphael to get me out of the room. Raphael went him one better and got me out of the house. We stole one of the People's vans, and we've been running ever since."

Jade stopped, her body suddenly motionless, and looked at Luke, trying to judge his reaction.

"So, now that you know...do you still want to be my friend?"

The tremor in her voice only added to the poignancy of her question. Luke leaned forward, wanting to touch her to add strength to his answer. Instead, he extended his hand toward her, palm up.

"I told you before," he said softly. "I will be what you need me to be."

Jade stared at him for a long, silent moment, then looked down at his hand. It was broad across the palm, with a faint scar near his thumb. If he'd made a fist, it would have been large—very large. She should have been terrified to even touch him, and yet there was something within her that kept telling her it would be okay.

Finally she extended her fingers, feeling the warmth and the strength of him against her flesh, and when his fingers curled around her hand, she barely flinched. When she spoke, her voice was so low that Luke had to lean forward to hear.

"What I need is someone I can trust."

"Trust me."

Finally she nodded, then asked, "Will you tell Sam?"

"Do you want me to?"

"I don't know. Let me think about it, okay?"

"It's your call," Luke said. "But remember what I told you before. Your father is overjoyed to have found you. He doesn't give a damn about anything else."

She nodded. "If I ask you something, will you promise to tell me the truth?"

"Yes."

"Now that you know…what do you think?"

"I think that if I ever get my hands on the son-of-a-bitch who calls himself Solomon, I will kill him."

Oddly, the violence in his answer satisfied something within Jade that she hadn't known was there. A yearning of her own, she'd stifled through the years, to enact some form of revenge. That Luke Kelly echoed the same feelings connected them in a way she hadn't expected.

"Okay, then," she said, and glanced at her plate. "The food is getting cold."

She needed to change the subject. Luke was willing to go along. He looked at his own food, congealing in its separate servings, and picked up his fork.

"Looks okay to me," he said, then forced a bite of his salad into his mouth. He chewed and swallowed, then gave her a wink. "It's not so bad—if you're into warm lettuce and cold chicken."

Jade made a face.

Impulsively Luke stuck his fork into the blob of whipped cream in the center of his pie and dobbed it on the end of her nose.

Jade was so stunned by what he'd done that for a moment she couldn't think what to do. Then she took the napkin from her lap and wiped off the whipped cream before looking around to see if anyone noticed.

"Why did you do that?"

He grinned. "Just sharing my food with my friend."

It was the smile that did it. If Jade could have put words to what she was feeling inside, she would have sworn that the old wall around her emotions had started to crack.

Twelve

Johnny Newton's rental car was a gray four-door sedan. It blended well with the neighborhood as he cruised past the Cochrane estate and then turned up the driveway of the house across the street.

The house was an old Tudor-style place built back in the early 1900s. The present owner, a seventy-seven-year old widow named Margaret Tyler, had lived there for more than forty years. According to Johnny's research, although Mabel was very wealthy, she'd become a bit of a recluse after her husband's death. She had no children, no living relatives in the area, and no regular routine. A cleaning service came once a week on Mondays, and since today was Tuesday, Johnny had almost an entire week before he needed to be concerned about being discovered, which made this location perfect for what he had in mind.

Without hesitation, he drove his car along the driveway that circled to the back of the house to the detached garages, then parked in one of the vacant spaces. After retrieving his suitcase from the trunk, he headed for the back door. It took less than a minute to pick the lock.

Once inside, he stood for a moment to get his bearings. The scent of coffee was still in the air, and there was a faint dusting of toast crumbs on the counter near a toaster. It seemed he'd missed breakfast with Mabel. Too bad. She might have been an interesting woman to know, but he didn't have time for chitchat. He carried his suitcase through the

house and then up the stairs. An array of bedrooms beckoned to be chosen, but he had to meet his hostess first.

"Mabel! Are you home?"

Seconds later, an elderly woman stepped out into the hallway, still holding a pillow and a pillow case in her hand.

"Ah, making the beds, are you?" Johnny said.

Mabel clutched the pillow against her breasts as the man started toward her.

"Who are you? How did you get in my house?"

He smiled. "Oh, that's easy. I'm Johnny Newton. I picked the lock on your back door."

Mabel gasped, then dropped the pillow as she moved back into the bedroom, toward the phone. Johnny caught her from behind before she could pick up the receiver and broke her neck with one vicious twist. As he threw her dead body over his shoulder, he paused for a moment to look around.

"Damn, Mabel...nice room," he said, and then headed back down the stairs.

Considering the heat this time of year, he needed to dump Mabel's body as far away from the main area of the house as possible. All old houses like this had full basements with lots of nooks and crannies. It should be perfect.

Sure enough, he found a door to the basement just off the laundry room in an area that had once been used as servants' quarters. He turned on a light at the head of the stairs, then carried her down.

The old coal furnace that had once heated the house had been replaced by central heat and air units, but there were several small closetlike rooms beneath the stairs. He chose the one farthest from the stairs and dumped her inside beside a box marked *Christmas tree ornaments,* then whistled as he returned to the main level.

Now that he had settled the question of his stakeout location, he felt much more relaxed. Rummaging through the fridge, he found the makings for a sandwich, poured himself

a glass of milk, and carried it into the living room, choosing a seat with a good view to the house across the street.

He set his milk on an end table, propped his feet up on an antique cherry-wood coffee table and took a bite of his sandwich. The turkey was seasoned to perfection, the lettuce and tomato crisp and fresh. He would have preferred mustard to mayonnaise, but obviously Mabel did not, because he hadn't been able to find any. Still, it was a good beginning to his day's work. He polished off the sandwich while watching the media circus outside and began making plans to add to the confusion.

Unaware of the fate of his poor neighbor, Sam Cochrane was busy making plans of his own. Ever since Jade's arrival, he had been cleaning out two large adjoining rooms on the third floor of his house. Since Jade was spending almost all her time at the hospital, it had been simple to do this without revealing his purpose.

Less than an hour ago, the art supplies that he'd ordered had been delivered. Velma had taken the curtains from the windows to let in more light, and polished the brass and the wood trim until all of it shined. Sam had moved all but a few chairs and a couple of small tables into other areas of the house, making room for the large storage cabinet, as well as an assortment of stretched canvases and easels.

Michael Tessler had warned him that it was only a matter of time before Raphael succumbed. Tessler had also warned Sam that because Jade and Raphael were so close, she was not only going to suffer normal grief, but that it was very possible she would suffer survivor's guilt, as well. Sam was heartsick for Jade and had spent many hours with her at Raphael's bedside, showing her in the only way he knew how that he cared. And while she'd nodded and smiled in all the right places and thanked him for what he was doing, they both knew the emotional bond that should have been there was missing. It was during one of those times that he'd re-

membered her skill as an artist, and thought that, maybe later, if she had a place of her own to practice that outlet, it might help with the grief.

And now it was finished. There was nothing left to buy. He shifted a stack of canvases from one side of the room to the other, then stepped back to admire what he'd done. His work here was finished. He felt sadness for the day when this would be revealed to Jade, because that would mean Raphael was gone, but if it gave her even a measure of relief, it would be worth it. Satisfied that he'd done what he'd set out to do, he left, quietly closing the door behind him.

Otis Jacks was scheduled for reconstructive surgery on Wednesday, then developed a toothache on Monday. After a quick visit to a dentist, he was informed that he had an abscessed wisdom tooth that needed to be pulled. But before that could happen, he was going to have to take a round of antibiotics to get rid of the infection. And because of the abscessed tooth, the scheduled surgery to change his face also had to be postponed.

So now he lay propped up in bed with an ice pack on his jaw and the remote control for his new plasma television in his hand, killing time until he could make his escape.

The forced inactivity had also given him time to think about the dangers of delay. A few phone calls had netted him information that made him realize how risky that delay might be.

"Damned tooth," he muttered, then aimed the remote and turned off the TV.

He reached for the bottle of painkillers on his bedside table, popped a couple in his mouth and downed them with a big swallow of water. He would have preferred bourbon, neat, but he knew from experience that codeine and whiskey didn't mix. He'd lost one of his best porn stars to just such an incident last year and was in no mood to follow her into oblivion.

Still, his nerves were on edge and would be until he got himself out of the States. As he lay there, waiting for the painkillers to start working, he couldn't help but curse the luck that had brought Jade Cochrane back into his life.

It had been three days since Big Frank Lawson had made the call that sent Johnny Newton to St. Louis. Three long days without a word. Each day Frank checked the papers and diligently watched all the national news broadcasts, hoping that the return of Sam Cochrane's daughter was becoming old news. To his dismay, it seemed to be just the reverse. There was news footage of a beautiful, dark-haired woman going in and out of a local hospital. Speculation as to why she was there ran the gamut of guesses, although the consensus was that the man she was living with when she was found was gravely ill. Although they did not mention the man's name, Frank suspected it was Raphael and wished them both to hell the hard way. Frustrated that all was not going according to his plans, he reached for his cell phone. He'd hired a man to do a job, and ineptitude was not something he tolerated. As far as he was concerned, Johnny Newton should have checked in with an update, but since he hadn't, Big Frank was going to check in with him.

Raphael's condition was stable, so at Sam's urging, Jade had taken time to come home with him this morning. When they'd walked out of the hospital, she'd been startled by the heat and clear skies. She'd been so focused on Raphael that she'd almost forgotten what it felt like to wake up to a normal day. And just for a while, she needed to pretend that everything was okay.

Sam cupped her elbow as they started toward the parking lot. When he did, she looked up at him and smiled. With each passing day, she was becoming more comfortable with him. A couple of times since she'd been home, she'd experienced what could only be called déjà vu. Once it had been

as she walked into the kitchen. The scent of cinnamon had been faint but persistent, and there had been a blue coffee cup sitting in a slice of sunshine on the countertop. She'd been staggered by the sight and the memory that had come with it. Her mother laughing as she stuffed an oversized bite of cinnamon roll into her father's mouth. A blue cup sitting on a counter just out of her reach.

The other time, as she'd been going up the stairs, she'd had the feeling that if she turned around, her father would be right behind her with his hand on her shoulder and a little pink blanket in his hand. She hadn't told him, but she'd thought about it. If the memories were real, then it was true that he'd loved her—loved them both.

Now, sitting beside him in the car as he maneuvered through traffic, she thought of it again and looked at him. He was a handsome man, with a full head of steel-gray hair. Despite what was happening, he seemed to handle each setback with clarity and purpose. Even more, he made Jade feel safe, which didn't make sense. Logically, he was a man she'd met only days earlier. With her history, every emotional warning bell should be going off, and yet it was just the opposite.

"Sam, can I ask you something?" Jade asked.

Surprised that she'd initiated a conversation, Sam could barely hide his joy.

"Of course," he said, then tapped the brakes as a light turned red at the intersection they were approaching.

"The other day…in the house…I think I remembered something. Well, actually, two somethings."

Sam's eyes widened. "Really? Like what?"

She shrugged. "It wasn't much. More like a picture that is flashed before your eyes and then taken away, but I've been wondering if it's something I really remembered or if it's just my imagination."

The light turned green. He accelerated through the intersection, then urged her to continue.

"Tell me," he said.

"We're all in the kitchen. My mother is laughing and stuffing a huge bite of cinnamon roll into your mouth. You have cinnamon and sugar on your chin, and you're trying to do the same thing to her, only she's avoiding the sweet roll that you're holding in your hand."

Sam inhaled slowly, then pulled over into a side street and parked. When he turned to look at Jade, there were tears in his eyes.

"That wasn't a dream, honey. It really happened. We used to play like that together a lot, especially in the beginning. That's why I was so stunned when she ran away. I didn't know she was that unhappy."

"I don't think she was unhappy," Jade said. "I think she was selfish and self-centered. If she'd been thinking about me, she wouldn't have wanted me within a thousand miles of the People of Joy."

Sam was startled by the anger. He hadn't realized that Jade blamed her mother for the hardships of her past. He should have, but he hadn't.

"I'm sorry," he said. "I don't know what she was thinking when she took you, but I truly believe that she loved you too much to leave you behind."

Jade's laugh was sharp and bitter. "Love like that can kill you." Then she waved her hand in the air, as if brushing away the past, and moved on to her other memory. "Remember the other day when you brought me home from the hospital so I could take a shower and change my clothes?"

"Yes?"

"Well, I was walking up the stairs when suddenly it seemed that I'd walked up those stairs a lot of times before and that you were right beside me with your hand on my shoulder. Oh...and you were carrying a little pink blanket. I think it was mine. Was that a real memory?"

Sam's breath caught at the back of his throat. She was remembering their night-time ritual.

"Yes, and when we get home, there's something I want to show you," he said, and pulled away from the curb.

A short while later they reached the house. There were still a couple of vans from local television stations, but the national news crews were starting to disperse, leaving the prodigal daughter story for something new. The media still in the area had been restricted from the immediate vicinity of Sam's home, so it was becoming easier for Jade to pretend they weren't even there. Still, it had been disconcerting to see herself on film on the evening news, going in and out of the hospital, or walking out of Sam's house to get in the car. And there had been the story of her homecoming on the front page of the biggest St. Louis paper with the picture that had run when she disappeared, as well as one of her now. It hadn't occurred to her that the story had been picked up and was running nationwide. If it had, she would have panicked for certain. The last thing she wanted was for Solomon to know where she was. Even now, she still feared his power.

Sam took her hand as they started toward the house, unaware that they were being watched from the house across the street. But as Jade got out of the car, the hair on the back of her neck began to crawl. She turned abruptly, expecting to see someone with a camera trained on them. Instead she saw nothing out of the ordinary.

"What's wrong?" Sam asked.

"I don't know," she said. "It just felt like someone was watching us."

Sam snorted beneath his breath. "That's because they probably are. Damned reporters have all kinds of fancy gadgets at their disposal these days. Telescopic lenses and the like. Come along, dear. Don't give them a thought."

Jade followed Sam's advice and hurried into the house. Once the door was shut behind them, the feeling disappeared, which convinced her that Sam had been right.

"What was it you wanted to show me?" she asked.

Sam took her by the hand. "It's upstairs."

She let him lead her up the stairs, then off to another wing of the house that she hadn't been in.

"What's down here?" she asked, as they started down a long hallway.

"It's the family wing," he said. "My bedroom is here." Then he stopped at a door and pushed it ajar. "This room was yours."

Jade gasped. "Why haven't you shown me this before?"

He frowned. "At first, you seemed so hostile at even being here, I was afraid you'd think that I was pushing you to remember."

"I'm sorry," Jade said. "May I go in?"

"It's why I brought you here," Sam said, and then stepped aside.

Jade walked in and was immediately struck with the sensation of having walked into a sort of museum. The furnishings were obviously for a little girl—a four-poster bed with pink and white decor. The pictures on the walls were of Winnie the Pooh, and there was a rag doll reclining against the pillows.

She picked up the doll, ruffling her fingers through the yarn hair, and then held it to her face. It smelled of furniture polish and age, with a faint whiff of lavender thrown in.

"You didn't change a thing, did you?"

"No."

"Why? Twenty years? What were you waiting for?"

Sam sighed, then briefly laid his hand on the back of her head. "I don't know…. A miracle, I guess. But it's not this room, precisely, that I wanted you to see." He crossed to a cedar chest beneath the windows and opened the lid. When he turned around, he was holding a bundle of pink. "It's your blanket. You never slept without it."

Jade took it, feeling the softness of the pink flannel against the palm of her hand. It smelled of cedar.

"It used to smell like roses. Why did it smell like roses?"

Sam sat down on the side of the small bed, because his legs suddenly felt weak.

"God. You do remember." Then he looked up at her. "It smelled like roses because your mother had a favorite perfume called Roses. You always begged her to spray it on your lovey." He pointed to the blanket. "That's what you called it."

Lovey. She sat down on the bed beside Sam. As she did, a sense of peace began to seep into her soul. For a long, long time, she hadn't belonged anywhere, or cared for anyone but Raphael. But coming back here had started a chain reaction of memories, memories that reminded her that she'd belonged here first—and to Sam.

She sighed, then slowly pulled the blanket up close to her chest and, without looking at Sam, leaned against him until their shoulders were touching.

It wasn't much of a gesture, but it was enough to convince Sam that his miracle had come true.

"How about I ask Velma to fix us some breakfast while you shower? Oh, and there are some new clothes for you in your closet. If they don't fit, or you don't like the styles, don't hesitate to tell me. They can go back to the stores as easily as they came."

Jade looked up. Sam was so earnest—so good. If only he never had to know what his baby girl had endured. If only the bubble never had to burst.

"Thank you for being so good to me," she said.

Sam put his arm around her then and gave her a quick hug.

"You're my daughter. If I could, I would give you the moon and Raphael back his health."

She smiled sadly. "Unfortunately, both are impossible."

"I know, dear, and I'm so, so sorry."

Jade relished the comfort of his strength as she leaned against him.

"I can never repay you for what you're doing for Rafie."

"The only thing I want from you is something you already have. When you remember it, too, then we'll both be happy."

She frowned. "Something I already have? What's that?"

"To remember how much I loved you...and how much you loved me." Then he stood abruptly, forestalling a response. "About that breakfast...do you fancy anything special?"

Jade shook her head. "Maybe waffles. She makes really good waffles."

Sam smiled. "With strawberries, right?"

Jade could tell that, for Sam, the connection between them was much stronger. But he had the memories of a father for his child.

"Something else I always ate, right?"

He laughed. "Mostly it was something I always ate. You sat in my lap and picked the strawberries off of my waffle, as well as your own."

"Uh, I think I'm too big to sit in your lap, but not to steal strawberries," she added.

"I'll be on my guard," Sam said. "Take your time with your shower. You deserve a little pampering."

He was gone before she could answer, leaving her alone in the room she'd slept in as a child. She started to get up, then impulsively rolled over on her side, curled her knees up toward her chest and pulled the blanket beneath her chin.

There was sunlight coming through a part in the curtains. She closed her eyes and, as she did, imagined she could hear her mother's footsteps coming down the hall. Jade pulled the blanket over her head just as she'd done the night that Margaret had taken her away. In the haste to escape, the blanket had been left behind. In that moment, Jade wished with every fiber of her being that she'd been left with it.

From the time the woman and the old man had gotten out of the car, Johnny Newton had had the back of her head in the cross-hairs of his rifle. All he would have had to do was

pull the trigger and it would be over. But there was no challenge in spilling gray matter onto concrete and grass, at least not until the victim saw his face. He wanted to see their fear and the knowing in their eyes that their time was up. It was why he did what he did, which meant that a quick bullet through Jade Cochrane's brain wasn't going to do it for him. Besides, his first target had to be the man. He'd followed them to the hospital yesterday. It had been easy to learn the identity of the man in the quarantine ward, but not so easy to get inside. He'd had to reassess his plans as to how to get rid of the son-of-a-bitch, although it was his personal opinion that if Big Frank would just bide his time, the man would die on his own. But Johnny didn't get paid for his opinions, only the fruits of his labors.

So he followed Jade's progress into the house through the telescopic sight on his rifle. When the door closed, he laid down the rifle, then leaned back in his chair and masturbated. The ritual was an old one, related to power and control, and was Johnny Newton's only weakness. He would never have admitted to having a sexual addiction, but it was true. Every time he played God by toying with the time and date of a person's demise, he followed it up by giving himself the ultimate high.

Right in the middle of his orgasm, his cell phone began to ring.

Big Frank expected to hear a hello, not some gut-wrenching groan.

"Hello? Hello? Newton, is that you?"

Still trembling from his sexual release, Johnny glanced down at the phone number displayed on the caller ID screen and knew it was Lawson.

Big Frank cursed. "Damn it, Newton, talk to me. Why haven't I heard from you? I'm not paying you all that money for nothing."

The rebuke pissed Johnny off. His parents had always yelled at him. He hadn't liked it then. He didn't like it now.

"Don't ever call me again," Johnny said. "You'll know what you need to know when it's over and not before."

Then he disconnected. As he turned off the phone, it occurred to him that if by chance he should get killed, there would be no way for anyone to know who'd hired him. And Johnny, being the man that he was, was always ready to shift the blame. Still weak from the climax, he crawled to his feet and dug through a desk drawer for a pen and some paper. He wrote down Frank Lawson's name, then his cell phone number beneath it, and stuck it in his wallet.

Jade had spent longer in her old bedroom than she'd intended, so she hurried back to her room, then went through her shower, suddenly anxious that she'd left Raphael alone too long. She towel-dried quickly, brushed out her hair, then fastened it at the back of her neck with a large tortoiseshell clip. She was stunned by the assortment of new clothes in her closet. It was more than she'd ever had in her life, but lingering over the soft, colorful fabrics and styles was a luxury she didn't have.

Choosing a blue short-sleeved shirt and a pair of white, cotton pants, she dressed quickly, then stepped into a pair of gold sandals. As she started out the door, she remembered her purse and ran back to the bed, where she'd tossed it earlier. While Sam had given her a half-dozen new ones in various colors, she'd chosen to keep the old beaded one that Raphael had given her years ago. It was her way of reminding herself of where she'd come from and what she'd survived.

She found Sam in the dining room, reading the morning paper. He gave her an appreciative smile as she entered the room.

"Darling…you look beautiful. I hope you brought an appetite."

She glanced at the food on the warming trays on the sideboard and was surprised when her tummy growled.

"Yes, I believe I did," she said.

"Then help yourself," he said. "I'm right behind you."

The doorbell rang just as Jade was spooning an extra helping of strawberries onto her waffle. Sam glanced at his watch and then frowned. It was just after eight-thirty. In his opinion, a little early for callers. A few moments later, Luke entered the dining room with an apology on his lips. Jade's presence took him by surprise.

"Uh…Jade. I didn't know you'd be here."

"I came home to clean up and change clothes."

Luke nodded, while frantically searching for something else to say. Sam saved him by inviting him to eat.

"Luke, have you had breakfast?" Sam asked.

"Yes, thanks."

"Then have some coffee with us while we eat."

Luke poured himself a cup of coffee. Sam was sitting at the head of the table, Jade on his left. Luke took the seat on his right, which was directly across the table from Jade. He didn't think he'd ever seen such a beautiful sight.

Sam could tell Luke was taken with his daughter. Hiding his delight, he took a couple of bites of his food to give Luke time to remember why he'd come.

Suddenly Jade felt awkward and clumsy. She fiddled with the napkin in her lap and then speared a thin slice of strawberry, hoping it didn't fall in her lap before she got it to her mouth. The last time she'd shared a meal with Luke Kelly, she'd spilled her guts about the sins of her past. Now she didn't know whether to be humiliated or relieved.

Luke saw the flush on her cheeks and knew she was embarrassed. Then he sighed. Hell, if the truth were known, he was the one who should be embarrassed for what he was thinking.

Finally he remembered why he was there.

"Hey, Sam, you were right about the Dawson Company."

Sam's attention quickly focused from matters of the heart, to business. The Dawson Company made valves. When he'd acquired the company, they'd been operating in the red for two years. Within nine months, he had pulled them from the verge of bankruptcy to showing a profit. And even though they were now running in the black, he didn't trust the general manager.

"It's Kilmer, isn't it?" Sam asked.

Luke nodded. "Yeah, he's taking kickbacks, but even worse, he's selling you out. The last two jobs that you lost with NASA were because he tipped off your competition as to the amounts of your bids."

"The bastard," Sam muttered, then remembered Jade was at the table. "Sorry, honey. I shouldn't have used that kind of language in your presence."

Jade almost laughed. If he only knew what she'd seen and heard in her lifetime, he would have refused to sit at the same table with her.

"Trust me," she said lightly. "I've heard worse."

Sam looked a bit startled, then nodded. "Of course you have. I just wasn't thinking, but it doesn't mean you ever have to hear it again. I'm still sorry, okay?"

"Okay," Jade said.

Sam glanced at his watch. "It's ten o'clock Eastern Standard Time. I should be able to catch him in the office about now." Then he turned to Jade. "Dear, will you please excuse me? I need to tend to this now before we lose another bid."

"Sure. Don't worry about me. I can always catch a cab back to the hospital."

"I'm on my way back to the office," Luke said. "I'd be happy to give you a ride."

"That's settled, then," Sam said, and got up from the table, giving his half-eaten breakfast a regretful look. "I guess you're going to get my strawberries again after all." He hurried from the room, anxious to confront the man who was selling him out.

Jade waved a goodbye, then glanced down at her plate. Thanks to Luke's unexpected arrival, she hadn't even eaten her own.

"That looks awfully good. Aren't you hungry?" Luke asked.

"I was," Jade said.

Luke sighed. "Please don't."

"Don't what?" she asked.

"Don't put any more walls up between us. Friends aren't supposed to have to climb walls just to say hello."

"I don't know how to have a friend, let alone be one," Jade muttered.

"You were doing all right yesterday."

She glanced up, looking to see if he was being sarcastic. He was not.

"Yesterday was yesterday."

He shrugged. "And today is today. So, like I said…the waffles look good. Aren't you hungry?"

"Yes, actually, I am.

"Then dig in," Luke said.

Jade forked a big bite of waffle, speared a strawberry on the end of the tines, then poked it in her mouth.

"Mmm," she said.

Luke watched as the tip of her tongue slid across the surface of her lips for the sprinkle of powdered sugar that she'd dropped, then reached for his coffee cup. He had to have somewhere to put his hands besides on her or he might very well lose his mind.

Thirteen

Jade was finishing her breakfast when she remembered something she'd wanted to do.

"The mall is on our way to the hospital, isn't it?"

Luke nodded as he finished his last drink of coffee.

"Could we stop there on our way? I want to get some warm socks for Raphael. His feet always feel cold."

"Absolutely," Luke said.

Then Sam came back into the room. "Shelly Hudson called. She wanted me to tell you that she's still thinking of you, and that if you need her for anything, you just have to call."

"She's a very nice lady," Jade said.

"Yes, she is. She used to baby-sit for Margaret and me sometimes."

"With me?" Jade asked.

Sam nodded. "From the time you were born until you disappeared."

Jade looked startled. "Good grief…she's changed my diapers."

Both men burst out laughing as Jade blushed.

"So laugh," she said. "It's a bit daunting."

Then Sam remembered something and pointed at Jade.

"Wait! Don't leave yet. I have something for you," he said, and hurried out of the room. He was back moments later with a pad of checks and a debit card. "Here,

honey...I've been meaning to give these to you and kept forgetting.''

''What are these?'' Jade asked.

Sam sat down beside her and put his arm around her shoulders.

''Temporary checks for the checking account I opened for you. Also, this is an extra debit card from my account. Use it until your own card comes in the mail. Five thousand dollars will be deposited each month in your account, so don't worry about running low.''

Jade's mouth dropped. Five thousand dollars? Each month? She'd never had that much in one year in her life. She kept looking down at the checkbook, then back up at Sam. Finally she shook her head in disbelief.

''Sam... I don't know what to say. I still have a little money from the last art show. You must know that I didn't expect this.''

Sam shook his head and then smiled. ''Bless your heart, honey. I know I don't have to, but I want to, understand?''

She glanced at Luke. He was eating the last bites of waffle that she'd left on her plate.

''Well, you're no help,'' she muttered.

He looked up and then grinned. ''What am I supposed to do? Unless Sam wants to adopt me, I'm afraid I'm out of this loop.''

There was a small drop of strawberry juice on the edge of his mouth. Jade stared at it, then at the curve of his bottom lip, until her face felt hot.

Since it was obvious that Luke was full of silliness, she was going to have to face this alone.

''I've never taken charity from anyone in my life.''

Sam frowned. ''It isn't charity, darling. You're my daughter. It's rightfully yours as much as mine.''

Jade fingered the checkbook cover, then opened it up.

''I've never written a check before.'' Then she sighed. ''Truth is, I've never had enough money at one time to even

open a checking account. We moved around so much, it didn't seem wise."

Sam hoped he didn't look as startled as he felt.

"I'm sorry. Obviously I wasn't thinking or I might have realized that. I don't suppose you have a driver's license, or any other form of picture identification, like an old school ID or something of the sort?"

"Driver's license? I can't drive, Sam. What would I have learned on? As for a school ID, I'm afraid I've never been in school…or at least a real school, like other kids."

"Never?" Luke asked. "Then how did you learn to read or count money or—"

"There was a woman in the People of Joy who'd once been a teacher. Solomon made her hold classes for all the children within the group. It wasn't constant, and there were lots of times when she was too stoned to come to class, but I learned what I learned. The rest came after we ran away. Raphael is smart…really smart. He taught me a lot—about everything. He can do… I mean he would have been able to do anything."

She felt sick to her stomach, guilty that, for a time, she'd almost forgotten Raphael's fate.

Luke's expression was somewhere between dismay and anger. Again he thought of what he would like to do to this Solomon character as Sam tried to smooth things over.

"Don't fret. We'll tend to all of that another day, so for the time being, don't worry about writing any checks. Just use your debit card. It's like cash. Luke will show you how it's done. You'll catch on in no time. Oh, yes…there's a pin number that goes with that. It's 7373. Luke, do you have time to take her to an ATM and show her how it works?"

"Absolutely," Luke said.

Jade's head was spinning as she repeated the pin number. Having money was more complicated than she'd thought.

"7373." Then she frowned. "But what if I forget it?"

Sam smiled. "It should be easy for you to remember. It's your birthday."

"My birthday is in July?"

For Luke, it was the last straw.

"Son-of-a-bitch," he muttered, and stalked out of the room.

Sam was stunned. "You didn't know your own birthday?"

"I guess I might have at one time, before Mother died, but if I did, I've forgotten it."

"We used to have the best parties," Sam said, and then he slapped the table with the flat of his hand. "And, by God, we will again! Go on with you now. Luke's probably waiting in the car."

Jade dropped the checkbook and debit card into her purse and got up from the table; then Sam walked her to the door. Just as they reached the foyer, she turned around and gave him a hug. Then, before he could say something that would rattle her even more, she ran out the door.

Luke was sitting on the front steps. He stood as she came out, then held out his hand. To his surprise, she took it and let him lead her down the steps to the car.

"Buckle up," he said, as he seated her in the car.

She reached for the seat belt as Luke circled the car and then slid behind the wheel. Even after they were both buckled in and ready to go, Luke still sat, staring blindly out the windshield.

"Luke?"

He jerked, as if coming out of a trance, then started the car but left it in Park.

"Jade, sometimes you just about break my heart. I hope to God that one day you'll let somebody love you the way you deserved to be loved."

She couldn't look at him for fear that he would see how badly she wanted that to happen, but she had to say what she was thinking.

"What if I'm not able to give that kind of love back?"

He looked at her then, his voice thick with emotion.

"It's in you, honey. You just need to trust enough to let it go."

"What if that never happens?"

"It will—when you're ready," Luke said, then put the car in gear and drove off.

Johnny Newton was dressed and sitting in his car. From where he was parked, he could see who came and went at the Cochrane home, although he could not be seen. He watched as a younger man came out of the house with Jade Cochrane, then waited as they got into a dark red sports car, then waited some more while they had some kind of conversation. He picked up a pair of binoculars from the seat beside him, training it on their faces, and watched as their expressions ran the scale of emotions.

"I think he wants to fuck you, baby," Johnny said, and made a mental note to learn how to read lips. Then he shifted the view to Jade's face and whistled softly between his teeth. "Sweet...you'd almost be worth taking the time to do it right."

As soon as the car started to move, Johnny dropped the binoculars onto the seat beside him and put his car in gear. He counted to three, then started down the driveway just in time to see the red car turning the corner up the block. Taking care not to be noticed, he began to follow. He had made no plans to take Jade Cochrane out today, but he'd figured out how to do Raphael. Trouble was, they never left the poor bastard alone. Someone was with him in that isolation room all the time, and Johnny liked privacy when he worked. But he was also getting bored and figured that if the opportunity presented itself, he would take the chance. It might be interesting to see just how close he could get to her without alerting her that she'd become a target. The more he thought about it, the more excited he became. And because he was thinking about how easily her soft flesh would yield to a

knife, he got careless. Had he known that the man with Jade Cochrane was an ex-cop with his own private security business, it might have made him think twice about what he was doing. But he didn't, and because he liked to play close to the edge, he got himself made.

Luke saw the flash of sunlight in his rearview mirror as it glinted off the windshield of the car behind him. Out of habit, he noted it was a gray, late-model sedan and then returned his attention to his driving. Jade was counting and recounting the twenty dollar bills they'd taken from an ATM. He wished he'd had a camera to capture the shock, then delight, when she came away three hundred dollars richer than she'd been when she arrived. It wasn't as if she'd never seen ATMs, but she'd never had the opportunity to see how they worked, and it was obvious she was fascinated.

"We're almost at the mall," Luke said.

"Oh! Okay," Jade said, and quickly put the money back in her purse.

As Luke turned off the street into the mall parking lot, he noticed that the gray sedan was still behind him. However, at least two dozen other cars were also signaling a turn into the mall, so he ignored its presence.

"We're looking for socks, right?"

She nodded. Conscious of the large amount of money in her purse, she clutched it close against her chest.

Luke circled an area of the parking lot twice before he found a parking place near the wing closest to JCPenney's. It was as good a place as any to buy some men's socks.

"Ha! There's one!" he crowed, and wheeled into an empty parking space that a woman in a PT Cruiser had just vacated.

Jade almost smiled. "It doesn't take much to please you, does it?"

Luke arched an eyebrow in pretend dismay. "You wound me, woman. Are you insinuating that I'm shallow?"

She laughed aloud.

Luke shuddered and then quickly looked away. Her laugh made him feel naked—stripped to the bone by the joy in the sound.

"Okay," he said shortly. "Let's go buy some socks."

Jade tightened her grip on her purse and got out of the car.

Johnny Newton saw them park and get out. He watched as they crossed the parking lot and then disappeared inside the mall. He'd had a brainstorm as he'd watched them circling the lot, but without knowing how long they would be inside, he didn't have time to waste. He knew they were on their way back to the hospital, but he needed to slow them down so he get to Raphael without interference. He parked in the first parking place he found, and as soon as they were out of sight, got out on the run. Moments later, he was beside their car. With a quick glance around to make sure he was unobserved, he took a knife from his pocket, dropped to the concrete, rolled onto his back and then pulled himself as far under the front of the car as he could go.

The concrete was hot against his skin, even through the layers of his clothing. The acrid scent of burning oil and hot rubber seared his nostrils as he reached for the brake line. He heard voices and the sound of someone laughing as he thrust the knife into the line. A thin smear of fluid coated the knife as he pulled it out. Without wasted motion, he closed the blade and slid out from under the car. As he jumped to his feet, he startled a pair of teenage girls who were on their way back to their car.

They gasped in unison, eyeing him nervously as they clutched their bags and increased their stride.

"Boo!" he said, and then wiggled his hands toward them, as if he were putting them under some spell.

They screamed and started to run.

Johnny laughed aloud and then cut across the parking lot back to where he was parked. He was in his car and gone

before the girls reached their vehicle. His plan hinged on getting in and out of Raphael's hospital room without having too many people running interference, and he had just given himself the time and space to do it.

Jade kept looking for a clock. The longer she stayed away from Raphael's hospital room, the more anxious she became.

"What time is it?" she asked, as they hurried down the mall with her purchases.

Luke glanced at his watch. "Almost ten."

"Oh God…I've been gone three…almost four hours. What if—"

"Raphael is all right," he said.

"How do you know?" Jade asked.

"Because if he wasn't, the hospital would have called Sam's house. And Sam knows you're with me, so he would have called my cell phone. So since Sam hasn't called us, we can assume Raphael is okay. That's how I know."

"Oh."

It made sense. It also gave Jade permission to relax.

"Sorry," she said. "But every moment I'm away from him is a moment I can never get back."

Her voice broke as she looked away, and when she did, she saw a little girl standing up against a storefront. She was standing with her back to the windows, and Jade could tell by the look on the child's face that she was frightened.

Before she could say anything about her, Luke saw her, too.

"Jade, look. I think that little girl is lost. Do you see any adults nearby that she might belong to?"

Jade quickly searched the area but didn't see anyone who fit the description.

"No, I don't, do you?" she asked.

"No," he said, and without hesitation, walked toward the girl. As soon as he reached her, he went down on one knee

so that they would be speaking face to face. "Honey...are you okay?"

The child couldn't have been more than four. When she saw Luke, she hid her face in her hands.

"My name is Luke," he said, then motioned for Jade to come closer. "This is my friend Jade. Are you lost?"

There was a moment when all they could hear were the quiet sounds of stifled sobs; then, slowly, she lowered her hands and studied Luke's face. Something she saw there prompted her to answer.

"No, but my mommy is," she said.

"Ah...so what's your name?"

"Melissa Joan Carter, but my daddy calls me Princess."

Luke dug a handkerchief from his pocket and carefully wiped at her tears.

"So, Melissa Joan Carter, what do you say we find a nice policeman who will help us find your mommy?"

"Yes, please," she said, and then snuffled through a few lingering sobs.

They led her to a nearby bench, then all sat down together.

"Do you know your mother's name?" Jade asked.

"Mommy."

Jade frowned, then thought to ask the question a different way. "What does your daddy call your mommy?"

"Sugar...but my Grammy calls her Faith."

"Good work," Luke told Jade, then he looked at the little girl. "We're going to find your mommy, okay? But first we have to tell a policeman that she's lost."

"Okay," the child said, and before Luke knew what was happening, she'd crawled up into his lap.

Without thinking, he swiped at a stray tear that he'd missed, then kissed the side of her cheek.

"Don't cry, baby girl. We'll make everything all right."

Then he turned to Jade. "Honey, run in that store and ask the clerk to call security, will you? I'll wait here with Melissa, just in case her mommy shows."

Luke watched as she hurried into the store, then began talking to the clerk. When they looked his direction, he waved. The clerk immediately waved back and reached for the phone.

Jade hurried back to where Luke and the child were sitting.

"He said for us to wait here."

"We're waiting, aren't we, Melissa?"

The little girl nodded.

"Want me to hold you?" Jade asked, thinking that the child might be afraid of Luke and be more comfortable with a woman.

"No," the little girl said. "I like him."

Jade was a bit startled, then smiled.

"You do, huh?"

"Yes."

"Why is that?" Jade asked.

"'Cause he's higher than you and he smells nice...like my daddy."

"Oh."

Luke winked at Jade and then smiled.

"As you can see, I *am* much higher than you."

"And you smell."

Luke looked a bit taken aback, and then it hit him that she was teasing. He thought it was a first.

"That's not what she said," he muttered.

"Sorry," Jade said. "I guess I didn't hear her right."

"Hey, look!" Luke said, pointing down the mall. "There comes a policeman now. I'll bet he's going to be able to help us find your mommy."

The child nodded sagely, as if suddenly Luke's word was law. Her innocence made Jade sick. She knew how naive a child that age was, and how easily it could have been someone less trustworthy than she or Luke who had found her.

Then the officer arrived and introductions were necessary again.

He eyed Luke closely. "I'm Officer Reyes. Who do we have here?"

Luke quickly flashed some identification. "My name is Luke Kelly, of Kelly Securities here in St. Louis."

"Oh! My brother-in-law, Mel Holmes, works for you!"

Luke nodded in recognition. "Yes, he does, in accounting," he added; then he turned to the little girl. "Tell the officer your name, sweetheart. He can help you find your mommy faster."

Suddenly intimidated by too many strangers, she ducked her head, hiding her face against the curve of Luke's neck.

Luke eyed the officer, then shrugged. "She was talking a few minutes ago. Said her name was Melissa Joan Carter but her daddy calls her Princess."

The officer smiled. "So, Princess, how about we see if we can find your mommy? Want to come with me?"

She clung to Luke's neck and shook her head.

Jade laid her hand on the little girl's back and felt her trembling. Her heart instantly went out to her. She could well remember what it felt like to lose Mommy. The only trouble was, hers never came back. She turned to the security officer.

"Maybe it would be okay if we went with you? Her mother is probably frantic."

"Oh, yeah...by the way," Luke added. "I think her mother's name is Faith. We're assuming that it's also Carter, although these days, you can't be too sure."

"Yeah, sure, why not?" the officer said, and led the way back down the mall toward the security office.

As they were walking, the officer's radio began to squawk. He slipped it out of the case on his belt and keyed up the mike.

"This is Dwight."

"Yeah. Dwight. We got a woman here who's reported a missing child. Thought I'd double-check and see if your kid is a match."

"What's her name?" the officer asked.

"Faith Carter."

The officer grinned at Luke and then gave him a thumbs-up.

"Yeah, tell her we got the kid. We're on our way now."

Luke breathed a sigh of relief and then winked at Jade.

"See, miracles do happen."

She nodded, yet all the way to the security office, she couldn't help but wonder what her life would have been like if Sam had been able to find her this easily.

By the time they reached the office, Luke and the child were fast friends. Her tiny hand was fisted in the collar of his shirt, and she was telling him about her pet fish named Harry.

Suddenly a woman darted out of the doorway and snatched the little girl from Luke's arms.

"Missy...missy...you scared Mommy to death." Then she looked at Luke and Jade and started to cry. "I can't thank you enough for finding her. One minute she was right beside me, and then she was gone." She closed her eyes momentarily and laid her cheek against the child's silky hair. "Oh God, oh God. I was so scared. I thought...I was afraid...I didn't know if I'd—"

Jade touched the woman. "You were lucky this time. A really nice man found her, but it doesn't always happen that way. Trust me, I know."

Suddenly the woman gasped. She looked at Jade as if seeing her for the first time.

"It's you, isn't it? I saw your picture in the papers. You're the little girl who's been lost all those years." Then she started to cry all over again. "Oh my dear, my dear...what you must have gone through." Still holding her daughter in one arm, she wrapped her other arm around Jade's neck and gave her a hug. "Welcome home, dear, welcome home." Then she turned Jade loose and hugged Luke, as well.

But it was Jade who was speechless as they walked away. It took her a few seconds to realize that Luke was holding

her hand, and when she did, she didn't bother to pull it loose. Instead she curled her fingers around his and held on tight.

Luke had been covertly watching her expression throughout the entire ordeal and had been fearful that it would resurrect some bad memories for her. He'd taken hold of her hand because taking her into his arms was out of the question, yet fully expecting her to pull back. Instead she'd tightened her grip, and when she did, he thought he knew what was going through her head.

"Hold on tight to me, honey," he said softly. "I'll make sure you'll never be lost again."

Jade took a deep, shuddering breath, shifted the sack with Raphael's socks to a tighter grip and led with her chin. He was right. She didn't have to be afraid. There was nothing left to hurt her but losing Raphael, and she wouldn't let her mind go there.

Johnny loved this part of his job. In another life, he wondered if he might have been an actor. He liked the costumes and the disguises that he often used to get to the hit. This time he had filched a lab coat, a pair of surgical gloves and a mask, and sauntered through the halls of the hospital, blending easily into the dozens and dozens of health care workers who, at any given time, would be on a floor. Knowing that the ward he needed to get to was a sort of quarantine, he even had some disposable footies over his shoes.

He did wonder why they had Raphael in quarantine, since he'd found out the guy was dying of liver cancer, then decided it was probably more for the patient's protection than the reverse. If he was critical, even a sneeze from an unwitting passerby could trigger a bout of pneumonia for him, and it would be all over. So he entered the ward without hesitation, confident that, within minutes, it would be all over. He thought about how he would tell Frank Lawson the job was done, and then decided that he might wait an extra day or so before letting him know, just to make him sweat.

When he reached the room, he pulled the mask up over his face, threw back his shoulders and pushed the door inward, striding as confidently as any doctor in the place. He was a bit taken aback by the presence of a private nurse, then decided it was all for the better.

She looked up and then, not recognizing Michael Tessler behind the mask, frowned.

"I'm sorry," she said. "How can I help you?"

Johnny pointed to the IV, then took an empty hypodermic syringe out of his pocket and held it to her.

"You can shove this in his arm, or get out of the way and let me do it," he said.

The nurse gasped as the masked stranger started toward her. She reached for the phone to call security but was not fast enough. Johnny broke her neck as silently and swiftly as he'd broken Mabel Tyler's, then let her limp, lifeless body drop beside the bed.

"Okay now," he muttered, as he fiddled with the IV attached to Raphael's arm. "One good shot of air into this baby and, buddy, you're toast."

Raphael had heard the stranger's voice as well as the implied threat. Struggling to pull himself out of a drug-induced haze, he felt along the side of the bed rail, trying to find the button that would ring the nurses' station. Instead the man shoved his hand aside and started to jab a needle into the IV shunt.

Raphael sensed something was terribly wrong and cursed his illness, as well as the medicine that had left him so weak.

"Who are you? What do you want?"

The man laughed, and the sound made the hair on the back of Raphael's arms stand on end.

"Don't take this personally," the man said. "It's just a matter of business."

Raphael finally focused just as the man thrust the needle of the syringe into the shunt. When he realized that there was nothing in it but air, he knew his time on this earth was over.

An Important Message from the Editors

Dear Reader,

Because you've chosen to read one of our fine novels, we'd like to say "thank you!" And, as a **special** way to thank you, we're offering you a choice of <u>two more</u> of the books you love so well **plus** an exciting Mystery Gift to send you — absolutely <u>FREE</u>!

Please enjoy them with our compliments...

Pam Powers

Lift here

What's Your Reading Pleasure...
ROMANCE? _OR_ SUSPENSE?

Do you prefer spine-tingling page turners OR heart-stirring stories about love and relationships? Tell us which books you enjoy – and you'll get 2 FREE "ROMANCE" BOOKS or 2 FREE "SUSPENSE" BOOKS with no obligation to purchase anything.

Choose **"ROMANCE"** and get 2 **FREE BOOKS** that will fuel your imagination with intensely moving stories about life, love and relationships.

FREE!

Choose **"SUSPENSE"** and you'll get 2 **FREE BOOKS** that will thrill you with a spine-tingling blend of suspense and mystery.

FREE!

Whichever category you select, your 2 free books have a combined cover price of $11.98 or more in the U.S. and $13.98 or more in Canada.

And remember. . . just for accepting the Editor's Free Gift Offer, we'll send you 2 books and a gift, ABSOLUTELY FREE!

YOURS FREE! *We'll send you a fabulous surprise gift absolutely FREE, just for trying "Romance" or "Suspense"!*

® and ™ are trademarks owned and used by the trademark owner and/or its licensee.

Order online at
www.FreeBooksandGift.com

The Editor's "Thank You" Free Gifts Include:

- *2 Romance OR 2 Suspense books!*
- *An exciting mystery gift!*

Yes! I have placed my
Editor's "Thank You" seal in the
space provided at right. Please
send me 2 free books, which
I have selected, and a fabulous
mystery gift. I understand I am
under no obligation to purchase
any books, as explained on the
back of this card.

**PLACE
FREE GIFT
SEAL
HERE**

▼ DETACH AND MAIL CARD TODAY! ▼

© 2003 HARLEQUIN ENTERPRISES LTD.

	ROMANCE
	193 MDL EE5A 393 MDL EE5X

	SUSPENSE
	192 MDL EE5M 392 MDL EE6A

FIRST NAME   LAST NAME

ADDRESS

APT.#   CITY

STATE/PROV.   ZIP/POSTAL CODE

Thank You!

(ED2-MI-06)

The Reader Service — Here's How It Works:

Accepting your 2 free books and gift places you under no obligation to buy anything. You may keep the books and gift and return the shipping statement marked "cancel." If you do not cancel, about a month later we'll send you 3 additional books and bill you just $5.24 each in the U.S., or $5.74 each in Canada, plus 25¢ shipping & handling per book and applicable taxes if any.* That's the complete price and — compared to cover prices starting from $5.99 each in the U.S. and $6.99 each in Canada — it's quite a bargain! You may cancel at any time, but if you choose to continue, every month we'll send you 3 more books, which you may either purchase at the discount price or return to us and cancel your subscription.

*Terms and prices subject to change without notice. Sales tax applicable in N.Y. Canadian residents will be charged applicable provincial taxes and GST.

If offer card is missing write to: The Reader Service, 3010 Walden Ave., P.O. Box 1867, Buffalo, NY 14240-1867

POSTAGE WILL BE PAID BY ADDRESSEE

BUSINESS REPLY MAIL

FIRST-CLASS MAIL   PERMIT NO. 717-003   BUFFALO, NY

THE READER SERVICE
3010 WALDEN AVE
PO BOX 1341
BUFFALO NY 14240-8571

NO POSTAGE
NECESSARY
IF MAILED
IN THE
UNITED STATES

Someone was going to kill him. But why? Immediately he thought of all the news coverage and of Jade and knew that it had to be someone from their past. Someone who didn't want them alive to tell any tales. Then he knew that if they were going to kill him, they would kill Jade, too.

Desperate to save her and knowing that it was going to be impossible, his last thought was to make the killer's life a living hell.

Before Johnny Newton could react, Raphael had yanked the IV needle out of his arm. Blood spurted everywhere. On the bedclothes. On the floor. And all over Johnny.

Johnny cursed. The air bubble he'd shot into the line was now as useless as a fart. Who could have known that this dying son-of-a-bitch would fight back?

"You stupid bastard," he growled, and yanked the oxygen tube from Raphael's nose, then threw it in the floor. Then he wrapped his hands around Raphael's neck and started to squeeze.

Raphael dug his fingers into the man's hands, peeling back surgical gloves and flesh with his nails. The blood was still spurting from the open vein that the IV needle had been in, and now it was all over them both.

Johnny suffered the pain in his hands as he tightened his grip around the man's neck. But instead of fighting, the man suddenly stopped. Then, even with the air being choked out of his body, he smiled. It rattled Johnny Newton more than staring down the barrel of a gun might have done, and still he squeezed. He pushed and pushed against the larynx until the smile was gone and the man's eyes had rolled back in his head.

Suddenly it was over as quickly as it had begun.

Johnny let go of Raphael's neck and stepped back, surveying the mess that they'd made, for the first time aware of the pain in his own hands and the blood all over his clothes.

He cursed beneath his breath. This hadn't been planned. He couldn't walk out of the ward with blood all over him

like this and not be noticed. He would have to ditch the disguise and hope for the best.

Quickly he stripped off the coat, gloves and mask, and dumped them in a large biohazard container near the door, then looked back at the man on the bed. He couldn't get the smile out of his mind. What the hell had the sorry bastard had to smile about?

Fourteen

Luke and Jade were only minutes away from the hospital when they began approaching a busy intersection. Luke tapped on the brakes to start slowing down but felt no resistance. He hit the brakes again, this time pumping them rapidly, and felt the brake pedal go all the way to the floor.

"Hell."

"What's wrong?" Jade asked.

"No brakes," he said. "Hold on."

Jade didn't have time to be afraid, but from the look on Luke's face, he was plenty afraid for them both. She braced herself against the dashboard with both hands and closed her eyes.

Luke swerved to miss a car already stopped at the light. Steering through the space between two other vehicles that were still moving, he let the car bump up onto the curb and begin dragging high center. Luke yanked on the emergency brake and slammed the car into park just as the gears on the transmission sheared smooth. The moments after the screech of metal and rubber were surreal. The silence was as comforting as the noise had been frightening. Before there had been no certainty that there would be another breath to draw, and now they sat, listening to the rapid beating of their hearts and seeing the hiss of steam coming out from under the hood.

Suddenly there were people everywhere, tapping on the windows and shouting to them, "Are you okay? Are you okay?"

Luke reached over and grabbed Jade's arm.

"Jade...honey...are you all right? God, please be all right."

Jade leaned back against the seat, then took a deep breath. Nothing hurt. Nothing bled.

"Yes... I think so. What happened?"

"I don't know, but you can bet I'll find out. Don't move. I'll help you out on the other side."

He got out in a hurry, circling the car on the run. There was so much smoke and steam coming from under the hood, he feared something leaking might cause an explosion.

"I called 911," a man told him.

Luke nodded his thanks as he grabbed the passenger side door and yanked it open. Seconds later, he was pulling Jade out of the car and into his arms. He carried her a distance away from the accident.

"I can walk," she said.

"Humor me," Luke said, as he sat her down beneath some trees. "Don't move around until a medic can look you over, okay?"

She grabbed his arm, trying to still his panic.

"Luke. Listen to me. I'm okay."

Luke stopped, then, for the first time, really looked at her. When she smiled, he exhaled slowly.

"See?" she said. "All my fingers. All my toes."

He shook his head, then leaned forward and kissed her squarely on the lips. Before she could react, his cell phone began to ring.

Jade was shocked by what he'd done but thought she understood the reason. He was just relieved that they were all right and had showed it with a kiss. Nothing personal about it. Just a gesture of relief. Still, as she watched him answering the call, she couldn't help but touch her fingers to her lips, just to see if they felt different.

They felt the same, but she did not. For the first time in her life, the feelings she had for a man weren't of fear and

loathing. And never having had a normal crush or a stirring of puppy love, she didn't know how to identify what she was experiencing.

She shoved a shaky hand through her hair, then leaned back against the trunk of the tree, trying to regain some composure.

Just when she was beginning to relax, someone recognized her. She heard the whispers starting. They rose to a murmur, spilling throughout the crowd; then everyone began to come closer. She could no longer see Luke. Panic struck, and she called out in distress.

"Luke! Luke!"

She was struggling to get to her feet when he came out of nowhere, pushing and shoving both men and women aside in an effort to get to her.

"Get back!" he shouted, as he pulled her to her feet, then pulled her beneath the shelter of his arms. "What's wrong with you people? Get the hell back!"

Within seconds, police cars began to arrive, along with an ambulance. One of the officers recognized Luke and quickly helped disperse the crowd.

"Hey, Kelly! Is that your car?"

"Yes, and I need you to do me a favor. Have it towed to police headquarters and have the crime lab check it out to see if someone messed with it."

The officer frowned. "You serious?"

"As a heart attack," Luke muttered. "I'll call you later."

It was the word "call" that reminded Jade his phone had rung. Still worried about Raphael, she wanted to make sure it hadn't been about him.

"Luke?"

Even with the noise of the wrecker backing up to hook onto his car, and the police sirens and people talking, he heard her say his name. She wasn't stupid. She had to know that something besides the accident had him concerned.

"What, honey?"

"What's happening?"

"Just a minute," he said as he flagged down an arriving police car, then quickly hustled her inside. But when the cruiser suddenly turned and headed back the way they'd come, Jade grabbed at Luke's arm.

"Luke! We need to go to the hospital. He's going the wrong way!"

Luke felt sick. He didn't know what the hell was going on, but if he was right, Jade's life was in danger.

"No, honey, we can't do that right now."

Confusion turned to anxiety. "Yes! We can! We have to! I need to see Raphael. I need to give him his socks." Then she remembered that they were still in Luke's car. "I forgot the socks. We have to go back and get them. I told you, Raphael's feet are always cold."

"Something happened," he said. "We have to go back to Sam's now."

Jade started to shake. "You're lying to me. You told me that you'd never lie."

Luke reached for her, cursing whatever fates continued to bring such hell into her life.

"I'm not lying. I said we can't go to the hospital because we can't."

Jade had scooted to the far end of the seat. Her arms were wrapped around her middle, her eyes brimming with tears.

"Then tell me why," she said. "Damn you, Luke Kelly. Tell me why."

Luke shuddered. He'd heard Sam saying the words and still could not believe what he'd been told.

"You heard the phone ring?"

She nodded.

"Well, it was Sam."

Jade was trembling now—trembling so hard that she could hardly breathe—but she still had to hear.

Luke felt sick. The moment he spoke the words, he would be giving them life. They would be impossible to take back.

"Sam said the hospital called."

Jade shuddered. Her face went blank; then she started to rock back and forth where she sat. Luke had seen her do this once before, when she'd been telling him about her childhood. He wished Michael Tessler were there, because he didn't know what was going to happen by the time he was finished.

"He's dead...isn't he? He died alone...without me."

Luke sighed. "Yes, Jade, he's dead."

For a moment she just sat there, mute and trembling. Trouble was, Luke wasn't through destroying her world.

"That's not all," he said softly. "There's more."

Jade shuddered. It was all she could do to focus on Luke's face.

"How could there be more? Dead is dead."

"He didn't die from natural causes. He was murdered."

Jade reeled as if somebody had just slapped her face.

"That's a mistake. It wasn't Raphael. They're wrong. We need to go to the hospital and see."

"No, we don't need to see any of it," Luke said. "And it's not a mistake. Somebody came into his room, killed his nurse, then him. There was a struggle. They don't know a lot of details right now, but the police are checking the security videotapes."

She shook her head, then put her hands over her ears.

"I can't hear you," she said softly, and bent her forehead to her knees. "I won't hear you."

"I'm sorry, Jade. So sorry."

Then she started to wail—a thin, high-pitched sound that ripped through Luke's head and straight into his soul.

He reached for and pulled her into his arms. She fought back, resisting both touch and sound, and still he held her until she suddenly went limp. When her forehead bumped against his shoulder, he thought that she'd fainted, but then she started to speak.

"All the newspapers…all the pictures…all these years we kept running and hiding. But as soon as we stopped…"

Luke frowned. "Are you telling me that you think the man you call Solomon did this?"

"I don't know…maybe…but I should have been there. If I'd been there, it wouldn't have happened."

"No, Jade, no. You couldn't have stopped it any more than Raphael's nurse could. She tried and she died. He would have killed you, too. In fact, I think he already tried. There wasn't a thing wrong with my brakes this morning. I've never had a bit of trouble with them until now. After what just happened to Raphael, I don't think this was an accident."

Jade pressed her fingers against her lips, stifling the urge to scream as Luke continued.

"I've got some friends at the police department looking over the car. If my suspicions are right, someone tampered with the brakes, hoping to cause a wreck."

She crumpled in his arms just as the policeman reached Sam Cochrane's home. Sam met them at the door as Luke carried her into the house.

"Call Tessler," Luke said, as he started up the staircase to Jade's room.

Sam followed Luke up the stairs, then pulled back the bedcovers as Luke laid her down. She was still unconscious.

"I can't call Tessler," Sam said. "He's tied up at the hospital with the police investigation. I called Antonia DiMatto instead."

Luke paused in the act of removing Jade's shoes.

"Who's she?"

"A psychiatrist, but also a friend."

Luke brushed the hair away from Jade's face, then pulled the sheet up over her legs. He kept hearing Jade say that they shouldn't have stopped running. He felt sick, wondering if she was right. He sat down on the edge of the bed, then looked up.

"God, Sam…what have we done?"

"What do you mean?" Sam asked.

"When Jade heard about Raphael, she went to pieces. She seems to think that whoever killed Raphael is someone from their past."

"Preposterous," Sam said.

Luke shook his head. "Maybe not. Think about it. They endured a true hell on earth. They saw things that no adults should have seen, never mind the fact that they were children."

"What are you saying?" Sam asked.

Jade had asked Luke if he was going to tell Sam what she'd just told him about her past. Then, he hadn't been sure, but he was now. If they were going to keep her alive, Sam had to know everything he knew.

"Come out into the hall with me," Luke said. "There's something you need to know."

Sam went.

Luke started to talk, and by the time he was through, Sam was pale and shaking. He stood for a moment, as if trying to gather his thoughts, then suddenly turned and headed down the stairs.

"Sam? Sam, what are you going to do?"

Sam didn't answer.

Luke hesitated, uncertain as to whether to follow Sam or stay with Jade. He peeked in on her. She was motionless on the bed. Still concerned about what Sam might do, he bolted down the stairs, taking them two at a time. He found Sam in the library, taking down the painting of Ivy that he'd hung on the wall.

"What are you doing?" Luke asked.

"She doesn't deserve to be remembered," Sam said. "I don't want to look at her face again and know that she chose to put our daughter in danger. If she was so goddamned stifled by living in this house...if she felt that her life was going to be enhanced by living with a bunch of fools who experimented with every drug they could get their hands on, then

fine. But she should have been woman enough...no...by God, she should have been mother enough not to take a child into such a place.''

Then his voice broke. He lowered his head. His shoulders started to shake.

"Oh God, Luke...oh God. If I could find them, I would kill every man who ever touched her with my bare hands.''

"I know, Sam. I feel the same way, only we can't change her past. What's done is done. What we can do is make sure she has a future.''

Sam swiped a hand across his face, struggling to pull himself together.

"Yes, of course. I'm just sick at heart. She was hardly more than a baby. How can a grown man do that?''

"I don't know,'' Luke said. "But God better help the offenders, because I won't. If I ever find myself face-to-face with one of the men who put his hands on her like that, I will make him sorry he was ever born.''

Then the doorbell began to ring. Luke hoped it was the psychiatrist Sam had sent for. If it was, Velma would let them know. All Luke knew was that he wasn't going to leave Jade alone.

"I'll get that,'' Sam said. "You go stay with Jade. I don't want her to see me like this. She'll think I'm upset with her, and that's the farthest thing from the truth.''

"Will do,'' Luke said, and hurried back up the stairs.

The wounds on the backs of Johnny Newton's hands had finally quit bleeding, but they still stung. When he got back to Mabel's house, he would doctor them. Mabel had struck him as the kind of woman who would probably keep a well-stocked medicine cabinet.

As he drove through the streets of St. Louis, he thought back over the event. It wasn't as satisfying a hit as he'd expected it to be, although the nurse had been a plus. He hadn't known she would be there, and the high he always

got from the power of ending a life had been more than satisfying. He'd expected more of the same from offing Raphael, but it hadn't happened. Who could have known that someone that sick would be so defiant? Not only had he fought back, but he'd made such a goddamned mess. Johnny didn't mind spilling blood, but he didn't like it spilled on him. Still, it was over, and he had the satisfaction of knowing that the bastard had known what was happening. He was still a little puzzled over the way Raphael had kept smiling, even though he was bleeding all over the place, but the way he figured it, he'd actually done the guy a favor. Instead of lingering with cancer and all the pain and sickness that comes with it, Johnny had put him out of his misery.

A few minutes later, he turned up the driveway and parked in the Tyler garage as he'd done before. He headed for the back door as if he'd lived here all his life and was just walking inside when someone hailed him from behind.

"Hey, mister!"

Johnny froze.

"Mister! Hey, mister!"

He turned slowly, his hand on the gun beneath his jacket. When he saw a bare-chested young teenager standing beside a lawn mower and realized he'd been smelling the odor of freshly cut grass without even realizing it, he relaxed.

"Excuse me? Were you speaking to me?" Johnny asked.

The kid nodded. "I'm Kevin. I just finished mowing the yard, but Mrs. Tyler isn't answering the door. She always pays me when I'm through."

Johnny stifled a frown. "Yes, of course. If you'll wait there, I'll see where Aunt Mabel has gotten off to. She's getting so hard of hearing these days that she probably didn't hear the bell."

"Sure, no problem," the kid said, and ambled over to a bench beneath some shade trees to wait.

Then it dawned on Johnny that Mabel wasn't going to be available to tell him how much was owed.

"Say, kid...how much does she owe you, anyway?"

"Forty bucks."

Johnny dug his wallet out of his pocket. "How about I just pay you myself, then I won't have to bug Aunt Mabel in case she's taking a nap?"

"Yeah, sure," Kevin said. "Wow, what happened to you?" he asked, as he took the money out of Johnny's hands.

"What do you mean?" Johnny asked.

Kevin pointed to Johnny's shirt and arms.

"You got blood all over you."

"Oh that. Nosebleed," Johnny said. "Happens a lot, thanks to a bad habit from my past."

"What do you mean?"

"I used to be too fond of the white stuff."

Kevin nodded, pretending that he understood, although Johnny could tell he was shocked.

"You know...nose candy," Johnny added. "Let it be a lesson to you. Don't snort the damned stuff. It fucks up more than your nose."

"Yeah. Right," Kevin said, as he pocketed the cash Johnny handed him and jogged back to his mower.

Johnny waited until the kid and his mower were out of sight; then he hurried inside. Locking the door behind him, he cursed all the way upstairs. He wasn't in the habit of missing the details, but he should have known that an old woman like Mabel Tyler wouldn't have done her own yard work. It reminded him that there might be other things he'd forgotten to take into account. The knowledge made him nervous. Maybe he didn't have as much time to off Jade Cochrane as he'd planned.

Knowing that his visit with Mabel needed to come to a quick end, he stripped off his clothes as he strode down the hall, then headed for the shower to wash off the blood.

Later, as he was showering, the soap stung the scratches on his hands, reminding him of the other bungle that he'd made today. With an angry curse, he rinsed, dried, then

quickly dressed. After retracing his steps down the stairs, he stopped off in the kitchen to get himself a snack, then grabbed his binoculars as he headed for his viewing window to see what was going on across the street.

He placed his plate of cold cuts and crackers on the table beside his chair, opened the can of pop that he'd filched from the refrigerator and took a big swig.

"Aaah," he said, burping loudly as the carbonated soft drink hit his empty stomach.

He put the binoculars to his eyes, adjusted them accordingly, then aimed them toward Sam Cochrane's house just in time to see a pair of city police cruisers pulling into the driveway. He arched an eyebrow, then, without taking the binoculars away from his face, felt for the plate of cold cuts and got himself a bite. He chewed quietly with his mouth closed as his mother had taught him to do. When another car pulled in behind the patrol cars, he turned the binoculars to the license tag.

HEADDR.

It took him a few seconds to decipher it; then he realized that the latest arrival was a shrink. He grinned, laid the binoculars in his lap, and picked up the plate and polished off the rest of the meat and crackers.

"I guess somebody got a little spooked by her boyfriend's recent demise. What a pity."

He downed the rest of his pop, then crunched the empty can between his hands before tossing it into the ornamental urn in the corner of the room.

"Two points!" he shouted when the can dropped inside, then laid the binoculars on the floor and carried his dirty plate into the kitchen.

Finished with doing the dishes, he searched through the various bathrooms until he found some antiseptic cream and small bandages. Once he'd doctored the deep scratches on his hands and covered them up, he was in a much better mood. His belly was full, his wounds no longer causing him

pain, and he was more than halfway through with the job he'd come to do.

Tonight he would find a way into the Cochrane house. It gave him a hard-on just thinking about the risks of walking into the enemy's camp and taking out the woman without detection. This was what had been missing over the last few years. The risks. He'd gotten too damned good at what he did, and it had taken all the fun out of killing. Shooting Jade Cochrane from a hidden location and with a rifle fixed with a telescopic sight would be as boring as white bread. But entering her house, walking in the same places she walked, breathing the same air, touching the same things, then killing her in her own bed while her family slept only a short distance away, was a high he could only imagine. For Johnny, it was crossing a line from professionalism to personal pleasure.

He could hardly wait.

Earl Walters had been a street cop the year Jade Cochrane disappeared. Now, pushing thirty years on the job, he was the chief of police for the St. Louis Police Department and a personal friend of Sam Cochrane's. Like everyone else in the city who remembered the desperation of a young father trying to find his family, he had rejoiced at Jade Cochrane's return. He didn't know the particulars of the man who'd come with her, but it hadn't mattered. The little girl who'd been lost had come home.

But today he was outraged by the murders that had taken place in the hospital. That some son-of-a-bitch could waltz into a ward that was off limits to the general public, then commit such heinous crimes without being seen, was not to be tolerated. The mayor was on his ass, and the phones on his desk hadn't stopped ringing since the bodies had been discovered. As if that wasn't enough, the incident had caused a new feeding frenzy for the media. Speculation was high as to why someone attached to the prodigal daughter would

have been murdered. Gossip abounded as to what they must have done in their past that would have made someone kill. Knowing Sam Cochrane the way he did, this was going to be touchy business, which was why he'd come out from behind his desk to ask the questions himself.

Velma was at her wits' end and had abdicated answering the door for her duties in the kitchen. Luke had made a call to his office, and thirty minutes later two very large, very determined men were stationed at both entrances to Sam's house, along with guards at the driveway leading up to the house and at the back gates. Now that they were confident no intruders could get through their defenses, all they had to do was ignore the phones, which meant they were also ignoring calls from the police, which accounted for the reason two city police cars were parked on their front lawn and Earl Walters was ringing their doorbell.

Earl ambled up to the front door and rang the bell. A very large man with a big head and no neck opened the door and basically told Earl to get lost, at which point Earl flashed his identification and told the man to go get Sam.

Earl waited in the foyer. He didn't have long to wait.

Sam came down the stairs in a hurry.

"Earl! I expected the police, but not you. You've been riding that desk for so long I didn't know you still knew how to dismount."

Earl grinned. The references to his being more cowboy than cop was an old joke between them. "Wish I could say this was a personal visit, but we both know it's not. We need to talk."

"Of course," Sam said. "Library okay?"

"Can your daughter join us?"

Sam's expression darkened. "Right now my daughter is debating as to whether she's still willing to join the human race."

"Damn. I'm sorry," Earl said. "But it's important. Will you let me try to talk to her?"

Sam shrugged. "There's a doctor with her now. If she says it's okay, then you can try."

"Thanks," Earl said. "Lead the way."

Sam went back up the stairs, with Earl right behind him. As they neared the second floor, Earl could hear someone crying. His stomach knotted. Now he remembered why he'd wanted off the streets and behind a desk. He hated facing the families of victims of crime.

Trying to regain some composure, he swiped a hand across his face and then popped a couple of breath mints in his mouth. The sobbing was louder now. He patted the pocket of his jacket, then cursed beneath his breath when he discovered he'd forgotten to get a handkerchief this morning. Already, beads of sweat were forming on his upper lip, a sure sign of anxiety.

"She's in here," Sam said. "Luke's with her."

Earl frowned. "Luke Kelly of Kelly Securities?"

"The same."

"He's the guy you hired to find her, right?"

"In a manner of speaking," Sam said.

"Still on the payroll, I see. So what are you and those guys outside protecting her from?"

Sam turned around. The congenial expression on his face was gone.

"The goddamned television crews...the reporters who won't take no for an answer. You name it. We haven't been able to show our faces in public without causing a stir."

Earl flushed. Sam was defensive. He should have expected it.

"Sorry. But we're trying to find a reason for the murders. She's the logical place to start."

"You're sure that the killer was after Raphael and not the nurse? Maybe Raphael was just a witness who the killer needed to shut up. Did you check that angle?"

Earl frowned. "You know we did, and I can promise you that the man was the target."

"How do you know that?" Sam snapped.

"Because the woman's kill was neat, quick and quiet. Raphael was all doped up. He wouldn't even have known she was dead if the killer had walked out then. But his death was brutal. He fought back. We have DNA beneath his fingernails, hemorrhaging beneath the skin and in his eyes. He was strangled, and it was not an easy way to die. He was the target."

"Oh Lord," Sam whispered, then laid the flat of his hand on the door to Jade's room, as if holding off the hell that had followed her here. Then he looked at Earl. "Don't tell her the details. She can't know. Not now. Maybe never."

Earl nodded.

Sam opened the door.

Earl saw a slim, dark-haired woman curled into fetal position in the middle of the bed. The man at the window was nothing but a dark silhouette against the sunlight until he moved. Earl recognized Luke Kelly.

"What's he doing here?" Luke asked.

"He wants to talk to Jade."

Luke lowered his voice. "Are you crazy? She's in no shape to talk to anyone."

"Look, the sooner I can get some answers, the better off we'll all be. Right now, we don't have anything except a faint image of some guy in a lab coat who nobody knows, walking down a hall toward the isolation ward."

Luke shook his head. "That's not true. You've got my car. Check underneath for fingerprints."

Earl frowned. "What do you mean?"

"They had a wreck at the same time the incident was happening at the hospital," Sam said.

"So what's one got to do with the other?" Earl asked.

"I think someone messed with my brakes. Whether it was

just to slow us down or in the hope of killing Jade, too, I don't know."

Earl dug in his pocket, popped another breath mint and wished it was an antacid instead.

"I didn't know about this," he said. "I'll look into it. In the meantime, I really need to talk to her. So where's the doctor?"

At that point the bathroom door opened and a woman came out with a towel in her hands. She was short and dark, just like her hair. Her olive-green business suit was expensive, her makeup flawless. Earl Walters recognized her and nodded a hello.

"Antonia."

She glanced at Jade, then frowned.

"This isn't a good time," she said.

His opinion of her was less than favorable after she'd once told him he needed his head examined. He'd taken it personally, and they'd been at odds ever since.

"Murder never is," he said, and stood his ground.

Jade rolled over on her side, then sat up on the side of the bed. Her eyes were swollen, her face streaked with tears.

Luke sat down beside her, then bent and whispered something in her ear that Earl couldn't hear. But whatever Kelly said, it captured her attention. She fixed him with a stare that made him wish he'd sent the homicide detectives, instead.

"Miss Cochrane, I am sorry for your loss."

Jade took a slow, shuddering breath and then covered her face with her hands.

Earl's stomach lurched. If she started crying again, he was going to make his apologies and get the hell out. To his surprise, she was trying to pull herself together.

"Thank you," she said.

Antonia DiMatto sat down on the other side of Jade and handed her the damp towel she'd brought from the bathroom.

"Here, dear. Wipe your face. It will make you feel better."

"No, it won't," Jade muttered.

''Do it anyway,'' Antonia said.

Jade wiped the damp towel over her hot, tearstained face, and to her surprise, it felt good.

Earl leaned forward, resting his forearms on his knees. ''I've got some things I'd like to talk to you about.''

Jade looked horrified. ''Are you a reporter?''

''Hell no!'' Earl blurted, then flushed. ''Sorry. That just slipped out.'' He pulled his badge. ''Earl Walters, Chief of Police. Your daddy and I are old friends.''

Jade looked to Sam for assurance. Sam nodded.

''I don't know who killed my Rafie,'' she said; then her voice broke.

Earl pulled his chair closer to the bed. ''Is there anything from your past that you can think of that would set someone off...? Maybe someone who might want either of you dead?''

''Yes.''

It was the last thing he'd expected her to say. He pulled out a notebook and pen.

''Can you give me a name?''

She sat for a moment, staring down at the carpet. Then she took a deep breath, as if she'd just made up her mind about something important, and looked up at Luke.

''There's an old shirt box in the bottom of the last dresser drawer. Would you bring it to me?''

''Sure, honey,'' he said softly, and did as she asked.

The moment the box was in Jade's hands, she felt the burden of it numbing her soul. If she kept this secret, Raphael's killer might get away, but Sam wouldn't have to know. But if she told, Sam wasn't going to want her anymore. She tried to think of how she would survive back on the streets without Raphael, and then knew it couldn't matter. Raphael had died trying to protect her—of that she was certain. Humiliating herself was the least she could do if it brought the killer to justice.

Her hands were shaking as she handed Earl the box.

He opened it, expecting almost anything except the dozens and dozens of drawings. He fingered through them, absently noting the skill of the artist but missing her intent.

"These are really nice," he said. "Are they your work?"

She frowned. "I'm sorry?"

"Your work? Are you the artist?"

She glanced up at Sam and then quickly looked away.

"Yes, but I'm also the victim."

Earl leaned forward. Now they were getting somewhere. "Victim" was a word he understood.

"How so, Miss Cochrane?"

"The faces…they're of some of the…uncles…but not all of them, you understand. Only the ones that I remember." Her finger was shaking as she pointed to the stack in Earl Walters' hand. "They're the ones who smiled. They're the ones who liked to inflict pain."

Antonia DiMatto quickly hid her shock. Now the blank spaces in Jade Cochrane's life were beginning to make sense, as was her reticence to trust.

Earl stared down at the drawings, then back up at Jade.

"I'm not following you."

Jade sighed. "I'm sorry. It's difficult to talk about."

"Tell it anyway," Antonia said. "If you want to get well, tell it anyway."

Sam sat on the bed behind her. Now Jade was surrounded. Luke on one side, the psychiatrist on the other, and Sam at her back. Instead of feeling crowded, it made her feel safe. Then Sam touched the back of her head.

"Honey, look at me," he said.

"I can't," she whispered.

"It's all right," he said. "I know."

She gasped, then looked at Luke as if he'd betrayed her.

"I didn't tell him until they killed Raphael," he said. "He had to know, honey, and you were in no shape for me to ask permission."

She turned around, unsure of what she would see.

Sam took her hands in his, then lifted them to his lips.

"Don't ever be afraid to tell me anything. I love you. Nothing is going to change that."

Jade sagged with relief. "I tried to get away," she said. "I kicked and begged for them to stop. They never did."

"I know, darling, I know. It wasn't your fault...ever."

Earl cleared his throat. "Hey, people. I'm still here, and I'd like to know what the hell is going on."

"Tell him, honey," Luke said. "The more you talk about it, the easier it's going to get."

"Everyone is going to know," Jade said.

"Everyone doesn't matter," Luke said. "The people who know you...the people who love you, will never judge you. Understand?"

She sighed, nodded, then looked at Earl and pointed to the pictures.

"A man named Solomon was the leader of the People of Joy. I lived with them from the time my mother took me away until I was twelve, only mother died about two years after we left here. I guess I was about six when it happened, but I'm not sure. The years all sort of ran together."

Earl nodded, encouraging her to continue.

"About a week after my mother left...I didn't know she was dead for several years until one of the women let it slip, because I thought she'd just run away again, only this time, leaving me behind like she had Sam. Anyway, one night Solomon got me out of my bed and carried me down the hall to the purple room. He laid me down on this bed. There weren't any lights in the room. Only candles. I thought that was where I was supposed to sleep now and told him that I wanted to go back to the other bed, that it smelled funny in there."

A muscle in Earl's jaw jerked. It was the only sign of any emotion. Antonia DiMatto was watching Sam's daughter for signs of a mental breakdown. What she saw was a very troubled, but a very strong woman who'd endured and prevailed.

"Go on," Earl said.

Jade nodded.

"Solomon got mad and told me that since my mother was gone, I was going to have to earn my keep. I told him that if I stood on a chair, I could reach the sink to wash dishes. He stroked my face, then pulled my gown up above my waist, put his hand between my legs and told me it wasn't enough."

"Christ," Earl muttered.

"The man came out of the shadows. I hadn't known anyone else was there. I cried to go back to my room. Solomon pushed me back down on the bed and then left. I...uh, he..."

Jade started to hyperventilate as she struggled for breath.

Luke cupped Jade's face.

"Look at me, honey. Look at me."

Jade's gaze focused.

"Now breathe," he whispered.

Antonia DiMatto moved closer now. "Jade. It's in the past. You are not in the purple room. You are in your own room with your father and with Luke. Do as he says, dear. Breathe."

Slowly the panic Jade felt began to subside. She shuddered, then moaned.

"I prayed to God. He didn't answer."

Luke cursed.

Sam was crying.

Antonia DiMatto knew Jade had a lot of work to do to get beyond the past.

Earl Walters stared at the drawings.

"These drawings..."

Jade shuddered. "The faces. They haunt my dreams. Maybe I haunt theirs, as well."

Suddenly Earl understood.

"Are you saying that the killer is one of these men?"

She shrugged. "It could be any of them...or someone I don't remember...or even Solomon."

"Is his picture in here, too?" Earl asked.

Jade nodded. "Several times. He's the one with the pointed beard."

Earl shuffled through the stack until he found the drawing. She'd drawn an interpretation of the Devil, with Solomon's face.

"Okay," he said softly, then leaned over and awkwardly patted Jade's knee. "Miss Cochrane... Jade... I'm as sorry as I can be that this happened to you. But to flush out the killer, I may need to release this information to the press."

"No," she said. "Please, no. People will think I'm—"

"A miracle," Luke said, and then pulled her close to his chest. "Think of the children you may be saving by doing this. If these bastards are still alive and not behind bars, I can guarantee that they are still molesting."

There was a moment of silence while Jade thought about what Luke had said; then her good sense faded as she focused on the sensation of Luke's arms around her and the rumble of his voice against her ear.

"Jade...answer me, honey."

She shuddered, then looked up. "Do what you have to."

Earl Walters took the drawings and left without looking back.

Fifteen

Once Jade had confessed to the shame of her past, it seemed as if a huge weight had been lifted from her shoulders. She knew that there might be a lot of gossip and curiosity from the press, but she no longer cared. Sam hadn't thrown her out in disgust, and Luke already knew and hadn't turned his back on her. For now, it was enough to get her through whatever else would come.

And another strange thing had occurred during her conversation with Earl Walters. When he'd taken away her drawings, Jade felt as if her guilt had gone with them. The burden of keeping the abusers alive in her mind was no longer needed. The police chief would make sure that justice was served in some way or another. All she cared about now was putting Raphael to rest.

Antonia DiMatto could tell that the need for her presence at Sam's house was past, at least for now. She began gathering up her things. She wanted to talk more with Jade, but now was not the time. Delving into the hell that had been her childhood would have to come after all this was over.

"Are you leaving?" Sam asked.

Antonia glanced at Jade, then nodded. "Yes, but I'll be back…when your daughter is ready. Won't I, Jade?"

Jade sighed. It was obvious the woman was determined. She was also right. It had to come when she could face it.

Right now, she had yet to face the fact that Raphael was really gone.

"I'll let you know," Jade said.

Antonia smiled. "See? She's just like you, Sam. Everything in its own time."

Sam glanced at Jade, then took Antonia by the elbow.

"I'll see you to the door."

"I'll be expecting your call," Antonia told Jade, and then waved goodbye.

As soon as they were gone, Jade turned to Luke.

"Will you take me to see Raphael?"

Luke had known this was coming, and, truth be told, he would rather have taken a beating than do it. But he couldn't tell her no.

"I'll have to check with the police first and see if—"

"I have to see him."

Her eyes were swimming in tears and her lower lip was quivering, but there was a finality in her voice he couldn't ignore. Every time he thought he had a handle on this woman, she blindsided him with nothing more potent than a look or a request.

"I'll make some calls."

"Thank you," she said.

She started to sit down, then lifted her hands to her face, running them over her features as a blind person might do in order to see.

"What's wrong?" Luke asked.

"I feel lost...almost weightless. Raphael was my rock...my anchor. I feel like I need to cry, but I can't. I'm empty. This doesn't seem real. Last week we were fine. At least, I thought we were fine, but it seems I didn't know him after all. I still can't believe he was sick for so long and didn't tell me."

"He was afraid for you, Jade. And I think he was afraid for himself, too. If he had ever admitted aloud how sick he was, he wouldn't have been able to deal with your pity or

his own fear. You not knowing was part of what kept him going."

For a while Jade was quiet; then she finally nodded.

"In a strange way, I guess that makes sense."

"I'll go make those calls now," Luke said.

"Luke? Wait!"

"Yeah?"

"How much danger am I in?"

"I don't know, but I'd guess enough."

"Maybe I should leave to keep from putting you and Sam in harm's way, too."

Shocked, he grabbed her forearms, yanking her toward him. "Hell no! Promise me you won't do anything like that."

"Promises are nothing but words. Action is the only promise I believe in," she said, then pulled out of his grasp.

Luke reached for her again, needing to make certain that she understood the seriousness of what she'd just said.

"Look at me! Whoever killed Raphael isn't through. You want to face him alone?"

"No, but saying that makes me feel like a coward. Before, I let Raphael stand between me and the world because I didn't want to face what had happened to me. I kept telling myself it was in the past and that I was over it. Except I wasn't. The faces…they haunt my dreams. I've let the memories keep me from living a full life. Every time I got spooked, we ran. Raphael kept trying to tell me there was a better way, but I wouldn't listen. You don't understand. I feel like I've killed him, and if something happened to you or Sam, I couldn't bear another man's death on my conscience."

"His death is not your fault, and staying in one place would not have changed Raphael's fate. He began dying the day an infected pedophile had sex with him. And if you haven't thought about it before, it's nothing short of a miracle that it didn't happen to you."

"How do I know it hasn't? I haven't been tested."

"Then we'll have it done today, okay?"

Jade sat with her head down, staring at the floor. Finally she looked up at Luke.

"Do you see what I mean? How ugly is that?"

"How ugly is what?"

"That I'd have to be tested for diseases before..." Suddenly she stopped, but Luke knew what she'd been going to say. She felt guilty that she would have to be tested before she even thought about trying something that, for her, was frightening—dangerous—like falling in love.

"No man is ever going to want someone like me."

"Well, that's blatantly not true," Luke muttered, then changed the subject before she realized he was talking about himself. "Look, honey, what happened to Raphael was horrible, and he paid for it with his life. I don't know how Raphael felt, but if it had been me, I would rather have died fighting as he did than lie in some bed waiting for weakness to claim my last breath."

A stillness settled over Jade as she thought about what Luke had said. She knew he was right. It was just so frightening to accept that someone from their past wanted them dead. She heard a phone ring in another part of the house and wondered how long it would be before that sound didn't make her think of disaster.

"I'm afraid," she said.

"I know," Luke said, and wanted to hold her.

"No...not like what you're thinking," Jade said, and then looked away, as if embarrassed to admit what was in her mind.

"Then what?" Luke asked.

"I'm afraid of going after what I want out of life."

Luke frowned. "How so? What is it that you want that you're afraid you can't have?"

"I want someone to love me." Then her voice broke. "Like a man loves a woman he wants to spend the rest of his life with. I want to be happy, not afraid. I'm so tired of

always being afraid. I want children, but I don't know if I could be a good mother. I don't even know what good mothers do.''

"Like hell," Luke said. "You would be the best, and you know why? Because you've seen the worst, so you already know what not to do."

He sat there with his heart pounding, wanting to tell her someone already loved her, but the knowledge was so painfully new, and he was so afraid of being rejected that he didn't think she was ready to hear it. Not yet. Maybe never.

"Did you and Raphael ever talk about getting married or having children?"

She frowned. "You mean together?"

He nodded.

"No...never. He was like my brother...my best friend...but we could never have been lovers. We'd seen too much of each other's pain." Then she took a deep breath. "And now I need to see him, if for no other reason than to know that for him, the pain is over. Can you understand that?"

He nodded.

"So will you help me?"

"Yes."

"I'm going to change clothes. When you come back from making your calls, we'll go see him, okay?"

Luke didn't know what it was going to take to make it happen, but make it happen he would.

"I'll be right back."

"I'll be ready."

Big Frank was in Nashville getting a haircut when the fishing show on the barbershop TV was interrupted by a bulletin with breaking news. There was a female reporter on the screen who was standing outside a hospital in St. Louis, Missouri, and police cars were everywhere in the background. Then it hit him—St. Louis, Missouri? That was

where Jade Cochrane had surfaced. Suddenly he felt light-headed. He wanted to hear what was being said but was almost afraid of what he might hear. He pointed toward the TV.

"Hey, Sonny...turn up the volume on that thing, will ya?"

The barber complied, then went back to snipping at the shaggy length of what was left of Frank Lawson's hair.

"Ladies and gentlemen, we have just learned of a rather strange twist in the story of St. Louis's own Sam Cochrane and the return of his prodigal daughter, Jade Cochrane. Less than an hour ago, the man with whom Jade Cochrane had been living for the past few years was murdered in his hospital room, as was the private duty nurse that the family had hired to attend him.

Authorities are still searching for clues to the identity of the killer, but right now we're told they have little to go on.

Hospital authorities are staying closemouthed as to the deceased's illnesses, or why the man had been hospitalized in an isolation ward. An unnamed source has told us that the murder victim was dying of cancer, but that doesn't explain why he was under virtual quarantine.

We'll update you with more information as soon as it becomes available. For now, all we can do is say prayers for the families who've lost loved ones and hope the police can track down the killer before someone else has to suffer.

This is Laura..."

Frank was so elated that he blanked out on the rest of the broadcast. Newton had done it! He'd gotten rid of one of only two people who could blow the whistle on him and screw up his chances at the governorship. He leaned back in the chair and closed his eyes as the barber continued to clip and snip. It wasn't until the barber was almost through that Frank realized he'd made a slight error in his counting. Killing this Raphael person, as well as Jade Cochrane, wouldn't do away with everyone who knew his nasty little habits. As long as Otis Jacks still drew breath, Big Frank was not safe.

"You 'bout done here?" he asked.

The barber gave Frank's hair a last snip, then brushed the loose hair from the cape before taking it from around Frank's shoulders.

"There you are, Mr. Lawson. You look fine…real fine."

"Thank you, Bob. Now don't forget who to vote for this fall."

The barber grinned and nodded as Frank tossed down a pair of twenties and sauntered out of the barber shop.

Frank moved through the parking lot, carefully dodging traffic as he headed for his car. He needed to give Johnny Newton a quick call and see what it would cost to add one more name to the list.

At the same time that Big Frank was learning of Johnny's success, Johnny was listening to the same news bulletin. He'd even gone so far as to get out the silencer for his handgun and strap on the knife he'd used to cut the brake line. He wouldn't know until he got there which weapon he might use on Jade Cochrane. Hell, he might even use both.

While he was thinking about finishing what he'd come to do, Luke and Jade were getting into Sam's car. All Johnny saw as he glanced out the window was a black Lexus rolling down the driveway with two people in it. He recognized the woman in the passenger seat and started to run for his car when he realized that following her twice in one day would be worse than careless. He had to assume that whoever she was with would be bringing her back.

Luke's cell phone rang as he was parking.

Jade was already nervous about coming to the morgue, and the sudden and strident ring made her flinch.

"Easy," Luke said.

Jade nodded, although it was not as simple as Luke made it out to be. There wasn't a thing about this whole nightmare

that was easy, especially this. Then she focused on what Luke was saying.

"Are you sure? Nine-point match on the prints? Yeah, I know that's good. Three-time loser? Is his DNA on file? Good. So if it matches what was found under Raphael's fingernails, we've got our perp. Yeah…thanks."

He disconnected. Obviously Jade had heard everything that he'd said, but not the whole conversation, and she deserved to know it all.

"The brakes on my car *had* been tampered with. They got a couple of good prints from underneath the car and got a nine-point match on one of them."

"What's a nine-point match? What does that mean?"

"It means that we know who messed with my car. He's a three-time loser…been convicted and incarcerated three times for everything from assault to assault with intent to kill."

"And he's not still in prison?"

Luke grimaced. "He's been out since '94, compliments of our screwed-up justice system. Earl also told me that the Feds believe he's been working free-lance as a hit man for several years but can't get enough evidence on him to make an arrest."

"What about now?" she asked.

"We can't put him at the murder scene…only messing with my car. At least, not yet."

"What are you saying?"

"The laws are changing. During his last incarceration, they took DNA from him. It's on file. If the DNA they found under Raphael's fingernails matches, then we've got our man."

"How long will that take?"

Luke shrugged. "Sometimes it can take months. Labs are backed up beyond belief. However, knowing Sam, if the cops will let him, he'll pay to have the tests run himself. If so, we

could know enough soon to either exclude him from being the killer or have enough on him to make an arrest.''

"His name…what's his name?" Jade asked.

Luke eyed her carefully, watching her face for a sign that the name might register.

"Johnny Newton."

"Never heard of him…but I didn't know the names, anyway. Maybe I could see his face?"

"As soon as we're through here, I'll make sure to get a copy of his mug shots."

"Okay."

"Okay," he echoed, then got out of the car and hurried to the passenger side. He opened the door, then extended his hand. "Come on, honey, it's time to go tell Raphael goodbye."

Jade clutched his hand while getting out of the car, then didn't let go. They had told her nothing specific about Raphael's defensive wounds, only that he had been strangled, so she was imagining the worst. In a perfect world, this wouldn't be happening, but the only perfection she'd ever known had been the beauty of his face. If the killer had destroyed that, too, she didn't think she could bear it.

Then, as if Luke had just read her mind, he bent down and whispered in her ear, "Are you afraid?"

She nodded.

"Don't be, honey. Raphael is gone. What's left is just a shell of the man you knew. I don't know what you believe about the afterlife, but I believe that wherever Raphael is now, his body is perfect. He's well, and he's home with the Father of us all."

Jade had proclaimed for years that she didn't believe in God; now Luke was asking her not only to believe, but to believe that the best part of Raphael was still living in a place she couldn't see.

She didn't argue the details with him, but thinking of Raphael like that was comforting.

"He never had a father before."

"Well, he does now, honey. Maybe it will be a little easier to think of him that way, okay?"

She pulled her hand out of Luke's grasp.

"Nothing about this is easy."

Luke sighed. There was no use talking anymore. Jade was putting walls between them to buffer the pain that she was feeling, as well as that she had yet to face. He didn't blame her. In her place, he might have done the same thing.

"This way," he said, and led the way inside.

A few minutes later, the chief medical examiners met them and led them deeper along the winding hallways.

"We have a viewing window right here. If you'll wait, I'll tell the—"

"Please...not like this," she said, and then pressed her fingers against her lips to keep from screaming. "I need to talk to him...to let him know that it's okay."

The medical examiner frowned, then glanced at Luke. "We're not allowed to—"

It was the words "not allowed" that fueled Jade's anger.

"Allowed? I'm not allowed to see him because of your rules? No! You're the one who shouldn't be allowed to touch him! I lived with him. I slept with him. I laughed with him." Then her voice broke. "I cried with him. Touching his body now is not going to damage your damned investigation."

"Let her in," Luke said. "What the hell is it going to hurt?"

The medical examiner shrugged, then opened a door and stepped aside.

"After you."

Luke stepped forward. Jade stopped him with a look.

"Wait here," she said.

"Are you sure?"

"No, but it's something I have to do."

He nodded, then stuffed his hands in his pockets and watched her disappear into the adjoining room.

A few moments later the medical examiner returned. He looked at Luke and then shrugged.

"She asked me to leave, too."

"This is really hard for her," Luke said.

"Sooner or later, death comes to all of us."

"Yeah, but we usually have some family left to fall back on. The man lying in there on that slab was the only family Miss Cochrane had for most of her life. In effect, his death is the death of all she's ever known."

The ME whistled beneath his breath. "That's tough."

"Tough doesn't cover it," Luke said, and wished she had not shut him out.

Jade stood beside the slab, trying not to think of the body beneath the sheet. Finally she laid her hand on his head.

"Oh, Rafie...why did it have to come to this?"

He didn't answer. That was the moment when she accepted that she would never hear his voice again. But even if he couldn't answer, there were things she needed to say. She straightened a slight wrinkle in the sheet, then laid her hand on his shoulder.

"I wanted you to know that you were right. I am going to get some counseling. The doctor's name is Antonia DiMatto. You would like her." She choked on a sob, then patted his arm. "Oh, Rafie... I never told you how much you meant to me. I never said the words that were always in my heart, but I'm saying them now. I just hope you can hear me. You saved my life, over and over, without ever asking for anything for yourself. Before I started painting...before I knew I could draw...I never asked you where the money came from that kept us fed and in warm shelters during the winters. I didn't ask, because I didn't want to know. I told myself you didn't—but you did, didn't you? You did, and it killed you didn't it?"

Jade lowered her head. "You were always the strong

one…always the one with the level head. I don't know how I'm going to live without you, but I'm going to try.''

Then she grabbed the edge of the sheet covering his head and started peeling it back. Inch by painful inch, she pulled until the whole of his face had been revealed. When she saw him, her legs went weak with relief.

Even in death, his face—the chiseled perfection of his features, which had always turned women's heads—was just as it had been in life. Unblemished.

She kissed him then, one last bittersweet goodbye. Her lips barely brushed the pale, cold skin of his brow; then she pulled the sheet back over his head and walked away.

Sixteen

Sam was in the living room, watching for Luke and Jade to return, when he happened to look across the street. He stared for a moment, then moved closer to the window. Something was different at Mabel Tyler's house, but he couldn't put his finger on what it was. The yard had been freshly mowed. The flowers in the large urns on her front porch were blooming nicely. Mabel always did have a green thumb. As he looked, it occurred to him that he hadn't seen her in days. Of course, he'd been so preoccupied with everything else, it stood to reason. And Mabel was a very private person. She would never have insinuated herself into the trauma that was going on in Sam's life. Still, he made a mental note to give her a call tomorrow, after everything settled down here. She and her husband had been good friends and neighbors, and even though Edward had been dead for years, he felt a responsibility to make sure Mabel was all right.

Before he could follow up his thoughts, a black Lexus turned the corner at the end of the street. That would be Luke and Jade! Breathing a sigh of relief, he headed for the door.

Someone had tipped off the media that Jade Cochrane had been to the morgue. As a result, they were once more gathering in the vicinity of the Cochrane home.

"Looks like the vultures are back," Luke said, as he turned the corner near Sam's property.

Jade was only vaguely aware of the camera crews lined

up on both sides of the street. Suddenly someone aimed a camera in her direction, and she flinched, as if they had pointed a gun.

Luke saw her jump. "Honey...you okay?"

"No."

He frowned. "Sorry. That was a stupid question."

She looked down at her hands, staring at the length and shape of them in the patch of sunlight coming through the windows.

"He used to tell me they were magic."

"What was magic?"

Jade blinked, a little startled. "I'm sorry. What did you say?" she asked.

"You said they were magic. I asked you what you were talking about.

"I didn't know I'd said that aloud," she said, then leaned her head against the back of the seat and closed her eyes. For a moment there was silence, then a quick, indrawn breath. "My hands. Raphael always said they were magic because I could draw."

"It's a gift," Luke said.

She shrugged off the compliment. "It kept us fed."

"It's more than that. It was also the impetus that enabled your father to find you."

"I suppose, but that gift also got people killed. I can't forget that."

"God forbid," he muttered.

Jade frowned. "What's that supposed to mean?"

"You aren't responsible."

"Yes, I am. Raphael is dead. So is the poor nurse we hired to tend him. They're dead because of me."

"Unless you're the person who hired the killer, you are in no way responsible."

"If you hadn't found us, then—"

"Oh...so now it's my fault? Why? Because I found you,

or because I talked you into coming back to St. Louis? No wait. I know. It's all of the above.''

"That's ridiculous," Jade said.

"Yes, it is, just like your reasons. Why do you always take responsibility for whatever's happening, even when it's out of your control?''

"I don't always do that," Jade said.

"Bullshit," Luke said.

Jade gasped, then glared.

He ignored her.

"We're here," he said, and wheeled into the driveway leading to Sam's house, then parked. He hurried around to Jade's door, but she was already getting out of the car. Luke knew he'd made her mad. He didn't care. At least it was an emotion he could deal with. Constantly blaming herself for the bad stuff that happened in her life was nothing more than a symptom of someone who'd been repeatedly abused.

She stalked toward the house without looking back at Luke. The pain in her gut was so fierce that she thought she might die, and he'd cursed at her. If she'd had something in her hand, she would have thrown it at him. How dare he belittle her part in this horror? How dare he belittle *her?*

Her hand was on the doorknob when Sam opened it. She hurried inside.

"Glad you're home," Sam said. "I'm so sorry you had to go through that. Are you all right?''

Jade stopped. Home? All right? She looked at him then, and the sympathy on his face was too much. It was either hysterics or anger. When Sam continued to talk, she opted for the anger.

"Is there anything I can do? We can talk about a funeral service when—''

She held up her hand, instantly silencing him.

"There will be no funeral service. It would be nothing but more fodder for those vultures out there in their vans, capturing grief with their cameras from people they don't even

know, then delivering it up to the country as they eat their evening meals. I will not be someone's entertainment! No one knew Raphael but me, and I will not see him put in a box and buried in the ground. He hated small spaces."

Luke walked into the foyer just as Jade delivered her ultimatum.

"Hey!"

She pivoted angrily, her eyes glittering with unshed tears.

"Don't take your anger out on your father just because you're pissed off at me," Luke said. "He offered help. Tell him what you want."

"What I want? What *do* I want? Since you know so much, then you tell me. What is it that I want, Luke Kelly?"

He stood for a moment, letting his own anger cool and, for the first time, seeing the barely hidden panic in her eyes. She was scared half out of her mind, but he couldn't help her if she wouldn't let him.

With a frustrated sigh, he tossed the car keys back to Sam.

"Thanks for the loan of the car. Call me if you need me."

"But how are you getting home?" Sam asked.

"That's my problem," he said, and then pointed at Jade. "She's yours."

He strode out of the house, slamming the door behind him as he went.

When the door slammed, Jade felt as if she'd just been slapped. It brought her back to her senses, but not in time to apologize to all concerned. She would start with Sam and deal with Luke Kelly later.

"Sam...I'm sorry. Luke was right."

"About what?" Sam said.

"I don't know why, but I keep shutting out the very people who keep trying to help me."

Sam shook his head. "No need to apologize, dear. I know you're hurting. If you need anything, will you let me know?"

She nodded, then impulsively hugged him. As soon as his

arms enfolded her, her panic began to fade. And because the fear was lessening, she felt comfortable enough to explain.

"Once, when we were much younger, Raphael and I were in L.A. We had no money, and we were camping out in the hills above the canyons. It was late summer, and everything was hot and really dry. Somehow a brush fire got started. I smelled the smoke and ran to the edge of the cliff and looked down. The fire was eating through the brush down in those valleys like crazy. I was so scared and certain we would die in it. But Raphael got me out of harm's way, then made me sit and watch it, pointing out the power of the blaze and then the aftermath of what was left behind. He said that fire wasn't always bad, that sometimes it was necessary to clean up things that had gone untended."

She pulled out of his embrace, then looked up, searching his face for understanding.

Sam recognized her anger as nothing more than a shield to hide how she really felt, and he understood what she was trying to say.

"Yes, fire can be cleansing. You want to have him cremated, don't you?" he asked.

She closed her eyes against the thought, then finally nodded.

"Then it will be done."

"I need to be alone. Can you understand?"

"Yes."

She started toward the stairs, then stopped and turned around. She'd forgotten something.

"Sam?"

"Yes?"

"Thank you."

"You're welcome."

She was halfway up the stairs when this time Sam called out to her.

"Jade?"

"Yes?"

"I'm not going anywhere, so if you need me, just let me know."

Her eyelids felt so heavy that she could barely keep them open. All the sounds around her mingled into a roar, until the only thing she could recognize was the erratic thump of her heartbeat in her ears. She tried to answer, then finally managed a nod. It took everything she had to get herself the rest of the way up the stairs and into her room. Once there, she wanted to undress. She needed to wash the smell of the morgue from her hair and her skin. Maybe then she could forget where she'd left Raphael. If so, then she could pretend this hell hadn't happened.

She got as far as stepping out of her shoes; then she moaned. The sound shattered what was left of her control, and she fell to her knees on the floor. The image of Raphael's face was haunting her as badly as the faces from her dreams, only this time for a different reason. Before, he had urged her to put the faces on paper so that she could forget about them. But this time she was afraid that, with the passage of time, Raphael's face would blur in her memory.

"Oh...oh... I cannot bear this."

She laid the palms of her hands against her breasts, but the pressure did nothing to stifle the pain. Slowly understanding came, and she knew what she had to do.

Draw him. Draw him so you never forget.

She crawled to the table, pulled her drawing pad and a charcoal pencil from off the top, and then sat cross-legged on the floor.

Within minutes, the face she was drawing became recognizable. She wouldn't draw him the way she'd last seen him—lying still and cold on that metal table. She would draw him alive...full of life. She started with the beginning of a twinkle in his eyes and a tilt to the corner of his mouth, just the way he always looked at her when she'd done something foolish. That was the Raphael she wanted to remember. That was the man she would never forget.

* * *

Johnny Newton walked through the darkened rooms of Mabel Tyler's house, turning on lights as he went. It was just after nine o'clock in the evening, and he was hungry. He thought about getting in his car and going out to have something to eat, but instinct told him to lie low.

Still riding on the high of a successful hit, he dug through Mabel's freezer, wanting something sweet. And he found it. A small carton of Chunky Monkey ice cream. He grabbed it and a spoon, then went back through the house, turning off lights, just as he'd turned them on before.

Once upstairs, he settled down in front of the television, opened the carton of ice cream and took his first bite. There was a bit of freezer burn on the surface, but he quickly ate past that. So the old lady didn't use up her food as quickly as she should. So what. He would do it for her.

He aimed the remote between bites, channel surfing for something interesting to watch, and finally settled for old game shows from the seventies and eighties.

"Those were the days," Johnny said to himself, then took another bite of ice cream.

He was almost through eating when his cell phone rang. He glanced at the caller ID and frowned. It was that damned Frank Lawson again. Didn't he watch the news? But the phone continued to ring, and finally he answered it with a curse.

"What the hell do you want?"

Big Frank was taken aback and for a moment couldn't think what to say.

"Look, I know it's you, so start talking before you totally piss me off," Johnny muttered.

Big Frank got a little pissed himself. "Look, you little asshole. I don't know what's got your tail in a knot, but it damned sure isn't me."

"Don't you watch the news?" Johnny snapped. "Your man is dead…just like you wanted."

"Yes, I watch the news, and yes, I already knew that. It's not why I'm calling."

"I'll do the woman by tomorrow," Johnny said. "Then I'm out of here."

"Fine," Frank said. "But the reason I called is to ask you how much it would cost me to add one more name to the list."

Johnny sat up straight and set the empty ice-cream carton aside.

"What's the name and where's the location?"

"Los Angeles. There's a man going by the name of Otis Jacks. Owns a film studio that makes porn. I want him gone."

Johnny smiled to himself. "It's gonna cost you."

"How much?"

"One hundred thousand."

"Fine."

Johnny frowned. From the sound of it, he could have asked for more and gotten it. Still, it was a nice chunk of change for the price of a bullet.

"Got an address on this Jacks fellow?" He reached for a pen.

A few minutes later, he hung up, then tossed the phone aside and took the ice-cream carton to the kitchen and dumped it in the trash. Tonight was going to be busy. He figured he'd better get some sleep now.

It had been hours since Luke had seen or heard anything from the Cochrane home, and he'd spent them in misery, wishing he and Jade hadn't parted company in anger, yet knowing that he could not, in good conscience, have responded any other way.

But now he had an excuse to go over there. He had just gotten a call from Earl Walters, telling him that he could pick up a copy of Johnny Newton's mug shot. They needed to know if he was someone Jade knew. If not, then he'd been

hired by someone else, which meant she needed to see the picture.

He reached for the phone and dialed Sam's number. The moment Sam answered, Luke could tell something was wrong.

"Luke…thank God. I've been on the verge of calling you, but I hated to bother you with family problems."

Luke's fingers tightened around the receiver.

"What's wrong?"

"It's Jade. She won't come out of her room. Every time I got up to check on her, I could hear her pacing…and talking to herself. A couple of hours ago, Velma tried to take her some food, but she didn't respond. I don't know when she last ate or slept, and I'm at my wits' end."

"Did you call Antonia DiMatto?"

"Yes. She says it's grief and to let Jade work it out her own way. But I'm afraid."

Luke frowned. "Are you saying you're afraid Jade will hurt herself?"

Sam's hesitation before responding was answer enough for Luke.

"Look," Luke said. "If I know one thing about your daughter, it's that she's a survivor. She hasn't quit on herself once, despite all that she's been through. Don't sell her short, Sam. She's grieving, not plotting suicide."

"Yes, I think I knew that, I just needed to hear someone else say it. Sorry to burden you with our troubles. Why did you call?"

"It's not a burden, Sam. I care, probably more than I should." Then he sighed and blurted it out, knowing what he'd been feeling had to be said. "I'm doing something Raphael told me not to do," he said.

"What's that?" Sam asked.

"Falling for your daughter."

Sam frowned. "Why on earth would he say something like that? I would be overjoyed."

"I think because he knew what a challenge it would be for Jade ever to trust, let alone be intimate with, another man. He didn't want her hurt. Neither do I."

Sam sighed. "Thank you for being so frank with me. I'm not doing so well as a father, so I'm hardly in a position to criticize."

"We're all off balance," Luke said. "Especially Jade. Her fragile world has been torn apart. It's going to be up to us to help her find a way to put it back together."

"And keep her in one piece in the process," Sam added.

"Exactly," Luke said. "Which is the reason for my call. I have a copy of Johnny Newton's mug shot. I'm not sure Jade will talk to me, but I need to know if she knows him."

"Come on over," Sam said. "Maybe, between us, we can get some answers."

"If you don't mind, I think a united front at this point in her life might seem as if we were ganging up on her. I'd like to try it alone."

"Of course."

"Fine, then I'll see you soon."

"Right," Sam said, and hung up the phone. As he was turning around, Velma came in the room.

"Mr. Cochrane, that yard boy, Kevin, is here. He wants to know if there is anything special you want him to do this time or just the usual?"

"Tell him to just mow and use the weed-eater. The hedges don't need to be clipped until we get some more rain."

"Yes, sir." Then she paused in the doorway. "About your girl..."

"Yes?"

"She hasn't touched the food I left in the hall. Should we do something?"

"Like what?" Sam asked. "We can't force feed her. She'll eat if she gets hungry. Besides, Luke is on his way over."

Thankful that the hard decisions were out of her hands, she went to deliver the instructions to Kevin.

Luke's car wouldn't be repaired until sometime the next day, so he was driving a rental. It was a white two-door Lincoln and smelled too much like pine aerosol for his liking, but it was his for the moment.

Despite what he'd told Sam, he was worried about Jade. If she'd shut herself off from everyone in the house, he could only imagine what devils she was battling alone, and if she wasn't sleeping, he knew why. Before, she'd had Raphael to help keep the demons at bay when she slept. But now he was gone and she was afraid to close her eyes for fear of what would come. "God help her...and me," Luke muttered.

When he got to Sam's, he grabbed the photo, waved to a couple of his employees who were still on duty outside, then rang the doorbell.

Velma let him in.

"He's in the library on a conference call," she said. "He said to tell you to call him if you needed him."

"Thanks. I'll be upstairs."

She shook her head. "Hope you have better luck than we did."

"It's not about luck. It's about perseverance," he said, then, worrying about her fragile mental state, he laid the photo on the hall table and headed up the stairs. The last thing Luke wanted was to confront her with a face from her past without a little preparation.

Jade shuffled from the bed to the table and back again, and everywhere she walked, a picture of Raphael smiled back at her. She'd drawn him in every way that she could remember. But the smiles never changed and the lips never parted and the words never came. Now, instead of drawing comfort from the pictures, she was becoming paranoid, imagining that his smiles turned to taunting laughter, but only after she

looked away. She didn't understand it. Rafie would never taunt her. He'd loved her. But then she would remember that he'd kept secrets—horrible secrets. He'd told everyone else before he'd told her. She wasn't sure she would ever be able to forgive him for that. And she wasn't sure she would ever be able to forgive herself for letting him die alone. It was a dichotomy that was driving her mad.

Then there was a knock on her door. She turned abruptly, her hands curled into fists.

"Go away."

Luke leaned his forehead against the door and closed his eyes. He hadn't expected this to be easy, but the pain in her voice was nearly his undoing.

"Can't do that," he said.

Jade inhaled sharply. It was Luke. Why was he here? He didn't belong here—not in this room. It belonged to her and to Raphael.

"Jade…let me in," he said.

She grabbed a small figurine from a shelf and flung it at the door. It shattered, just as Jade's life had done.

"I said, go away," she repeated.

Luke gritted his teeth and grabbed the doorknob, only to find it locked.

"Open the goddamned door before I break it down," he warned.

For a moment there was silence; then, from the sound of her voice, he could tell Jade was standing near the door.

"You wouldn't dare."

"Try me," he warned.

"You don't belong in here."

It hurt to know that whatever little bit of headway he'd made with her was not only gone, but she'd begun to shut him out.

"I'm not leaving until I see you."

She shuddered, then covered her face with her hands. See

her? She couldn't bear to look at herself. Why would anyone want to see her?

"There's nothing to see."

"Prove it," Luke said. "Open the door now, or I'm coming in my way."

She looked up, defiance in every line of her posture. Then she shouted.

"No, damn you, no!"

The door rocked against his first kick, and when it did, Jade realized he was serious.

"Wait!' she screamed. "Wait!"

Luke paused, his heart pounding, his breath coming in short, angry gasps. He heard the click of a lock being undone and watched as the doorknob began to turn. Then he saw her, and all the anger he'd felt turned to shock.

She was wearing the same clothes she'd had on earlier in the day when he'd brought her home from the morgue. Her hair was wild and tumbled all about her shoulders. It looked as if she'd combed her fingers through it countless times. Her body was trembling—he guessed from physical exhaustion—and the look on her face was one he would never forget. She looked just like that little girl they had found in the mall—the one who'd gotten separated from her mother. Her expression was somewhere between desperation and despair. He took a deep breath, girding himself for whatever might come, and then walked into her room and shut the door.

For a few moments there was nothing between them but two feet of silence. Then he let himself look at what she'd done. Images of Raphael stared back at him from all over the room. And they, like the faces the police chief had taken away, were smiling. It didn't make sense. She'd said that the only uncles whose faces she'd drawn were the ones who'd caused her pain. And then it hit him.

"Oh, honey," he said softly. "Raphael didn't mean to hurt you. But the business of dying is very personal. It's something we all have to do alone. Even if you'd been there—

even if Raphael had died of natural causes—you couldn't have changed what was. You couldn't go where he was going.''

She swayed on her feet. ''I don't know how to do this by myself. I thought I did, but I don't.''

He moved closer. ''Do what?''

''Live.''

He touched her face with the back of his hand, and when she didn't move away, he turned it palm upward and cupped her cheek.

''Oh, baby...it's easy. You just breathe in and breathe out.''

She swayed. Luke picked her up and carried her to the bed, then swept aside the pictures she'd drawn. He drew the covers up to her waist, then pulled a chair up close to the bed.

She watched his every move until he sat down.

''What are you doing?'' she asked.

''Close your eyes,'' he said softly.

''I can't.''

''Yes, Jade, you can. You have to.''

Tears rolled from the corners of her eyes.

''What if I dream?''

''I'll be here.''

''Oh God,'' she said.

''I thought you didn't believe in God?''

''I don't, but on the off chance that He's out there, I don't want Him to forget I'm here.''

Luke scooted out of the chair, then slid onto the side of her bed.

''When you were little, do you remember ever saying your prayers?''

''No.''

''It's real easy...and it will make you feel good. Want to try?''

She shrugged as more tears followed the first.

"I don't know what to say."

"I do," Luke said, and then got down on his knees beside the bed. "You don't have to get up," he said. "Just close your eyes."

Seconds passed, then turned into minutes as Jade thought about what he'd said. Just when Luke thought she was going to refuse, she reached for his hand and then shut her eyes.

Way to go, baby. "Repeat this after me, okay?"

"Okay."

"The Lord is my shepherd…"

"The Lord is my shepherd."

"I shall not want…"

She echoed each phrase that Luke uttered until they had gone all the way through the twenty-third psalm.

"Amen," Luke said.

"Amen."

She was silent for a few seconds; then she opened her eyes and looked at Luke.

"Do you believe that…about walking through the valley of the shadow of death and fearing no evil?"

He nodded.

She sighed. "Okay, I'll give it a try."

Luke got to his feet and had started to sit back down in the chair, when Jade reached for his hand.

"Do you remember when you promised to be my friend?"

"Yes."

"So, if I asked you…as one friend to another…would you do something for me?"

Luke's stomach knotted. Something told him this wouldn't be easy, and still he said yes.

"Would you lie down beside me? I've pretty much never never slept alone, but I'm so tired. If you would only—"

Luke kicked off his shoes as he walked to the other side of the bed. Then he crawled in beside her, and with the covers between them, spooned himself up against her back and then laid his arm across her waist.

She stiffened almost immediately.

Luke sighed.

"I'm not Raphael."

"No," she said quietly. "I can tell."

"If I frighten you, I'll move."

She thought about it for a moment, trying to figure out exactly what it was she was feeling, then decided it wasn't that kind of fear.

"No, don't move," she said. "I just have to think about this a minute."

Luke felt for her in every way there was for a person to feel empathy for another human being, and at the same time, wanted nothing more than to have her turn in his arms and look at him with love and not fear.

He laid his chin against the crown of her head and then whispered softly next to her ear, "Jade, I swear to God, I will never do anything to frighten you or hurt you...not in any way. Please know that you can trust me."

She didn't answer, but she did slide backward just a fraction of an inch, settling into a more comfortable position against him.

Luke closed his eyes and willed himself to stay motionless. If ever he'd needed his body under control, it was now. As Jade settled into an uneasy silence, he forgot about everything—even the photo downstairs in the hall.

Seventeen

Sam came out of the library just as Velma was setting a fresh bouquet of flowers on the table in the foyer. Then he saw an unfamiliar car in the driveway.

"Whose car?" he asked.

"Mr. Kelly drove it here."

"Ah…of course," Sam said. "Must be a rental. His wouldn't be fixed yet. Where is he?"

Velma pointed upstairs. "There was some yelling, then I think he kicked the door. Haven't heard anything since."

Sam shook his head as he looked up the stairs.

"I've never felt so helpless. She's my daughter, and yet she feels like a stranger."

"That's because she is a stranger," Velma said. "You only knew her for four years. She's spent the last twenty on her own. That's going to take some time to get past."

"Mentally, I know that. Still…"

"You're too impatient. Always were," she stated succinctly, then frowned when the doorbell rang. "That's probably the boy wanting his money for mowing."

"I'll get it," Sam said. "Why don't you go on home for the day?"

"Are you sure?" she asked.

"Yes, I'm sure," he said, and went toward the front door as she headed for the back of the house to get her things.

As Velma had predicted, it was the teenager from down the street, coming to collect his pay.

"Afternoon, Mr. Cochrane. Been a hot one, hasn't it?"

"Sure has, Kevin. Come in where it's cool while I write your check."

"Thank you, sir," Kevin said, and sat down in a chair beside the hall table while Sam went to get his checkbook.

As always, he eyed the furnishings with interest. The house was grand, and his dad said Mr. Cochrane's family had lived there since the beginning of St. Louis. He'd heard about the long-lost daughter and had hoped to get a glimpse of her, but no such luck.

The scent of the bouquet near his shoulder kicked up his allergies, reminding him that he'd forgotten to take his medicine that morning before he'd left the house. As if that wasn't enough, his bare legs were itching. His mom had told him not to wear shorts when he was cutting grass, but he'd ignored her. He was a growing young man, but not quite grown up enough to know that sometimes, mother still knew best. He bent down to scratch an itch near his ankle, and as he sat back up, the picture Luke had left on the table caught his eye. He was looking at it when Sam came back with his money.

"Hey, where did you get the picture of Mrs. Tyler's nephew?"

Sam frowned. "I'm sorry? I don't know what you're talking about."

Kevin handed him the picture.

"This guy. He's Mrs. Tyler's nephew."

Sam took it, and as he did, he realized that this was the mug shot Luke had brought for Jade to look at.

"What on earth makes you think this man is any relation to Mrs. Tyler?"

"Well, because yesterday after I mowed her yard, he's the one who paid me. He asked me how much she owed me, then said he didn't want to wake up Aunt Mabel and paid me in cash. That's when I figured he was her nephew." Then he added, "He's not what you'd think, either. He had blood

all over his clothes. He said it was nosebleeds from being a druggie. Man...you wouldn't think Mrs. Tyler would have family like that, would you?''

Sam's heart skipped a beat. Blood? Nephew? He walked back to the window and looked across the street. It was the same scene as the day before. The same yard, the same flowers, the same...

Sam groaned.

"The mailbox."

"Sir?" Kevin asked.

"The mailbox on the street. It's full of mail. I can see it from here."

Kevin followed him to the window.

"Yes, I see. Maybe I'd better go over and get it for her. Her arthritis must really be acting up for her to have left her mail in the box."

Sam's hands were shaking as he handed Kevin the check, then shoved him back down in the chair.

"No. Under no circumstances do you go back to her house. In fact, don't leave this house. Don't move," he said sharply. "I'll be right back."

"But I still have three yards to—"

"Not yet!" Sam said, grabbed the photo and started up the stairs on the run.

He burst into Jade's room.

She was on the verge of sleep when the sound of the door hitting the wall startled her awake.

"What the hell?" Luke said, as he sat up in bed. "She was almost asleep."

"Sorry," Sam said. "But I think you'd better get downstairs fast."

Luke rolled out of bed on the run.

"What's happening?"

"You know Kevin...the kid who mows yards in this neighborhood?"

"Yes, I know him. What about him?" Luke asked.

"It's about this picture you left on the table when you came in. Jade, honey, do you recognize it?"

She leaned forward, then shook her head. "No."

Luke frowned. "That shoots down one theory."

Sam took a deep breath, trying to slow the thunder of his heart.

"But that's not the worst. Kevin says that he's staying across the street in Mabel Tyler's house. He told Kevin he was her nephew."

Luke felt sick. He thought about how easily the killer had eliminated Raphael's nurse. He couldn't imagine Mabel's fate being any kinder.

"Call Earl," he said.

"Kevin is downstairs," Sam said. "Go talk to him."

"Tell him I'll be right there," Luke said, as Sam ran from the room.

Jade staggered as she stood up. "What's going on?"

"There's a good possibility that the man who killed Raphael has been staking us out from across the street in the neighbor's house."

The horror on her face mirrored the horror within. Her eyes widened; her voice started to shake.

"You mean he's been watching us...? All this time he's—"

Luke grabbed her by her shoulders. "Jade! Don't! I need you to keep it together. Don't fall apart on me now."

"Go! I'll be fine. If he's the one who killed Rafie, don't let him get away."

"We won't. But I need something from you first."

"Anything," she said.

He started to touch her, then stopped and shoved his hands in his pockets instead.

"I need to know that you are going to do what I say. You need to promise me that you'll stay right here, inside Sam's house. He'll be with you. Not for any reason do you come

outside. You stay away from the windows. Don't let him get a clear shot at you, understand?''

It was the word "shot" that made Jade realize the danger Luke could be in. And when she thought of losing him, too, she got sick to her stomach. She put her hands on his chest, slightly startled by the warmth, and by the steady rhythm of his heartbeat when hers was going wild.

"I *will* be careful, but what about you? I couldn't bear it if something happened to you, too."

The tenderness of her touch made Luke ache. He wanted so much from her, but he would settle for one sweet kiss.

"Forgive me, Jade."

"For what?" she asked.

"For this," he whispered, then lowered his head.

Before she knew it, he was kissing her.

Jade jerked; then her muscles started to tense. But Luke didn't move. Slowly she began to feel the contact of their lips, then the warmth of his breath against her face. There was no threat, no fear, only an overwhelming need to get closer. She'd never known that touching a man could bring pleasure and not pain.

When he broke the contact, she actually moaned.

Luke deciphered it as fear and instantly regretted his lack of restraint.

"God...I'm sorry, honey. Don't be afraid. I didn't intend to scare you. I just wanted to—"

She put her hand on his mouth.

"You didn't scare me."

Luke's heart skipped a beat. "You swear?"

"It was...it was nice."

Sam yelled at him from downstairs.

Luke stifled a groan. "I've got to go."

Then Jade remembered where he was going. She didn't know how to say what she was feeling, because she didn't recognize the emotions. All she knew was that she didn't want him to go.

"Please," she begged. "Please come back."

"Count on it," Luke said, and then ran out the door and down the stairs.

Jade followed him as far as the hallway, then, remembering her promise, went back inside her bedroom and closed the door. Only this time she wasn't shutting herself in. She was shutting a killer out.

Luke had spoken quickly with Kevin, who had repeated what he'd told Sam, confirming their worst fears.

"Can you drive?" he asked.

Kevin nodded.

He handed Kevin his keys.

"Take my car and go home. Leave your mower here, and when you get home, tell your mother I said for both of you to stay inside and lock all the doors and windows."

Kevin's mouth dropped.

"Sir?"

"Do it," Luke said. "In a few minutes, there will be police everywhere."

"Why? What's happening?"

"That man across the street isn't Mrs. Tyler's nephew. He's a hired killer. I don't want you to get caught in any cross fire."

"Oh man," Kevin said. "He looked so ordinary." Then it dawned on him what hadn't been said. "What about Mrs. Tyler?"

Luke shook his head. "I don't know, but he isn't in the habit of taking prisoners."

Kevin's eyes filled with tears.

"I'm sorry, son," Luke said, and clapped him roughly on the shoulders. "But you need to understand the seriousness of what's happening. Now get home and do as I said."

Kevin nodded, but his hands were trembling as he headed out the door.

Sam came running into the hall just as the door shut.

"Where is Kevin?"

"I gave him the keys to my rental and told him to go home and tell his mother to lock themselves in."

"Good," Sam said. "I was going to tell him to stay here, but maybe that's for the best."

"What about Earl?" Luke asked.

"The police are on the way. A SWAT team is coming, too." Then he shook his head. "I knew something was off at Mabel's, but I ignored it."

"Don't you go getting all guilty on me, too," Luke said. "You read Newton's rap sheet. Whatever he did to Mabel, he did it days ago. It's over and done with, no matter what."

"You don't think she's alive, do you?"

"No."

Sam groaned. "Poor Mabel."

"Mabel is in God's hands," Luke said. "You go stay with Jade. Don't let her out of your sight."

"Where are you going?" Sam asked.

"I've got to let my men know what's going on. There's no reason to assume that Newton knows he's been made. We'll be fine…at least until the cops show. Oh…Sam…do you still have that handgun?"

"Yes."

"Good. Mine's at home. I had no idea this was going to happen or I would have come better prepared."

"Wait here," Sam said. "I'll go get it."

He was back within the minute, handing Luke both the gun and a box of ammunition.

Luke loaded it while he stood, then slipped it behind his back into the waistband of his pants and dropped an extra handful of shells into his pocket as he started for the door.

Sam was sick at heart. "Dear God, how has this all come about?"

Luke paused with his hand on the doorknob. What he was going to say was beyond the bounds of friendship, but it had to be said, whether Sam liked it or not.

"Because twenty years ago, your wife rejected her marriage vows and abducted your child. That's how it came about."

A muscle jerked at Sam's right temple. It was the only sign of emotion he showed, and Luke couldn't tell if it was directed at him or his deceased wife. Then Sam moved.

"I'll have my cell phone with me. Call me if we need to do something different other than stay here."

"I will."

"Uh…Luke?"

"What?"

"Thank you for taking care of us."

Luke shrugged. "I have no choice. If anything happens to me—"

"Then I'll take care of her—for both of us."

Luke stared at Sam for a moment, then smiled. Moments later, he was gone.

Sam started toward the stairs, then paused at the first step. His fingers curled around the newel post, as if gathering strength for the climb ahead of him. His shoulders slumped; his chin dropped toward his chest.

"Oh, Margaret, Margaret…do you know what you've done?"

Then he heard Jade calling from above. He lifted his head and gritted his teeth. The time for worrying about the dead was over. It was time to concentrate on the living.

"I'm coming, sweetheart."

Otis Jacks took the last round of his antibiotic and then winked at himself in the mirror. In thirty minutes, he would leave for his dental visit. He never went early to appointments like this, because he hated to wait. By the time he was through today, the decayed tooth would be gone. After that, he didn't give a fuck what excuse the plastic surgeon came up with next. He would have a new face by the end of the week or he would give the doctor a reason to have to practice

on himself. As soon as he could travel, he would be setting up his new residence in a country that did not have an extradition agreement with the U.S.

He switched on the television and then, out of habit, began surfing channels. Curiously, it was a crawl at the bottom of the CNN screen that captured his attention, rather than the lead story on a crisis in the mideast.

"Man and his nurse murdered in St. Louis hospital. Authorities suspect link to the return of business magnate Sam Cochrane's kidnapped daughter."

Otis's mouth dropped open; then he jumped to his feet. Someone—probably that loser who had called—had blown it for everyone. All he'd had to do was lie low. But hell no. What he'd done was going to unload a closet full of skeletons for sure.

Suddenly the idea of a new face was less important than getting the hell out while the getting was good. He pulled his cell phone out of his pocket and made a quick call.

"Francoise…it's me, Jacks. Are my papers ready?"

"Not quite. You said—"

"Plans change. I need them by tomorrow morning," Otis snapped. "Finish them now. I'll make it worth your while."

He hung up, then grabbed his car keys and headed out the door. He was going to be early to his dental appointment after all.

Johnny Newton's hand wasn't doing so good. The wounds were red and puffy, and there was a red streak running from one of them toward his wrist. Despite his meager attempts at doctoring, it had gotten infected. He'd always heard that fingernails carried loads of germs. Obviously the old saying was right.

"Sorry son-of-a-bitch," Johnny muttered, as he dug through Mabel's medicine chest for something stronger than alcohol. His constant use had depleted the stash. He found

nothing left but an out-of-date tube of antiseptic ointment. 1992? Fuck.

With no other options but the nearly empty bottle of alcohol, he poured what was left over the festering wounds, then tossed the empty bottle in the trash. He glanced at his watch. There were only a couple of hours left until nightfall, which he'd decided would be the time to strike. Carefully he parted the bathroom curtains just enough to look at the house across the street. The guards were still there. He frowned. It was too late to rethink his options, but if he had it to do over, he would have popped the woman when he had the chance and taken the guy out on his way out of town.

Never one to dwell on a mistake, he moved away from the window, still confident that he could make all this work. Besides, he had the chance to make an easy hundred thousand just for offing one man when this job was done. Once it got dark, he was going to pay a little visit to the house across the street, then head to L.A. But he wouldn't do the job there until he knew for sure the money was in the bank. No sir. Johnny Newton's father might have been a fool, but he hadn't raised one.

He moved through the second story of the house, poking in drawers and cubbyholes, more out of boredom than with intention to steal. A few minutes later, he heard a car starting up across the street. He picked up his binoculars and, out of curiosity, looked to see who was behind the wheel.

It was a kid. He shrugged and started to turn away when it dawned on him that he'd seen that kid before. He was the kid who'd mowed Mabel's lawn. He trained the binoculars on the kid's face. He looked weird, all wild-eyed and slack-jawed.

"What the hell?" he muttered, and shifted his gaze a little bit to the left. "His lawn mower? Why is he leaving without that?"

A few seconds later, a tall, dark-haired man came out of the house and walked down the driveway to the street and

spoke to one of the guards. Johnny frowned. Something was going on. He could feel it.

The man stayed at the street with the guard, then suddenly took his leave. Johnny watched the man disappear around the back of the house, but he never returned. Finally he convinced himself that what he'd seen meant nothing. He laid down the binoculars and thought about calling pizza delivery. He'd been thinking about one all day. Trouble was, he doubted if Mabel was in the habit of calling out for her meals, and he didn't want to draw undue attention. Cursing the state of affairs in which he now found himself, he went downstairs to raid Mabel's kitchen one more time.

The skin on Luke's neck was still crawling, even after he'd gone around to the back of Sam's house. He couldn't prove it, but he would have been willing to bet that Johnny Newton had been watching them from a window of Mabel's house. It made him sick to his stomach, just thinking of what must have happened to her, but common sense told him that Johnny Newton would not have saddled himself with a hostage.

He quickly explained to the guards in the back about the imminent arrival of the police and also told them to stay out of the way. They were there as protection for the Cochranes and nothing else. As soon as they understood what was going on, he slipped out the back gate and ran down the alley. If he was lucky, he could circle around to the back of Mabel's house before the police appeared. That way, if Newton got wind of what was happening before they arrived, maybe he could head him off.

Sam knocked on Jade's door. "Honey, it's me. May I come in?"

Jade ran to the door and opened it wide. "I'm so scared."

He nodded. "So am I. I thought, if you didn't mind, I'd wait it out in here with you."

Her expression betrayed her relief. "No, I don't mind. In fact, I'm grateful."

"Sorry about disturbing your rest a while ago," Sam said. "I know you didn't sleep last night."

Jade could tell how hard Sam was trying to help. She could only imagine how he felt as she constantly shut him out. Raphael had begged her to be open to belonging to her family again. Now she knew how right he'd been. If it wasn't for Sam and Luke, she would have been lost through all of this. She wrapped her arms around his waist and leaned her head against his chest.

"No, I didn't sleep. I kept imagining Raphael on that metal table in the morgue, remembering what his last moments had been like, then knowing he'd faced them alone. I took my grief out on you and Velma…and then Luke, and I'm so sorry. I know you're getting tired of hearing me constantly apologizing for my behavior. I don't want you to think I'm ungrateful, because I'm not. You made Raphael's last days bearable, and for that I will always be grateful."

Sam took her in his arms. "Honey…I did it because I love you, and I knew you loved him. It's that simple."

Jade sighed. "Simple was not a word in our vocabulary," she said. "Everything we did was such a struggle."

Sam hugged her, then urged her over to the bed.

"Why don't you lie down…at least for a bit? I promise I won't leave you alone, and if you happen to fall asleep, so much the better."

Jade shook her head. "I'll sit down if you will, but there is no way I'll be able to sleep. Not as long as I know Luke is in danger."

"You like him a little, don't you?" Sam asked.

Jade looked startled. "Who? You mean Luke?" Then she quickly looked away. "Sure I like him. He's been very good to me."

"Is gratitude all you feel?"

Jade shrugged. "I don't know."

Sam sat down on the bed beside her, then took her hands.

"We missed so many firsts with each other, didn't we?" he said.

Jade nodded.

"No first day of school. No first roller skates or first bike. No first date or first prom."

Jade saw his eyes fill with tears.

"I am so sorry I didn't find you," Sam said. "I feel such horrible guilt for what happened to you. I should have seen Margaret's unhappiness. I should have looked for you longer…tried harder…something…anything." Then he shuddered. "Anything to avoid what happened to you."

"It happened. I survived it. I'm past it."

Sam looked up. "Are you? I mean, really past it?"

Jade shrugged. "I don't know. I like to think I am. But I've never tested myself to see if I could have a normal relationship with anyone."

"Would you want to?" he asked.

Jade looked down at the floor, then up at a shadow in the corner of the ceiling.

"I wonder what's happening across the street. Do you think it would be safe if we peeked out to—"

"Jade?"

She frowned. Sam wasn't going to let her change the subject. So be it.

"You're talking about Luke, aren't you?"

"You may call this meddling, but since I never got to be a father in all the ways that count, I would like to think that I can be a friend."

"Anyone can be a friend," she said. "I think I'd like you better as a father."

Suddenly Sam's vision was blurred. He tried to speak but couldn't get past the tears. Then Jade laid her head on his shoulder and patted his knee.

"If you don't mind…I think I might try calling you Dad."

"Mind? Oh, honey…" He put his arms around her and then pulled her close. "It would make me very happy."

"I think it would make me happy, too," she said. There was a long silence, then she added, "As for Luke, he frightens me a little. But I've already lost Raphael, and it frightens me even more to think of life without Luke, too."

Sam smiled to himself as he pulled her close.

Had Luke known what Sam and his daughter were discussing, he might have hesitated at what he was about to do. But the thought of Johnny Newton escaping from the police was enough to keep him moving. Soon he had circled the block and was coming in at the edge of the Tyler property from the back.

He was behind the detached garage and trying to figure the best way to get into the house when he saw a strange vehicle parked in Mabel's garage.

With a quick glance toward the house, he slipped inside, then moved between the cars, breaking off all four of the valve stems on the rental's tires. The quiet hiss of escaping air was all he needed to hear. Newton wouldn't be going anywhere in that car.

Once again he glanced toward the house. All was still silent, but as he was contemplating his first move, he saw the first police car pull up in front of the house. He lost count after the sixth car and knew that an equal amount or more would have arrived from the other direction.

It was only a matter of time before Newton saw them. Which meant he would do one of three things. Take a stand and negotiate—possibly claiming he had Mabel as a hostage—make a run for it, or shoot it out. Without waiting to see what he would do, Luke slipped out of the garage, then headed for the back door.

It was locked, which didn't surprise him. He didn't have his lock picks with him, and shooting his way in, or breaking a window, would only alert Newton. On the off chance that

Mabel was still alive, he needed to find a way to get into the house before Newton took her as a shield and started shooting at the cops.

The Tyler house had a full basement and the windows were old. All he had to do was find one that no longer locked and come in from below.

Newton was polishing off a can of Vienna sausages when he happened to glance out the kitchen window. A police car sped past. His heart thumped; then he reminded himself that cops had been coming and going across the street ever since his arrival. It didn't mean a damn thing. But when the second, then the third flew past, his instinct for survival kicked in. He tossed the can into the sink and ran toward the front of the house, pulling his gun as he went. What he saw made him panic. The cars hadn't gone across the street. They were gathering in front of this house.

"Fuck, fuck, fuck," he muttered, as he headed for the back of the house. But before he could get out the door, he saw an armed man climbing onto the top of the garage, then dropping out of sight. A sharpshooter. Johnny's luck had run out.

"Come on, Johnny boy...you've been in worse spots than this and come out smelling like a rose. Just think. Think. There's got to be a way."

Then it hit him. There were a thousand places to hide in this old house. But he had to make them think he was gone. He dashed back through the rooms and then upstairs, threw everything he'd brought back into his suitcase, then ran back downstairs. They would probably check the attic, but once they found Mabel's body—and they would find it, of that he was certain—they would never suspect he was hiding in the same place. Without hesitation, he headed for the kitchen. Just as he started down the stairs, he remembered the Vienna sausage can and ran back to the sink. He took it, and the lid, and then dug through the trash can, burying them deep within the depths.

There was motion toward the front of the house, and he thought he could hear them running on the roof. It was time to go to ground.

The moment Luke dropped through the window to the basement floor, he knew Mabel was dead. The heat of a Missouri summer and the dark, enclosed cellar had enhanced the putrefaction process. Stifling the need to gag, he took out his handkerchief and held it against his face as he started toward the stairs. Then, to his shock, the door above suddenly opened. He froze, highlighted by the sudden light, then grabbed his gun and took aim. To his surprise, the footsteps that had started his way suddenly stopped. He could hear someone moving around in the room above. It was all the break he needed to take cover. Hoping that Newton would be afraid to turn on any lights in the cellar, he ran for the stairs, then flattened himself in the corner against the wall.

Johnny grabbed his suitcase and started down the stairs. Mabel's stench hit him square in the face before he'd pulled the door shut.

"Oh crap," he muttered, then coughed and gagged as he stumbled down the stairs on the run.

There was just enough light coming through the basement windows for him to see the outlines of the doors. He remembered where he'd put Mabel. He damned sure wasn't opening that one. But there were dozens of cubbyholes. What he needed was a way to get between the walls. He'd seen old houses like this before. In fact, he'd grown up in one. Years of remodeling always left nooks and crannies that no one would suspect were there. All he had to do was find the right—

"Newton! Drop your gun and don't move!"

Johnny squealed out in shock and dropped his suitcase. He spun toward the sound but saw nothing except darkness.

"Who the hell are you?" he said, waving his gun in front of him as he continued to move back.

Luke could see the faint outline of a gun and dropped to his knees. He stretched out on the floor until he was flat on his stomach and as far below the range of flying bullets as he could get.

His finger was steady on the trigger as he waited for a clear shot. Seconds later, Newton silhouetted himself against one of the windows. Luke rose up on his elbow, judged the distance from Newton's waist to where his knees should be and shot twice.

Pain splintered Johnny's mind as he fell. He heard someone screaming as he emptied his gun. But he was unaware that the screams were his own and that his shots had all gone into the ceiling. It wasn't until he tried to get up and run that he realized he couldn't move. He started beating his empty gun against the floor and screaming for help.

Suddenly a long shadow separated itself from the space beneath the stairs and came toward him.

"Who are you? What the hell have you done?"

Luke could hear footsteps running through the rooms. They would have heard the shots. It was only a matter of time before they found them. But before they did, he wanted to pass on some good news to Johnny Newton.

"You looked better in your mug shot," Luke drawled, as he kicked aside Newton's empty gun and then leaned over, so that Newton could more clearly see his face.

"You!" Johnny groaned, and then arched off the floor as the pain from the shattered bones in his knees began to increase. "Fuck, oh, fuck, you sorry bastard. What have you done?"

"I didn't kill you," Luke said; then he pointed his gun at Johnny's hands. "Someone else has already done the job for me."

"Get me a doctor. I'm bleeding to death," Johnny screamed.

The footsteps were in the room above them. Luke walked to the foot of the stairs and yelled up.

"We're down here!" he called. "Newton is down. I'm unarmed."

Then he laid his gun on the stairs and hurried back to Johnny. There were things he wanted to say before they carted the man off.

"Raphael didn't die without a fight, did he?"

"I don't know what you're talking about," Johnny said. "If you're a cop, you gotta get me some help."

"That's just it. I'm not a cop," Luke said. "I'm a friend of Jade Cochrane's. You killed someone she loved. Who hired you?"

"Fuck you!" Johnny screamed.

Luke kicked Johnny's leg just above the knee. The man screamed at the same time that the cellar door flew open.

"It's me. Luke Kelly. Turn on the lights as you come down. My gun is on the last step."

Newton cursed as the room filled with cops.

"He shot me!" he screamed. "Help me before I bleed to death!"

Luke straightened, then looked at the SWAT team, along with at least a half-dozen cops, all with guns trained on him, as well as Newton.

"As you can tell from the smell down here, our friend Newton has done away with his hostess before the party was over. I don't know where she is, but the body you find down here is what's left of Mabel Tyler, the owner of this property. She was a nice old lady and didn't deserve to die like this. Also, when you compare DNA, I'm quite certain you will discover that this is the man who murdered Raphael and his nurse at St. Louis Memorial."

"To hell with you!" Newton shrieked. "To hell with all of you. I need medical attention."

One of the cops got on his radio and told the paramedics, who were waiting above, that the scene had been secured and

where to come to find their patient, while the others began a search for Mabel Tyler's body.

A couple of cops stood guard over Newton. But Luke wasn't through with the man yet. He was going to give him something to think about before he left.

He squatted down beside Newton and pointed to his hands.

"Raphael got a piece of you before he died, didn't he?"

Newton was half out of his head with pain.

"You mean my hands? Fuck my hands! I'm bleeding here," he moaned.

"You're also dying," Luke said.

Newton moaned. "Damn you."

"Oh, not from the gunshots. They'll fix you up. I don't know whether they can save your legs or not, but they'll probably save your life…so you can die later."

Johnny began to claw at his legs as the paramedics arrived and began mopping up the mess Luke had made of Newton's body.

"Shut him up. Make him stop. I don't know what he's talking about," Newton moaned.

"Sorry, I thought I'd made myself clear," Luke said. "Those cuts on your hands…they're from Raphael's fingernails, right? Well, remember the blood that was all over his body when you were through choking the life out of him? I'd bet my life that a good portion of it got on you…and in those scratches he left on your hands."

"So what? So what? The bastard was dying of cancer. I just hurried the process along. Now shut up and leave me alone!"

"Johnny, Johnny…you're still missing the point. Yes, Raphael had cancer, and yes, he was dying. But the cancer was just a sidebar to the real reason he was sick. He had full-blown AIDS. Remember all that blood? I'd lay odds it's now in you, too."

The shock of what he'd been told was enough to momentarily block out all Johnny's pain. In that moment, time

seemed to stand still. He thought back to the hospital and the look on that sick bastard's face as he'd dug his fingernails through the surgical gloves into Johnny's flesh. Now Johnny knew why he'd been smiling.

He closed his eyes and started to scream.

Eighteen

Sam was sitting quietly, still savoring the joy of hearing his daughter call him Dad. Then he glanced down at Jade. Despite her insistence that she was too worried to sleep, her eyes were closed and she'd gone very still.

He was thinking about the best way to lay her down without waking her up when suddenly he heard the sounds of what appeared to be a car backfiring. But he knew better. Before he could move, Jade was on her feet. She'd heard it, too.

She grabbed his arms, her eyes wide with sudden fear.

"Did you hear that? Were those gunshots?"

"I think so," he said.

"It's Luke," she said, and then bolted from the room.

Sam caught her in the hall and pulled her back against his chest.

"Wait! You have to wait, remember? We have no way of knowing who's firing at whom. It's safer up here, away from the possibility of stray bullets."

"What if the police didn't come? What if—"

"We can see if they're there from my bedroom window."

"Show me," she begged.

They both ran to the other wing, uncertain of what they might see.

"No! Look! It's okay," Sam said, as he peered through the drapes. "There are police cars everywhere...and look,

there's the SWAT team van. Luke is certainly not alone. They have everything under control."

"Thank God," she whispered.

"Come away from the windows," he said. "It's not safe."

She did as he asked and followed him back to the head of the stairs. When he would have urged her back to her room, she refused.

"I'll just wait here," she said, and sat down on the top step. "That way we can see him when he comes through the door."

Sam sat down beside her without comment. He'd already seen through her act. Jade cared more for Luke Kelly than she was ready to admit. All they needed now was for Luke to come back through that door.

Luke watched the paramedics as they started an IV in Johnny Newton's wrist, then did what they could to stop the bleeding before they loaded him on a stretcher and carried him up the basement stairs.

Newton screamed and cursed all the way up and then out of the house, while the officers and detectives who'd stayed behind continued searching for the source of the foul odor in the basement. Luke kept remembering the last time he'd talked to Mabel Tyler. It had been just after Easter, and she'd been telling him a story about the egg hunt they'd had for the children at her church. She'd gotten so much fun out of the children's antics, which had sent her into a state of reminiscing about her own childhood days, and her regrets that she and Edward had never been able to have children of their own.

Now, because of Johnny Newton, she was rotting away in some corner of her own basement. It was enough to make Luke regret not killing the sorry bastard.

Thomas Haley was a homicide detective who'd known Luke for years. He walked over to the steps where Luke was sitting and then thumped him roughly on the back.

"Damn, Kelly, you did a number on him, didn't you?"

"I'm thinking I should have killed him."

"But you couldn't, because he's not the end of this, is he?"

"We don't think so," Luke said. "Until we know who hired him, Sam Cochrane's daughter is still not safe."

"The chief has been circulating the drawings in the department," Haley said, and then glanced at Luke to gauge his reaction. "It's a damn shame what happened to her. It's a lot worse to think that when all of that comes out, the media is going to have a field day with her."

"They already are," Luke said.

"Still, it's damned gutsy of her—and smart, too. Those are almost as good as snapshots. Problem we're gonna have is that so much time has elapsed. Way I understand it, this happened to her in the span of about six years...from the age of six to about twelve. Is that right?"

Luke nodded.

"So we're looking at almost a twenty-year difference, in some cases. Our problem is going to be that these men will have aged tremendously. Hell, some will have died, others gone bald, gotten fat. You name it."

"We can hope that some of them have already been incarcerated."

"Yeah," Haley said. "There's that. Still, she must be quite a woman to be willing to tell the world."

"She's that and then some," Luke said.

Before Haley could say more, one of the officers suddenly gave out a shout.

"Over here," he yelled.

Luke looked up. The officer had opened a small closet door. From where he was sitting, Luke could see the toe of a shoe.

"Damn it," he muttered, and then went up the stairs.

He walked through the rooms, his stride lengthening as he neared the front door. By the time he was outside, he was

jogging. As he started across the street, he started to run. He'd dealt with enough death for today. He needed to see Jade, and to tell Sam about Mabel. Damn Johnny Newton. Damn him to hell.

When Jade heard the front door open, she jumped to her feet.

Luke was coming through the door as she started down the steps. When he looked up and saw her, the expression on his face made her stumble. But then she caught herself and kept moving toward him.

Luke took the stairs two at a time. He met Jade halfway and then stopped. She began touching his shoulders, then his chest, running the flat of her hands along his body to assure herself that he was unharmed.

"We heard shots," she said softly.

Luke nodded.

"Is he dead?"

"No."

"Are you all right?"

"Yes."

Jade sighed, then leaned forward and put her arms around his neck and laid her cheek against his shoulder.

Luke was stunned. For a moment he was afraid to move for fear of messing up a good thing, but when she didn't pull back, he took it as a positive sign and wrapped his arms around her waist.

Luke heard footsteps on the stairs. He looked up. Sam was coming toward them.

"Mabel?" he asked.

"Sorry, Sam. My best guess is that he killed her within minutes of entering her house."

"Poor Mabel," Sam said. "She was probably scared out of her mind." He passed Luke and Jade on the stairs as he descended. "I've got to call Brooks Bentley. I think he's still her lawyer. He'll know what to do."

"Dad?"

The word lifted Sam's sorrow. "Yes, honey?"

"I'm sorry about your friend."

He touched her briefly, stroking her hair, then the side of her face.

"And I'm sorry about yours," he said, then continued down the stairs.

As soon as they were alone, Luke shifted so that he could see Jade's face.

"You called him Dad."

"Yes."

"Good for you," he said softly, then kissed the side of her cheek. "At the risk of getting my face slapped, I'm going to remind you that you need to be in bed."

"Surely you didn't expect me to sleep while you were being a hero?"

Luke shook his head, then ran his finger down the curve of her cheek, marveling at the softness of her skin and the startled expression in her eyes.

"I need to tell you something."

"Okay."

"I wanted to kill him. I've never had that feeling before. For what he did to Raphael and his nurse, and what he did to Mabel, he deserved to die."

"But you didn't do it."

"No...because we need to know who hired him."

"He didn't say?"

Luke thought about Raphael and the wounds he'd inflicted on Newton's hands. He'd been fighting back the only way he'd known how. He admired him for that. And he remembered the satisfaction he'd felt in giving Johnny Newton the news about Raphael's parting gift.

"We talked about other things," Luke said. "If the police find out anything, they'll let us know."

"What if he won't talk? What if whoever hired him finds out he failed and then sends someone else to finish the job?"

"That's why I'm here," Luke said.

Jade looked startled. "Is Sam paying you?"

"In the beginning, he offered. I turned it down."

"And now?"

Luke slipped a thumb across the inside of her wrist. Her pulse was rapid and irregular. He didn't like that any more than he did the dark, haunted shadows in her eyes.

"I'm here because I want to be," he said gently, then picked her up. "Honey, you're about to pass out from exhaustion."

"I know."

"You have to sleep."

She laid her head on his shoulder. "Yes... I know that, too."

"Are you afraid?" Luke asked.

When she answered, her voice was so soft he had to lean over to hear what she said.

"I don't think I can sleep without Raphael."

Luke started up the stairs with her head bobbing limply against his arm.

"First time for everything," he said, and toed the door of her room open, then carried her to the bed.

Jade rolled over onto her side. Her eyes were closed before Luke finished pulling up the covers.

Then he leaned over, brushed the hair from her face and kissed the side of her cheek.

"Luke?"

"Yes, baby."

"Will you stay...at least until I go to sleep?"

"Yes."

"Okay then," she said, and fell through the hole in her mind.

A few minutes later, Sam tapped lightly on the door. Luke got up from the chair and hurried to answer.

"She's asleep," he whispered, and then stepped out into the hall.

"Thank God," Sam said. "I don't know how to thank you for all you've done. You don't have to stay any longer. I can sit with her now."

"No. I promised her I'd stay." Then it dawned on Luke that Sam might not want him there. "If it's okay with you."

"Anything that makes her happy pleases me," Sam said. "On another note, I talked to Bentley. He was still Mabel's lawyer and is as horrified as the rest of us are at what's happened. Also, the coroner has released Raphael's body. I called a crematorium. They'll call when the ashes are ready to be picked up." Then he shuddered. "I hear myself saying this, but it doesn't seem real. You found Jade, and I cannot express in words the extent of my joy. But there's been nothing but despair since her return. I'm so afraid that she's going to think of this place as...as...I don't know...bad luck. What if she wants to leave me? I don't think I could bear to lose her again."

Luke touched Sam's shoulder in a comforting gesture.

"You still think that? After the breakthrough you had today, with her calling you Dad? Think, man. Because of all the hell that's been happening, you and this home have become her refuge. Don't you see, the tragedies have brought you both together sooner than might have happened otherwise."

Sam leaned against the wall, then shoved his hands through his hair.

"You're right. Of course you're right. But sometimes I'm almost afraid to go to sleep for fear that it will be a repeat of the first time when she disappeared."

"I give Jade more credit than that," Luke said. "You should, too." Then he glanced at his watch. "It's almost eight. Why don't you have an early night?"

Sam rolled his eyes. "I almost forgot why I came up. You

haven't had a bite of food for hours. Can I bring you something?"

"No. I'm fine. Are you okay with me staying here with Jade?"

Sam nodded. "I'm okay with anything that will make her happy again. So I'll see you in the morning. You know where my room is if you need anything."

"Don't panic if you see someone moving around outside in the night. I left a couple of men on guard. One in front, the other in back, although I don't think it's necessary."

"Thank you, Luke, for being more than a good friend."

"Sleep well," Luke said.

Sam waved goodbye.

Luke slipped back into Jade's room and quietly closed the door. He started back to his seat by her bed when he stopped, retraced his steps and turned the lock.

Satisfied that they would not be bothered any further tonight, he stepped out of his shoes, tossed his shirt on the table, then sat back down near her bed. The springs squeaked softly as the chair absorbed his weight; then, once again, the room was silent.

"Come here, baby girl...let Uncle Peter see what you've got under that pretty robe. Ooh yeah...what a pretty nightgown. I like pink, don't you?"

"Your breath smells funny," Jade said.

The smile on Peter's face slid sideways. So the little bitch doesn't like the smell of brandy?

"You're not supposed to criticize your elders. Uncle Peter is gonna have to spank you for that."

Jade woke up in a sweat, her heart pounding. She turned to look for Raphael and in that second remembered. But before the sadness could engulf her, she realized that Luke was still there. He'd fallen asleep, chin forward, long legs sprawled.

She took a deep breath and made herself relax. It was okay.

She wasn't alone. Then she looked at Luke again, this time from a different perspective. There was a faint light coming through the windows, as well as a pale yellow glow from the night-light in the bathroom. In the shadows, he took on a completely different persona—one that she'd shied away from looking at before. But now, when he was unaware that she was looking, she sat and gazed her fill.

His feet were bare, as was his chest. She could tell from the strain of muscles against his pants that his body was very well toned. Unlike Raphael, his face was not perfect, but there was a strength and assurance in it that Raphael would never have had. It came from always knowing who he was, and that he was loved.

His hair was thick and dark, and she wondered what it would feel like to touch. Would it be springy, or would it curl around her fingers? Her gaze slid to the waistband of his pants. He'd undone the button, but not the zipper. The waist lay slack against his belly. She wondered if his legs were as long as they looked, and then suddenly imagined him naked.

An odd, unfamiliar ache suddenly drew at the muscles deep in her belly, hitting quick and hard and making her breath catch in the back of her throat.

She clasped her hands to her mouth, quickly stifling a soft groan. She'd seen Raphael naked before. It had never made her feel this way. So she sat and she stared until her fingers began to twitch. Quietly she crawled out of bed, got her sketch pad and her pencil from the floor beneath the table, and then got back into bed. Sitting cross-legged on the mattress, she began to draw.

Luke didn't know how long he'd been aware of the sound, but he thought it had been penetrating his dreams for some time. It was an intermittent scratch—like a rat trying to eat through the outer wrappings of a box—interspersed with the sounds of someone's breath. Without moving, he opened his eyes, and then he saw her.

Jade was awake, and not only that, she was drawing. At first he thought she'd had another bad dream and was drawing the face, as he'd seen her do before. But then he realized that every so often she would glance over at him, study him for a moment, then return her attention to the drawing pad. She was drawing *him*.

He didn't move and tried not to change the pattern of his breathing. It was strange, knowing that she was looking at him without really seeing—oblivious to the fact that he was watching her face.

And such a face. Expressive—shaded with the lingering remnants of exhaustion—yet still so very beautiful. Her hair was a jumble around her face, and her clothes were all crumpled, as if she'd slept in them, which she had.

And so Luke turned the tables on Jade and, unbeknownst to her, became the voyeur.

Jade's back was starting to ache. It was the first sign she had of how long she'd been bent over the drawing pad without proper light or a table. She looked at the drawing one last time, swiped the charcoal pencil sideways on the paper to give a darker shadow to the valley between Luke's pecs, and then stifled a groan as she stretched.

"Are you through?"

She gasped. Luke's eyes were open.

"How long have you been awake?"

"Long enough."

Luke sat up, then stretched his arms above his head and yawned.

Again that funny ache dug a little deeper into Jade's belly. Suddenly the room was too crowded and too warm.

"May I see?" he asked.

Jade closed the drawing pad and then tossed it and the pencil on the floor on the other side of the bed.

"It's not finished," she said, then made a face at the mess

on her hands. "Charcoal. I need to wash." She got up slowly, keeping her distance from Luke.

He listened to the sound of running water in the bathroom, then waited for her to come out. The silence afterward was long and deafening, but she didn't appear.

"Jade?"

"What?" she called.

"Do you want me to leave?"

The door flew open. She was standing in the doorway with her hands clutched against her belly.

"No."

"Then come back to bed. You must be exhausted."

Still she stood.

He got up. "Is something wrong? Are you ill? If you are, I can call Sam. He said to let him know if—"

"No. I'm not ill."

He sat back down to give her space and tried to smile.

"Good. So if you're not sleepy, do you want to talk? Or maybe you're hungry? I'll bet you haven't eaten."

"I'm not hungry."

He sighed in frustration. "I'm running out of questions. You're going to have to give me some hints."

She took one step into the room, then stopped in the moonlight. The breath caught in the back of Luke's throat.

"Do you know how truly beautiful you are?"

"We never see ourselves as others see us," she said, then started to tremble. It was what she had wanted to hear, but she didn't know if she should be afraid of where it would lead.

"I was very afraid for you when you left the house today."

"I know," Luke said. "But I was a cop for years before I began Kelly Security. I knew what I was doing."

"That doesn't absolve us of worry."

"I know. I'm sorry you were frightened. Would you like to sit down?" Luke asked.

She crossed the floor quickly and then jumped into bed.

But now she was closer than ever. She could smell his body heat. It had always been something that triggered bad memories. However, in this instance, she still felt anxious, but in a different way.

"Am I making you uncomfortable?" Luke asked.

"Yes."

A small word, yet as painful as a kick to the gut. "Sorry. Maybe if I put on my shirt?"

"No. Leave it off," she said, and was thankful for the shadows that hid the sudden flash of heat on her face. "What I meant was…it's too hot to sleep in your clothes."

Luke grinned. "You are."

Her mouth dropped as she looked down at herself in disbelief. Then she fixed him with a cool, pointed stare.

"You're making me crazy," she muttered.

The smile died on Luke's face. "Yeah? Well, join the club."

"What do you mean?" she asked.

"Nothing," Luke said, and this time he was the one to stomp into the bathroom and close the door.

Jade's eyes teared up. She'd made him mad, but she didn't know why. Damn it, this man/woman stuff was something she should have learned years ago. She flopped backward on the bed, then rolled over on her side and squinched her eyes tightly shut. It was stupid and awful of her to be thinking like this when Raphael was dead.

Why, honey girl? There's nothing stupid about you except your refusal to admit that you can sometimes be wrong.

She opened her eyes with a jerk. Although she knew it was impossible, she would have sworn she'd just heard Raphael.

The toilet flushed on the other side of the door; then she heard the shower go on. She thumped her fist against a pillow and then settled a little deeper into the covers. Just when her heart had stopped rattling against her ribs and her pulse was settling into a normal rhythm, she heard him again.

I can't live with you anymore, honey girl. But he can. Trust him. Trust yourself. It's all you have left.

Jade sat up in bed, her face streaked with tears. *Oh Rafie… I feel lost without you.*

No, you don't. You just feel different. It's time you let go of the past and grabbed hold of the future.

Is Luke my future?

There was a long stretch of silence, and then she heard Raphael's voice as clearly as if he were standing beside her.

Don't ask me. I can't feel what's in your heart.

You can't?

No. Not anymore. I'm gone. You're not. Live for the both of us, baby. Live long and prosper, and make me proud.

I love you, Rafie.

I know. I loved you, too.

Jade shuddered, unprepared for his answer to come in the past tense.

She heard the shower go off, then the sound of a sliding door. She closed her eyes and fisted her hands, picturing his wet, naked body as he emerged from the tub.

She wanted to know what it was like to make love and enjoy it, even revel in it, the way women were supposed to do. There had been nothing but violation in her life, and then, only as a child. Would she ever be able—as a grown woman—to be that intimate with a man?

Then the bathroom door opened. Luke came out freshly showered but once again wearing his slacks.

"I think it would be a good idea if I slept in the adjoining bedroom. I won't be far. All you have to do is just call my name and I'll come running, okay?"

She nodded.

Luke wanted to touch her but settled for a smile as he walked into the other room.

Jade leaned over the side of the bed, watching as he pulled back the bedclothes and then tossed a couple of pillows against the headboard. She saw him start to undo his pants,

then stop. His shoulders slumped; then he sat down on the side of the bed, put his elbows on his knees and stared at the floor. He looked so lost. So sad. So hurt. It hurt her heart to realize that he was feeling this way and that she might be partly responsible. She wanted to go to him, to put her arms around him and coax a smile back on his face. With that moment of understanding came another, even more frightening, and that was when she knew.

"Um…Luke?"

"Yeah?"

She had expected him to come into the room. Instead, he was still sitting on the bed—still staring at the floor. She sighed. He wasn't making this easy.

"Luke!"

His voice rose. "Yes?"

"Damn it, Luke. I called your name. You're supposed to come running."

Seconds later Luke was standing in the door, staring at her face in disbelief.

"What are you saying?" When she didn't answer, he tried again. "Let me rephrase that. What aren't you saying?"

"I'm not telling you that I want you to sleep with me."

He frowned. "Okay. I told you I was fine sleeping in the other bed."

She rolled her eyes and thumped the bed with both fists.

"I don't know how to do this," she muttered. "You're going to have to help me."

Suddenly contrite, he sat down on the side of her bed.

"I'm sorry, baby. Maybe I'm punchy from lack of sleep, too, but I don't know what you're trying to do. Of course I'll help you. That goes without saying."

Jade rocked back on her heels. "Are you sure?"

"Of course. You name it."

"It's something I've never done before…at least not as a grown woman."

She looked up at him then, studying the contours of his

features, as well as the shadows beneath, and saw a face that she knew she could love. What remained to be seen was if she could give to him that which he so deserved.

"I've never been in love before, so I'm not sure what it feels like. But I think it might be happening."

Luke felt as if he'd been poleaxed. His ears were ringing, and his head was feeling light. He opened his mouth, but nothing came out except a groan.

Jade frowned. "Isn't this where you're supposed to say something? Anything? Maybe a thank you, but no thank you? Even a 'Really, my dear, I had no idea' would be preferable to this."

"Help me, Jesus," Luke mumbled, and then felt his lips to see if they'd moved or if he'd just thought the quick prayer.

Jade was frowning. He figured he'd better say something fast, even if it was wrong.

"I'm not so sure that I'm not still in that bed in there, and that I've already gone to sleep and what I'm hearing is just a dream."

Jade shifted nervously. She didn't know whether what he'd said was a good sign or not, but just in case it was, she took a chance and brushed the flat of her hand across his chest.

Luke couldn't have been more shocked if she'd punched him in the gut. He grabbed her hand, then lifted it to his lips. She tasted awfully sweet and way too solid to be a dream.

"Okay, since this is my dream," Luke said, "I'm going to unload it all. I've been falling in love with you since I first saw you in New Orleans, sitting on the floor in the middle of those kids and drawing pictures on their faces. Not only that, but I dream about making love to you all the time. Only I understand how you feel about men, and I want you to know that I would wait a lifetime on the chance that you might one day change your mind."

Jade felt as if all the bones in her body had suddenly gone

missing. Oh God. So this was what it felt like to want someone to touch you so much that it ached.

"This isn't a dream," Jade said. "And what I want is for us to make love…or at least try. I don't know if I can do this. I want to, but I don't know what's going to happen. It might set off all kinds of alarm bells from my past, and if it does, please know that it's not because of anything you did. It will be because of what someone else has already done."

Luke's focus shattered. "Oh, honey," he whispered, then touched her hands, her face.

"Call it a test drive," Jade said. "If you don't like the model, then we've lost nothing but a few minutes of time."

Luke took a slow deep breath.

"If you're serious about this—and trust me when I pray to God that you are—then there's something I think you should know."

"What?"

"If I'm going to be wasting time…"

Jade gulped. "Yes?"

"It's going to be a hell of a lot more than a few minutes."

Nineteen

Jade's gaze was fixed on Luke's face. She needed to see the tenderness and the warmth in his eyes to remind her that this was not a mistake.

"Who goes first?" she asked.

Luke was a little taken aback by the question. In that brief moment, he flashed on a small child standing naked before some deviant and being subjected to only God knew what. She would have no idea that the joining of a man and woman could be a truly beautiful thing.

"No, baby, it isn't about taking turns. It's touching..." He brushed the back of his hand beneath the curve of her chin.

"And stroking..." He took her hand and put it on his chest. "And tenderness..." Their lips touched, at first just a butterfly kiss, then a nibble with a quick return for a second taste.

Jade shuddered.

Immediately Luke moved back.

"Sweetheart...at the risk of sounding a bit corny, you're the driver here. All you have to do is tell me to stop."

She licked her lower lip, carefully tasting where his mouth had just been. It felt hot and moist, and she wanted to know more.

"What comes next?"

He traced the curve of her chin with the tip of his finger. "The possibility of internal combustion."

"What?"

"Never mind," he said softly. "I was teasing."

"I thought we were being serious?"

Luke's eyes darkened. "Honey, this is about as serious as it gets, but there's nothing better than being able to laugh with someone you love. So, are you still with me?"

"Yes."

He pointed to her clothes. "You're sort of overdressed for the moment."

She grabbed the collar of her shirt in reflex to what he'd said and pulled it tighter beneath her chin than it already was.

Luke held up his hands and backed completely away.

"Here's the deal," he said. "How about I take off all my clothes, you check out the goods, and if you're still okay with all of this, then you make the next move?"

"Uh…"

Luke unzipped his pants. Jade wanted to look away, but she couldn't, and when he tossed them aside and then took off his briefs, as well, she went weak in the knees. The muscles in her stomach began to pull, then ache. She'd seen far more naked men than she cared to remember, and yet looking at Luke was like seeing one for the very first time. His muscles were well-toned. His body was perfectly proportioned. She already knew that his chest was broad and firm, with a slight dusting of very black hair. Now she could see that it spiraled down the middle of his belly, then surrounded a growing erection.

Luke watched her carefully, afraid to dwell on what she might be thinking.

"I can't stop this from happening. It's not a weapon or a means to cause you pain. It's just a man's normal reaction to a very desirable woman."

"In my head, I know that," Jade whispered.

"I'm going to lie down now. Come sit beside me. I promise I won't touch you in any way until you tell me otherwise."

Without waiting for her permission, he lay down on the

bed, stretched out on his back and pillowed his hands behind his head.

"Tell yourself it's something like the petting zoo."

Jade laughed before she thought, then gasped and covered her mouth. When he grinned, then winked, she began to relax.

"See, I told you there's nothing better than laughing with someone you care for. Add some sweet loving to that and you've got the makings of a real good thing."

"Oh, Luke… I so want this to be all right."

"I know you do, honey. I wish your life had been different, but it wasn't. However, thanks to Sam, you have the chance to change it. All you have to do is take what's being offered."

"Like you?" she asked.

"It's a start."

Her chin jutted just the tiniest bit. "I don't want to do this alone."

Luke rose up on one elbow.

"Then come lie with me, Jade."

Sheltered by the darkness, she stood up, turned her back and started taking off her clothes. If she was going to do this, she was going to do it right.

The thunder of her heartbeat was not evident as she methodically undressed. When she was completely naked, she braced her shoulders and then turned around.

The smile on Luke's face froze as his gaze slid from her face downward. A thin, white scar began on her left breast and then followed the curve of her body to just below her navel.

Before Luke could pull himself together, Jade splayed her fingers across as much of it as she could touch and took a step back.

"Jesus," Luke muttered, then bounded from the bed and took her hands, gently pulling them away from her body. "Don't."

"It's ugly."

"The only thing ugly is the bastard who did it."

Slowly he traced the length of the scar with his finger. "Such a little warrior you must have been." Then he picked her up and carried her to bed.

She rolled over onto her side, subconsciously concealing another man's mark.

Luke lay down beside her, then slid his arm beneath her neck to pillow her head.

"Look at me," he said softly.

Jade did.

"Tell me his name."

"I don't know it. I never knew their names. Solomon just called the men uncles."

"Why did he do this?"

"I think because I was no longer a little girl. My breasts were growing, and my body was changing. It turned him off instead of on, and when he couldn't...you know...he took it out on me."

"Christ Almighty," Luke whispered, and then cupped her face with his hands. "Know this...if I ever find the man who did this to you, I will kill him."

"I don't know his name, but he called himself Uncle Frank. Probably a made-up name." Then Jade laid a finger over his mouth, then slid the palm of her hand along the side of his face. She could feel the beginnings of a beard and a muscle twitching near his jaw.

"I hate enough for both of us. What I need from you is a lesson in how to make love."

Luke sighed, then leaned forward until their foreheads were touching.

"Okay, honey...and like I told you before...I'll be anything you need me to be."

They lay on their sides, facing each other, and she let the dance begin.

"A kiss...just a kiss," he said softly.

Instinctively her lips parted. She felt the warmth of his breath on her face and then closed her eyes. Mouths merged—gently, at first. She slid a hand behind his neck.

Luke was struggling to balance caution with desire. With each move that she made, he could feel her hesitation. But she was so very, very sweet. He slid his mouth from her lips to her chin, then the hollow at the base of her throat.

Jade rolled over on her back, giving him access to her body. When she felt his lips at the valley between her breasts, she shivered.

Luke paused and rose up on one elbow.

"Don't stop," she whispered.

His nostrils flared slightly. It was the only sign he gave her of his emotional state of mind.

Afterward, Jade's senses seemed to go out of control. She would feel his mouth on her body, then his hands, then his mouth once more, always moving downward in gentle strokes and tender kisses. As his tongue dipped into the valley of her navel, an answering fire began to heat inside her. Somewhere deep—somewhere low. She reached for him, her fingers digging into the muscles of his shoulders, uncertain of his next move.

Again he rose up. There was moisture glistening on his lips. A bead of sweat had run from his hairline and then down the side of his face. Without thinking, she caught it on the tip of her finger, then lifted it to her mouth. It was warm and salty, and she wanted this feeling inside her to go on forever.

When Jade touched her finger to her tongue, Luke's mind went blank. Already aching for her to the point of physical pain, he almost lost it. Then she shifted restlessly beneath him, and as she did, a small beam of moonlight slipped through the curtains, spearing through space and then highlighting the scar. It was as effective a set of brakes as Luke had ever known, reminding him that this night wasn't about what he wanted from her but what she needed to learn. That this act—the act of making love—meant pleasure, not pain.

"Spread your legs," he said.

Her breathing staggered, stopped, then resumed in a ragged effort. This was where passion ended and panic began. Every image she'd been trying to forget for the past eighteen years slammed back into her mind with brute force. She tried to move and could do nothing but shake. Just the thought of being touched there made her want to throw up.

"Oh, Luke… I'm sorry… I don't think I can."

Luke stopped, then turned his head and laid his cheek on the flat of her belly. She was shaking so hard that he thought she was going to pass out.

"Easy, baby, it's okay, it's okay. You don't have to do a damned thing you don't want to do."

Then, to prove his point, he slid his arms beneath her hips and just held her close, binding her legs together with the weight of his body. Her skin was hot, her muscles trembling. He could smell the soap on her body from her last bath, as well as her musky, woman smell.

At that moment, Jade hated herself for what had been done to her and for what she'd become.

"I'm sorry," she mumbled. "I'm sorry. I tried."

"I know you did, and I'm telling you it's okay."

Jade hated this part of herself. She was nothing but an emotional cripple.

"But it's not," she said, and then started to cry.

Luke rolled over, then sat up and pulled her across his lap. She laid her head on his shoulder while his arms held her close, and together they sat as Luke rocked her like a baby.

Seconds passed into minutes; then they lost track of time. Jade had heard the thunder of his heartbeat and knew what strength it had taken for him to pull back. Now she knew she could trust Luke. If only she could trust herself. She'd come so close. As they sat in the quiet, Jade started to consider another try.

"Luke?"

"Yes, baby?"

"Can we give this another go?"

Luke groaned. "Oh, baby, I want to, but I don't know if I can without—"

"Maybe if I was the one in control?"

"You're always in control."

"That's not what I mean," she said, and then slid off his lap and gave his shoulders a push.

He dropped flat on his back.

Jade sat up, then tentatively ran her hands down the length of both legs, feeling the muscles jumping beneath the skin.

"Oh, man…if this is you in control, be my guest," Luke said.

Her fingers moved past his groin, then across the flat of his belly, testing the texture and tension of the muscles beneath his skin. In a way, Jade felt as if she was painting him, but with her fingers instead of paint on canvas.

She closed her eyes, mentally mapping the conformation of his arms and legs, subconsciously storing the information, as if she were making a sketch.

Luke was sweating now, and his breath was coming in short, frantic gasps. He'd never thought that he would lose his mind in a sweet woman's bed, but there was a good chance that it was going to happen tonight. When her fingernails raked across his nipples, he arched off the bed.

"Sweet mother of—"

Jade inhaled slowly, then opened her eyes. She felt weightless—almost mindless. Everything around her seemed to be happening in slow motion. Her mind went on hold as she straddled Luke's thighs. His erection was hard and pulsing. She didn't have to touch him to know what it felt like. But this wasn't like before. For the first time in her life she felt like a woman, not a victim. She so wanted to be a woman, and she wanted to be one with this man.

Her movements were slow and studied as she rose up on her knees. She could feel him against the inside of her leg.

"Luke."

His answer was little more than a grunt.

"Don't...move," she said.

With the fluidity of cold sorghum on a winter morning, she began to lower herself onto his erection. Slowly, slowly, she slid downward, giving her body time to adjust to the unfamiliar intrusion. Where she'd been empty, now she was full. Where she'd been alone, she was now part of him. And without fear. Without pain.

Luke's hands were shaking as he fitted them to her waist. The need to drive himself deeper into her was like a bloodlust. If she didn't do something, he would go insane.

"Move with me, baby," he begged.

Jade leaned forward. Planting her hands on either side of his shoulders, she began to rock. Without the weight of his body as a reminder of all the years of her helplessness, she let herself fly as only a woman can fly.

All too soon, the sensations of pleasure went from good to meltdown. Suddenly every pulse point in her body was splintering into a thousand pieces, shattering like breaking crystal from a musical note pitched too high.

"Ooooh...ooooh no...oooooh God."

At the same time, Jade's climax grabbed Luke, pulling him under so fast that he forgot to hold on. One second he'd been riding the high. Then he fell without warning—without ropes or nets. He spilled himself in her until there was nothing left of him to give, and still he couldn't break free.

Finally it was Jade who broke the spell. When she collapsed on his chest, her body limp and spent, he managed to roll over with her still in his arms. With his last ounce of strength, he reached down and pulled up the covers.

The peace that came afterward was a combination of silence and satisfaction. Luke was drifting between heaven and sleep when he realized Jade was crying.

"Talk to me," he said softly.

"I never knew. All these years, and I never knew."

"What?"

"That it didn't have to hurt."

He held her tighter. The words he was thinking were locked deep inside his heart. And that night, after she'd finally gone to sleep, he lay vigilant beside her, watching the shadows for the demons that had yet to be slain.

Earl Walters had a vested interest in closing the file on Jade Cochrane, and even though they had the man responsible for murdering Raphael, as well as the nurse and the Tyler woman, Earl knew he was just the gun. They wanted to know who'd aimed it.

He picked up the phone and put a call in to the captain of the homicide division.

"Charlie...it's Earl. Bring me up to speed on what we know about the Newton case."

Charlie Black reached for a file, then flipped it open as he leaned back in his chair.

"Myers is lead on this, so his file is probably more complete than what I have here, although we just finished an update. Newton came out of surgery around eleven last night. He's in critical care but expected to make a full recovery. He's not a happy camper, though. Seems he's real indignant about his last victim. That Raphael fellow had AIDS. Mr. Newton would like to complain that his rights have been violated, but he can't figure out how to make it work, considering the fact that he did go into an isolation ward without permission and off the two people in Room 342. He's trying to make a case that someone should have 'told' him ahead of time that the guy he killed had AIDS. Now he's almost certainly been infected, and he's scared shitless."

Earl chuckled. "Feels pretty good when the perp gets a dose of his own medicine, doesn't it?"

"And then some," Charlie said. "Myers said there wasn't anything in Newton's suitcase that would lead them in the direction of who'd hired him. However, someone happened to mention in the meeting this morning that since he was

taken straight from the scene to E.R., we never had the chance to go through his clothes. So Myers and his partner are on their way to the hospital as we speak to take the clothing into evidence.''

"Let me know what you find," Earl said. "I've got a personal interest in seeing this whole ugly thing resolved. Oh, one other thing… those drawings I gave you…the ones that Miss Cochrane drew of the men who'd molested her…what's happening there?"

"We turned them over to Vice. Last I heard, they were running them through some national database, trying to match up the drawings with the mug shots of known molesters, but it's gonna be tough. As I understand it, the drawings are the way the men looked fifteen to twenty years ago. Most of the mug shots will be more recent. It's gonna be difficult to get matches. And even if we did, we'd need proof besides her word against his…and, we're looking at different laws in different states. For some of them, the time has lapsed for charges to be filed."

"Yeah," Earl said; then he spun his swivel chair toward the window, squinting against the daylight. "You know… that damned bunch of newshounds has been plaguing us and the Cochranes ever since this mess came to light."

Charlie frowned. "Yes, but don't they always?"

"You also know it seems like someone's always leaking info that we don't want told. I'd hate to think what might happen if those drawings ever fell into the wrong hands. *We* might never be able to identify them, but I'll bet there are some people out there across the nation who could. Before they started fucking children, they were someone's sons and brothers and friends. Now, if they're still alive and they're not in jail, they're probably someone's husbands and fathers and bosses. It would be a crying shame if someone accidentally knocked over the rocks they've been hiding under."

Charlie started to smile.

"It would be a shame, wouldn't it? Of course, we can't

do that. Infringing on civil rights without proof, or something like that.''

"Yeah…civil rights," Earl echoed, then turned his back to the window. "Keep me posted on what Myers and his partner find out."

"Will do," Charlie said.

Larry Myers had been a homicide detective for eight years. Before that, he'd been a uniformed street cop. He'd seen his share of neglected and abused children, but what he'd learned about Sam Cochrane's daughter made him sick. He'd seen her twice in public. Once going into the morgue. Once coming out. It was his personal opinion that there should come a time in one's life when your dues got paid in full—when the crap that comes with everyday living has come and gone and what's left of your life is pure gravy. Except, of course, for the day that you die. That was something that comes to everyone. If ever a person deserved some happiness, it was Jade Cochrane. And he wanted to find the person who'd put out the hit more than he'd ever wanted to do anything in his life. Because of that, he had been saying prayers all the way to the hospital that they would get the break they'd been waiting on. If there was nothing in the clothes, maybe Newton would be ready to talk. Maybe he would give up the man who'd hired him. And maybe hell would freeze over before dark.

Myers flashed his badge at the nurses' station. "We've come to pick up Johnny Newton's personal belongings," he said.

A few minutes later, a nurse came back with a plastic sack full of bloody clothes, a pair of equally bloody shoes, and a cell phone and watch. Myers put on latex gloves and grunted to himself as he sorted through the lot. If they were lucky, Newton might have some numbers stored in the cell phone's memory that would take them in the right direction. He dug

through the pockets, counting out a dollar and forty-three cents in change. There were several hundred dollars in his wallet, no credit cards, and a fake driver's license. There was nothing in there that would give away his true identity, but that didn't matter. They knew who he was, just not who'd sent him here.

"Hey, Bradley, you go through the pants and shirt pockets," Myers said.

Wearing a pair of surgical gloves, Harry Bradley searched Newton's pockets with careful precision. He didn't want to make contact with any of the contaminated blood any more than Newton had.

"Whatcha' got?" Myers asked.

"An unused toothpick, still encased in the cellophane. A half a pack of sugarless chewing gum. A receipt for gas…and some trash. Wait. There's a name and phone number on the back of this one."

Myers' interest was piqued. "What's it say?"

"It ain't talkin'," Bradley drawled.

Myers frowned. "Damn it, Harry, you know what I mean. Whose name and number is on the paper?"

Harry Bradley grinned, then turned his attention to the paper.

"The name is Frank Lawson. Ever hear of him?"

Myers thought for a minute, then shook his head. "I don't think so. What's the number?"

Bradley repeated it.

Myers' frown increased. "That's a Tennessee area code."

"How do you know something like that?" Bradley asked.

"I have an aunt and uncle who live outside of Nashville. Same area code."

"I'll be damned," Bradley muttered. "Wonder what that could mean?"

"I need to make a couple of calls," Myers said.

"To who?" Bradley asked.

"First call is to Nashville. Think I'll give the chief a little call. See what he can tell us."

He got information, and within a minute or so was being connected to Nashville's chief of police.

"Chief Randall, my name is Larry Myers. I'm a homicide detective with the St. Louis P.D."

"Hello, Detective. Is old Earl still behind the desk over there?"

"Yes, sir, that he is."

"So, what can I do for you?"

Myers quickly explained the situation about the murders and taking Newton down.

"Good work," Randall said. "We've been hearing about that on the news. Nasty piece of business."

"Yes, sir, and that's why I'm calling. We found a name and a phone number in the pocket of the man we took into custody yesterday. I was wondering if it might ring a bell."

"What's the name?" Randall asked.

"Frank Lawson."

The congenial smile on Chief Randall's face disappeared as his feet hit the floor.

"Big Frank?"

Myers frowned. "I don't know who that is. All we have is Frank Lawson and then a phone number. It's within the Nashville area code is why I called."

"Hell yes, I know him. He's running for governor."

Myers' heart rate accelerated as his body went still.

"He's what?"

"Big Frank is quite a popular guy. It's common knowledge that he's pretty much a shoo-in come election day."

"What do you know about his past?" Myers asked.

Randall frowned. "There was talk that he lived pretty rough in his younger days, but he's been a household name for years. A few years back, he single-handedly saved a woman and her kids from a killer. Took the shooter down

by himself and then called 911. He's pretty much a hero around here."

"Well, my instincts tell me there's a good chance that your hero might have some big flaws. Do you know where Lawson is?"

"At this moment?" Randall asked.

"Yes, sir…at this moment."

"I'd hazard a guess that if he's not home, he's on the road campaigning."

"Want to do me a favor?" Myers asked.

"Always happy to help a fellow officer in a murder investigation."

"Thank you, sir. I really appreciate this."

"Don't thank me yet. What is it that you need, boy?"

"I'm going to give Mr. Lawson a call, but I'd like to think I had some long-distance backup on the premises, just in case he decides to run before we can question him."

"Give me thirty minutes," Randall said. "I'll find out where he is and give you a call to see if we can make this happen."

"Yes, sir, and thank you," Myers said, and then gave the chief the number of his cell phone.

"Let's head back to headquarters," Myers said. "I'm thinking the captain needs in on this."

With only thirty minutes to spare, they jumped in their car and headed back to the station.

Charlie Black was finishing off a tuna melt when Myers and Bradley knocked on his door. He motioned them in as he wiped his mouth, then eyed the plastic bag and the bloody clothes with distaste.

"Damn, Myers, shouldn't that be logged into evidence?"

"Sir, I think we may have found the break we've been looking for."

Charlie's disgust turned to glee, imagining how pleased Earl Walters was going to be if they broke this case.

"Tell me," he said.

"We found a piece of paper in Newton's pocket with a name and phone number. It's a Tennessee phone number...the same area code as Nashville. I know because I have family in the area. Anyway, I called the chief of police, told him the name in question, and he nearly blew a fuse."

"So who's the guy...some country music star?"

"Better. A big shot of some kind who's running for governor. Frank Lawson."

"Big Frank Lawson?"

"You know him?" Myers asked.

"I know of him," Charlie said. "Are you saying that Lawson is the man who wanted Raphael and Jade Cochrane dead?"

"Don't know yet, but I didn't want to call this number until we had some backup in place. Chief Randall is supposed to call back in just a few minutes. Once he's got men posted in Lawson's location, I thought I'd give him a ring...just to see what he has to say."

"Good idea," Charlie said.

A couple of minutes later, Myers' phone rang. It was Randall.

"He's still at his home," the chief said. "I have three patrol cars parked in the vicinity of his house. If he decides to take an unexpected vacation, we'll be detaining him for a few more questions. How's that?"

"Perfect," Myers said. "And, sir, if he gets hinky while we're talking, my captain will let you know. You can relay the message to your patrolmen so they'll know he's likely to go on the run."

"Good luck," Randall said.

"Yes, sir," Myers said. "Same to you."

"Is it going down?" Charlie asked.

"Yes, sir. Now for the final touch."

Myers took out his handkerchief and carefully picked up Newton's phone with it, then took the paper from his partner, Bradley.

"What are you doing?" Charlie asked, when Myers used Newton's phone to call Frank Lawson.

"I'm making a call," Myers said.

"With Newton's phone?"

"If this Lawson fellow has caller ID on his own phone, it might be interesting to see what he has to say when he thinks Newton is the one making the call."

Bradley grinned. "Damn, Myers, wish I'd thought of that. Get it on tape."

"Will do," Myers said, and set about making it happen.

A few moments later, he dialed the number then put his finger to his mouth to indicate silence as the call began to ring through.

Frank Lawson was stepping out of the shower when his cell phone began to ring. He had a television interview in a couple of hours and no time to waste, but then he saw who was calling and quickly picked up.

"It's about time you called," Frank said. "Did you finish the job? And don't give me any shit about it, either. Remember, you've got Jacks to do next, and time's wasting."

Myers was grinning from ear to ear. They'd hit pay dirt.

"Mr. Lawson?"

Big Frank choked. He was a man who thought fast on his feet, but even as he was talking, he knew that it was too late.

"No, Frank isn't here."

"So if you're not Frank, who are you and why are you answering his phone?"

"Who the hell are you?" Frank countered.

"I'm Detective Myers with the St. Louis homicide division. We have arrested a man here for the murders of three people, and we'd like to know why he had your name and phone number in his pocket."

Frank heard the word "three" and immediately thought that the third victim was Jade. He was mentally congratulating himself while knowing that he would have to make other

arrangements about Otis Jacks. But right now, he had to get himself out of the faux pas that he'd made.

"I told you, I'm not Frank Lawson. He's on his way to the studio for an interview."

"Then I suppose you wouldn't know why that name and this number would be in his pocket?"

"No, sir, I don't."

"Then maybe you can tell me who you are and why you're using Lawson's phone?"

There was a moment of silence, then a very distinct click. Myers looked up. He was grinning.

"Captain, I think you'd better call Chief Randall in Nashville. Lawson just hung up on me."

Frank had dressed, packed a small bag and emptied the safe in his bedroom. His world was crumbling. He didn't know how long he had, but run he must.

He dashed through the house and then into the garage, tossed his bag in the back seat, then opened the garage door. Within seconds, he was behind the wheel and backing out. Halfway down the driveway, he saw a police car pulling into position to block the exit.

"No," he moaned, as his mind went blank. It couldn't end like this. Not after all he'd accomplished. Damn Johnny Newton. Damn Otis Jacks. And damn that little bitch, Jade, for not dying when he'd tried to cut out her heart.

He pulled to a stop at the end of the driveway, then got out, wearing his famous smile.

"Hey, boys, what's goin' on here? Am I in some danger? Has there been some kind of threat I don't know about?"

Another two police cars pulled into view. At that point Frank knew that the brand of bullshit he'd been spreading for years had just gone out of style. He frowned. Ever the optimist, he switched from jovial to indignant, yanked his cell phone from his pocket and dialed the police.

"I need to speak to Marty Randall. Tell him it's Big Frank Lawson."

Almost immediately, Randall came on the line.

"Hello, Big Frank, what can I do for you?" Randall asked.

Big Frank huffed, then he puffed. "For starters, you can tell me what the hell three police units are doing blocking my driveway. I've got an appointment, and they're making me late."

"Well, they're there because I sent them," Randall said.

"You? What the hell for?"

"I think I'd like to ask *you* a question instead," Randall said. "Why are your name and phone number in the pocket of a man who's just been arrested for murder?"

"I don't know what you're talking about."

"I think you do," Randall said. "So what I want you to do is play nice and get in the patrol car. Let the boys give you a ride on down to the station. We've got some more talking to do."

"I'm not talking to anybody but my lawyer!" Frank yelled.

"That's fine with me," Randall said. "But you're still coming down."

This time Big Frank was the one who got disconnected. He watched in horror as the policemen got out and came toward him. One had a pair of handcuffs. The other had his hand on his service revolver.

He groaned.

God, please let this be a bad dream.

But when the handcuffs snapped around Big Frank's wrists, sharply pinching a bit of his skin, he knew he wasn't dreaming.

Twenty

Jade woke up in increments, with an awareness of her body that she'd never had before. She lay motionless, her eyes still closed, and felt the throb of her heartbeat. The friction of the sheets against her skin was almost sexual, reminding her of the feel of Luke's hands and mouth. She tested the tenderness of her lower lip with the tip of her tongue, wondering why it felt sore, then vaguely remembered biting down on it at the height of her climax.

She shivered.

Last night a great wall had been breached, and by nothing more than the tenderness and patience of Luke's love. She remembered listening to his voice against her ear as she'd drifted off to sleep, focusing more on the sound of his voice rather than the promises he had made. For the first time in as far back as she could remember, she had slept through the night without nightmares. She rolled over on her belly and buried her face in the pillow.

As she did, she felt a hand in the middle of her back.

"Jade?"

She groaned and then slowly rolled over onto her back. She had no idea that her wild, tousled hair and the smoky quality of a sleep-heavy voice would be enticing. If she had, she might have contemplated testing the waters again with Luke Kelly, but she was not confident in social etiquette for the morning after, and so she waited for him to speak.

Luke smiled at her, then teasingly poked at her hair, pushing stray strands from her forehead and around her eyes.

"Are you all right?"

She nodded.

His smile softened. "So am I. Very all right."

It was his tenderness that gave her ease. Tentatively she touched his face, rubbing her thumb against the curve of his chin and feeling the sharp prick of whiskers. It was such an ordinary, yet intimate, gesture. And what was most amazing of all was that she felt perfectly confident in doing so. Then she thought of yesterday and all that had transpired. It seemed like a lifetime ago, and yet her life was still in a rather precarious position. Until they found out who had hired Newton, she would never feel completely safe. Needing to say what was on her mind, she sat up. The covers fell down around her waist. She was not as daring in the bright light of day as she had been last night and reached for the sheets.

Luke stayed her intent with a touch, then a look.

"It's just me," he said softly.

Subconsciously her fingers went straight to the scar.

Luke frowned. "Don't worry about it, honey. It's just a map to your heart."

"Oh, Luke."

"See," he said, and ran his finger along the faint white line up from her belly to the place where the mark began. "Right over your heart. Now, if I ever lose my way, I'll know how to get back."

She stared at him for a moment, and then suddenly choked on a sob and covered her face with her hands.

Luke sat up, then put his arms around her.

"It's okay, honey. It's okay. Cry all you want. Cry until all the pain is gone, and when it is, we're going to start over."

Jade looked up, her eyes swimming with unshed tears.

"Start over on what?" she asked.

"On building memories. Only this time, they will be good ones…happy ones."

She sighed. "Oh, Luke."

"You already said that," he teased.

She made a face at him. "And it's entirely your fault that I'm speechless."

"I was that good, was I?"

Her mouth dropped—her eyes widened with surprise. Then she saw the twinkle in his eyes and started to grin.

"You're teasing me."

"Yeah. So what are you going to do about it?"

She threw her arms around his neck and wrestled him back down onto the bed.

Luke was laughing when she finally pulled back.

"Do you give?" she asked.

Suddenly all the playfulness was gone from his face. He tightened his grasp and pulled her close, until she was lying across his chest with her head beneath his chin.

"Yes, I give…. I give to you for always and whatever you ask."

Jade snuggled against him, taking comfort in the love and the protection. Then she thought about Raphael and closed her eyes. How could this be? How could she feel these moments of joy when he was gone from her life forever?

Not as long as you remember my name.

She flinched. The shock of hearing his voice—now, when she was lying in another man's arms—was unnerving. Then she thought of what she'd heard and relaxed. He was right. As long as someone remembered his name, he would never really be gone.

"Luke…?"

"What, baby?"

"I talked to Sam."

"Yeah…what about?" Luke asked.

"Things…mostly about Raphael. No funeral. No box in

the ground. When I can, I want to spread his ashes somewhere beautiful. He would have liked that.''

Luke took her hand and lifted it to his mouth, kissing each fingertip, then the center of her palm.

''You are a remarkable woman, Jade Cochrane. He was blessed to have you as a friend.''

''And I was blessed to have him,'' she said; then she shifted her gaze to a spot on the wall. ''What's going to happen?''

He frowned. ''Are you talking about us or—''

''No. I mean that man…that killer. Do the police know who hired him? Do you think the danger to my life is over?''

Luke thought of Mabel Tyler, then tunneled his fingers in her hair and momentarily closed his eyes. Lying to Jade was not an option.

''I would like to say that you're safe, but until we know the whole story, I don't think we should assume anything, do you?''

''No. We should not assume.''

Luke glanced past her to the clock on the wall. It was almost half past eight. He gave her a quick hug and a kiss.

''As much as I would like to spend the day in bed with you, I don't think Velma's heart could stand the shock. And maybe after I talk to Chief Walters, I'll have some answers to your questions.''

The mention of getting caught with him like this was enough to send Jade packing. She was out of bed and heading for the shower before Luke could call her back. He stifled a groan at the sight of her lush, naked body, and then got out of bed and began to dress. By the time Jade came out, he was already downstairs.

She frowned, then saw the note on her pillow and picked it up.

Sam wants to have breakfast with us. I'm in the library making calls.

Her frown lightened. Okay, so she hadn't been abandoned

after all. She quickly dressed, taking care with her makeup and hair. As she started down the stairs, she found herself hurrying. It startled her to realize that she was actually running to meet a man.

Luke had called his office first, gone through the cases with his second in command and then told him to call if he ran into any complications.

After that, he made a call to Earl Walters.

"Chief, it's Luke Kelly. I guess you know why I'm calling."

Earl shifted a stack of mail to the side of his desk and leaned forward.

"I suppose that I do," he said. "I was actually going to give Sam a call in a few minutes. Why don't you put him on an extension and you can both hear this at the same time?"

"Hang on," Luke said. "He's in the other room. I've got a portable with me. I'll tell him to get on an extension."

Luke hurried out of the room, yelling Sam's name as he went.

Sam had been in the dining room pouring himself a cup of coffee. When he heard Luke's voice, he set down the cup and came running.

"Get on a phone," Luke said. "Earl Walters is on the line."

Sam turned quickly, ran back into the dining room and picked up the extension.

"Earl. I'm here. What's going on?"

"Luke there, too?"

"Yes. We're listening."

"Okay, here's what we know. The lead detective on the hospital murders picked up Newton's personal property from the hospital this morning. There was a cell phone, the usual clothing, and a piece of paper with a name and phone number in one of the pockets. To make a long story short, he set up

a sting with the chief of police in Nashville, then they used Newton's cell phone and called the number on the paper. A man named Frank Lawson saw the caller ID and spilled his guts before he knew it wasn't Newton on the phone.''

"Frank? You said his name was Frank?" Luke asked.

Earl frowned. "Yes. Does that mean something to you?"

"I don't know…maybe," Luke said. "Jade has a scar. She said that a man who called himself Uncle Frank did it."

Sam didn't know about the scar, and the fact that Luke did told him the relationship between his daughter and Luke Kelly must have moved in a new direction. That part of it pleased him. It was the image of something splitting his baby's flesh to the extent that it would leave a scar that made him sick. He felt like throwing up.

"Jesus," Earl said.

"So tell me they have the bastard in custody," Luke asked.

"Oh, yeah, they picked him up as he was making a run for it."

"I'm going to Nashville," Luke said.

Earl shifted in his seat. "Now look, Kelly, there isn't anything you can do down there."

Luke thought of the shame on Jade's face and the pain of what she'd been forced to endure. His chin jutted mutinously.

"Yes, there is," he said. "I made Jade a promise that I'm not going to take back. I'd appreciate it if you'd call the powers that be and give them the heads-up that I'm on my way."

"Not until you make me a promise," Earl said.

"Like what?"

"You won't do something stupid like hasten Mr. Lawson's demise."

When Luke didn't immediately reassure Walters, Sam looked at Luke and then stood abruptly.

"No one wants to see the people responsible for Jade's horrors get what's coming to them more than I do, but what

good would it do her if we both wound up in prison and she was once again left to live her life alone?''

Luke cursed beneath his breath then turned away.

''Fine,'' he snapped. ''You both have my word that I won't lay a hand on the son-of-a-bitch.''

''Okay,'' Earl said. ''I'll make the necessary calls. Oh. I'll be damned. I almost forgot one of the twists in this whole mess.''

''Like what?'' Luke asked.

''Frank Lawson is—or maybe I should say 'was'—the front runner for the governorship of Tennessee.''

Sam spun toward Luke, his expression one of shock.

''Governor? I find that hard to believe.''

Luke shook his head as he spoke into the phone.

''I find it a damned good reason to hire a hit man, especially if there's something in your past that you're trying to hide.''

Earl started to smile. ''Kelly, I'm beginning to remember what a good cop you were.''

''What do we know about Lawson's past?'' Luke asked.

''Not nearly enough,'' Earl said. ''But I'll put a bug in my detective's ear. There's no telling what else we might turn up.''

''What's the police chief's name in Nashville?'' Luke asked.

''Randall. I'll give him a call right now.''

''You tell him I'll be there today…at the latest, this afternoon.''

''What if you can't get a flight?''

''He'll be arriving in my corporate jet,'' Sam said. ''If there are any more developments, you'll be sure to let us know?''

''Count on it,'' Earl said. ''Like I told my men, I've got a personal interest in this one. It's been an open sore on the department record for too many years. It's time to close it.

And, Sam, before I forget, you might want to brace your daughter for some more flak from the media.''

"Why?" Luke asked.

"You remember those drawings she gave us?"

"Yes."

"There's a possibility that someone leaked their existence to the press. If so, we're guessing there's going to be mass hysteria among a large number of child molesters once word hits the news."

Luke stood still for a moment, absorbing what Earl had said. Then it hit him.

"You couldn't find a way to use them legally, could you?"

"We had…options," Earl said.

"Earl, you're a scary man," Luke said.

Earl grinned. "I'll take that as a compliment."

They all three disconnected at the same time, but Sam was confused.

"I don't get it," he said. "What's going on with those drawings?"

"Remember when Jade gave them to him? She said she didn't care if the press found out about what had happened to her if it would stop other children from being harmed? Well, I'm guessing that the police ran into difficulties identifying the faces, because the images are so old. They don't have names, and they don't know where those men might be living now. Coupled with that, the law varies from state to state regarding the statute of limitations. Some of them, even if identified, couldn't be prosecuted because of the time issue alone. But…if the media got wind of them…and if someone just happened to sell copies of the drawings to some tabloid…"

Understanding dawned. "Just because the authorities wouldn't be able to identify them, that doesn't mean other people won't. People who knew those man when they were younger."

"Exactly."

"Brilliant," Sam muttered. "And I hope it scares the hell out of every mother's son of them."

Luke patted Sam on the back.

"I need to go tell Jade."

"Tell me what?" Jade asked.

Luke jumped. Sam gasped.

"I didn't know you were there," Luke said.

Jade frowned. "Obviously. So what is it you need to tell me?"

"They've arrested the man they think hired Johnny Newton."

Impulsively she clapped her hands in a gesture of relief.

"You're kidding! So soon? Does this mean the danger is passed? What's his name?"

"Maybe," Luke said, then took a deep breath, carefully watching Jade's face as he answered the last part of her question. "His name is Frank. Frank Lawson. He's running for governor of Tennessee."

Jade heard the name, but from a distance. Already the room was starting to spin. She was reaching for Luke's arm when everything went black. She never knew that he caught her before she hit the floor.

"In here!" Sam cried, and led the way into the living room, where he tossed the throw pillows on the sofa into the floor. "Do you think we should call someone?"

Luke laid her gently down on the sofa, then smoothed the hair back from her face. Only seconds before, she had been so at ease. Now they were back to square one.

"No. She just fainted. Maybe if we had a wet cloth?"

Sam hurried out of the room, calling for Velma as he went.

Within seconds of Sam's exit, Jade began coming around. The first thing she felt were hands on her face, then her body, and she began pushing them away in an effort to escape.

"No, no...get away from me."

Immediately Luke turned loose of her.

"Easy, honey, it's okay. It's me, Luke. Take it easy. You just fainted."

She groaned, then rolled over to the side of the sofa and sat up.

"What happened?"

"I mentioned Frank Lawson's name. You fainted."

"Oh God." She started to tremble.

"Do you think it's the same man?" Luke asked.

"I don't know. I'd have to see his face."

"Did you draw a picture of the man who cut you?"

Jade gasped, then nodded. "Yes. The police have it. The name on it is Uncle Frank."

"I'll have Earl fax a copy of the picture to my apartment," Luke said. "I'll take it with me when I go to Nashville. I'll bring back a picture of the man they arrested."

"Should I go with you?"

"Hell no. The media would have a field day with that." Then he sighed. He had to tell her the rest, so she could at least be prepared. "There's something else," he said. "Earl hinted that someone might have leaked the existence of your drawings to the press. If so, don't be surprised if they start showing up in the tabloids."

"I don't care," she said. "They've haunted me for far too long. Let someone else live with those faces for a while."

Luke grinned. "Way to go, Jade!"

"What?"

He cupped her face, then leaned down and gave her a kiss.

"Because after grief, one of the next steps to healing is anger, and God knows you have a right to be pissed."

"I do, don't I?"

At that point Sam came running back into the room, with Velma on his heels carrying a handful of damp washcloths and a large fluffy towel. When Sam saw Jade sitting up, he dropped onto the cushion beside her.

"Darling, are you all right?"

Her chin jutted angrily. "Yes. Sorry I upset you. It was just such a surprise."

"Then I take it you don't need reviving," he said.

"Not at all. What I need is some justice, and you and Luke are doing all you can to see that happen."

"All right, then," Sam said, then grabbed a wet cloth from the stack in Velma's hands and slapped it on his own forehead. "You may not need this anymore, but I do."

They all looked at him and then burst out laughing. He grinned wryly, then leaned against the sofa and scrubbed the wet cloth over his face.

Luke left within the hour. Jade stood at the window, waving as he drove away. She waved until she could no longer see his car, then glanced at the house across the street. A shudder ran through her as she thought of that poor little woman. What a horrible end to what had been a long and happy life.

Somewhere in another part of the house a phone began to ring. She turned around, then paused in the foyer, staring at the surrounding opulence. It was still difficult to believe that she had the right to take all of this for granted.

"Jade...honey...have you got a minute?"

Sam was halfway up the stairs, standing on the landing.

She shrugged. "Time is about all I do have." Then she made herself smile. "And it's all yours."

Sam held out his hand. "Come with me. I have something to show you."

Jade let him lead her up the stairs. "Where are we going?" she asked.

"You'll see," he said, and led her past her old bedroom to another set of stairs. They went up yet another story.

Jade gasped in surprise. "Oh my, I guess I thought this level of the house was just an attic."

Sam smiled as he took her hand. "When my grandfather was a little boy, it was the servants' quarters. Once your

mother and I had plans to fill this house with children.'' The smile shifted slightly as sadness came and went on his face. ''But of course that didn't happen. Years back, I used to host the occasional house party, and these were the guest rooms. But no more. I don't have the stomach for all the fuss and bother. Lately it's just been gathering dust.''

''So why are we here?'' Jade asked.

''You'll see. It's right behind this door. Now close your eyes.''

Jade's eyes widened. ''You mean it's a surprise?''

Sam chuckled. ''Yes. For you. Your eyes, please.''

She closed her eyes. Sam took her hand and led her forward.

''Careful here. There's a small threshold. Step over it. And don't peek.''

Jade giggled.

The sound brought tears to Sam's eyes, but he quickly brushed them away. Today was a day of joy, not for reminders of all they'd lost.

''Okay. Now you can look.''

Still smiling, Jade opened her eyes. Then she gasped and took a sudden step back.

''Oh! Oh, no.'' She clasped her hands over her mouth and then looked at Sam in disbelief. ''You did this? For me?''

''You don't like it? You're such a powerful artist, I thought you—''

''Like it? Oh, Dad…you don't understand. It's like something out of a dream. I always wanted…I thought maybe one day I…''

She covered her face and then started to cry.

Sam smiled with relief. A crying woman made him nervous, but a woman crying from happiness he could handle. He gave her a hug, then handed her his handkerchief and tugged her forward.

''Look. See here by this bank of windows? You'll have good morning light. There are dozens and dozens of different

sizes of canvases, and a supply of paints and brushes in the cabinet in the next room. Oh...and I didn't know about easels, so I got several. One is for very large canvases, the others, I'm told, are adjustable.''

Jade kept moving from one thing to another, picking it up and then putting it down as something else caught her eye. Finally she remembered where she was and that Sam was still there.

''This is the most marvelous thing anyone has ever done for me. I don't know how to thank you.''

Sam let out a big sigh of relief.

''Paint me a pretty picture.''

She laughed, and then ran toward him, threw her arms around his neck and soundly kissed his cheek.

''Oh, Sam... Daddy...thank you, thank you a thousand times.''

Sam froze. He had heard her say it once before, but he had begun to believe it would never happen again. Now he was the one in tears.

''Jade, darling, it was a pleasure. Don't you know how much you are loved?''

''You know... I think I'm beginning to find out.''

''Okay then,'' Sam said. ''Why don't I leave you to look around on your own?''

''Yes, all right, but where will you be?''

''Oh, honey, don't worry. I'll be right here in the house. If you need me, call out. I'll come running.''

''I'll be fine. I just...just wanted to know, that's all.''

''Of course. You hardly had time to settle in here before everything came undone. In time, you will feel comfortable here again, just as you did when you were a child.''

She thought about what he'd said and knew that would never happen unless she came to terms with her past. But she didn't know how.

''Daddy?''

''Yes?''

"You know that doctor...Dr. DiMatto?"

"Antonia?"

Jade nodded. "So, do you think it would be possible if I saw her sometimes? You know...just until I can get a handle on things?"

"I think that's a very good idea. Would you like me to call her for you?"

"Raphael always wanted me to get help. I would never listen to him. I wish he was still alive so I could tell him I understand, and that I know he was right."

"He knows, Jade."

"Yes, maybe he does at that," Jade said.

"I'll go make that call."

"Okay, and if Luke happens to call, will you let me know?"

Sam hid a smile. "Yes. I'll let you know."

Twenty-One

Sam Cochrane's jet arrived in Nashville just after two in the afternoon. Luke was out of the plane and in a cab within minutes of landing. He gave the address to the driver, then settled back for the ride. A short while later, he dumped a handful of bills over the seat, grabbed his own suitcase and hurried into the building. After that, it was just a matter of getting to the police chief's office.

"Chief Randall, I'm Luke Kelly. Thank you for seeing me on such short notice."

Randall met him at the door.

"Earl Walters called. I've been expecting you."

Luke set his suitcase down, then followed the chief back to his desk.

"Have a seat," Randall said. "So, I understand you want to interrogate one of our prisoners?"

"Frank Lawson."

Randall leaned back in his chair and crossed his hands over his chest.

"Yes, Big Frank himself. If someone had told me two days ago that this would be happening, I would have called them a liar. Now…" He shrugged.

"It's important," Luke said.

Randall's good old boy attitude quickly vanished.

"Everything regarding the law in my city is important to me, too, son. But I understand you have a personal interest in this?"

Luke nodded. "You're familiar with the Cochrane case in St. Louis?"

Randall nodded. "Everyone is, if they watch any television. Earl Walters is a good friend. He said you could be trusted. I am assuming you're not planning to let him down?"

"No, sir. But our best interests are aimed at Jade Cochrane's welfare. Someone put a hit out on her childhood friend, Raphael, and we think on her, too. She and I had a near miss with some tampered brakes. But Raphael was brutally murdered, as were his private nurse and an elderly woman who lived in the house across the street from Sam Cochrane. The killer was a man named Johnny Newton. I trust you've already been told all this?"

"Yes, but please continue. You're putting it into a much clearer perspective for me."

"When Newton was taken down, we found a piece of paper in his clothes with Frank Lawson's name and private cell phone number on it. We took Newton's own phone and made the call so that his name would show up on caller ID. Frank Lawson basically spilled his guts before he realized he wasn't talking to Newton. Then he tried to lie his way out of it. Obviously our men didn't buy it, and then your men stopped him from flight. So what I need to know is if he's the end, or if there's someone farther up who's calling the shots."

"And you think you can get answers from him that we can't?"

Luke leaned forward.

"Oh yes."

Randall frowned. "Why you?"

"Because I'm in love with Jade Cochrane. And I want to know if he's the son-of-a-bitch who put a scar on her that nearly killed her. I want to know if he was one of the men who paid money to be with her when she was a child."

Randall was shocked and made no attempt to hide it.

"Are you saying that Frank Lawson is a child molester?"

Luke took the photocopy of the picture of the man Jade had called Uncle Frank from his jacket and laid it on Randall's desk.

"Is this man Frank Lawson?"

Randall picked up the picture. Despite the years between, it was definitely recognizable.

"Good drawing."

"Jade Cochrane is a professional artist."

"She drew this?"

"And a whole lot more."

Randall whistled softly through his teeth as he kept looking at the drawing. "Yes, I'd say that's Lawson. A much younger version, but Lawson just the same."

Luke felt a surge of justification as he put the picture back in his pocket, then took out the other one he'd brought.

"This is the drawing she did of the bastard who called himself Solomon. He was the supposed leader and pimped the kids in the cult to pedophiles. She was six when it started and twelve when she ran. Thanks to your ID, we can pretty much assume that Lawson was one of the customers."

During his career in law enforcement, Randall was a man who'd often been exposed to the darker side of society, but this story turned even his stomach.

"Christ! And we almost elected him governor."

"So do I get to talk to him or not?"

"I'd like a couple of my detectives to sit in."

"I don't care if you televise it to the whole city," Luke said.

Randall nodded. "Okay, let's get this show rolling." He picked up the phone and made a call. "Captain, this is Chief Randall. I'm sending a man named Luke Kelly over to your office. I would take it as a personal favor if you would have a couple of your detectives escort him to an interview room and provide him with Frank Lawson's presence. Oh, yes. It might be a good idea if the detectives stayed with him. He

seems like a nice enough man, but he's real pissed right now, not that I blame him. However, we wouldn't want to have to put a good man in jail.... Yes. Thank you.''

Luke breathed a quiet sigh of relief. It was going to happen.

"International flight passengers traveling to New York City with connecting flights to Lisbon or Antigua, please begin boarding at Gate...."

Otis cursed beneath his breath and then shifted his carry-on to the other side of his seat. He'd been waiting for the better part of two hours to board his flight to Geneva at LAX, but it kept showing up on the departure board as a delay. He'd questioned the gate attendants so many times that now they glared at him every time he moved. The only good thing about the departure of this latest flight was that the woman and her three screaming kids who had been sitting beside him would be leaving, too. No wonder her husband was getting on that plane without her. If she was his wife, he would leave her and those brats behind—permanently. Then he amended the thought. If she'd been his wife, he would have made damned sure she'd never gotten with child. He didn't like kids. Never had. Except as a commodity, but even that had run its course.

Which reminded him that it was because of kids that he was, once again, on the run. Starting over in life had been easy, even fun, when he was younger. But he was getting to the age where he liked his creature comforts more than excitement. Hell, he'd screwed more women in his lifetime than a thousand men put together, then made a fortune selling films of them screwing others. It had been a damned good run, but thanks to Jade Cochrane's tenacity, that was now over, too.

Slowly the area began to clear, and for a time the only things to be heard were the distant rumble of voices and the occasional squawk of the P.A. system announcing another

arrival or departure. In boredom, he glanced up at the television mounted on the wall above him and then grunted as if he'd been punched.

It was a close-up of Frank Lawson's face. Only it wasn't one of his prerecorded political spots. According to the news anchor, the film they were showing had been recorded earlier this morning. It was of Lawson being arrested, handcuffed and taken to jail. Rumors abounded as to why it was happening, but the one that seemed to have the most credence had him connected to a hit man and three murders in Missouri.

Otis groaned. This sucked. If they'd already tied Lawson to that, then it stood to reason that they would find out why Lawson wanted them dead. And if they found that out, then it also stood to reason that they would want to know the name of the man who'd provided Lawson with his...entertainment years ago. And if Lawson knew or could find out where "Solomon" had gone... Otis Jacks' days were numbered—unless, of course, his flight finally took off.

Then he took a slow, calming breath. They could look for both Solomon and Otis Jacks until the end of time but wouldn't be able to find them. Solomon had vanished years ago, and Otis Jacks, too, had dropped off the face of the earth as abruptly as he had arrived. Otis wasn't Otis anymore. He was Myron Handelman. He owned property in Switzerland in that name. He had money in a Swiss bank under that name, and he had purchased his ticket under that name. He had a passport, a driver's license and credit cards to prove it. The only thing that bothered him was that he hadn't had time to get the new face. That would have to wait until he got to Geneva.

Frank Lawson had lost all his bluster. For a man who had spent the past few months making speech after speech, he was unusually silent. When he'd been told that someone from St. Louis was coming to talk to him, he'd insisted that his

lawyer be present. Now, while he was waiting for everyone to arrive, he kept thinking back over the last week, trying to figure out what he could have done differently, wondering if it would have made any difference if he'd simply gone to St. Louis and done the job himself. He knew he was capable of murder. He just hadn't been certain he could get close enough to Jade or Raphael, so he'd hired Newton, which had proved to be a fiasco. How could he have known that Newton was such a screw-up? Hired killers were supposed to be cold and calculating—and careful. Newton had proved to be the exception to the rule. And that had brought both of them down.

And Frank Lawson *was* down—as down as he'd ever been in his life—but he wasn't out completely. At least, not yet. He would wait to see what this St. Louis cop had to offer, then make his decision as to the wisest course of action.

"Hey, Governor, you've got a visitor. Get up and step away from the door."

Frank ignored the snide reference to his defunct political aspirations and pretended it was an everyday occurrence to be wearing prison orange as he received guests. Ignoring the handcuffs the guard snapped around his wrists, he let himself be led to the visiting area.

He was swaggering as he walked into the room. He recognized two of Nashville's homicide detectives and nodded cordially. Then his gaze slid to the tall, dark-haired man in the corner of the room. He was standing with his feet apart and his arms folded across his chest, and he was staring at Frank with what could only be described as complete antipathy.

Frank stared rudely. The man didn't so much as blink. But in the ensuing seconds, Frank would have sworn that the air in the room suddenly became too dense to breathe. He wanted to look away but found himself locked into the stranger's stare.

"Mr. Lawson, please sit down."

Frank blinked, then realized one of the detectives was speaking. He sat.

"Where's Gorman? Where's my lawyer?" he asked.

"I'm right here," Paul Gorman said as he was ushered into the room. "Sorry I'm late. Got caught in traffic."

Bolstered by his lawyer's presence, Frank settled back in the chair.

"So what's up?" he asked.

One of the detectives, a man named Art Brewster, noticed they were now a chair short and motioned to the guard who'd brought Lawson in.

"Would you tell someone outside to get Mr. Kelly a chair?"

"I'll stand," Luke said.

Frank frowned. It was an intimidation tactic. Determined to control the situation, he spoke up first.

"Mr. Kelly, is it? I don't believe we've met."

"Jade Cochrane sends her regards."

The blood drained out of Lawson's face so fast he felt light-headed. He knew he should respond, but he couldn't find the words.

"What's wrong?" Luke asked. "Surely you haven't forgotten her? Pretty little girl. Black hair. Blue eyes. Begging for you to let her go. But you couldn't, could you? You like them fragile and helpless. The flat chest and tiny hands and feet turn you on, don't they."

Lawson swayed, as if Luke's words were actual physical blows, then looked wildly about the room, only to be met with horrified stares. He'd been riding out the accusations of hiring a hit man with aplomb, but having the world know his dirty little secret was like having his legs cut out from under him.

"Shut up," he mumbled. "Shut up. You don't know what you're talking about."

Luke moved then. Only one step, but it was enough to make Frank panic.

"Keep him away from me," Frank said.

"I told Jade that if I ever found the man who cut her, I would kill him."

Both detectives jumped, their hands automatically going to their guns.

"But then I decided there was a better punishment for him than a quick death."

The detectives relaxed. Frank did not.

"Gorman...do something! You can't let him talk to me like that."

Gorman was already waffling between his conscience and the money Lawson was paying him. He'd represented plenty of people accused of murder, some who had actually done the deed. But Paul Gorman had three little girls, ages twelve, seven and six, and Luke Kelly's accusations had literally turned his stomach. He couldn't find the words to answer.

"Lawson!" Luke barked.

Frank's frantic gaze slid back to Luke Kelly.

"Leave me alone," Frank whined. "You're no cop. I don't have to talk to you if I don't want to."

"Me leave you alone?" He grinned. "You need to practice that phrase, because where you're headed, you're going to use it more than you can imagine."

"What are you talking about?" Frank asked.

"Do you know who inmates hate worse than the people who put them behind bars? Perverts. Child molesters. Pedophiles. That's who. I don't have to live with your blood on my hands, because once you're inside, someone is bound to do the job for me, and with a whole lot more originality."

Suddenly Frank's lunch was at the back of his throat, threatening to come up. Someone was whimpering. It took him a few moments to realize the sounds were coming out of him. If ever there was a time to play his hole card, this was it.

"I want to make a deal," he mumbled, the handcuffs

banging against the top of the table as he reached toward Detective Brewster.

"You don't have anything I want," Luke said.

"Yes, yes, I do," Frank said. "I know Solomon. I know where he is."

Luke's expression sharpened. "Like hell."

"It's true! I swear!" Frank cried. Then he grabbed Paul Gorman's arm. "Tell them! Tell them we'll deal. I'll give them Solomon if they'll keep that part of my business out of the papers."

Luke had his hands on Lawson before the detectives even knew he'd moved.

"You'll tell me where he is, or you won't live to go to trial," Luke whispered.

"Not until we deal. Not until we deal!"

Both detectives grabbed Luke and pulled him back. He immediately turned Lawson loose.

"He's fine," Luke snapped, as he shrugged out of their grasp.

"He threatened me," Lawson whined.

"That wasn't a threat. It was a promise," Luke said.

Frank looked wild-eyed from one man to the other. None of them were saying anything. Finally he threw up his cuffed hands in self-defense.

"Look! Jade wasn't the only one he sold. There were dozens of kids in that cult. Boys and girls. And I wasn't the only one who knew what was going on. Solomon had plenty of customers."

Brewster was frowning as he looked at Luke.

"Who the hell is Solomon?"

Luke sighed, then shoved his hands through his hair in mute frustration. He didn't want to make any kind of deal with Frank Lawson, but he could see one coming.

"Back in the seventies, there was a commune...a cult...call it what you want, but they called themselves the People of Joy. They were led by a man named Solomon.

Margaret Cochrane, Jade's mother, got involved and took her daughter with her when she ran away with them. Jade was four. Two years later, Margaret died of some drug overdose, leaving her little girl in the hands of those people. Instead of getting the child back to her father, Solomon took her, as well as the other children there, and repeatedly sold them to pedophiles. Jade said the children called them uncles. When she was twelve, a man she knew only as Uncle Frank cut her, damn near killing her. After that, she and another kid, a boy named Raphael, ran away. They'd been on the move until…well, the media took the story of her being reunited with her father and plastered it all over the national news. I'm guessing that when good old Uncle Frank, who had an agenda all his own, realized that same little girl was alive and all grown up, he panicked. It wouldn't do to have skeletons like her rattling around in his closet this close to election day, right, Frank?"

Brewster eyed Frank.

"Is this true? Did this Solomon keep the children prisoners?"

"I don't know what he did with them. I didn't live there," Frank said. "But I know where he is, and I know the name he's living under."

Luke's heart skipped a beat, but he wouldn't let himself hope. "If Solomon is as tuned in to current events as you were, there's no guarantee he's still there."

"Mr. Kelly, we're now looking at Federal kidnapping charges," Brewster said. "I'm going to ask you to leave now. We need to question Mr. Lawson further regarding this turn of events."

"Where is he?" Luke asked, completely ignoring Brewster's demands.

Frank looked wildly from one cop to the other. "Do we have a deal?"

"Tell me," Luke said. "Do it now, or I go to the papers with everything."

Brewster was pushing Luke toward the door.

"Lawson, if I walk out of here, your days of breathing are numbered," Luke warned.

"Los Angeles!" Frank yelled. "He owns a porn studio called Shooting Star or Rising Star or something like that. He goes by the name of Otis Jacks. And I know he's going to leave the country."

Luke groaned, wondering if it was already too late. "What country? Where was he going?"

Frank grabbed his lawyer's arm again. "For God's sake, speak up you son-of-a-bitch! What the hell am I paying you for if I'm the one who's doing all the negotiations?"

"Good question," Gorman said. "I cannot, in good faith, represent you anymore. I have three daughters, which biases me against giving you fair representation. And off the record, if you did what that man says you did, then I hope you rot in hell."

Lawson gasped. He jumped up from his chair.

"You can't do this!" he shrieked. "You're all railroading me. I have a constitutional right to fair representation."

Brewster's partner grabbed Lawson by the arm and yanked him back toward the chair.

"Sit down, Mr. Lawson, before I put you down."

"I can get a phone number." Luke said. "I want more."

Frank moaned. "You can't do this to me. It's not fair."

It took every ounce of control Luke had not to put his hands around Lawson's throat and squeeze the life out of him.

"You had your chance," Luke said. "And just so you know, there's a rumor that someone has already leaked the faces to the media."

"What faces?" Frank asked.

Luke grinned. "Oh. Didn't anyone tell you? Jade Cochrane grew up to be quite an artist. She has a formidable file of drawings of the men who defiled her. They're very good.

Close to photographic in quality.'' Then he stuck his hand in his pocket. ''Here, want to see yours?''

He tossed the picture down on the table.

Frank took one look at it and started to cry. ''You don't understand. I don't do that sort of thing anymore. I was into drugs back then. I did things I don't even remember. It was the drugs. Not me. I would never—''

Luke opened the door and walked out.

Frank started yelling.

''323-555-2390. It's Jacks' cell phone number. Call it. You'll see. Just don't let them put me in prison with... I don't want to die.''

Luke kept on walking. The two detectives were right behind him.

''Listen, Kelly. This has become a federal investigation. Sounds like the kid was held hostage after her mother's death. If so, that becomes kidnapping, which is a federal offense. Stay out of it. It's none of your business.''

Luke just kept walking.

''Where are you going?''

''And that is none of *your* business,'' Luke said, then he took out his cell phone, glanced at his watch, and called the pilot of Sam's jet. If they were lucky, they should arrive at LAX before dark.

As soon as they were in the air, Luke made a call to Earl Walters, filling him in on everything that had taken place. Earl quickly transferred Luke to Detective Myers of the St. Louis P.D., who was heading the Newton investigation.

''Detective, I'd really appreciate any help you can give me. If Frank Lawson is telling the truth, then we probably have a very narrow window of time in which to get Otis Jacks before he disappears. From what Lawson said, he must be a master at reinventing himself.''

''Happy to oblige,'' Myers said. ''How can we help?''

''I'm on my way to L.A. now. Call the LAPD, tell them

the situation, maybe fax them a copy of the drawing Jade did of Jacks, the man she calls Solomon. He runs some porn studio by the name of Rising Star or Shooting Star.... Lawson wasn't clear on that. See if they can get an address for his home or office and pick him up. If you would keep me posted as to their progress, I would appreciate it.''

''Will do,'' Myers said. ''And good luck.''

''Oh, by the way,'' Luke said. ''How is Johnny Newton?''

''He'll live to go to prison.''

''Pity,'' Luke drawled.

Myers grinned. Normally he wouldn't have appreciated someone outside the precinct involving himself in their business like this, but Kelly had been a cop. And this was a personal mission. He understood that.

''Yeah, a real pity,'' Myers said. ''I'll keep you posted.''

They disconnected quickly, after which Luke promptly made a call to Jade.

Jade hadn't intended to do anything more than look through the art supplies in her new studio. But the moment she'd picked up some of the brushes and felt the soft, perfect sable bristles, she'd been lost. She'd gone back to her room, found the sketch pad with the drawing she'd done of Luke asleep by her bed and hurried back upstairs.

Within the hour, she'd started a portrait of him. Just the simple act of recreating his face was comforting. The scent of oil paint filled the air. The only sounds that could be heard were the sweep of brush to canvas and the occasional squeak of a loose board beneath Jade's feet as she moved around the easel. It was her habit to study a work from every angle as she painted, making sure that no matter where a person stood, it seemed the subject was looking straight at him. It was a trick of light and shadow and had to do with the eyes, but it was something in which she took pride.

As the face began to take shape, Jade would occasionally speak to Luke, as if he were sitting for the portrait. They

were nothing but small, offhand remarks that required no answers but were soothing to her just the same.

It wasn't until her head began to hurt that she realized she'd been squinting. She looked up and then around, surprised to see that the sun was close to setting. Stretching her back, she gave the unfinished portrait a judgmental look, then began to clean her brushes.

She was on her way downstairs to clean up before dinner with Sam when she heard him calling up to her. She leaned over the landing.

"I'm here."

"Darling... Luke is on the phone. He wants to talk to you."

"I'll take it in my room," she said, and then dashed back down the hall. Her heart was pounding as she picked up the receiver. "Hello?"

Luke began to smile. "Hello, honey. I miss you."

She hugged herself as she crawled up on the bed. "I miss you, too," she said shyly. "What's happening? Are you on the way home?"

"No, but I wish I was. I'm on my way to L.A."

"You didn't go to Nashville?"

"I did."

There was a catch in her breath, then Luke heard her ask, "Did you see the man...the man named Frank Lawson?"

"Yes."

"Was it...is he...?"

"Yes."

Without thinking, she laid her hand over the top of her scar.

"Oh my God." Her voice started to shake. "All these years, and I thought maybe Raphael had killed him. He beat him so bad. We never talked about it, but we thought it just the same. Is he...did he hire that man to kill us?"

"Yes, but he's locked up, baby, and he's not going anywhere."

"You're sure?"

"Absolutely."

She started breathing a little easier. Luke hadn't lied to her yet, and she had no reason to think he would start now.

"So why aren't you coming home?"

"It's a little complicated. Frank Lawson had some information we hadn't expected."

"Like what?"

"He says he knows where Solomon is."

Luke heard her gasp, then nothing.

"Jade? Honey?"

"I'm here." Then she shuddered. "I feel like every nightmare I ever had is coming to life."

"I know, and I'm sorry I'm not there to help you through this. But this is important. There's a chance he's trying to get out of the country and I can't let that happen."

"I just want you to come home."

"I know, honey, and so do I. We have lots of things to talk about."

"I'm painting again...and I asked Daddy to call Dr. DiMatto. I thought maybe I should...you know."

Luke sighed. He knew how hard it was for her to talk about her past. But it was going to be the key to her recovery.

"I'm so proud of you, baby."

"I want to be well."

"And you will be. Tell Sam I'll call him when I know something more."

"Yes. All right."

"Jade...honey?"

"Yes."

"I love you."

She closed her eyes, hugging the words close to her heart.

"I love you, too," she said softly.

The line hummed in her ear.

Twenty-Two

Otis was watching the departure board when the signs began to change. He stared at the words in disbelief as, one by one, the post next to all flights changed to read Canceled. Canceled. Canceled. Canceled.

He jumped to his feet in disbelief.

"No," he moaned, and dashed toward the gate. "What's happening? You can't do this! You don't understand! I've got to leave for Switzerland today!"

The attendant pointed to the television screen.

"Sir, you're the one who doesn't understand. Haven't you been watching the news?"

Otis turned around and then dashed toward the set, standing close enough so that he heard the news anchor's voice.

"A major storm front is moving down out of the mountains and into L.A. All flights in and out of L.A., as well as the surrounding areas, have been delayed."

Otis shook his head in disbelief, then started to curse. He beat his fists against his legs, then threw his carry-on as far as it would go. He was still cursing when airport security grabbed him from behind.

"Sir. You need to come with us."

Otis jerked, then started to struggle. "No, no, I can't. I've got a flight to catch."

"No, sir. You're not going anywhere right now."

As they began to lead him through the airport, he remembered his bag—the one he'd thrown.

"My bag! My bag! I need to get my bag!"

"We have it," the guard said, and held up Otis's carry-on.

Otis stumbled. "Look. I'm sorry, okay? I was upset because my flight was canceled. I just lost my temper, you know?" Then he tried to laugh. "You guys know how it is. You have a bad day…you let off a little steam…and it's over, right? Well that's all it was…just letting off a little steam."

They didn't answer, but they took his identification, and they didn't let him go.

He muttered to himself all the way through the terminal, but when they took him through a door that was off limits to everyone but security, he knew he was in trouble.

"I'm calling my lawyer," he threatened. "You can't treat people like this and get away with it."

One of the guards pushed him through a pair of double doors and then unlocked another door to a small room, while another got on a call phone, verifying his ID.

"Actually, sir, yes we can. At the least, you disturbed the peace. At the most, your rampage frightened passengers and gave us reason to suspect that you may be unstable and a danger to others."

Then the other guard spoke. "Sir, there seems to be a question about your identity. You will be detained here until the arrival of Federal agents, at which time, they will question you further. Apparently, 'Mr. Handleman,' you've been dead for six years."

At that moment, Otis knew he was fucked.

He sat down in the only chair in the room, leaned his head back against the wall and started to laugh. He had to. It was either that or off himself. And since his hands were cuffed behind his back and his natural instinct for survival precluded him from holding his breath long enough to die, that wasn't going to happen.

* * *

"Captain Warren, there's a call for you from a Captain Myers with the St. Louis P.D."

"I'll take it in my office," Warren said, and hurried inside. He tossed a stack of paperwork on his desk and then leaned across a lamp to reach the phone. "Captain Myers, this is Joe Warren. How can I help you?"

"Captain Warren, I'll be brief, because we have reason to believe that time in this situation is at a minimum. We have information that a man living in your city under the name of Otis Jacks is connected to a case we're working, which includes three murders, kidnapping and pimping children to child molesters."

"Good God," Warren muttered. "Is that all?"

"We're not sure. Our information is sketchy, but we believe he's trying to leave the country. He supposedly was running a porn studio named Shooting Star or Rising Star. During the late seventies and early eighties, he headed a cult that called themselves the People of Joy. This is where the kidnapping and pimping took place. Are you familiar with the Jade Cochrane case out here in St. Louis?"

"Is that the prodigal daughter story…some kid returned after twenty years?"

"Yes. From the age of six until twelve, when she finally escaped, Jade Cochrane was at the mercy of this man who called himself Solomon. We've already arrested a man in Tennessee for hiring a hit man to kill both Jade and the friend who helped her run away. He allegedly molested her over a period of time, and when he heard that she'd been returned to the fold, so to speak, he was afraid she'd ruin his career. If you can believe it, the bastard was running for governor. The hit man, a man named Johnny Newton, got to Jade's friend. Newton killed him and his nurse, as well as an elderly woman whose home he used for a stakeout."

"What do you want us to do?"

"There's a man named Luke Kelly who's flying in on private jet. He should be landing at LAX within an hour o so. Once he arrives, he will corroborate what I'm telling you He's an ex-cop with a personal interest in Miss Cochrane However, if you could locate Otis Jacks and pick him up fo questioning, it would save us all a lot of time and worry. I this bastard gets out of the country, it will be a terrible in justice to all the children he helped to destroy."

"I'll put my best men on it," Warren said. "In the mean time, fax me everything you have."

"Pictures of Solomon are already being faxed as we speak They're of the man as he looked twenty years ago, bu they're all we have."

"I'll let you know what we find out," Warren said, the hung up the phone, walked out of his office and pointed two of his best detectives.

"Ruiz. Drury. We need to talk."

Amelia Ruiz and Fred Drury got up from their desks an followed the captain into his office. Within minutes, the were on their way out with the fax of Jade's drawing c Solomon.

Amelia Ruiz was a short, slim Latino with a body tha wouldn't quit. She had worked vice before she'd transferre to homicide and knew of Otis Jacks by reputation. She als knew where Shooting Star Productions was located, so sh and her partner headed toward the Hollywood hills.

Drury was fond of teasing Ruiz about her previous wor He knew that she'd often gone undercover as a prostitut She ignored his teasing, just like she'd ignored the remark about her looks and her body. It wasn't easy being a co when you looked like a miniature centerfold.

"So, do you know this Jacks by sight?" Drury asked.

"No."

"That drawing is good, but a man's looks can change after all those years."

"I'd sure like to take him down," Ruiz said. "I know the seventies were all about free love and drugs, but what this Solomon did to those kids is disgusting. Do we know for sure that Otis Jacks is Solomon?"

"The captain said their information came from a man who's already been arrested for murder. I'm thinking maybe he wanted to make a deal just to lighten his sentence."

"Maybe, but then how would he have known about Solomon's existence?"

"Oh. Yeah. Right. Captain did say that he brought that up himself, didn't he?"

"Yep."

"Okay, so let's see what we see and hope for the best," Drury said.

A short while later, they pulled up to the iron security gates at Shooting Star Productions and buzzed the intercom.

"Shooting Star Productions. Do you have an appointment?" a woman asked.

Drury leaned out the window and flashed his badge toward the security camera.

"LAPD. We need to talk to Otis Jacks."

"Oh, Mr. Jacks isn't here anymore," she said. "He put the studio up for sale about three days ago. McAfee and Sons are handling the sale. I don't know where Mr. Jacks went."

"Do you have a home address or phone number for him?" Drury asked.

"Is he in trouble?" she asked.

"Are you?" Drury countered. "I can get a search warrant and put everyone in there out of a job pretty quick if I want to."

There was a brief shuffling of papers, then the woman answered.

"His address is 15582 Canyon Drive in Encino."

"How about a phone number?"

She rattled that out quickly, then clicked off.

Drury glanced at Ruiz and then shrugged. "Well, we can hope she doesn't call him and warn him we're coming, or we can call this in and see if the local P.D. will do a drive by and see if he's home."

"I vote for the drive by. I'd really hate to lose this character."

"Me too. Call it in."

Ruiz made the call as Drury started back down the hillside from the studio. While Ruiz was on the radio, Drury got on his cell phone and had the office pull all the records on Otis Jacks' phones. It would be interesting to see who he had called in the past few days.

They were on the freeway and heading to Encino when they got the word that Otis Jacks' apartment was vacant. Some of his belongings were still there, but a large portion of his clothes looked to be gone. They had also found a scratch pad with the phone number of LAX.

Ruiz quickly began making calls, trying to find out if there was a man named Otis Jacks scheduled to go out on any flights. When she learned the flights had been delayed, she grinned.

"We just got ourselves a break," she said. "Look at the sky."

Drury glanced up, then out the window. "Storm is coming. So what?"

"Flights have been delayed, but there's no Otis Jacks scheduled to travel. Gives us time to follow up on something else."

"Like what?" Drury asked.

"Like maybe he's using another identity," Ruiz said. "He used to call himself Solomon. Then Otis Jacks. Maybe he's branching out again."

"Yeah, maybe," Drury agreed. "So who do we know

who's capable of forging prime IDs to get someone overseas?''

"I know of one or two," Ruiz said. "Let's get copies of those phone records and see if we come up with a match."

"Good idea," Drury said, and took the exit off of the freeway and headed back to the station.

Sam was on his way up to his room to change for dinner when he noticed the door to Jade's old room was ajar. He started to close it; then something told him to look inside. She was sitting on her bed with her legs crossed and her old pink blanket clutched under her chin. She jumped when the door moved, then relaxed when she saw it was him.

"Hello, darling," Sam said. "Are you okay?"

"I don't know," she said.

"Want some company?"

She nodded.

He sat down at the foot of the bed, then turned to face her.

"Luke told you about Solomon and Frank, didn't he?" she asked.

"Yes. Is that what's bothering you?"

She laid the small blanket aside, then leaned forward, resting her elbows on her knees.

"I'm overwhelmed. I've spent most of life in hiding, only to have most of my ghosts show up all at once."

"I can only imagine how you feel. I don't think I can grasp the immensity of what it means to you."

She looked down at the tiny print on the coverlet, absently rubbing her fingers over the slightly raised designs.

"You used to do that when you were little," Sam said.

She looked up. "Do what?"

"Feel textures and shapes. Your mother had a pale blue chenille robe that you used to love. She wore it most nights when she was putting you to bed. You used to run your fingers over and over it."

Jade smiled. Even though she didn't remember doing that, it was comforting to think she had a history with this man. Then her thoughts shifted as she sat up straight and looked—really looked—at her dad.

"You know something, Daddy? You're very handsome."

Sam was a bit taken aback. "Why, thank you, honey."

"I'll bet you had lots of opportunities over the years to remarry. Why didn't you?"

He took her hand then, unaware that his smile was as sad as, if not sadder than the expression in his eyes.

"I guess because I loved your mother."

"Do you still?"

He thought about it, then frowned. "I love the memories of the times we had, but since your return, my feelings for her have certainly gone through a transformation."

"I'm sorry."

"Don't be," Sam said. "All those years, I consoled myself with the thought that you two were alive and well and, if not living together, were in constant contact as parents and children should be. What she did to you was so careless…so thoughtless…and brought you to such unimaginable harm that I can never think of her the same way again." Then he patted her hand to soften the blow. "Having said that, I must congratulate you on growing into such a marvelous woman. She would have been proud of you, as I am."

"Oh, Daddy, I wish I was as proud of myself as you are."

"You will be," Sam said.

She glanced at him quickly, then looked away. The silence grew between them until she finally spoke.

"There was a large free-standing mirror in Solomon's room in the house we lived in last…before Raphael and I ran. He used to take us, one by one, into that room and stand us naked before it. We couldn't look away from our own image or get away from his voice. And he would tell us over and over as we looked that we were ugly and that no one

loved us but him." Jade looked up then, managing a smile to soften what she was saying. "But even then, I knew he was wrong. You know why?"

Too upset by what she was saying, he could only shake his head.

"Because someone else did love me."

Understanding dawned. "Raphael."

She nodded. "Yes, Raphael. My Rafie. He was my brother, my family, my best friend. He never knew where he came from, but we suspected later, when we were older, that he was someone like me...someone whose mother had fallen in with the People, then died, or maybe just left, leaving him behind without caring what might happen. He didn't even have a last name. At least I knew that much about myself."

"I'm so sorry he's gone," Sam said. "I know what a hole that left in your heart."

Tears welled but didn't fall. "I want you to know how wonderful he was and how much he cared, because the more people who know about him, the less likely it is that he'll be forgotten. I don't think I could bear that." Then she laughed softly. "There were times all through our lives when I thought he might have wished he'd left me behind when he ran."

"Why?"

"Think about it," she said. "I was barely twelve when we got away from Solomon. My body was changing, both inside and out." Then she laughed aloud. "Oh, I knew about what would happen when I reached puberty. One of the women with the People had taken it upon herself to tell me that. But I didn't know how to go about doing anything for it. When I started my period, somehow Rafie came up with the necessary goods, but neither of us really knew what to do with them. You should have seen us reading those instructions, then trying to figure it out. Oh Lord, he was red in the face for days afterward." Her smile ended. "But he never

quit on me. Somehow I got through that, as well as first bras and learning how to shave my legs…and, well, the memories go on and on. Always him. Always there.''

Sam felt sick, but he made himself smile with her. His baby girl had literally grown up without him. Then he amended the thought. Thank God she'd lived to grow up.

''When did you first know you could draw?'' he asked.

''Oh, way back. When I was still with the People. There was a man who called himself Love Bug. Can you believe it? Anyway, he was always painting whatever vehicles we drove…you know, those horrible bright colors with the flowers and psychedelic designs? One day he caught me painting the fender of the van, but instead of getting me in trouble he encouraged me. Said it was good. After that, they let me decorate the walls inside the houses, at least, as far up as I could reach.''

''Amazing.''

''No. What was amazing was that it kept Raphael and me alive.''

''There's something I've wanted to ask you, but—''

''Ask,'' she said. ''It makes it easier for me if you know what I know.''

''You have a scar. I didn't know.''

Her expression went flat, but she didn't look away.

''I don't remember much about being cut, only knowing afterward that it had happened. I was almost unconscious from the beating before Raphael stopped…Uncle Frank. If he hadn't, I don't think I would have survived.''

''Did Solomon take you to the hospital?''

Jade rolled her eyes. ''You've got to be kidding. Someone would have asked him how it happened, then someone else would have wanted to know if he was my father, and he knew that I wouldn't lie for him.''

''Then how—''

''When Raphael took me away, we stole one of the Peo-

ple's vans. He also stole some of Solomon's money. I have
a vague memory of being treated at some emergency room
in a huge hospital. The waiting area was so crowded that
some people were standing, while others were sitting on the
floor. Rafie told me that when he came running in with me,
they snatched me out of his hands and took me away. He
followed, told them he was my brother and that our father
had done this while he was drunk. They had seen worse.
They sewed me up, treated the bruising and abrasions, and
told him to wait with me, that a policeman was on the way
to take our story. Then they got busy, and as soon as he
could, he stuffed his pockets with all the antibiotic ointments
he could find, pocketed some syringes and some penicillin,
and carried me out without anyone noticing.''

Sam's shoulders slumped. ''I am so sorry that his life had
to end as it did, but I want you to know. Had he been well,
I would have been proud to have him as a member of our
family.''

Jade threw her arms around Sam's neck and then just held
on. There were no words for what she was feeling—only love
and pride. Despite the hardships she had endured, she considered herself very blessed for the three remarkable men in
her life. Her father, then Raphael, and now Luke.

One had given her life, then loved her enough to never
quit looking for her. The second had loved her and kept her
alive at the expense of himself. And Luke had looked beyond
her emotional scars to the woman beneath and was teaching
her how to live again.

Now it was up to her to do her part. Tomorrow was her
first session with Antonia DiMatto, and no matter how painful it was, she was holding nothing back.

It was nearing sunset when Fred Drury and Amelia Ruiz
pulled up in front of a building down on the Sunset Strip.
The faint lettering on the brick above the doorway told them

it had once been a tailoring shop. But from the look of it now, it was, at best, a flop-house.

Otis Jacks' phone records had turned up an interesting co-incidence that they couldn't ignore. It was the phone number for a man who called himself Leonardo Da Vinci. Forger by name and by trade, since his given name was Truman Hollowell. The address that coincided with the phone number was on the third floor of this building.

"Don't touch the walls," Ruiz warned, as she and Drury started up the stairs to the third floor landing.

"Shit...don't breathe the air," Drury countered.

Ruiz grinned. "Sissy. This is nothing. You should have started out in Vice, like me."

"Just knock on the damned door," Drury whispered. "I've got you covered."

Ruiz doubled up her fist and then pounded on the door.

"Who is it?" a man called.

She shifted her voice to a higher pitch and let her speech flow back into a streetwise cadence.

"Señor...you let me in. I need some papers...the INS...they on my tail."

Due to a lack of physical exercise, given both his job and his love of food, Truman Hollowell was a very obese man. It took him a couple of minutes to get up from his chair and to the door. He wasn't expecting the badges Ruiz and Drury shoved in his face.

"We need to talk," Drury said, as he pushed his way past Truman and into the room.

"You got a search warrant? You need a search warrant!" Truman shouted.

"Why?" Ruiz asked. "We don't want to search you. We just need to ask you some questions."

"I ain't talkin' to no cops," Truman said.

"You either talk here or down at the station. It's your call," Drury said.

Truman cursed. He hadn't left his apartment in years and wasn't even sure he could get through the door.

"What the hell do you want, then?" he asked.

"You know a man named Otis Jacks?"

"No."

"That's strange. According to his phone records, he called you three times last week."

"Maybe it was a wrong number," Truman said.

"Look, Da Vinci, tell us what we need to know and we'll forget we were here. Fuck with us, and we'll get that search warrant, and I'm willing to bet you'll be spending the next few years in another kind of cell."

Truman glared. He hated mouthy women, but she had a point.

"So what if I know Jacks?"

"What do you think, Drury? Do you think he's trying to be helpful, or do you think we oughta call for that warrant?"

"I'm not hearing anything helpful," Drury said.

"Fuck!" Truman yelled. "Quit playing with me and ask me the goddamned questions."

Drury leaned forward, getting in Truman's space.

"You did a job for Otis Jacks. We need to know the name of his new identity, and we need it now."

Truman frowned. "What do I get if I tell you?"

"Peace and quiet," Ruiz said.

"Truth?" Truman asked.

She shrugged. "If you tell us what we want to know...truth."

He turned back to his worktable, holding on to the back of his sofa until he reached it. Then he pulled out a stack of papers, shuffled through it and then removed a single sheet.

"Myron Handleman. Credit cards. Driver's license. Passport."

"No social security card?" Drury asked.

"Social security doesn't exist where he's going," Truman said.

The moment Ruiz heard the name, she was back on the phone to LAX. It didn't take her long to get the info she needed. She gave Drury the thumbs-up.

Drury eyed the stack of papers in Truman Hollowell's hand. Truman saw the look and stuffed them back underneath the desk.

"You promised," he warned.

"Come on, Drury, let's get out of here," Ruiz said.

Drury shrugged, then took a handful of the pens Truman used to perform his craft and dropped them in the floor at Truman's feet.

Truman started to curse. Drury was still grinning as he shut the door behind him, knowing how difficult it would be for a man Hollowell's size to pick up anything off the floor.

"Did you have to do that?" Ruiz asked as they hurried down the stairs.

"He's lucky we didn't arrest him," Drury said.

"We're the lucky ones," Ruiz said. "I don't think we could have gotten him out of the door."

Drury's eyes widened; then he grinned. "Damn. I didn't think of that."

"That's why I'm here," Ruiz said. "Someone has to have the brains."

"Where to?" Drury asked, as he slid behind the wheel.

"LAX," Ruiz said. "And you'll never guess what. Our man is already in custody, awaiting the arrival of the Feds."

"Why?"

"Caused a ruckus when he found out his flight had been canceled, and then it turned out his ID was phoney."

Drury's grin widened. "And got himself arrested?"

"The term they used was 'detained.'"

"Call Captain Warren," Drury said.

Ruiz took her cell phone back out of her pocket and called the station.

"Captain, it's Ruiz. We've located Otis Jacks."

"Great. Are you bringing him in?"

"I'm not sure," she said. "He's at LAX, being detained by security. The Feds are on their way to interrogate him."

"Why?" Warren asked.

"He threw some kind of fit when his flight was canceled, then gave them a phony ID."

Warren chuckled. "I'll bet he did. Go to LAX. Stay with him. Luke Kelly will be there soon. Have security meet him and take him in. Don't leave Kelly alone with him. He has a personal interest in seeing this man come to justice, and he might not want to wait for the judicial system to do its thing."

"Yes, sir," Ruiz said. "What about the Feds?"

"I'll make some calls."

"Yes, sir," then she disconnected.

"What?" Drury asked.

"Keep driving. Kelly is going to meet us there, and the Captain is trying to delay the Feds."

Drury nodded and stomped on the accelerator.

Sam's jet was on the ground and had taxied to a stop when Luke's cell phone rang.

"Luke Kelly."

"Mr. Kelly…Captain Warren here. We have some good news for you. Airport security has Otis Jacks in custody."

Luke couldn't believe it could be this easy. "What? Why?"

"He lost his cool when all flights were delayed due to weather. The Feds are on their way to interrogate him, but so are two of my people. Detectives Ruiz and Drury will be meeting you at the security office."

"Thank you, Captain Warren. More than you can know."

"No problem," Warren said. "Happy we could help get filth like that off the streets."

Luke hurried through the plane to the cockpit. The pilot turned around.

"Do you need something, sir?"

"Fuel up and then get some rest. I want to get out of here as soon as we can."

"Yes, sir. But…we were one of the last planes allowed to land, because of the storm. We may be delayed in leaving."

Luke glanced up at the sky and frowned. "Do what you can," he said.

The pilot nodded. "I'll file the flight plans now. We'll be ready to leave when you say."

"Thanks," Luke said, and then headed for the terminal.

Twenty-Three

Otis was convinced his luck couldn't get much worse, and then the door opened. He looked up. He didn't recognize the trio that came in, but he assumed they were FBI.

"Sorry I can't offer you any refreshments, but I'm otherwise occupied," he drawled, and then showed him his handcuffs, as if they were a joke.

Luke stayed where he was, staring intently at the man, as Ruiz and Drury moved forward. Jade's drawing might be of a much younger man, but the resemblance was unmistakable. The hate that came with that knowledge was startling. He could have killed him where he sat and never looked back. But that wasn't going to happen.

Ruiz and Drury got to the table, flashed their badges and identified themselves, then pulled out two chairs and sat down.

"Otis, you're a hard man to run down," Ruiz said.

Otis was relieved to see that they were LAPD, rather than Feds. Given this situation, he wasn't ready to admit to being Otis Jacks, since he had a wad of identification that said otherwise. He frowned, then leaned forward, putting himself in their space.

"I'm sorry, my name is Myron Handleman. You have me confused with someone else."

"That's not what Truman said."

Otis frowned. "Who?"

"Oh…sorry…maybe you call him Leonardo. He's such a faker."

Otis blanched. Leonardo had double-crossed him.

"I still don't—"

Luke moved into Otis's view.

"Save it," he said, then slapped Jade's drawing on the table before him.

Otis stared at the picture in disbelief. "Where did you get that?"

"From the artist."

"I never sat for any artist," Otis said.

"Then you admit that's you," Ruiz said.

Otis gasped. He'd just screwed himself.

"I—"

"Save it, Mr. Jacks. You're not going anywhere, and we all know it. My suggestion would be to start thinking of your best way out of this mess, and lying isn't going to do it."

Otis shuddered. He had a sudden need to pee.

"I need a bathroom," he mumbled.

"We don't always get what we need, do we?" Luke asked.

"What do you mean?" Otis asked.

"Remember a little girl named Jade?"

Otis felt sick. Black hair, blue eyes. Tiny, fragile body. "Never heard of her."

"That's strange," Luke said. "She remembers you very well. So well that she drew that picture of you as you were during your years with the People of Joy."

Now nausea was warring with his need to urinate.

"I don't know what you're talking about," he mumbled. "I need to go to the bathroom *now*."

"How many times did Jade and all those other children beg you for mercy? How many times did they plead with you not to take them to the purple room?"

Otis groaned. No one knew about that purple room—no

one except the People and the children he'd taken there. He started to stand up. Luke shoved him back in the chair.

"Don't move," he said. "Don't you fucking move. You don't know how easy it would be for me to kill you where you sit."

Now Jacks began to panic. He looked frantically from Ruiz to Drury and back again. "You have to protect me. He can't kill me!" he cried. "I know my rights. I have a right to legal representation, and the right to a trial, if it's deemed necessary. I—"

Luke leaned forward, bracing himself with the flat of his hands on the tabletop until he was only inches away from Otis's face.

"They can't hurt you, but I can. I'm not a cop."

Otis felt the heat before the moisture, but he knew the moment it started running down his leg that he'd done the unforgivable. He'd wet himself.

"Goddamn you!" he screamed. "I told you I needed to pee. Now see what you made me do!"

Ruiz made a face, then got up and moved away.

"Damn it!" Drury yelped, and scooted back from the table and headed for the door. "Hey!" he yelled to the guards outside. "Somebody get a mop. This sorry bastard peed himself."

Luke smelled the acrid stench of fresh urine, but he wasn't through with Otis Jacks yet. Now, while everyone was out of hearing distance, he gave Otis a final parting shot.

"I'm telling you like I told Frank Lawson. You'll go to prison, and a Federal one at that. And don't think that your money or your fancy talk will get you anywhere in there, because I'm going to make sure that wherever you two go, the inmates know what you are."

Otis swung his handcuffed hands up in a defensive gesture.

"Get him away from me!" he screamed.

"Hear me," Luke whispered. "If you believe in a god,

say your prayers. If there's anyone in this world who you care about, make a will. You won't live a year behind bars. I'll make sure of that.''

Luke handed Ruiz the drawing.

"You might want to keep this. There's no telling what else you'll turn up on this snake. When the Feds get here, tell them, if they don't already know, to call the St. Louis Police Department and speak to Captain Myers. They want Jacks for kidnapping, as well as a number of other ugly little charges.''

Otis heard enough to know his days as a free man were over. He didn't even want to think about how many days he might have left to live. But he hadn't devoted his life to being a con man to quit now without giving it one last try.

"Listen to me! All of you! I have millions of dollars in a numbered account in a Swiss bank,'' he said. "If you three let me go, it's yours. No one would have to know.''

"Naw, the LAPD has a real good pension plan,'' Drury drawled. "I'm not interested. Ruiz, how about you?''

Amelia Ruiz glared at Jacks, her nose twisted in disgust from the stench of his urine-soaked clothes.

"No deal. Dirty man. Dirty money. Kelly?''

Luke shoved his hands in his pockets to keep from putting them around Otis Jacks' neck. Otis was staring up at him. The desperation on his face was easy to read, and he wondered how many children had looked at Jacks with the same expression.

"Don't look at me,'' he said. "Don't even say my name. God forgive me, but I can't think of you without wanting to watch you die.''

Otis groaned in disbelief.

"Forty-three million dollars? You'd throw away forty-three million dollars for *that?* It wasn't such a big deal. Hell, they were only kids. They get over it.''

Before the thought had gone completely through Luke's

head, he had already doubled up his fist and hit Otis in the mouth. Blood spurted from between Otis's teeth as he went backward out of the chair.

Ruiz jumped toward Luke, but he was already turning away, as if the touch of what he'd done had contaminated him beyond recovery.

Luke looked at Amelia Ruiz, unashamed of his emotion. His body was shaking with rage, and his voice was gruff and thick with tears.

"They don't get over it," he said. "They live with the pain and degradation every day of their lives, and when they close their eyes at night, they relive it some more. And those are the ones who don't die. He put those children with men who were sick and diseased, and didn't give a fuck as long as he got paid. Raphael was murdered, but you want to know the irony of that? If Frank Lawson had left well enough alone, none of this would have happened. Jade just wanted to put the past behind her, and Raphael was already dying of AIDS. Then Frank Lawson got nervous."

Otis recognized the name immediately and reeled from the words, then groaned aloud.

"Damn Frank Lawson's sorry ass. Damn him, damn him, damn him."

If it hadn't been for Lawson's panic, they would have gotten away with it after all. Before he could think what to do next, the door opened again. This time, a man with a mop and bucket led the way for two men in dark suits. He groaned again, then closed his eyes.

The Feds were here. It was over.

Luke nodded to the men as he strode past them.

"Who are you?" one of them asked.

"The Lone Ranger," he muttered. "Hi-yo Silver, away."

"What the hell?" the agent asked, as Luke walked out the door without looking back.

Ruiz flashed her badge. "Detective Ruiz, LAPD. This is

my partner, Detective Drury. Let him go," she said. "He's done what he came to do. Now the rest is up to us."

But the agent wasn't satisfied with the answer. He walked to the door just in time to see Luke disappearing into the throng of people hurrying to catch planes. When he came back, he cornered Ruiz.

"Exactly what was it that he came to do?"

Ruiz sighed. "He wanted revenge, but he settled for letting the law enact justice instead. So I strongly suggest that you boys don't mess up this arrest, or the ensuing gathering of evidence for this bastard's trial. If you do, and Otis Jacks goes free, you'll live the rest of your life looking over your shoulder." She pointed at Otis. "And that pissy bastard won't live past the courthouse door. I'm also supposed to ask you if you've spoken to a Captain Myers with the St. Louis P.D."

While the first agent was digesting the thinly veiled warning, the other was corroborating her assumption.

"Yes. We have a Federal arrest warrant for Otis Jacks aka Solomon, for kidnapping as well as a few other associated charges."

She nodded. "Good. Then we're outa here. Drury...you're driving, and it's time to go. We'll let the big boys handle ole pee-pot here. I think we can find better things to do."

Otis heard them leaving, but he couldn't watch. He kept telling himself that if he kept his eyes closed, this would be nothing but a bad dream. Then the strong smell of disinfectant filled his nostrils. He opened his eyes just as the janitor swung a soaking wet mop across the top of his feet.

"God damn it!" he shrieked. "You're getting my shoes wet!"

"All the better to match your pants," the agent said, and pulled Otis to his feet.

Luke had every intention of flying home, but when he called the pilot, he'd been told that due to weather, all planes

had been grounded again. He checked his watch, calculating the time between California and Missouri, and then sighed. It was after midnight there. Too late to call. All he could do was check into a hotel, and hope they could start home in the morning.

"Sir, what about your luggage?" the pilot asked.

"Hang on to it," Luke said. "I'm on my way over. It's a ten-minute walk. I'll get it and then catch a cab."

"I already have a rental car. I'd be happy to drop you wherever you need to go," the pilot said.

"Hey, thanks, buddy," Luke said. "I'll be right there."

At the same time and half the country away, Jade was dressing carefully for dinner with Sam, wearing a pale blue cotton sundress that he'd purchased for her, and white backless sandals with silver heels. She pulled her hair up off her neck and fastened it back with a tortoiseshell clip, then added a little bit of lipstick before coming downstairs.

Sam met her at the foot of the stairs with a smile on his face.

"Jade…you look stunning!"

Still a little uncomfortable with such compliments, she smiled shyly.

"Thank you," she said, eyeing Sam's beige slacks and pale yellow shirt. "You don't look so bad yourself."

"One does what one can," he teased, and then offered her his arm. "Would you care for a glass of wine before dinner?"

"Is it proper?"

Sam grinned. "Oh, yes, it's very proper."

"Then, thank you, I believe I will."

He led her into the library, then seated her in a chair near the bookcase before going to the bar and pouring them each a drink.

"Try this," he said, as he handed her a fragile, long-stemmed glass half-filled with one of his best vintages.

Jade took her first sip, then made a face. "Sorry," she said. "I'm afraid I'm socially inept. Is this supposed to be good?"

Sam laughed out loud. "Would you prefer a soft drink?"

She grinned. "Please."

He took the wine from her and returned with a glass of cola.

"Try this," he suggested.

She sipped, then smiled. "Better, thank you."

He was still chuckling when Velma came in to tell them that dinner was ready.

Sam stood and once again offered his arm.

"My lady, will you join me?"

She slipped a hand in the crook of his arm and then briefly laid her cheek against his shoulder. There were no words to describe her sense of finally belonging somewhere and to someone.

The lights in the dining room had been dimmed. A beautiful centerpiece of fresh flowers adorned the table. On either side of the flowers were long white tapers in silver candlesticks, and the air from Jade's passing caused the flames to shimmy.

Sam seated Jade to his left, then sat down.

"Comfortable, darling?"

Still taken aback by the casual elegance of the man and his home, she sighed.

"Not yet...but I will be," she promised.

It was enough to satisfy Sam.

Their time together passed easily. Sam soon had Jade smiling and laughing as he shared anecdotes about things from his travels and his past. Little by little, Jade was coming to know the man who was her father and to appreciate his wisdom. He'd accumulated great wealth in his lifetime, and yet

it seemed to have no negative influence on him. Even though Sam had made it very clear in the beginning, it was staggering to know that one day this would all be hers.

They were just finishing dessert when Jade put down her fork.

"Have you heard from Luke?"

"Not since you did."

"Do you think everything is okay?"

"Yes. Luke can take care of himself. You like him, don't you?"

Jade felt the heat rising on her neck, but she wouldn't lie. "Yes."

"He will never hurt you."

She sighed. "I know that…or at least, I do now. But I'm so flawed."

"The flaws are only in your mind."

She was quiet for a few moments more; then she looked up at Sam, unaware of how frightened and helpless she looked.

"Do you think it would be all right if I slept in my old room? Just for tonight? With your room right next door, I wouldn't feel so—"

"Absolutely," he said.

"I feel like such a baby, but I've never slept alone since—"

"Don't apologize to me—ever," Sam said. "Not about that. Never about that."

She nodded. But there was relief in her voice as she kissed him on the cheek.

"Thank you, Daddy. Maybe one of these days I'll be as old in my mind as I am in real years. Imagine, being afraid to sleep alone. Isn't that crazy?"

Sam wished he could answer, or at least smile—anything to dislodge the knot in his throat, but he couldn't, not without breaking down in tears. She couldn't know how deeply he

hurt for what she'd endured, and he prayed she never would. All he could do was shake his head in denial. There wasn't anything crazy about Jade.

After dinner, they spent the evening in the library, supposedly watching television, but Jade, growing up without constant access to televisions, had not developed the habit. Instead she'd gotten up from the sofa and wandered over to the book-burdened shelves. Despite her lack of schooling, she was a voracious reader, and when she saw one of her favorite stories, she took it from the shelf and headed for an overstuffed chair beneath a Tiffany reading lamp.

It wasn't until a commercial that Sam realized Jade was engrossed in the book.

"What are you reading?" he asked, as he got up to get himself a cold drink.

"*The Boxcar Children*. It's a story for kids, but it's one of my favorites."

Sam frowned, trying to remember the story line, but couldn't.

"What's it about?"

"There are these children who have no home, and they find and live in an abandoned railroad car. It's sad and it's wonderful, all at the same time."

Sam touched her hair as he passed. "I'll have to read it when you've finished."

She nodded.

"Want something cold to drink?"

"No, thank you," she mumbled.

He grinned. She was already engrossed in the story again. It dawned on him, as he watched her turning the pages, that she read very quickly. For having no formal education at all, it was a miracle in itself that she could read, let alone with skill.

The grandfather clock in the corner was striking eleven

when the phone suddenly rang. Jade flinched as Sam answered.

"Luke! We've been waiting to hear from you. Is it over?"

Luke sighed. "Pretty much. We stopped Jacks—he's in custody, too. Is Jade still up?"

Sam smiled and handed Jade the phone.

"Luke?"

Just hearing her voice eased the rage he'd been carrying. "Yes, it's me, baby. Just wanted you to know that it's over. You're safe, and I'll be home as soon as I can." Then he added, "I love you."

She sighed. "I love you, too."

Then Jade stood up and stretched. After hearing Luke's voice, all her tension had eased.

"I think I'm going to bed," she said. "Do you mind if I take this up to read?"

"Darling, there's nothing in this house that is off-limits to you. This is your home, remember?"

She smiled her thanks and started toward the door.

"I'll be up in a bit," Sam said. "I've got some overseas calls to make. Would you like me to look in on you when I come up?"

"That would be nice," she said, then waved goodbye as she left with her book.

The phone calls took longer than Sam had expected, and it was after midnight when he finally started up the stairs. He was tired, but his heart was full to overflowing. It was going to take time, but today had been a turning point for all of them. He could tell that something had happened between Jade and Luke. He hoped it was something on which they could build a life together. But even better for Sam, something had happened between him and his daughter. Today she had called him Daddy, and it was as special now as it had been the day she learned to talk.

As he neared her room, his steps slowed. The door was

closed, but he'd told her he would check on her, and he wasn't about to break his word.

The door opened silently on well-oiled hinges. The book she'd carried upstairs was on the bedside table beneath the lamp. She lay facing the door with her knees bent toward her chin and her head tucked near her chest. Even in sleep, she assumed a position of defense—curled in upon herself for optimum protection.

Emotion swept over him as he stepped into the room. The covers had slipped off her shoulders, and although it was hot and steamy outside, the central air kept the rooms quite cool. Carefully, so as not to disturb her, he lifted the covers and pulled them back up. As he did, he noticed she had something clutched in her hands. When he bent down for a closer look, he saw it was the little pink blanket that had been left behind when Margaret had taken her away.

Oh, baby…my sweet, sweet baby…it may take you a while to realize it, but it's finally safe to grow up.

He turned out the lamp and tiptoed quietly from the room.

Jade never knew when Sam came and went, but sometime toward morning, she began to dream. And as always, it started off the same way: with Solomon coming to the bedroom and waking her up, then dragging her down the hall toward the purple room. Her heart began to pound, her hands started to sweat, and, as always, there was that overwhelming need to pee that came from ungovernable fear.

In her sleep, she began to struggle and beg, fighting the bed and the covers as he dragged her nearer and nearer. Then, suddenly, she was holding Raphael's hand and Solomon was gone.

Her heartbeat evened, and the panic she was feeling subsided, even though something still wasn't right. She wasn't yet at the part in the dream where Raphael always came to save her. That came later, after all the pain. But this time he

was smiling at her, and she could feel the brush of his lips as he bent and kissed her cheek. Because of that, she told herself it was going to be okay.

In the dream, he tugged at her hand impatiently, just as he always did when she dawdled. She smiled as they started to move. Then she saw herself turning around. The door to the purple room was swiftly disappearing, and suddenly it was gone. When she turned to see where they were going, she saw a long narrow hallway with a light up ahead.

"Rafie…where are you taking me?"

He smiled. "Home."

"But aren't we already home?"

"Not yet, but we soon will be."

Jade pulled her knees a little closer toward her chin and let herself fall deeper into the dream.

Suddenly the hallway ended and they were walking out into a light. Before she could ask Raphael where they were, Luke was suddenly standing before them. She felt the smile spreading on her face and the joy growing in her heart and remembered what it felt like to make love to this man.

She turned to Raphael.

"It's over, isn't it, Rafie? Now we can all live happily ever after."

But Raphael shook his head, and to Jade's dismay, he began to fade before her eyes.

"We can't live anywhere," he said. *"But you can…and with Luke. He loves you, honey. Trust him enough to love him back."*

Raphael was fading swiftly now. Jade could still see him, but she could also see through him. It was enough to send her over the edge of panic.

"No! Rafie, no! Don't go. Please don't go!"

Now he was completely gone. Although she could still hear his voice, there wasn't a wisp of him left.

"Live your life to the fullest, Jade Cochrane. Live for yourself...and for me."

Then Jade felt Luke's hand on her arm and the rush of his breath against her cheek.

"Sweetheart...it's time to go. Are you ready?"

Jade felt torn between the past and the future, caught between betraying Raphael and following her heart to Luke. She turned to face Luke and saw the love on his face and the truth in his eyes, and still she couldn't make her feet move.

Then, suddenly, she felt a pressure in the middle of her back, as if someone was pushing her forward. Tears filled her eyes, then spilled down her face, because she knew it was Raphael, still giving her a nudge in the right direction.

In the dream, she reached for Luke's hand, taking comfort in the warmth and strength of his touch as he led her forward toward the light. She wanted to turn around, to make sure that Raphael was truly gone, but something inside told her not to look back.

She took a deep breath and opened her eyes.

It was morning.

Despite Luke's best efforts, the storm front refused to budge, and he accepted the fact that it was going to take him longer to get home. So bright and early that morning, he made a call to Jade.

"Cochrane residence."

"Hey, Velma, it's Luke. May I please talk to Jade?"

"Yes. I'll have to give her a buzz on the intercom. I think she's in her studio, and my knees aren't up to those third floor stairs."

"Studio? Third floor? What's been going on?"

"Oh, the Mister has been plotting a surprise. He took the two biggest room on the top floor and made an artist's studio

for Jade. She was so pleased. My, but that girl can paint, can't she?''

''Yes, she can.''

''Okay, hang on. I'll get her on the phone.''

A few seconds later, he heard an extension pick up, and then the hesitancy in a very beloved voice.

''Luke?''

Just the sound of her voice made him smile.

''Hello, baby...how ya' doing?''

''I'm good, Luke. Really, I am. I have an appointment with Dr. DiMatto today, and last night I had a dream that was different...even good.'' She paused, then added, ''You were in it.''

His smile widened. ''I was?''

''Yes. You came and took me out of the dark.''

His vision blurred, and he was glad she couldn't see his face.

''Jade, darling...''

''It's okay,'' she said quickly. ''Now tell me about L.A. Last night you were so brief. It was Solomon, wasn't it?''

He had to gather his thoughts, because he knew she would want to know everything.

''Yes, it was him. He didn't mean to, but he gave himself away.''

''What's happening? Can they do anything? It's been so long.''

''The Feds arrested him. He'll be charged with kidnapping, and a host of other things that will keep him behind bars for the rest of his life.''

''Was he connected to Frank Lawson's hit man?''

''I don't think so. They're still in the investigation phase, but I'd say not. It's storming here, so planes aren't flying. Even if I rent a car, I can't be there before Saturday at the earliest. Are you all right with that?''

She knew he was referring to her fear of sleeping alone.

"I slept in my old bedroom last night. It's next to Daddy's room. Even though I didn't have nightmares, I knew he was nearby. But I will get better. I *am* getting better. I know and accept that it's going to take time."

"I'm with you, baby. You know that, don't you?"

"Yes."

"Truly? You know in your heart that I will always be there for you?"

"Yes, Luke. I do."

"So when I get home, we'll talk about us, okay?"

She hugged the promise to herself as she leaned against the window.

"Yes. We will talk about us."

"Tell Sam I called. Tell him what's going on. I'll call you tonight when I stop to get a room."

"I wish it would be here," she said softly.

Luke groaned. "Not half as much as I do, sweetheart." Then he glanced at his watch. "Okay. I gotta go. As my granddad used to say, 'I'm burning daylight.' Love you."

"Love you, too," she said softly, and visibly winced when the connection ended.

Luke headed due east. The days passed slowly, marked by his phone calls to Jade and the times when he had to stop for food and gas, or to sleep. He caught a plane in Denver, then had another long layover in Oklahoma City, when the storm caught up with him again. Finally his plane took off, and he relaxed, knowing he would be with Jade before dark.

During the same time, Jade had gone through two sessions with Antonia DiMatto, finished the painting of Luke and started studying for her GED. Her goals were simple. Education, healing and Luke, and not necessarily in that order.

As predicted, her drawings had hit the tabloids, causing a stir all over the country as women recognized husbands, sis-

ters recognized brothers, and parents recognized sons. Some of the faces belonged to men who, like Margaret Cochrane, were already dead. Others were already incarcerated for similar crimes against other children. But there were a few, like Frank Lawson, whose lives had been carefully crafted lies, lies that had come tumbling down around them like the proverbial house of cards.

The pictures spawned a melee of separations and divorces—even a couple of arrests.

Jade felt vindicated in a way that nothing else could have done. She felt no pity for the men who'd created perfect worlds for themselves, only for the women who'd married them and the children they'd continued to molest.

Luke had called her at least twice a day since he'd started home, and today, he was due to return. She didn't know how to say what she felt in her heart, but she knew that she wanted him home. She needed to see his face, to know that he'd seen the worst of her life and to accept that he still loved her in spite of it.

And there was another milestone that had happened since he'd been gone. After that night, when she'd slept in her old room and dreamed that last dream, the dreams hadn't come again. Not even the nightmares—not even Raphael.

She didn't hear him in her head anymore. He was just a memory in her heart. It was Luke's voice that called to her from the miles and through the phones, making her laugh, teasing her into embarrassed giggles and praising her for staying so strong.

But three days was a lifetime for a woman trying to be reborn. Even though her father stood strongly at her side, she needed reassurance from the man who held her heart.

Twenty-Four

It was just after four in the afternoon when Luke pulled into Sam's driveway and started toward the house. The noticeable absence of media on the way through the neighborhood had been startling, and then he realized that eventually the news of something new had inevitably superseded the drama of one woman's long journey home.

He'd thought long and hard, on the long drive home, about what he should do to keep Jade become the woman he knew she could be, and though it hurt him to think that absenting himself from her, even for a short while, would be helpful, he knew it was true. She would never be able to completely trust herself until she learned how strong she really was. And that wasn't going to happen if he stepped into Raphael's shoes and began cosseting her from any- and every-thing she didn't want to face.

So it was with mixed feelings that he pulled up to Sam's house and parked. Before he could gather his thoughts, Jade was at the door. He saw her and waved as he got out.

And then she was coming toward him on the run, with the sun on her face and the wind in her hair. He caught her in midstep, lifted her off her feet and then swung her around. Her arms snaked around his neck. Her head dropped back against his arm as they circled in place. Then he felt her lips on his mouth and heard her laughter as she called out his name.

He was home.

* * *

Luke had stayed for dinner with Sam and Jade. Paul and
helly Hudson had come over, and he could tell that Shelly
as doing what she could to reassure Jade that she was spe-
al to all of them.

Their questions had come at him fast and furious all
rough the meal. He'd done his best to answer without
romising something out of his control, but he was confident
at both Lawson and Jacks would go to prison. What Luke
adn't known until his arrival in St. Louis was that the draw-
gs had gone national.

"Jade, how do you feel about that?" he asked.

"What? You mean am I worried about people seeing me
d knowing that all those men—"

"No!" His answer was abrupt and ended her train of
ought. "What I should have said was, are you expecting
ose men to be brought to justice, too?"

"Oh." She thought about it for a moment and then shook
r head. "Not really. I mean, I wasn't the only one. The
her girls with the People went through the same things I
d. What's happening is good enough for me. I understand
out the statute of limitations, and I know that proving my
aims would be next to impossible. However, guilt is its own
and of justice, right, Daddy?"

Sam's pride in Jade grew with each passing day. While he
ould have liked to see each and every mother's son of them
ucified, he was willing to settle for the man who'd scarred
r and the one who'd sold her.

"You're right about that, honey. Now how about some
ssert? Velma made chocolate cake."

"I'm in," Luke said.

"Me too," Jade said.

"I shouldn't," Shelly said. "But I'm going to anyway."
Paul patted his stomach. "Never too full for cake."

"I heard that," Velma said, as she entered carrying a tray

with five hefty servings of chocolate cake with a scoop o
vanilla ice cream on each plate.

"What if we hadn't wanted any dessert?" Sam asked.

"Then I'd be eating good tonight, wouldn't I?" sh
quipped, and smirked when everyone laughed.

Later, the Hudsons left with promises to return the favo
of a meal soon. Shortly afterward, Velma went home, an
Sam retired to his room to read before going to sleep. Luke
and Jade finally had time to themselves. Luke knew he coul
stay, but he didn't think he should. Jade had embarked on
mission to regain control of her life, and if he behaved as i
she needed to be protected again, it wouldn't be sending he
a positive message. The only problem was, he didn't kno
how to tell her. Oddly enough, it was Jade who showed hir
how.

"I want to show you something," she said, and led th
way upstairs to her new studio.

Luke didn't let on that Velma had already spilled the bean
about Sam's surprise.

"Oh…man…this is amazing," he said, as he move
around the rooms, admiring all that she showed him.

Then he realized there was a canvas on an easel near th
window.

"Is that the painting you were doing?"

"Yes."

"May I see?"

She nodded, then turned away, unwilling to look at Luke'
expression as he saw it for the first time.

He hadn't known it was of him. He studied the portrai
realizing that she'd done it from that sketch she'd made th
night he'd stayed by her bed. In it, she had portrayed him a
someone weary, but faithful—ever watchful toward the cov
ered figure lying alone on the bed.

He turned toward her.

She was still looking away.

"Jade."

"What?"

"Look at me."

She did.

"Is this the way you see me?"

She nodded.

He took her in his arms, then hugged her.

Tears shimmered in her eyes, but she wouldn't cry.

"You humble me. I am honored, more than you will ever now."

"You watched over me…like Rafie used to do." Then her xpression changed. "Only Raphael lied to me. You don't."

Luke sighed. She was still transferring her grief into anger, ut not in a positive way.

"Raphael didn't lie to you."

"But he didn't trust me enough to tell me the truth."

"Well, maybe he tried so hard to protect you as a child hat he never gave you credit for growing up. It wasn't that e didn't trust you, it was just that he didn't know he could ean on you, as you had once leaned on him."

The tears in her eyes welled and spilled over. "Then that's ny fault, not his, because I was always leaning on him. Every ight. Every time a strange man got too close. Every time I anicked and wanted to run."

"So you're not really mad at him."

She swiped angrily at the tears, scrubbing them away as f they offended.

"I think the person I'm maddest at is me."

"Do you know why?"

"Because I've leaned on everyone in my life except my-elf."

"So what's your solution?"

She sighed. "Depend on me first."

"And that's my signal to go home," he said gently.

"But I didn't mean… I don't want…"

"Yes, you did," Luke said gently. "And yes, you do. I won't be any farther away than a phone call. And I fully expect to be taking you to dinner soon. We'll talk and go places and everything a man and woman do when they're falling in love."

Now the tears fell, silently and swiftly.

"Promise you aren't mad at me."

"God no," Luke said, and took her in his arms. "I'm so in love with you that I ache. I want to marry you and make love to you for the rest of my life. I want babies and grandchildren and laughter...." Then he swiped his thumb across her cheek, momentarily stalling the flow from her eyes. "Even tears. It's what living is all about, and I want to do it with you. Only you're not there yet, and we both know it."

"How will I know when it happens?" she asked.

"You'll know. And when you do, you'll tell me, and then I'll give us both something to dream about. Right now, you need to learn to trust yourself before you give your trust to me."

She nodded.

He touched the canvas again, feeling the love with which she'd painted it.

"Is this mine?" he asked.

"Yes," she said, and tried to smile, then gave up and buried her face against his shirtfront.

"Love you, Luke Kelly."

"Love you, too, darling. Sweet dreams."

Then he picked up the painting and made his way home.

October: St. Louis, Missouri

It started raining in the night. Jade heard the rumble of thunder and rolled over in bed long enough to see a brief flash of lightning.

She could almost hear Raphael telling her that rain washes

all the troubles away, but he wasn't around to remind her, and anyway, she knew that was no longer true.

She got out of bed and stumbled to the windows, then pulled the curtains shut. The room seemed chilly, so she got another blanket from the closet and spread it at the foot of her bed before crawling back between the covers.

Now she was warm and settled back in the bed, but she couldn't find her comfort spot. Frustrated that she'd awakened so early, she glanced at the clock. It was a little after four. It would be daybreak before long, the first day of October. She pulled the covers up close around her ears and then snuggled deep down in the pillows.

Almost immediately, her thoughts went to Luke. It had been a week since she'd talked to him, and it had probably been the longest week of her life. Over the past two months, he'd taken her to dinner, laughed with her, teased with her, and at the end of each evening, deposited her safely on Sam's doorstep, then waved as he drove away.

Then, seven days ago, he'd called her unexpectedly, and told her he would be gone to Alaska for most of the week and that he would stay in touch. She hadn't talked to him since, part of which was her fault.

The first time he'd called, she'd been in a session with Dr. DiMatto and had turned off her cell phone. When she'd tried to return the call, his phone had been off. They'd been playing phone tag ever since.

But his absence had only confirmed something she'd known for some time. She didn't want to live her life without him. Antonia DiMatto had told her she was ready to move on. Her father kept telling her over and over how proud he was of her. And last month, her grief had come to a point where she could face doing a painting of Raphael.

There had been an aspect of the portrait that she hadn't seen until it was done. It had been her father who'd been the one to call it to her attention, but now, every time she looked at it, it stunned her. No matter where you stood, Raphael's

eyes always seemed to be looking just beyond the viewer's shoulder, as if he was looking at something that no one else could see. She didn't know how she'd done it. It had been unintentional, and something she doubted she could ever duplicate.

Thunder rumbled again. She rolled over onto her back and thumped the covers again but couldn't get comfortable. The bed seemed too large—too empty to sleep in alone.

She'd learned to live with herself—even be comfortable with herself. Only now and then did a twinge of anxiety surface, but then she would think of what she'd been through and know there wasn't anything she couldn't do on her own. But out of that had come another realization. She'd come to understand that she didn't want to live alone. She loved Luke Kelly, as fully and completely as any woman could love a man. It was time to make that call.

She didn't know what time it was in Alaska, but she knew it was a whole lot earlier than it was here in Missouri. Hopefully he wouldn't have gone to bed, but even if he had, something told her that he wouldn't mind waking up.

Luke was finally home. His flight had been delayed twice for bad weather, and then the stormy landing in St. Louis had been hairy at best. It had been a few minutes after one when the plane touched down; then they were not allowed to get off until the worst of the thunderstorm had passed. Lightning kept striking all around them, until Luke was of the opinion that they would probably be just as safe making a run for the terminal as sitting and waiting for the bus to come and get them. But rules were rules, and the small jet he'd flown in on was not one with access to the covered exits.

By the time he reached the terminal, it was close to 2:00 a.m. Walking past the closed shops on his way to baggage claim was like walking through a ghost town. The rain hammering against the windows only added to the gloom. He thought about calling Jade just to hear the sound of her voice.

then chided himself for being selfish. What he wanted to tell her could wait until morning. By the time he got his luggage, then his car out of airport parking, it was ten minutes until three. As tired as he was, it was a relief to be in charge of his own momentum.

The rain-washed streets were nearly empty as Luke headed home. Although the rain continued to fall, it seemed to have lessened in intensity. He glanced off to the east as he turned the corner. The worst of the storm was passing. It wasn't until he began looking for his apartment building that he realized he'd driven into Sam's neighborhood, instead of his own. Cursing himself for the blunder, he knew it had been instinct that had led him here. He'd thought of nothing but Jade all the way from Alaska, and now here he was, pulling to a stop in front of her home.

"Lord have mercy," he muttered, and for a moment gave himself permission to close his eyes. He was so tired. All he wanted to do was rest.

It was the ringing of his cell phone that startled him awake. He jerked, then looked up, half expecting to see the oncoming headlights of an approaching car. To his relief, he was still parked, and it was his cell phone that had awakened him and not the blaring of another driver's horn. He fumbled in his pocket, then flipped it open and answered without looking at caller ID.

"Hello?"

"Honey…"

He sat straight up in the seat.

"Jade? Is that you?"

"Remember when you told me that one day I would know when I was healed…and when it happened I was supposed to call and let you know?"

The breath caught in the back of Luke's throat. Over the past few months, he'd begun to fear that this call might never come.

"Yes, I remember," he said, and put the car in gear.

"So...I'm letting you know. I miss you, Luke Kelly, and I love you madly, and although I'm perfectly capable of living life on my own and sleeping all alone, I find that I don't like it one bit."

Luke approached the iron gates, then braked.

"Well, if you'll buzz me in, we can talk about this in a much dryer location."

There was a moment of silence while Jade grasped what he'd said; then she squealed.

"Are you here? I mean at the gates? I'm not talking to you in Alaska?"

"Hell no. Fact is...we never did get to talk in Alaska, did we? And just for your information, I'm not going that far away again without taking you with me. So, are you going to let me in? I'm warning you, I've already fallen asleep once in this car, so if I sit out here much longer, just tell Velma to cook a couple of extra eggs in the morning, because I'll be there for breakfast."

"Just a minute!" she cried. "I don't know how to take off the security code. I've got to wake Sam."

Luke grimaced. Lord. Nothing like waking up his future father-in-law so he could watch them go to bed. He heard her throw down the phone, then heard her running out of the room. After that, there was silence.

Suddenly the gates began to swing inward. He put the car in gear and then drove through. Within seconds, he was pulling up to the front of the house. Before he could get out, the exterior lights came on and Jade came running through the open doorway. She had on a long white robe over something blue. Her feet were bare, and her hair was loose and tangled as she came down off the porch and into the rain.

Luke got out laughing, caught her on the run, and swung her into his arms. He groaned and then kissed her, tasting the rain on her lips, before he scooped her up and began running to get her out of the rain.

"You're crazy, woman. Where are your shoes? Can't you see that it's raining?"

"That's not rain," she said, as Luke carried her into the house.

Luke set her down, then quickly closed the door behind him, shutting them in and the rain out.

"If that wasn't rain, then I'd like to know what it was," he said, as he took off his raincoat and hung it on the hall tree.

"Rain isn't rain, it's angel tears."

He shrugged off the odd reference, thinking it was something from her childhood, then took out his handkerchief and wiped the raindrops from her face. When she shivered, he hurried her up the stairs.

"Good to have you home," Sam called out, as they reached the landing.

"Good to be here," Luke said.

"I'll talk to you in the morning," Sam added, and then shut his door and went back to bed.

"It's already morning," Jade said, as they ran down the hall to her room.

Once inside, Luke shed his wet clothes and, at Jade's urging, took a warm shower. By the time he came out, she was wearing a fresh nightgown and fuzzy slippers on her feet.

He kissed her again, and when her arms slid around his neck, he kissed her longer, then deeper—each time waiting for her to call a halt or pull back. When she didn't, he thought he would die from the joy of loving her.

"Are we going to make love?" Jade asked.

Luke sighed. "I would dearly love to, but I think this one's up to you."

"I would dearly love to, also," she said. "Come lie with me, Luke, and be my love."

His heart soared as she urged him toward the bed.

"You've been reading poetry again, haven't you?"

She smiled, unaware of how seductive her smile had become.

"Some of that stuff is pretty sexy."

"No more than you," Luke whispered.

He lay down beside her, then slipped his arm beneath her shoulders and started to roll onto his back; then she stopped him with a touch.

"No. Not this time. This time you're making love to me." She tugged at his shoulders, urging him to come to her.

"Are you sure about this?"

"As sure as I can be until it happens."

He took a deep breath. "Just let me know if anything scares you."

"The only thing frightening about this is if it never happens again."

He shook his head. "Then, darling, you can lay your fears to rest."

Luke's weariness was forgotten in the tenderness of her touch. Every tentative gesture she made toward him was reciprocated double-fold. If she caressed his face, he smothered hers with kisses. If she stroked his chest, he lay tender siege to her breasts. But when she spread her legs beneath him, he was afraid to move.

"Please," she whispered. "It's all right. It's all right."

Luke slid between her legs, then into her body as fluidly as water flowing down glass.

For Jade, there was no panic or pain at the point of entry, only a steadily building warmth that was coiling itself up through her heart. She moved with him instinctively, letting the motion build the tension and the tension stoke the fire. Over and over, she took his weight without flinching, lost in sensations that took her farther than she'd ever thought she would go. Everything was Luke, and Luke was everything, and he was giving her joy.

Then suddenly it shifted, moving her to a different level,

where thought ended and nothing mattered but chasing the push of blood thundering through her veins.

She arched her body toward the motion, meeting it head-on as it slammed into her with unbelievable force. For a few seconds she would have sworn that she'd imploded, but then her mind let go, and her body soon followed, as she sank into the mattress with a deep, weary groan.

The moment of her climax had been the beginning of the end for Luke. He let it take him over the edge into his own mindless pleasure, and when it was over, he collapsed. Almost immediately, he realized his entire weight was on her and panicked.

"Oh Lord...oh, Jade...I can't move. Give me a minute...just don't be afraid."

She was laughing softly as she held him close. Nothing had prepared her for this. Not even the time before when they'd made love. Then she'd been so afraid of failure that she'd forgotten to focus on what making love was all about.

But now she knew. It wasn't just about trusting her body to a lover, it was trusting herself enough to let go. She'd known she was in love with Luke, but she hadn't fully understood the depth of her feelings until now. She loved a man who'd given her back herself.

"Afraid? Never with you. That was beautiful, so beautiful. Thank you for loving me, but more importantly, thank you for letting me grow up enough to appreciate the gift."

"You're very welcome," he whispered. "Although somehow, after the way I feel, I think I should be thanking you."

She shivered from the joy of knowing that she'd given him pleasure, then wrapped her arms around his neck and sighed, totally replete.

Luke held her without mercy, refusing to let her go. It seemed like a lifetime since he'd first seen her on the floor in the New Orleans YMCA, and maybe it had been. Certainly a lifetime for her. The child she'd been at six had died with Margaret as surely as if her heart had stopped beating, leav-

ing behind a mere shell of a soul to endure the ensuing years alone. But she'd survived and endured, and in doing so, had learned how to be a woman.

Luke sighed. "I was going to ask you to marry me," he mumbled.

"Yes."

His pulse jumped; then he grinned. "I said I was going to…I haven't done it yet."

"I just saved you some time," she answered, then reached down and pulled the covers up over their bare bodies.

His smile softened as he watched her eyelids fluttering, and her mouth go slack. Suddenly he remembered something he had wanted to ask.

"Jade?"

"Hmm?"

"Before, when you said that rain was angel tears?"

"Mmm-hmm."

"So…why would you think the angels cry? Heaven is supposed to be a happy place."

She sighed, then rose up on one elbow so that she could look him in the face.

"Look…I didn't mean that angels *really* cry. It was just a figure of speech. I guess it's just the artistic side of me that sees everything as a drama, but when it's raining, in my mind, I see angels' tears."

"If this is what you see, then why do they cry?"

"They cry for all the lost children who can't cry for themselves."

"I cried for you," Luke said.

She touched his face, then his heart, feeling the steady, rhythmic thump.

"I know, darling. I heard and was healed."

Epilogue

It had taken Sam Cochrane most of his life to amass the fortune that was now his. His daughter, Jade Cochrane Kelly, had made her own in five years. Her art was in high demand, the unique thumbprint signature impossible to forge, and it had all started after the birth of Amy Ann.

Luke and Jade had married before her first Christmas home and, at Sam's invitation, made the decision to live in the Cochrane home. As Sam had pointed out, the house was enormous, and it was going to be Jade's one day, anyway. He admitted that it was a selfish invitation on his part, and that his feelings would not be hurt if they declined. But Luke had seen the yearning on Sam's face and known how hard it was going to be for Sam to give her up so soon after their brief reunion.

So they'd stayed, and thrived, and ten months after their wedding day, Jade had given birth to their daughter, Amy Ann.

Jade was a typical new mother: a little anxious, a trifle teary, and proud beyond words. And even though Amy Ann was a good baby and was soon sleeping through most of the night, Jade would still get up in the quiet of early morning and go into the nursery, just to make sure that her baby was all right. It was during one of those times that Jade realized she wasn't the only one keeping watch over Amy Ann.

Sometime after midnight, Jade woke. Quietly, so as not to waken Luke, she slipped out of bed and tiptoed into the ad-

joining nursery to check on the baby. It was then that she saw motion in the air near the foot of her baby's crib. It was neither substance nor light, and yet Jade knew it was Raphael—following the path in spirit that he'd followed in life.

She thought his name without speaking it and felt the answer in her heart.

Yes, honey, it's me. She's so beautiful. Just like you.

Then she whispered softly. "Keep her safe for me, Rafie."

Always.

Her heart was easy as she went back to her bed. And even as she settled back within the shelter of Luke's arms, she couldn't quit thinking about what she'd sensed. The next day, when Amy Ann was taking her nap, Jade took the baby monitor up to her studio and picked up a brush. She'd been so moved by what she'd seen and heard that she wanted to capture it on canvas.

And so she'd painted him, giving him the shape that she'd remembered, but transparent, and with sheltering wings as he stood at the foot of a baby's crib. In the crib, a very small baby with dark curly hair slept peacefully, bathed in the angel's inner light. She'd called it The Guardian. Within months she'd done seven more. Each time with a different child, but always with the Guardian on duty, watching over those who could not take care of themselves.

By the end of the first year she'd painted a dozen of the Guardian paintings, and as an afterthought, hung them with other pieces of her work in her first professional show.

To her shock and Luke's delight, every one of the Guardian paintings sold at top price. The uproar for more took her by surprise, but she did what she could to keep up with the demand, although being Luke Kelly's wife and Amy Ann's mother was her first priority.

Now, five years later, the Guardian paintings were famous worldwide. Through countless interviews, it had become ap-

parent to the world that the angel in the paintings was her old friend Raphael—the man who'd been murdered. It gave Jade a sense of satisfaction in knowing that, because of the paintings, neither he nor his name would ever be forgotten.

But this morning her fame was taking a huge back seat to one of the more complicated milestones of life. It was her daughter's first day of school.

Amy Ann was ready to begin kindergarten, and Jade's old anxieties had begun to surface. It was the first time that her daughter would be in the care of someone other than family or friends, and she couldn't stop thinking of how innocent and fragile children were.

Luke knew she was worried, although she'd done a good job of hiding it from their child. He'd cornered her outside their bedroom door, seen the stricken look on her face and taken her in his arms.

"Honey, you're only feeling what all mothers feel." Then he sighed. "I'm not so happy about this myself."

"You're not?"

"No. I like knowing that you and Amy Ann are here in this house when I come home. I like knowing that we can do things together at the drop of a hat. But that's all over now. She's growing and changing, just as you did when we first met. Change is part of living, even though it's often uncomfortable for those who love us best."

Jade made a face, then smiled. "I guess you're right."

"I *know* I'm right."

She laughed.

"Mommy. Daddy. I'm ready to go."

They turned to see Amy Ann running out of her room and into the hall. She was dragging her backpack by one strap, and the neat little ponytail that Jade had made in her hair had already loosened and shifted to the side of her head.

Jade looked properly horrified.

"She might look like Mommy, but she's her daddy's girl all over," Luke said, and then burst out laughing.

"Wait," Jade said. "I need to fix your hair."

Amy Ann frowned and grabbed at her ponytail, unwilling to go back under the brush.

"You already fixed my hair."

"Yes, well, you unfixed it," Jade said, and quickly restored it to a proper do as Luke went to get the car.

Amy Ann frowned and then puffed out her cheeks as Jade tossed her hairbrush aside.

"Now can we go?"

"Yes, we can go." Then she held out her hand, and together, they hurried down the stairs.

"Bye, bye, Grandpa!" Amy Ann shrieked.

Sam came hurrying out of his office and gave his granddaughter a big kiss.

"You look great," he said. "Have a wonderful day."

"Oh, yes, I will," she said.

"You're going to be a big girl for me, aren't you?" he asked, referring to an earlier conversation they'd had regarding her reluctance to leave Mommy behind.

"Oh, yes," Amy Ann said. "Besides, I'm not going by myself."

Jade frowned. "I'm only going as far as the classroom door, darling. You know I can't stay."

"Oh, I know," Amy Ann said. "I didn't mean you."

"Then who do you mean?" Jade asked.

"My friend will be there."

At that moment Luke honked.

"Daddy!" Amy Ann squealed. "Hurry, Mommy! We're gonna be late."

Jade smiled at her father and then shrugged off Amy's comment, before following her daughter out the door.

A short while later, Luke and Jade, along with a half-dozen

other parents, were making the long walk down the school hallway toward the kindergarten room.

"Never thought this day would come," one weary mother muttered, as she waved goodbye to her youngest and fourth child.

"Hallelujah."

Luke chuckled. Jade frowned.

"Easy, honey," Luke said. "She's obviously been at this longer than we have."

She shrugged, then gasped when Amy Ann suddenly pulled loose from her hand and ran into the room without her.

"Amy Ann! Wait!"

"It's okay," Luke said. "Let her go. Be glad she's not crying like him."

He pointed to a little blond-headed boy who was clinging tearfully to his mother's leg.

"You're right—again," Jade said, and then grinned. "That's getting to be a habit."

"Hey, Kelly! Didn't expect to see you here," a man called.

Luke turned around, recognized a man who was also a client. "Honey, I'm going to go say hello."

"Sure," she said. Despite knowing that her daughter was fine, she still had to see for herself.

She walked to the door and peeked in. Amy Ann was already at a table near the back of the room, engrossed in play with two other little girls. Jade assumed one of them must have been the friend who would be there, but she didn't know them and was trying to remember where Amy Ann would have met them without her.

Jade stood for a moment, watching the teacher's interaction with the children, seeing how tenderly she was speaking to the ones who were upset.

She sighed, ignoring the twinge of hurt in her heart that

Amy Ann hadn't cried for her, too. But Luke was right. It was good that her child was independent and fearless.

The teacher looked up, smiled and winked a goodbye, and Jade waved. Then, just as she was turning away, she saw him, in the corner of the room near the table where Amy Ann played.

Raphael.

As she thought his name, he looked up. She thought she saw his lips move; then she thought she saw him smile. She lifted her hand to wave, then watched him fade away.

Sudden tears shimmered in her eyes. But she knew he wasn't gone, only nearby, as he'd been since the day Amy Ann had been born. That was when it hit her.

He was the friend—a friend who would always be there. Only she hadn't known that Amy Ann knew him, too. Her eyes filled with tears as she quickly looked away.

Then Luke was putting his arm around her and pulling her close against his side.

"Sweetheart...don't cry. She's going to be okay."

Jade looked up at him, then smiled.

"Yes, I know, darling." *At least, I do now.*

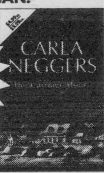

Praise for *New York Times* bestselling author

SHARON SALA

"Well-developed secondary characters and a surprising ending
spice up Sala's latest romantic intrigue."
—*Publishers Weekly* on *Snowfall*

"Spellbinding narrative...Sala lives up to her
reputation with this well-crafted thriller."
—*Publishers Weekly* on *Remember Me*

"Wear a corset, because your sides will hurt from laughing!
This is Sharon Sala at top form. You're going to love this
touching and memorable book."
—*New York Times* bestselling author
Debbie Macomber on *Whippoorwill*

"Ms. Sala draws you in from the very beginning.
She delivers main characters who will touch your hearts
and quirky secondary characters who will intrigue you
as you try to figure out whodunit."
—*Romantic Times BOOKclub* on *Butterfly*

"*Whippoorwill* is a funny, heartwarming story,
set in a raw, untamed land and rich with indelible
characters that will stay with you long after the last
page is turned. I didn't want it to be over."
—Deborah Smith, *New York Times* bestselling author of
A Place to Call Home

"Once again, Sharon Sala does a first-rate job at
blending richly developed characters and inspired
plotting into an unforgettable read."
—*Romantic Times BOOKclub* on *Dark Water*